APPARATUS

Cinematographic Apparatus: Selected Writings

Edited by Theresa Hak Kyung Cha

TANAM PRESS NEW YORK 1980

ACKNOWLEDGEMENTS

Upon Leaving the Movie Theater by Roland Barthes first appeared in *University Publishing,* Winter 1979.

The Vertov Papers first appeared in *Film Comment,* Spring 1972 and is © 1972 by Film Comment Publishing Corporation.

Ideological Effects of the Basic Cinematographic Apparatus by Jean-Louis Baudry first appeared in *Film Quarterly* Vol. XXVIII, No. 2 and is © 1974 by the Regents of the University of California.

The Apparatus by Jean-Louis Baudry first appeared in *Camera Obscura* No. 1.

An Anagram of Ideas on Art, Form, and Film first appeared in *Film Culture* No. 39, Winter 1965.

A Work Journal of the Straub/Huillet Film, Moses and Aaron by Gregory Woods and *Notes on Gregory's Work Journal* by Daniele Huillet first appeared in *Enthusiasm* No. 1 and is © 1975 Enthusiasm.

Le Defilement: A View in Closeup by Thierry Kuntzel and The Défilement *Into the Look* by Bertrand Augst first appeared in *Camera Obscura* No. 2.

The Fiction Film and Its Spectator: A Metapsychological Study by Christian Metz first appeared in *New Literary History,* Fall 1976.

The Lure of Psychoanalysis in Film Theory by Bertrand Augst first appeared in *University Publishing,* Winter 1979.

Manufactured in the USA. First printing, 1981

ISBN 0-934378-47-9(cloth) ISBN 0-934378-46-0(paper)

Tanam Press 40 White Street New York, NY 10013

Preface

—You have repeatedly defined the difference between making a political film and making a film politically.

—Yes, these two things are completely different. As Brecht already said, it's not important to know what are the real things but rather how things are real. The relation is in that reality.

An image is nothing. It's the relationships between the images that matter. Why are these relationships important? Marxism indicates what is the nature of the relationships between things. They are relations of production. A machine is not or a worker is not important by themselves, what matters is the relationship between the machine and the worker and the relationships between that worker and the other workers who from their own positions have relationships with the machine.

—Jean-Luc Godard

This book is conceived as a collection of Autonomous Works on the apparatus of cinema. The intention is to identify the individual components and complete film apparatus, the interdependent operations comprising the "film, the author of the film, the spectator."

The selection of works was made to approach the subject from theoretical directions synchronously with work of filmmakers who address and incorporate the apparatus—the function of film, the film's author, the effects produced on the viewer while viewing film—as an integral part of their work, and to turn backwards and call upon the machinery that creates the impression of reality whose function, inherent in its very medium, is to conceal from its spectator the relationship of the viewer/subject to the work being viewed.

The essential element of the project is to reveal the process of film and make accessible the theoretical writings and materials of filmmakers. Finally, I hope that this book in its totality will serve as an object not merely enveloping its contents, but as a "plural text" making active the participating viewer/reader, making visible his/her position in the apparatus.

It is necessary to emphasize the vastness of the subject, the cinematographic apparatus. This anthology is one orientation.

The achievements of this book are more profoundly expressed by the contributors themselves. With this statement I would like to offer my thanks to all the contributors for their generous support of the project, and to Teiji Ito, Catrina Neiman, Susan Wolf, Lee Hildreth, and Stephen Dodson.

My very special thanks to Bertrand Augst and Reese Williams for making this book possible.

Theresa Hak Kyung Cha
August, 1981

Contents

Upon Leaving the Movie Theater

Roland Barthes

The subject who speaks here must admit one thing: he loves leaving a movie theater. Finding himself once again outside in the illuminated and half-empty street (somehow he always goes to the movies on week days, and at night), limply heading toward some cafe, he walks in silence (he does not care much to talk after seeing a film); he is stiff, a little numb, bundled up, chilly: he is sleepy. That must be it, he must be sleepy; his body has turned into something soft, peaceful, sopitive; limp as a sleepy cat, he feels a little out of joint, or (because, for a moral organization, it is only in this way that he can find a little rest) irresponsible. In short, he is coming out of hypnosis. And from hypnosis, that old psychoanalytic saw which psychoanalysis disdains, he seeks the oldest of its powers: the cure. That reminds him of music, are there not hypnotic musics? Farinelli, the castrato whose incredible *messa di voce,* incredible both because of its length and of its "emmission," lulled the morbid melancholy of Spain's Phillippe V by singing the same romance every night for fourteen years.

This is how we often leave a movie theater. But how do we enter? With one exception—a more and more frequent one, it is true—of a specific cultural quest (when a film is chosen, sought, desired, the object of a genuine anticipatory anxiety), we go to movies through sloth, out of an inclination for idleness. It is as though, before even entering the theater, the traditional prerequisites for hypnosis were met: a feeling of emptiness, idleness, inactivity: we dream, not by viewing the film or by the effect of its content, rather, we dream, unwittingly, before becoming its spectator. There exists a "cinematic condition" and this condition is prehypnotic. Like a metonymy become real, the darkness of the theater is foreshadowed by a "crepuscular reverie," (preliminary to hypnosis, according to Freud and Breuer) which precedes this darkness and draws the subject, from street to street, from poster to poster, to abandon himself into an anonymous, indifferent cube of darkness where the festival of affects which is called a film will take place.

What is the significance of darkness in the cinema (and when I say cinema, I can't help think "theater" more than "film")? Darkness is not only the very essence of reverie (in the prehypnoid sense of the term), it is also the color of a very diffuse eroticism. In its human condensation, its lack of ceremony (contrary to the ritualistic "making an appearance'' in the theater), the relaxation of postures—how many spectators slip into their seat as they slip into bed, coat and feet on the seat in front of them—the ordinary movie theater is a place of disponsibility (even more than ''cruising''), with the idleness of bodies that best characterizes modern eroticism (not the eroticism of advertisements or of strip joints, but the eroticism of a large city). It is in this urban darkness that the body's freedom luxuriates. The invisible work of the potential affects proceeds from what is truly a cinematographic cocoon. The film spectator might adopt the silk worm's motto: *inclusum labor illustrat;* because I am shut in I work, and shine with all the intensity of my desire.

Submerged in the darkness of the theater (an anonymous, crowded darkness: how boring and frustrating all these so called ''private'' screenings), we find the very source of the fascination exercised by film (any film). Consider, on the other hand, the opposite experience, the experience of TV, which also shows films: nothing, no fascination; the darkness is dissolved, the anonymity repressed, the space is familiar, organized (by furniture and familiar objects), tamed. Eroticism, or, better yet in order to stress its frivolity, its incompleteness, the eroticization of space is foreclosed. Television condemns us to the Family, whose household utensil it has become just as the hearth once was, flanked by its predictable communal stewing pot in times past.

Inside this opaque cube, a light: the screen? Yes, of course, but also, visible and yet unnoticed, the dancing cone which drills through the darkness of the theater like a laser beam. This beam transforms itself according to the rotating movement of its particles into changing figures. We turn our face toward the traces of a flickering vibration whose imperious thrust grazes our head from behind, or obliquely, a hair, a face. As in the old hypnosis experiments, we are entranced by this brilliant, immobile and dancing surface, without ever confronting it straight on. This beam of light seems to bore a keyhole for our stupefied gaze to pass through. Are we, then, to understand that sound, music, speech play no part in creating this stasis? For the most part, in commercial productions, the sound formula cannot produce an aural fascination. Meant to strengthen the verisimilitude of an anecdote, sound is merely a supplementary support of representation: it must integrate itself dociley with the mimed object; it is in no way detached from that object. And yet, it would take very little to peel this sound stripe off: a sound slightly out of synch, or amplified; a voice whose graininess grinds right up against our ear—and once again the visual fascination gets hold of us, because it can only be produced artificially, rather, it itself is the artifact, like the flickering light of the projector that, over or next to it, blurs the scene mimed on the screen—but without distorting the image.

For such is the narrow space where the filmic paralysis, the cinematographic hypnosis takes place—at least for the subject who speaks here; I must be in the story (verisimilitude needs me), but I must also be *elsewhere:* an imaginary slightly detached, this is what I demand of the film and of the situation where I have come to find it, being a scrupulous fetishist, conscious, organized, in a word, hard to please.

A filmic image (sound included), what is it? *A lure.* This word must be taken in its psychoanalytic sense. I am locked in on the image as though I were caught in the famous dual relationship which establishes the imaginary. The image is there before me, for my benefit: coalescent (signifier and signified perfectly blended), analogical, global, pregnant; it is a perfect lure. I pounce upon it as an animal snatches up a "lifelike" rag. Of course, the image maintains (in the subject that I think I am) a miscognition attached to the ego and to the imaginary. In the movie theater, regardless of the distance I find myself from the screen, I glue my nose, to the point of disjointing it, on the mirror of the screen, to the imaginary other with which I identify myself narcissistically (reportedly, the spectators who insist on sitting closest to the screen are children and cinephiles): the image which ensnares me, captures me. I am riveted to the representation, and it is this bond which is the basis of the naturalness (pseudo-nature) of the filmed/represented scene (a bond made out of the ingredients of technique): the Real, for its part ignores distance. The Symbolic only knows masks; alone, the image is genuine (it can produce the ring of truth). In final analysis, does not the image have, by statute, all the characteristics of the ideological? The historical subject like the filmgoer I am trying to picture is also glued to the ideological discourse. He experiences its coalescence, its analogical security, the pregnance, the naturalness, the "truth": it is a lure (our lure, who can escape it?). Ideology is, in effect, the imaginary of an epoch, the Cinema of a society. Like a film which knows effectively how to draw a public, it even has its own photograms: the stereotypes with which it articulates its discourse: isn't a stereotype a still image? Do we not have a dual relationship with platitudes: both narcissistic and maternal?

How does one pry oneself from the mirror? Let me risk a response that will be a play on words: it is by "taking off" (in the aeronautic and the hallucinogenic sense of the term). It is true that it is possible to conceive of an art that would break the circle of duality (dual circularity), filmic fascination, and would loosen the glue's grip, the hypnosis of verisimilitude (of analogy) by resorting to some (aural or visual) critical faculty of the spectator—isn't that what is involved in the Brechtian effect of distancing? There are many things that could facilitate the awakening from hypnosis (imaginary/ideological); the very technique of epic art, the spectator's culture, or his ideological vigilance; unlike classical hysteria, the imaginary disappears the moment it is observed.

But there is another way of going to the cinema (other than going armed with the discourse of counter-ideology); it is by letting myself be *twice* fascinated by the image and by its surroundings, as if I had two bodies at once: a narcissistic body which is looking, lost in gazing into the nearby mirror, and a perverse body, ready to fetishize not the image, but precisely that which exceeds it: the sound's grain, the theater, the obscure mass of other bodies, the rays of light, the entrance, the exit: in short, in order to distance myself, to "take off," I complicate a "relationship" with a "situation." What I make use of to take my distance with respect to the image is what, in final analysis, fascinates: I am hypnotized by a distance, and this distance is not an intellectual one. It is, so to speak,an amorous distance: could there be, even in the cinema (and taking the word in its etymological profile), the possibility of deriving pleasure from discretion?

Translated by Bertrand Augst and Susan White

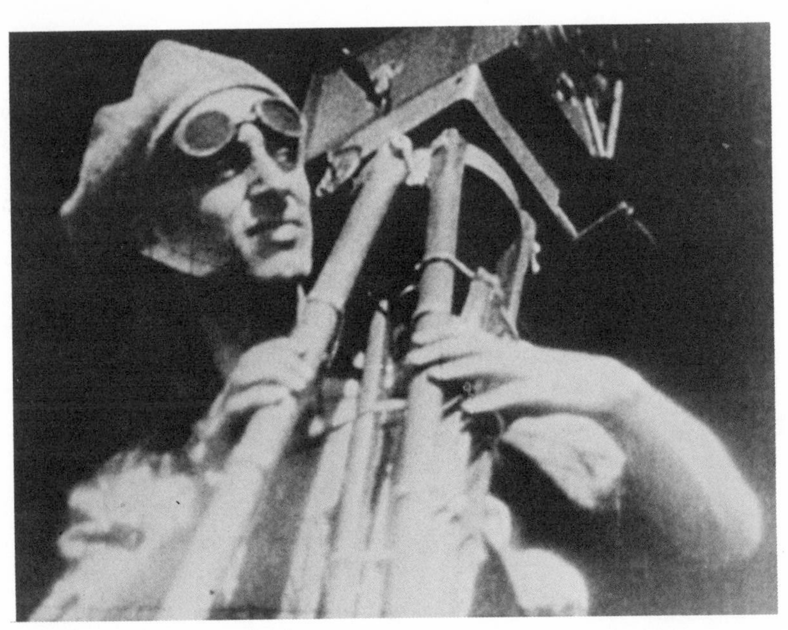

The Vertov Papers

THE MAN WITH THE MOVIE CAMERA
(A Visual Symphony) [19 March 1928]

The Man with the Movie Camera is an experiment in conveying visual phenomena without the aid of titles (a film without titles), scenario (a film without a scenario), or the theater (a film without actors and sets).

Kino-Eye's new experimental work aims to create a truly international film language, an absolute kino-chronicle, and to separate the cinema completely from theater and literature.

On the other hand, *The Man with the Movie Camera,* like *The Eleventh Year,* is closely related to the Radio-Eye period, which the Kinoks see as a new and higher stage in the development of unplayed film.

First. You find yourself in a small but strange country where all experiences and actions and even natural phenomena are strictly controlled and occur at precisely determined times. At any moment you can order rain, thunder, or a seastorm.

If you like, the deluge will stop. Puddles will immediately dry up. The sun will shine forth. You can even have two or three suns.

If you want it, day will turn into night. The sun will turn into the moon. Stars will appear. Winter will replace summer. Snowflakes will fall. Streams will freeze over. Frost will cover the windows.

You can, if you choose, sink or save ships at sea. Start fires and earthquakes. Make wars and revolutions. You control human tears and laughter. Passion and jealousy. Love and hatred.

According to your schedule, people fight or embrace. Marry and divorce. Are born and die. Die and come to life. Die again and again come to life. Or kiss endlessly into the camera until the director is satisfied.

We are at a film studio where a man with a megaphone and a script directs the life of this window-dressing country.

Second. This is no castle, merely a front of painted plywood. And those aren't ships at sea, but toys in a tub. Not rain, but a shower. Not snow, but down. Not a real moon, but painted.

None of this is life—it's a game. Play rain and snow. Make-believe castles and cooperatives. Toy villages and towns. Pretend love and death. A game of counts-and-robbers. Dressing up as tax-collectors and Civil War guerrillas.

Playing at revolution. Make-believe foreign lands. Playing "the new life" and "Socialist construction."

Third. High above this land of make-believe with its mercury lamps and electric suns, high in the real sky burns a real sun. The film factory is a miniature island in a tempestuous ocean of life.

Fourth. Streets and trolleycars intersect. Buildings and buses cross. Feet and smiling faces. Hands and mouths. Shoulders and eyes.

Steering wheels and tires turn. Carousels and organ grinders' hands. Seamstresses' hands and lottery drums. Workers' hands and bicycle riders' shoes.

Men and women meet. Birth and death. Divorce and marriage. Slaps in the face and handshakes. Spies and poets. Judges and defendants. Agitators and the agitated. Peasants and workers. Working students and foreign delegates.

A whirlpool of contacts, blows, embraces, games, accidents, athletics, dances, taxes, spectacles, robberies, and incoming and outgoing papers against a background of seething human labor.

How is the ordinary unarmed eye to make sense of this visual chaos?

Fifth. A little man, armed with a movie camera, leaves the make-believe world at the film factory and heads for real life. It throws him to and fro like a ship. He's a fragile toy boat on a stormy sea. The violent currents of city life swamp him again and again. Mobs of people surge around him at every turn.

Wherever he appears crowds of curiosity-seekers surround like an impenetrable wall, stare into his lens, feel the camera, and peer into the film cans. Obstacles and surprises at every turn.

Unlike the film factory, where the camera is immobile, where "life" moves toward the lens in the strict order of shots and scenes, here life doesn't wait to listen to the director's instructions. Thousands and millions of people go about their jobs. Spring follows winter. Summer follows spring. Thunderstorms, rain, and snow do not appear according to a scenario. Fires, weddings, funerals, anniversaries—everything occurs in its own time, and not according to a calendar invented by the author of the film.

The man with the camera must give up his usual fixed position. He must exert his powers of observation and his agility to the maximum in order to keep up with the speed of life.

Sixth. The first steps of the man with the camera end in failure. He is not upset. He patiently learns how not to lag behind. He gains experience. He becomes used to the circumstances, moves ahead, and employs a whole bag of tricks (candid camera, distraction of the subject, etc.). He tries to go unnoticed, to shoot in such a way that he doesn't interfere with the work of others.

Seventh. The man with the camera marches in step with life. To the bank and the club. The beer-cellar and the hospital. The Soviet and the housing council. The cooperative and the school. The demonstration and the party meeting. The man with the movie camera goes everywhere.

He is present at military parades, at congresses, and in workers' flats. He stands watch at savings banks, visits dispensaries and train stations. He surveys harbors and airports. He travels by car, by train on the roof, by airplane, by glider, by submarine, by battle cruiser, by hydrofoil.

Eighth. The chaos of life gradually becomes clear as he observes and shoots. Nothing is accidental. Everything happens according to law. Every peasant with his seeding machine, every worker at his lathe, every student over his books, every engineer at his drafting table, every Pioneer making a speech is doing the same necessary job.

All this—the rebuilt factory, the improved lathe, the new dining hall, the village day-care center, the high grade on the test, the new road or highway, the new bridge, the repaired locomotive—all this has its purpose. Small or large, these are all victories in the struggle of the new with the old, of the Revolution with the counterrevolution, of the cooperative with the private businessman, of the club with the beer-cellar, of athletics with debauchery, of the dispensary with the disease. All this is a forward position in the struggle for the land of the Soviets, the struggle with lack of faith in Socialist construction.

The movie camera is present at the supreme battle between the world of capitalists, speculators, factory owners, and landlords and the world of workers, peasants, and colonial slaves.

The movie camera is present at the crucial battle between the unique land of the Soviets and all the bourgeois countries.

Visual Apotheosis. Life. Film studio. And the movie camera at the Socialist post.

Note: a secondary theme of production—the passage of the film from camera to laboratory and editing room to screen—will be included through montage at the beginning, in the middle, and at the end of the picture.

FROM KINO-EYE TO RADIO-EYE [1929]
(The Kinoks' ABC's)

I

The village of Pavlovskoye. Not far from Moscow. A cinema show. The small auditorium is jammed with peasants and workers from the neary-by factory. *Kino-Pravda* is being shown without music. The noisy projector can be heard. A train sweeps past on the screen. A little girl appears and comes right up to the camera. Suddenly a scream from the audience. A woman rushes forward to the girl on the screen. She cries and stretches out her arms and calls the girl by name. But the little girl disappears. The train sweeps past again. The lights are turned on. The unconscious woman is taken out. "What is it?" asks the correspondent. "They filmed the little girl before she took ill and died. The woman who ran up to the screen was her mother."

A bench in a park. The assistant director of a trust and his typist. He asks permission to embrace her. She looks around, then says, "Please." A kiss. They stand up, look each other in the eyes, and walk down the lane. They disappear from view. The bench is deserted. From behind a lilac-bush appears a man dragging some sort of apparatus on a tripod. The gardener, who has been watching the scene, asks his helper, "What's this?" The helper replies, "It's Kino-Eye."

A fire. The inhabitants of the burning house throw out their belongings. They wait for the firemen. Militiamen. An excited crowd. At the end of the street speeding firetrucks appear. At this moment a car drives into the square from a side street. Standing in the car a man cranks the handle of some apparatus. Next to him stands a man who says, "We're just in time. Be sure to get the firetrucks when they pull up." The crowd buzzes, "Kino-Eye, Kino-Eye!"

Lenin's body in a raised tomb in Moscow. The working people of the city file past day and night. The entire square and all the adjacent streets are jammed with people. In Red Square a mausoleum is being erected at night under floodlights. Thick snow is falling. A man covered with snow watches the whole night with a camera in order not to miss anything important or interesting. This, too, is Kino-Eye.

"Lenin is dead, but his cause lives," say the working people of the Soviet Union as they strain to build the Socialist country. Two men, a director and a cameraman, on a cable trolley at a cement factory in Novorossiysk on the Black Sea. Both men have cameras, and both are shooting. The trolley moves swiftly. Looking for a better angle, the director climbs up on the side of the trolley. In the twinkling of an eye an oncoming steel beam hits him on the head. The cameraman turns and sees his comrade bloody and unconscious, his camera clutched in his hands, hanging over the sea. He turns his camera, films his comrade, and only then comes to his aid. This, too, is the Kino-Eye school.

Moscow. The end of 1919. An unheated room. A casement window with a broken pane. A table by the window. On the table stands yesterday's glass of tea, frozen. Near the glass lies a manuscript. We read: "Manifesto on Disarming Theatrical Cinema." A variant of this manifesto, titled "We," was subsequently published (1922) in *Kinofot* (Moscow).

The next major theoretical statement by the Kinoks was the well-known manifesto on the unplayed film which was published as "Kinoks Revolution" in *Lef* (1923).

These two manifestoes were preceded by the author's work on newsreels (from 1918), during which he released a number of issues of *Cinema Weekly* and several thematic newsreels.

In the beginning, from 1918 until 1922, the Kinoks existed in the singular, i.e., there was only one Kinok. From 1923 until 1925 there were three or four of them. Since 1925 the Kino-Eye idea has been widely disseminated. Apart from the growth of the basic group, there appeared many popularizers of the movement. Now one may speak not merely of a group, not merely of a Kino-Eye school, not merely of a sector of the front, but of an entire front in the battle for the unplayed documentary film.

II

Kino-Eye: *kinoglaz* or *kinooko*. Hence *Kinoglazovtsy* or *Kinoks*. The Kinoks' ABC's define Kino-Eye by the formula: Kino-Eye = cinechronicle of facts.

Kino-Eye = kino-see (I see through a camera) + kino-write (I record with a camera on film) + kino-organize (I edit).

The Kino-Eye method is a scientific, experimental method for researching the visible world:

a. on the basis of systematic fixation of facts on film;

b. on the basis of systematic organization of the documentary material fixed on film.

Hence, Kino-Eye is not merely the name of a group of filmmakers. Not merely the name of a film *(Kino-Eye* or *Life Unawares)*. And not merely some current in so-called Art (left or right). Kino-Eye is a continuously growing movement for exerting influence with facts against the influence of fiction, no matter how strongly the latter may impress.

Kino-Eye is a documentary deciphering of what is visible, as well as of what is invisible, to the unarmed human eye.

Kino-Eye is the overcoming of space, a visual bond between the people of the world on the basis of continuous exchange of visible facts, film documents, in contrast to exchange of staged films.

Kino-Eye is the overcoming of time, a visual bond between chronologically separated phenomena. Kino-Eye is concentration and decomposition of time. Kino-Eye is the opportunity to see the processes of life in any chronological order and at any speed.

Kino-Eye uses all the shooting methods available to the camera. Rapid shooting, micro-shooting, reverse shooting, animated shooting, shooting in motion, and shooting from completely unexpected angles are handled not as tricks, but as normal, widely used methods.

Kino-Eye uses all available means of editing, juxtaposing and uniting any points in the universe in any chronological order—breaking, if need be, all laws of editing.

Slicing into the seeming chaos of life, Kino-Eye attempts to find the answers in life itself. To find the resultant force among the millions of phenomena related to any given subject. To mount, to tear away with the camera what is most characteristic and expedient, to organize the fragments torn from life into a visually meaningful rhythmic order, a visually meaningful formula, an extracted "I see."

III

To edit means to organize pieces of film (shots) into a film, to "write" a film with the shots, and not to select pieces for "scenes" (the theatrical deviation) or for titles (the literary deviation).

Each Kino-Eye piece is edited from the moment the subject is selected until the film is released in its final form, that is, it is edited during the entire process of making a film.

We can distinguish three stages in this continuous editing:

First stage: editing as a stock-taking of all the documentary data that have a direct or indirect relation to the given subject (in the form of manuscripts, objects, pieces of film, photographs, newspaper clippings, books, etc.). The result of this editing/stock-taking through selection of the most valuable data is that the thematic plan is crystallized, made apparent, edited into shape.

Second stage: editing as a compendium of the eye's observations on a given subject (whether of personal observations or of those reported by scouts and informants). The shooting plan as the result of sorting and selecting observations by the eye. During this selection the author takes into account the indications of the thematic plan as well as the peculiarities of the "machine-eye" or Kino-Eye.

Third stage: central editing. A compendium of observations recorded on film by the Kino-Eye. Computation of editing groups. Joining (addition, subtraction, multiplication, division, and opening of parentheses) of homogenous pieces. Continuous transposition of pieces until they are arranged in a rhythmical order where all the semantic couplings correspond with the visual couplings. The result of all this blending, rearranging, and cutting is a kind of visual equation or formula. This formula, obtained by editing all the documents recorded on film, is the 100% film piece, the extracted, concentrated I see—I kino-see.

Kino-Eye is:

editing when I select a subject (select one from the thousands of possible ones);

editing when I observe the subject (make an expedient selection from the thousands of possible observations);

editing when I choose a sequence for showing the shots of the subject (determine the most expedient combination from the thousands of possible combinations of shots, on the basis of the qualities of the footage as well as of the requirements of the given subject).

The Kino-Eye school requires construction of a film by "intervals," that is, by inter-shot movement, by visual correlation of one shot to another, by transitions from one visual stimulus to another.

The inter-shot displacement (the visual interval, the visual correlation of shots), according to Kino-Eye, is a complex number. It is made up of the sums of various correlations, the chief of which are:

1. correlation of shots (close-ups, long shots, etc.);
2. correlation of foreshortenings;
3. correlation of movements within the shot;
4. correlation of light and shade;
5. correlation of shooting speeds.

Proceeding from a certain combination of these correlations, the author determines: 1. the sequence of pieces; 2. the length of time for each shot. Here both the inter-shot movement (the interval between adjacent pieces) and the visual relation of each individual shot to every other shot are considered.

Finding the most effective route for the viewer's eyes among all these interactions, attractions, and repulsions of shots, reducing this great number of intervals (inter-shot movements) to the simple visual equation or formula that best expresses the basic idea of the film—that is the author-editor's chief and most difficult task.

This theory of intervals was proposed by the Kinoks in the 1919 variant of the manifesto "We."

The work on *The Eleventh Year* and especially on *The Man with the Movie Camera* most clearly illustrate the Kinoks' position on intervals.

IV

On Radio-Eye.

Already in their statements on the coming, but still uninvented sound-film the Kinoks (now Radioks) declared that their path was from Kino-Eye to Radio-Eye, that is, to an audible and radio-transmittable Kino-Eye.

My article *"Kinopravda* and *Radiopravda"* in *Pravda* several years back speaks about the Radio-Eye as an elimination of distances between people, as an opportunity for the workers of the whole world not only to see, but simultaneously to hear one another.

The Kinoks' statement on Radio-Eye was hotly disputed in the press. But then the question was put aside as a matter of the distant future.

Not limiting themselves to a struggle for the unplayed film, the Kinoks simultaneously armed themselves for work on Radio-Eye as the unplayed sound-film.

Already, in *A Sixth of the Earth,* the titles have been replaced by contrapuntally constructed word-radio themes. *The Eleventh Year* is constructed as an audio-visual film: it is edited for both sound and images.

The Man with the Movie Camera is being constructed in the same movement from Kino-Eye to Radio-Eye.

The theoretical and practical research of the Kinoks (unlike the play cinema, which has been caught sleeping) has outpaced our technical possibilities, and now is waiting for the tardy technical basis of sound-film and television to catch up.

The latest technical discoveries in the field give the supporters and makers of sound documentary chronicles the most powerful weapon in the struggle for an unplayed October.

ANSWERS TO QUESTIONS [1930]

To the Editors of *Kinofront:*

There has been so much work lately that I have been writing in fits and starts. My answers to the questions should be published without any changes and in their entirety. The thing is that the preposterous attempts to indict me in formalism are continuing, and I cannot explain them as anything except total ignorance on the part of the people who write on the subject.

With fraternal greetings—D. Vertov

QUESTION: *Do you still stand on the artistic platform that was published in your manifesto of 1922?*

ANSWER: The question concerns the manifesto on the unplayed cinema, "Kinoks. Revolution," which was written in 1922 and published in *Lef,* No. 3, at the beginning of 1923. This manifesto, which declared the advance of newsreels and radio newsreels, cannot be taken statically, as if there were no subsequent statements and declarations.

"Instructions to the Kino-Eye Group," "Design for the First Experimental Station of Documentary Filmmaking," "Proposal for Organizing a Factory of Documentary Films," "Design for Reorganizing Soviet Cinema According to Leninist Proportion," and other of our articles in *Pravda, Kino,* and various anthologies *(Proletcult* and others) and our simultaneous practical work (about 150 documentary films of all kinds, lengths, and forms) have continuously refined and perfected our declaration, which already in 1924-1925 expanded into a program for advancement and which had a considerable influence on both the documentary and "play" sectors of our cinema.

We, Kinoks, agreed to consider as genuine only that cinema which is based on organization of camera-recorded documentary material.

The cinema that is based on organization of camera-recorded actors' play we decided to consider second-rate and theatrical.

We admit that in the struggle against bombastic subdivision of play-films (art—nonart, art film—non-art film) we put quotation marks around these expressions and poked fun at "so-called art," "so-called art films."

By no means did this contradict our respect for individual examples of acted films (admittedly very rare). Of course, we never gave total praise: a good film all in all. A good actors' film, a good play-film, we would always say with reservation.

We admit that, in the struggle for the right to develop documentary film, we did not cover ourselves with the widely used, but differently interpreted terms "art" and "artistic." At the same time we sharply emphasized the inventive, revolutionary (in form and content) nature of the Kino-Eye documentaries. We spoke about our documentaries as a pathos of facts, an enthusiasm for facts. To the attacks of critics we replied that the Kino-Eye documentary is not merely a documentary record, but a revolutionary beacon in the darkness of worldwide theatrical film cliches.

Even now we consider the documentary film method to be the basic method of proletarian cinema, and fixation of the documents of our Socialist advancement to be the basic task of Soviet film.

This hardly means that the theater or the affiliated play-film are in any way released from the struggle for Socialism. On the contrary, the sooner the played, theatrical cinema gives up falsifying reality and impotently imitating documentary film and takes up genuine, total play, the more honest and more powerful will its contributions to the Socialist front be.

QUESTION: *In your opinion, do such films as* The Man with the Movie Camera *satisfy the political demands made of revolutionary cinema?*

ANSWER: The political demands made of the revolutionary

cinema have still not been completely satisfied by a single documentary or play-film. *The Man with the Movie Camera,* released at a moment of crisis in film (not so much a crisis of themes—there were plenty of themes—as a crisis in means of expression), released as a film with the special purpose of eliminating the gap in film language and making the stilted cinema more cinematic, does not claim to replace all our other work. But even the entire sum of these films can hardly hope to have satisfied the sum of political demands made of revolutionary cinema by the Party.

Our energies must be tripled, our film industry must be reorganized according to Leninist proportion, factories of documentary films must be set up, the cadres of film-workers must be distributed along the entire front of the Five-Year Plan. Socialist competition will help documentary film-workers come closer to a better and more complete fulfillment of the political demands made by the Party.

This applies to the sound film also (replying to the question about documentary sound films). Radio-Eye anticipated Leninist proportion for radio-theater programs.

In the question about the role of sound in documentaries we have not changed our position. We see Radio-Eye as a powerful weapon in the hands of the proletariat, an opportunity for the workers of all nations to hear and see one another, an opportunity unlimited by space to agitate and propagandize with facts, an opportunity to oppose the radio-film documents of the capitalist world—documents of oppression and exploitation—with the radio-film documents of our Socialist construction.

Declarations about the need to keep visual moments from coinciding with audible moments, just like declarations about the need to have only sound-films or only talkies, aren't worth a bean. In sound-film, as in silent film, we distinguish only two kinds of film: documentaries (with real conversations and sounds) and play-films (with artificial, specially prepared conversations and sounds).

Neither documentaries nor play-films are obligated to have visible moments coincide with audible moments. Sound shots and silent shots are edited alike; they can coincide in montage or they can intertwine with each other in various combinations.

QUESTION: *Do you propose to change your method and your general views on the cinema in connection with the new tasks set by the period of Socialist reconstruction?*

ANSWER: The documentary film method, the Kino-Eye and Radio-Eye method, brought to life by the October Revolution and matured on the fronts of the Civil War and the Socialist construction, cannot but blossom in the period of Socialist reconstruction, when the establishment of Leninist proportion in cinema shows will allow factories of documentary films to grow, when competing film brigades will multiply and be tempered in the continuous documentary struggle for Socialism.

ON ORGANIZING A CREATIVE LABORATORY [1936]

Man, liberated from capitalist slavery. Man, liberated from the necessity to be a robot. Man, liberated from abasement, hunger, unemployment, poverty, and ruin. Man with his right to labor, rest, and education. Man with his right to be creative. Man in his luxuriant creative growth, his mastery of technology, science, literature, and art.

To show the behavior of this man on screen. Can there be a more noble task for the artist? Yet to fulfill this task we must understand that it is supremely difficult. The solution depends not on good intentions, but on sheer hard work and the technology of organization. Not with naked enthusiasm and bare hands, not with commotion and overexertion will the task be fulfilled.

To do the job and to get our group to stop making poetic survey films and start making films about man's behavior outside the studio, in natural conditions, we must descend from heaven to earth and do some preparatory work. The proposal for organizing a creative laboratory has been elicited by the necessity to put an end to wasting time and energy, to establish an intelligent order in all our work, to set up the technical basis properly, to make the work rhythmical, and to eliminate all obstacles. Persistence and firmness of character in overcoming these obstacles are needed.

The first obstacle we encountered was the impossibility of recording synchronous sound outside the studio. The apparatus at Mezhrabpomfilm could be used only with three-phase current. It could not be used to film people in the country, outdoors, in natural conditions. We realized that this obstacle was paramount and directed all our efforts toward it. But as things go in our industry, we succeeded in solving the problem only in words—promises and resolutions were made. In fact, we didn't get anything except postponement of the promises until "tomorrow." That tomorrow approached us with all the speed with which parallel lines draw together.

In our laboratory the first step will be to overcome this difficult but not insurmountable obstacle as quickly as possible.

The shooting work in our laboratory should fulfill the following technical requirements:

1. The shooting should be soundless so as not to distract the subject and not to leave a hum on the tape.

2. The shooting should be instantaneous—simultaneous with the action.

3. The shooting should be technically feasible in any location (cottage, field, airport, desert, etc.).

4. Both camera and recorder should be connected so that there is no need for special efforts to synchronize them.

5. The sound should be up to the demands that will be made of it when our best films are finished.

6. The apparatus for sync-shooting should be compact and have its own power supply.

7. There must be no possibility of accidents since we are filming unrepeatable moments.

8. The actions of the cameraman and soundman must be unified and simultaneous. This will be best achieved if sound and image are recorded by one unit on two tapes.

9. The laboratory will also work on the other technical questions that our group faces: kinds of stock and lenses needed, shooting indoors or at night, shooting from concealment at a distance, etc.

10. To do competent filming of human behavior outside the studio in natural conditions, we must concentrate in one place all the special effects and devices that have been invented. This can be done only in such a laboratory.

The second major obstacle has been the difficulty of setting up our editing work properly. It has been impossible to preserve rough cuts from film to film. The right to make new cuts has not been given. There has been no permanent housing for our editing work.

All this has reduced our editing to spurts and fits. What had been done before had to be repeated again and again. Each time the work had to be started from scratch.

Our laboratory solves these problems by moving from disjointed editing work to a continuous editing process, from systemless preservation of individual pieces to an author's film library.

The creative laboratory puts an end to systematic destruction of our preliminary work, just as it preserves our preliminary shooting work.

The third serious obstacle has been the impossibility of training and keeping experienced people.

When a film was finished the crew would be reassigned and the training of people for our special type of work would have to begin over again. Again, loss of time and energy.

In our laboratory the cameraman, sound mixer, director, assistant, informer, organizer, and other workers will continually perfect themselves from film to film. Instead of holding up the work, they will speed it up.

Analogous obstacles have stood in our way in all aspects of the information-gathering and organizational work. They created a thick wall which blocked all our attempts to make films about human behavior.

The contradictions between the organizational forms set for us and our own creative ideas have reduced our efforts to zero. No matter how much we increased our attempts in the existing conditions, the result was always the same. Zero destroys any number it is multiplied by.

The creative laboratory will make films of a special type about human behavior, not in the midst of organizational cliches, but in the peculiar conditions that this kind of work requires.

First task: creative cadres. Not indifferent, but enthusiastic for this new and difficult job. Not by assignment, but by calling. Not casual, but selected by the director of the workshop. Not transient or temporary, but permanent, each growing in his specialty from film to film, each dedicating all his ability and strength to the work, each given the opportunity to perfect himself and to implement his proposals.

Second task: shooting basis. Not accidental, but adapted to our special work. Not temporary, but permanent. Not rigid, but growing. Not stationary, but mobile. Not tied down to power lines, but able to sync-shoot at any time and place, under any conditions.

Third task: editing basis. Not temporary, but permanent. Not casual, but thoroughly prepared. Not anonymous, but signed by an author. Not fixed, but continually in action. A film library of rough cuts.

Fourth task: information-gathering basis. Not accidental scraps of information, but a system of continuous observations.

Fifth task: organizational basis. Not rush work (one alarm after another), but a constant preparedness for scouting or shooting at any moment.

Sixth task: work on developing not one isolated film, but on developing several related topics. Not a preliminary scenario about the future actions of the observed person, but a synthesis of filmic observations, a synthetic consideration of rough cuts, which is impossible without analysis of what is to be synthesized. Unity of analysis and synthesis. Script, shooting, and editing processes simultaneous with observations of the actions, behavior, and surroundings of the subject. Analysis (from the unknown to the known) and synthesis (from the known to the unknown), not opposed to each other, but inseparably linked. Synthesis of the subject's behavior as an integral part of the analysis.

Seventh task: influence the general level of Soviet film production by setting examples of various kinds of creative cinema.

Eighth task: gradually increase the quantity and improve the quality of the exemplary films, not by increasing estimates or enlarging the staff of the laboratory, but by continually perfecting the information-gathering, organizational, shooting, and editing work.

Ninth task: eliminate rejection of footage by director by making it possible to use material not included in one topic in a parallel or upcoming assignment.

Tenth task: eliminate the usual idle time by making the process of production continuous, by being prepared for shooting at any time, by being able to go from an interrupted session to work on another topic.

Note: to my knowledge, quarters for the laboratory can be found at Potylikha, in the Mosfilm studio. They also have there an Eclair camera, which comes closest to what we need in our work.

Translated by Marco Carynnyk

Next, said I, here is a parable to illustrate the degrees in which our nature may be enlightened or unenlightened. Imagine the condition of men living in a sort of cavernous chamber underground, with an entrance open to the light and a long passage all down the cave. Here they have been from childhood, chained by the leg and also by the neck, so that they cannot move and can only see what is in front of them, because the chains will not let them turn their heads. At some distance higher up is the light of a fire burning behind them; and between the prisoners and the fire is a track, with a parapet built along it, like the screen at a puppet show, which hides the performers while they show their puppets over the top.

I see, said he.

Now, behind this parapet imagine persons carrying along various artificial objects, including figures of men and animals in wood or stone or other materials, which project above the parapet. Naturally, some of these persons will be talking, others silent.

It is a strange picture, he said, and a strange sort of prisoners.

Like ourselves, I replied; for in the first place prisoners so confined would have seen nothing of themselves or of one another, except the shadows thrown by the fire-light on the wall of the cave facing them, would they?

Not if all their lives they had been prevented from moving their heads.

And they would have seen as little of the objects carried past.

Of course.

Now, if they could talk to one another, would they not suppose that their words referred only to those passing shadows which they saw?

Necessarily.

And suppose their prison had an echo from the wall facing them? When one of the people crossing behind them spoke; they could only suppose that the sound came from the shadows passing before their eyes.

No doubt.

In every way, then, such prisoners would recognize as reality nothing but the shadows of those artificial objects.

Plato, The Republic, vii, 514
Trans. by Francis M. Cornford

Ideological Effects of the Basic Cinematographic Apparatus

Jean-Louis Baudry

At the end of *The Interpretation of Dreams,* when he seeks to integrate dream elaboration and its particular "economy" with the psyche as a whole, Freud assigns to the latter an optical model: "Let us simply imagine the instrument which serves in psychic productions as a sort of complicated microscope or camera." But Freud does not seem to hold strongly to this optical model, which, as Derrida has pointed out,[1] brings out the shortcoming in graphic representation in the area earlier covered by his work on dreams. Moreover, he will later abandon the optical model in favor of a writing instrument, the "mystic writing pad." Nonetheless this optical choice seems to prolong the tradition of Western science, whose birth coincides exactly with the development of the optical apparatus which will have as a consequence the decentering of the human universe, the end of geocentrism (Galileo).

But also, and paradoxically, the optical apparatus *camera obscura* will serve in the same period to elaborate in pictorial work a new mode of representation, *perspectiva artificalis.* This system, a recentering or at least a displacement of the center (which settles itself in the eye), will assure the setting up of the "subject"* as the active center and origin of meaning. One could doubtless question the privileged position which optical instruments seem to occupy on the line of intersection of science and ideological products. Does the technical nature of optical instruments, directly attached to scientific practice, serve to conceal not only their use in ideological products but also the ideological effects which they may provoke themselves? Their scientific base assures them a sort of neutrality and avoids their being questioned.

But already a question: if we are to take account of the imperfections of these instruments, their limitations, by what criteria may these be defined? If, for example, one can speak of a restricted depth of field as a limitation, doesn't this term itself depend upon a particular conception of reality for which such a limitation would not exist?

*The term "subject" is used by Baudry and others not to mean the topic of discourse, but rather the perceiving and ordering self, as in our term "subjective."—Ed.

Signifying productions are particularly relevant here, to the extent that instrumentation plays a more and more important role in them and that their distribution is more and more extensive. It is strange (but is it so strange?) that emphasis has been placed almost exclusively on their influence, on the effects they have as finished products, their content, the field of what is signified, if you like; the technical bases on which these effects depend and the specific characteristics of these bases have been ignored, however. They have been protected by the inviolability that science is supposed to provide. We would like to establish for the cinema a few guidelines which will need to be completed, verified, improved.

We must first establish the place of the instrumental base in the set of operations which combine in the production of a film (we omit consideration of economic implications). Between "objective reality" and the camera, site of the inscription, and between the inscription and projection are situated certain operations, a *work** which has as its result a finished product. To the extent that it is cut off from the raw material ("objective reality") this product does not allow us to see the transformation which has taken place. Equally distant from "objective reality" and the finished product, the camera occupies an intermediate position in the work process which leads from raw material to finished product. Though mutually dependent from other points of view, *découpage* [shot breakdown before shooting] and *montage* [editing, or final assembly] must be distinguished because of the essential difference in the signifying raw material on which each operates: language (scenario) or image. Between the two complementary stages of production a mutation of the signifying material takes place (neither translation nor transcription, obviously, for the image is not reducible to language) precisely where the camera is. Finally, between the finished product (possessing exchange value, a commodity) and its consumption (use value) is introduced another operation effected by a set of instruments. Projector and screen restore the light lost in the shooting process, and transform a succession of separate images into an unrolling which also restores, but according to another scansion, the movement seized from "objective reality."

Cinematographic specificity (what distinguishes cinema from other systems of signification) thus refers to a *work*, that is, to a process of transformation. The question becomes, is the work made evident, does consumption of the product bring about a "knowledge effect" [Althusser], or is the work concealed? If the latter, consumption of

* *Travail*, the process—implying not only "work" in the ordinary sense but as in Freud's usages: the dream-work.—Tr.

the product will obviously be accompanied by ideological surplus value. On the practical level, this poses the question of by what procedures the work can in fact be made "readable" in its inscription. These procedures must of necessity call cinematographic technique into play. But, on the other hand, going back to the first question, one may ask, do the instruments (the technical base) produce specific ideological effects, and are these effects themselves determined by the dominant ideology? In which case, concealment of the technical base will also bring about a specific ideological effect. Its inscription, its manifestation as such, on the other hand, would produce a knowledge effect, as actualization of the work process, as denunciation of ideology, and as critique of idealism.

THE EYE OF THE SUBJECT

Central in the process of production of the film[2], the camera—an assembly of optical and mechanical instrumentation—carries out a certain mode of inscription characterized by marking, by the recording of differences of light intensity (and of wavelength for color) and of differences between the frames. Fabricated on the model of the *camera obscura,* it permits the construction of an image analogous to the perspective projections developed during the Italian Renaissance. Of course the use of lenses of different focal lengths can alter the perspective of an image. But this much, at least, is clear in the history of cinema: it is the perspective construction of the Renaissance which originally served as model. The use of different lenses, when not dictated by technical considerations aimed at restoring the habitual perspective (such as shooting in limited or extended spaces which one wishes to expand or contract) does not destroy [traditional] perspective but rather makes it play a normative role. Departure from the norm, by means of a wide-angle or telephoto lens, is clearly marked in comparison with so-called "normal" perspective. We will see in any case that the resulting ideological effect is still defined in relation to the ideology inherent in perspective. The dimensions of the image itself, the ratio between height and width, seem clearly taken from an average drawn from Western easel painting.

The conception of space which conditions the construction of perspective in the Renaissance differs from that of the Greeks. For the latter, space is discontinuous and heterogeneous (for Aristotle, but also for Democritus, for whom space is the location of an infinity of indivisible atoms), whereas with Nicholas of Cusa will be born a conception of space formed by the relation between elements which are equally near and distant from the "source of all life." In addition, the pictorial construction of the Greeks corresponded to the organization of their stage, based on a multiplicity of points of view, whereas the painting of the Renaissance will elaborate a centered space. ("Painting is nothing but the intersection of the visual pyramid following a given distance, a fixed center, and a certain lighting."—Alberti.) The center of this space coincides with the eye which Jean Pellerin Viator will so justly call the "subject." ("The principal point in perspective should be placed at eye level: this point is called fixed or subject."[3]) Monocular vision, which as Pleynet points out, is what the camera has, calls forth a sort of play of "reflection." Based on the principle of a fixed point by reference to which the visualized objects are organized, it specifies in return the position of the "subject"[4] the very spot it must necessarily occupy.

In focusing it, the optical construct appears to be truly the projection-reflection of a "virtual image" whose hallucinatory reality it creates. It lays out the space of an ideal vision and in this way assures the necessity of a transcendence—metaphorically (by the unknown to which it appeals—here we must recall the structural place occupied by the vanishing point) and metonymically (by the displacement that it seems to carry out: a subject is both "in place of" and "a part for the whole"). Contrary to Chinese and Japanese painting, Western easel painting, presenting as it does a motionless and continuous whole, elaborates a total vision which corresponds to the idealist conception of the fullness and homogeneity of "being,"[5] and is, so to speak, representative of this conception. In this sense it contributes in a singularly emphatic way to the ideological function of art, which is to provide the tangible representation of metaphysics. The principle of transcendence which conditions and is conditioned by the perspective construction represented in painting and in the photographic image which copies from it seems to inspire all the idealist paeans to which the cinema has given rise [such as we find in Cohen-Seat or Bazin].[6]

PROJECTION: THE DIFFERENCE NEGATED

Nevertheless, whatever the effects proper to optics generally, the movie camera differs from still photography by registering through its mechanical instrumentation a series of images. It might thus seem to counter the unifying and "substantializing" character of the single-perspective image, taking what would seem like instants of time or slices from "reality" (but always a reality already worked upon, elaborated, selected). This might permit the supposition, especially because the camera moves, of a multiplicity of points of view which would neutralize the fixed position of the eye-subject and even nullify it. But here we must turn to the relation between the succession of images inscribed by the camera and their projection, bypassing momentarily the place occupied by montage, which plays a decisive role in the strategy of the ideology produced.

The projection operation (projector and screen) restore continuity of movement and the temporal dimension to the sequence of static images. The relation between the individual frames and the projection would resemble the relation between points and a curve in geometry. But it is precisely this relation and the restoration of continuity to discontinuous elements which poses a problem. The meaning effect produced does not depend only on the content of the images but also on the material procedures by which an illusion of continuity, dependent on the persistence of vision, is restored from discontinuous elements. These separate frames have between them differences that are indispensible for the creation of an illusion of continuity, of a continuous passage (movement, time). But only on one condition can these differences create this illusion: they must be effaced as differences.[7]

Thus on the technical level the question becomes one of the adoption of a very small difference between images, such that each image, in consequence of an organic factor [presumably persistence of vision] is rendered incapable of being seen as such. In this sense we could say that film—and perhaps in this respect it is exemplary—lives on the denial of difference: the difference is necessary for it to live, but it lives on its negation. This is indeed the paradox that emerges if we look directly at a strip of processed film: adjacent images are almost exactly repeated, their divergence being verifiable only by comparison of images at a sufficient distance from each other. We should remember, moreover, the disturbing effects which result during a projection from breakdowns in the recreation of movement, when the spectator is brought abruptly back to discontinuity—that is, to the body, to the technical apparatus which he had *forgotten*.

We might not be far from seeing what is in play on this material basis, if we recall that the "language" of the unconscious, as it is found in dreams, slips of the tongue, or hysterical symptoms, manifests itself as continuity destroyed, broken, and as the unexpected surging forth of a marked difference. Couldn't we thus say that cinema reconstructs and forms the mechanical model (with the simplifications that this can entail) of a system of writing [écriture] constituted by a material base and a counter-system while also concealing it? On the one hand, the optical apparatus and the film permit the marking of difference (but the marking is already negated, we have seen, in the constitution of the perspective image with its mirror effect). On the other hand, the mechanical apparatus both selects the minimal difference and represses it in projection, so that meaning can be constituted: it is at once direction, continuity, movement. The projection mechanism allows the differential elements (the discontinuity inscribed by the camera) to be suppressed, bringing only the relation into play. The individual images as such disappear so that movement and continuity are the visible expression (one might even say the projection) of their relations, derived from the tiny discontinuities between the images. Thus one may assume that what was already at work as the originating basis of the perspective image, namely the eye, the "subject," is put forth, liberated (in the sense that a chemical reaction liberates a substance) by the operation which transforms successive, discrete images (as isolated images they have, strictly speaking, no meaning, or at least no unity of meaning) into continuity, movement, meaning; with continuity restored both meaning and consciousness are restored.[8]

THE TRANSCENDENTAL SUBJECT

Meaning and consciousness, to be sure: at this point we must return to the camera. Its mechanical nature not only permits the shooting of differential images as rapidly as desired but also destines it to change position, to move. Film history shows that as a result of the combined inertia of painting, theater, and photography, it took a certain time to notice the inherent mobility of the cinematic mechanism. The ability to reconstitute movement is after all only a partial, elementary aspect of a more general capability. To seize movement is to become movement, to follow a trajectory is to become trajectory, to choose a direction is to have the possibility of choosing one, to determine a meaning is to give oneself a meaning. In this way the eye-subject, the invisible base of artificial perspective (which in fact only represents a larger effort to produce an ordering, regulated transcendence) becomes absorbed in, "elevated" to a vaster function, proportional to the movement which it can perform.

And if the eye which moves is no longer fettered by a body, by the laws of matter and time, if there are no more assignable limits to its displacement—conditions fulfilled by the possibilities of shooting and of film—the world will not only be constituted by this eye but for it.[9] The movability of the camera seems to fulfill the most favorable conditions for the manifestation of the "transcendental subject." There is both fantasmatization of an objective reality (images, sounds, colors) and of an objective reality which, limiting its powers of constraint, seems equally to augment the possibilities or the power of the subject.[10] As it is said of consciousness—and in point of fact we are concerned with nothing less—the image will always be image *of* something; it must result from a deliberate act of consciousness [visee intentionelle]. "The word intentionality signifies nothing other than this peculiarity that consciousness has of being consciousness *of* something, of carrying in its quality of *ego* its *cogitatum* within itself.[11] In such a definition could perhaps be found the status of the cinematographic image, or rather of its operation, the mode of working which it carries out. For it to be an image of something, it has to constitute this something as meaning. The image seems to reflect the world but solely in the naive inversion of a founding hierarchy: "The domain of natural existence thus has only an authority of the second order, and always presupposes the domain of the transcendental."[12]

The world is no longer only an "open and unbounded horizon." Limited by the framing, lined up, put at the proper distance, the world offers up an object endowed with meaning, an intentional object, implied by and implying the action of the "subject" which sights it. At the same time that the world's transfer as image seems to accomplish this phenomenological reduction, this putting into parentheses of its real existence (a suspension necessary, we will see, to the formation of the impression of reality) provides a basis for the apodicity* of the ego. The multiplicity of aspects of the object in view refers to a synthesizing operation, to the unity of this constituting subject: Husserl speaks of " 'aspects,' sometimes of 'proximity,' sometimes of 'distance,' in variable modes of 'here' and 'there,' opposed to an absolute 'here' (which is located—for me—in 'my own body' which appears to me at the same time), the consciousness of which, though it remains *unperceived,* always accompanies them. [We will see moreover what happens with the body in the *mise-en-scene* of projection.—J. L. B.] Each 'aspect' which the mind grasps is revealed in turn as a unity synthesized from a multiplicty of corresponding modes of presentation. The nearby object may present itself as the same, but under one or another 'aspect.' There may be variation of visual perspective, but also of 'tactile,' 'acoustic' phenomena, or of other 'modes of presentation'[13] as we can observe in directing our attention in the proper direction."[14]

For Husserl, "the original operation [of intentional analysis] is to *unmask the potentialities implied* in present states of consciousness. And it is by this that will be carried out, from the noematic point of view, the eventual *explication, definition,* and *elucidation* of what is meant by consciousness, that is, its *objective meaning.*"[15] And again in the *Cartesian Meditations:* "A second type of polarization now presents itself to us, another type of synthesis which embraces the particular multiplicities of *cogitationes,* which embraces them all and in a special manner, namely as *cogitationes* of an identical self which, *active* or *passive,* lives in all the lived states of consciousness and which, through them, relates to all objects."[16]

Thus is articulated the relation between the continuity necessary to the constitution of meaning and the "subject" which constitutes this meaning: continuity is an attribute of the subject. It supposes the subject and it circumscribes his place. It appears in the cinema in the two complementary aspects of a "formal" continuity established through a system of negated differences and narrative continuity in the filmic space. The latter, in any case, could not have been conquered without exercising violence against the instrumental base, as can be discovered from most of the texts by film-makers and critics: the discontinuity that had been effaced at the level of the image could have reappeared on the narrative level, giving rise to effects of rupture disturbing to the spectator (to a *place* which ideology must both conquer and, in the degree that it already dominates it, must also satisfy: fill). "What is important in a film is the feeling of continuity which joins shots and sequences while maintaining unity and cohesion of movements. This continuity was one of the most difficult things to obtain."[17] Pudovkin defined montage as "the art of assembling pieces of film, shot separately, in such a way as to give the spectator the impression of continuous movement." The search for such narrative continuity, so difficult to obtain from the material base, can only be explained by an essential ideological stake projected in this point: it is a question of preserving at any cost the synthetic unity of the locus where meaning originates [the subject]—the constituting transcendental function to which narrative continuity points back as its natural secretion.[18]

THE SCREEN-MIRROR: SPECULARIZATION AND DOUBLE IDENTIFICATION

But another supplementary operation (made possible by a special technical arrangement) must be added in order that the mechanism thus described can play its role effectively as an ideological machine, so that not only the reworked "objective reality" but also the specific type of identification we have described can be represented.

No doubt the darkened room and the screen bordered with black like a letter of condolences already present privileged conditions of effectiveness—no exchange, no circulation, no communication with any outside. Projection and reflection take place in a closed space and those who remain there, whether they know it or not (but they do not), find themselves chained, captured, or captivated. (What might one say of the function of the head in this captivation: it suffices to recall that for Bataille materialism makes itself headless—like a wound that bleeds and thus transfuses.) And the mirror, as a reflecting surface, is framed, limited, circumscribed. *An infinite mirror would no longer be a mirror.* The paradoxical nature of the cinematic mirror-screen is without doubt that it reflects *images* but not *"reality";* the word reflect, being transitive,* leaves this ambiguity unresolved. In any case this "reality" comes from behind the spectator's head and if he looked at it directly he would see nothing except the moving beams from an already veiled light source.

*It is always a reflection *of* something.—Tr.

The arrangement of the different elements—projector, darkened hall, screen—in addition from reproducing in a striking way the *mise-en-scene* of Plato's cave (prototypical set for all transcendence and the topological model of idealism[19]) reconstructs the situation necessary to the release of the "mirror stage" discovered by Lacan. This psychological phase, which occurs between six and eighteen months of age, generates *via* the mirror image of a unified body the constitution or at least the first sketches of the "I" as an imaginary function. "It is to this unreachable image in the mirror that the specular image gives its garments."[20] But for this imaginary constitution of the self to be possible, there must be—Lacan strongly emphasizes this point—two complementary conditions: immature powers of mobility and a precocious maturation of visual organization (apparent in the first few days of life). If one considers that these two conditions are repeated during cinematographic projection—suspension of mobility and predominance of the visual function—perhaps one could suppose that this is more than a simple analogy. And possibly this very point explains the "impression of reality" so often invoked in connection with the cinema for which the various explanations proposed seem only to skirt the real problem. In order for this impression to be produced, it would be necessary that the conditions of a formative scene be reproduced. This scene would be repeated and reenacted in such a manner that the imaginary order (activated by a specularization which takes place, everything considered, in reality) fulfills its particular function of occultation or of filling the gap, the split, of the subject on the order of the signifier.[21]

On the other hand, it is to the extent that the child can sustain the look of another in the presence of a third party that he can find the assurance of an identification with the image of his own body. From the very fact that during the mirror stage is established a dual relationship, it constitutes, in conjunction with the formation of the self in the imaginary order, the nexus of secondary identification.[22] The origin of the self, as discovered by Lacan, in pertaining to the imaginary order effectively subverts the "optical machinery" of idealism which the projection room scrupulously reproduces.[23] But it is not as specifically "imaginary," nor as a reproduction of its first configuration, that the self finds a "place" in the cinema. This occurs, rather, as a sort of proof or verification of that function, a solidification through repetition.

The "reality" mimed by the cinema is thus first of all that of a "self." But, because the reflected image is not that of the body itself but that of a world already given as meaning, one can distinguish two levels of identification. The first, attached to the image itself, derives from the character portrayed as a center of secondary identifications, carrying an identity which constantly must be seized and reestablished. The second level permits the appearance of the first and places it "in action"—this is the transcendental subject whose place is taken by the camera which constitutes and rules the objects in this "world." Thus the spectator identifies less with what is represented, the spectacle itself, than with what stages the spectacle, makes it seen, obliging him to see what it sees; this is exactly the function taken over by the camera as a sort of relay.[24] Just as the mirror assembles the fragmented body in a sort of imaginary integration of the self, the transcendental self unites the discontinuous fragments of phenomena, of lived experience, into unifying meaning. Through it each fragment assumes meaning by being integrated into an "organic" unity. Between the imaginary gathering of the fragmented body into a unity and the transcendentality of the self, giver of unifying meaning, the current is indefinitely reversible.

The ideological mechanism at work in the cinema seems thus to be concentrated in the relationship between the camera and the subject. The question is whether the former will permit the latter to constitute and seize itself in a particular mode of specular reflection. Ultimately, the forms of narrative adopted, the "contents" of the image, are of little importance so long as an identification remains possible.[25] What emerges here (in outline) is the specific function fulfilled by the cinema as support and instrument of ideology. It constitutes the "subject" by the illusory delimitation of a central location—whether this be that of a god or of any other substitute. It is an apparatus destined to obtain a precise ideological effect, necessary to the dominant ideology: creating a fantasmatization of the subject, it collaborates with a marked efficacity in the maintenance of idealism.

Thus the cinema assumes the role played throughout Western history by various artistic formations. The ideology of representation (as a principal axis orienting the notion of aesthetic "creation") and specularization (which organizes the *mise-en-scène* required to constitute the transcendental function) form a singularly coherent system in the cinema. Everything happens as if, the subject himself being unable—and for a reason—to account for his own situation, it was necessary to substitute secondary organs, grafted on to replace his own defective ones, instruments or ideological formations capable of filling his function as subject. In fact, this substitution is only possible on the condition that the instrumentation itself be hidden or repressed. Thus disturbing cinematic elements—similar, precisely, to those elements indicating the return of the repressed—signify without fail the arrival of the instrument "in flesh and blood," as in Vertov's *Man With a Movie Camera*. Both specular tranquility and the assurance of one's own identity collapse simultaneously with the revealing of the mechanism, that is of the inscription of the film-work.

The cinema can thus appear as a sort of psychic apparatus of substitution, corresponding to the model defined by the dominant ideology. The system of repression (primarily economic) has as its goal the prevention of deviations and of the active exposure of this "model".[26] Analogously one could say that its "unconscious" is not recognized (we speak of the apparatus and not of the content of films, which have used the unconscious in ways we know all too well). To this unconscious would be attached the mode of production of film, the process of "work" in its multiple determinations, among which must be numbered those depending on instrumentation. This is why reflections on the basic apparatus ought to be possible to integrate into a general theory of the ideology of cinema.

Translated by Alan Williams

NOTES

1. Cf. on this subject Derrida's work "La Scène de l'écriture" in *L'Ecriture et la Différence* (Paris: Le Seuil).
2. Obviously we are not speaking here of investment of capital in the process.
3. Cf. L. Brion Guerry, *Jean Pellerin Viator* (Paris: Belles Lettres, 1962).
4. We understand the term "subject" here in its function as vehicle and place of intersection of ideological implications which we are attempting progressively to make clear, and not as the structural function which analytic discourse attempts to locate. It would rather take partially the place of the ego, of whose deviations little is known in the analytic field.
5. The perspective "frame" which will have such an influence on cinematographic shooting has as its role to intensify, to increase the effect of the spectacle, which no divergence may be allowed to split.
6. See Cohen-Seat, *Essai sur les principes d'une philosophie du cinéma* (Paris: Corti) and Bazin, *What Is Cinema?* (Berkeley & Los Angeles: University of California Press). In the French text Baudry includes lengthy quotations from these two works at this point as examples of "idealist paeans" to cinema.—Tr.
7. "We know that the spectator finds it impossible to notice that the images which succeed one another before his eyes were assembled end-to-end, because the projection of film on the screen offers an impression of continuity although the images which compose it are, in reality, distinct, and are differentiated moreover by variations in space and time.

"In a film, there can be hundreds, even thousands of cuts and intervals. But if it is shown for specialists who know the art, the spectacle will not be divulged as such. Only an error or lack of competence will permit them to seize, and this is a disagreeable sensation, the changes of time and place of action." (Pudovkin, "Le Montage" in *Cinéma d'aujourd'hui et de demain,* [Moscow, 1956].)

8. It is thus first at the level of the apparatus that the cinema functions as a language: inscription of discontinuous elements whose effacement in the relationship instituted among them produces meaning.

9. "In the cinema I am simultaneously in this action and *outside* of it, in this space and out of this space. Having the power of ubiquity, I am everywhere and nowhere." (Jean Mitry, *Esthétique et Psychologie du Cinéma* (Paris: Presses Universitaires de France, 1965), p. 179.

10. The cinema manifests in a hallucinatory manner the belief in the omnipotence of thought, described by Freud, which plays so important a role in neurotic defense mechanisms.

11. Husserl, *Les Meditations Cartesiennes* (Paris: Vrin, 1953), p. 28.

12. *Ibid.,* p. 18.

13. On this point it is true that the camera is revealed as incomplete. But this is only a technical imperfection which, since the birth of cinema, has already in large measure been remedied.

14. *Ibid.,* p. 34, emphasis added.

15. *Ibid.,* p. 40.

16. *Ibid.,* p. 58.

17. Mitry, *op.cit.,* p. 157.

18. The lens, the "objective," is of course only a particular location of the "subjective." Marked by the idealist opposition interior/exterior, topologically situated at the point of meeting of the two, it corresponds, one could say, to the empirical organ of the subjective, to the opening, the fault in the organs of meaning, by which the exterior world may penetrate the interior and assume meaning. "It is the interior which commands," says Bresson. "I know this may seem paradoxical in an art which is all exterior." Also the use of different lenses is already conditioned by camera movement as implication and trajectory of meaning, by this trancendental function which we are attempting to define: it is the possiblity of choosing a field as accentuation or modification of the *visée intentionelle.*

No doubt this trancendental function fits in without difficulty the field of psychology. This, moreover, is insisted upon by Husserl himself, who indicates that Brentano's discovery, intentionality, "permits one truly to distinguish the method of a descriptive science of consciousness, as much philosophical and trancendental as psychological."

19. The arrangement of the cave, except that in the cinema it is already doubled in a sort of enclosure in which the camera, the

darkened chamber, is enclosed in another darkened chamber, the projection hall.

20. Lacan, *Ecrits* (Paris: Le Seuil, 1966). See in particular "Le Stade du miroir comme formateur de la fonction du je."

21. We see that what has been defined as impression of reality refers less to the "reality" than to the apparatus which, although being of an hallucinatory order, nonetheless founds this possibility. Reality will never appear except as relative to the images which reflect it, in some way inaugurated by a reflection anterior to itself.

22. We refer here to what Lacan says of identifications in liaison with the structure determined by an optical instrument (the mirror), as they are constituted, in the prevailing figuration of the ego, as lines of resistance to the advance of the analytic work.

23. "That the ego be 'in the right' must be vowed, from experience, to be a function of misunderstanding." (Lacan, *op.cit.*, p. 637.)

24. "That it sustains itself as 'subject' means that language permits it to consider itself as the stagehand or even the director of all the imaginary capturings of which it would otherwise only be the living marionette." (*Ibid.*, p. 637.)

25. It is on this point and in function of the element, which we are trying to put in place that a discussion of editing could be opened. We will at a later date attempt to make some remarks on this subject.

26. *Méditerranée,* by J.-D. Pollet and Phillipe Sollers (1963) which dismantles with exemplary efficiency the "transcendental specularization" which we have attempted to delineate, gives a manifest proof of this point. The film was never able to overcome the economic blockade.

...I had the impression of being inside a place that is called this philosopher's cave (Plato's). It was a long and dark cave. I was seated among many men, women and children. We all had our feet and hands chained and our heads so tightly fitted between wooden vices that we were unable to turn them. However, what was surprising to me is that most of these people were drinking, laughing, singing without seemingly being encumbered by their chains, and you might have thought that those who tried to recover the freedom of their feet, hands and head were frowned upon, cursed, avoided, as if they were infected with a contagious disease, and whenever some mishap occurred in the cave, they were invariably blamed for it. Harnesses in the manner I have just mentioned, we all had our backs turned to the entrance of this place, and it was not possible to look in any other direction but towards the inside of the cave where a large cloth was hung.

Behind us stood kings, ministers, priests, doctors, apostles, prophets, theologians, politicians, rogues, charlatans, illusion makers, and the entire troupe of merchants of fear and illusions. Everyone of these people had a supply of small transparent colored figures suited to his condition. And they were all so well made, so well painted and in such quantity and variety that there were enought to supply the representation of all the comic, tragic and burlesque scenes of life.

Later on, I noticed that these scoundrels had placed between them and the entrance of the cave, behind them, a large hanging lamp in front of which they put their little figures, and these shadows cast over our heads, enlarged in the process, came to rest on the stretched cloth at the bottom of the cave creating scenes (tableaux), but scenes that appeared so natural, so lifelike, that we assumed that they were real. Sometimes they made us laugh without restraint, and at other times they made us cry effusively. This will not seem so unusual when you realize that behind the cloth there were other scoundrels, hired by those standing behind us, who gave these shadows the accents, the real voices of the parts they were playing.

Diderot

The Apparatus

Jean-Louis Baudry

One constantly returns to the scene of the cave: real-effect or impression of reality. Copy, simulacrum, and even simulacrum of simulacrum. Impression of the real, more-than-the-real? From Plato to Freud, the perspective is reversed; the procedure is inverted—so it seems. The former comes out of the cave, examines what is intelligible, contemplates its source, and, when he goes back, it is to denounce to the prisoners the apparatus which oppresses them, and to persuade them to leave, to get out of that dim space. The latter, (on the contrary,—no, for it is not a matter of simple opposition, or of a simplifying symmetry), is more interested in making them go back there precisely where they are; where they didn't know how to find themselves, for they thought themselves outside, and it is true that they had been contemplating the good, the true and the beautiful for a long time. But at what price and as a result of what ignorance; failure to recognize or repress, compromise, defense, sublimation? Like Plato, he urges them to consider the apparatus to overcome their resistances, to look a little more closely at what is coming into focus on the screen, the other scene. The other scene? What brings the two together and separates them? For both, as in the theater, a left side, a right side, the master's lodge, the valet's orchestra. But the first scene would seem to be the second's other scene. It is a question of truth in the final analysis, or else: "the failure to recognize has moved to the other side." Both distinguish between two scenes, or two places, opposing or confronting one another, one dominating the other. These aren't the same places; they don't respond point-by-point although, in many respects, we who come after Freud would not be unjustified in superimposing more or less grossly the solar scene where the philosopher is at first dazzled, blinded by the good, on the scene of the conscious and its well-meaning exploits—we who, as a result of this very discovery of the unconscious, or of the other scene, could be induced to interpret the move, the exit, ascension, an initial blinding of the philosopher in a totally different manner. "Suppose one of them were set free and forced suddenly to stand up, turn his head, and walk with eyes lifted to the light; all these movements would be painful, and he would be too dazzled to make out the objects (...) And if he were forced to look at the fire-light itself, would not his eyes ache, so that he would try to escape and turn back to the things which he could see distinctly?" But the philosopher's cave could certainly not be superimposed unto that other scene, the scene of the unconscious! That remains to be seen. For we are dealing here with an apparatus, with a metaphorical relationship between places or a relationship between metaphorical places, with a topography, the knowledge of which defines for both philosopher and analyst the degree of relationship to truth or to description, or to illusion, and the need for an ethical point-of-view.

So you see, we return to the real or, for the experiencing subject (I would be able to say, for the subject who is felt or who is acted,) the impression of reality. And one could naively wonder why, some two and half thousand years later, it is by means of an optical metaphor —of an optical construct which signals term for term the cinematographic apparatus—that the philosopher exposes man's condition and the distance that separates him from 'true reality'; and why it is again precisely by means of an optical metaphor that Freud, at the beginning and at the end of his writings, tries to account for the arrangement of the psychical apparatus, for the functioning of the Ucs and for the rapport/rupture Cs-Ucs. Chapter VII of the *Traumdeutung:*

> What is presented to us in these words is the idea of a *psychical locality*. I shall entirely disregard the fact that the mental apparatus with which we are concerned is also known to us in the form of an anatomical preparation, and I shall carefully avoid the temptation to determine psychical locality in an anatomical fashion. I shall remain upon psychological ground, and I propose simply to follow the suggestion that we should picture the instrument which carries out our mental functions as resembling a compound microscope or a photographic apparatus, or something of the kind. On that basis, psychical locality will correspond to a point inside the apparatus at which one of the preliminary stages of an image comes into being. In the microscope and telescope, as we know, these occur in part at ideal points, regions in which no tangible component to the apparatus is situated. I see no necessity to apologize for the imperfections of this or of any similar imagery.

(Sigmund Freud, *The Interpretation of Dreams*, (Avon Edition) pp. 574-5.

However imperfect this comparison may be, Freud takes it up again 40 years later at the very beginning of the *Abriss:* "We admit that psychical life is the function of an apparatus to which we attribute a spatial extension which is made up of several parts. We imagine it like a kind of telescope, or microscope or some similar device." Freud doesn't mention cinema. But this is because cinema is already too-technologically-determined an apparatus for describing the psychical apparatus as a whole. In 1913, however, Lou Andreas Salome remarked: "Why is it that cinema has been of no use to us analysts? To the numerous arguments that could be advanced to save face for this Cinderella of the artistic conception of art, several psychological considerations should be added. First, that the cinematographic technique is the only one that makes possible a succession of images rapid enough to roughly correspond to our faculty for producing mental images. Furthermore," she concludes, "this provides food for reflection about the impact film could have in the future for our psychical make-up." Clearly, Lou Andreas Salome seems to envision a very enigmatic track, unless we have misunderstood her. Does she mean that film may bear some sort of likeness to the psychical apparatus, that, for this reason, it could be of interest to those who, because of its direct relation to their practice, are immediately affected by a theorisation of psychical operation linked to the discovery of the Ucs? And is it not rather the apparatus, the cinematographic process itself than the content of images—that is, the film—which is under scrutiny here? She only points out that there might be correspondences between cinematographic technique and our ability to produce mental images. But there are many aspects of film technique, many different connections, from the recording of the images to their re-production—an entire process which we have named elsewhere the *basic cinematographic apparatus*. And certainly such a technical construct—if only as examples and metaphor—should have interested Freud, since the major purpose of metapsychological research is to comprehend and to theoretically construct devices capable of recording traces, memory traces, and of restoring them in the form of representation. He admits: the concept of the "magic writing pad" (which he substitutes for the optical metaphor to which he later returns) is missing something: the possibility of restoring inscribed traces by using specific memory mechanisms which are exclusively constituted by living matter, but which a certain number of technical inventions at the time already mimic: the phonograph and cinema, precisely. The advantage of the magic writing pad is that since the external surface doesn't retain any trace of the inscriptions, it is best-suited to illustrate the system perception-Cs; in addition, the waxy substance inside preserves, superimposed and to some extent associated, the different traces which have inscribed themselves throughout time, preserves them from what could be called historical accidents. Obviously, nothing prevents the same thing from applying to the material of the record or to the film stock of the film if not that such reproduction would be confusing and indecipherable to us: the inscription follows other tracks, which are organized according to other principles than those of inanimate matter.

Yet, there is something there which should capture our attention: the place doubled by the constituted subject (on the other hand by the system perceptions and representations; on the other, by the Ucs system traces-inscriptions, characterized by permanence) finds itself once more within an idealist perspective considerably displaced with respect to the unconscious in Plato. But as we have learned from Marx, there is often a truth hidden from or in idealism, a truth which belongs to materialism, but which materialism can only discover after many detours and delays—a hidden or disguised truth. In Plato, something haunts the subject; something belabours him and determines his condition (could it be the pressure of the 'Ideas'?) As for Freud, the subject which Plato describes, the prisoner in the cave, is deceived (this whole theme of the mistaken subject which runs through the history of philosophy!); he is the prey of illusions, and, as for Freud, these illusions are but distortions and symptoms (gradations, the idealist would say—and admit this changes everything) of what is happening somewhere else. Even though Ideas take the place of the Ucs for him, Plato confronts a problem equivalent to that which at first preoccupies Freud in his metapsychological research and which, precisely, the cave myth is presumed to resolve: the transfer, the access from one place to another, along with the ensuing distortions. Plato's prisoner is the victim of an illusion of reality, that is, of precisely what is known as an hallucination, if one is awake, as a dream, if asleep; he is the prey of an impression, of an impression of reality. As I have said, Plato's *topos* does not and could not possibly correspond exactly to Freud's and surely, although it may be interesting to show what displacement occurs from one *topos* to the other (the location of reality for Plato obviously doesn't correspond to what is real for Freud); it is still more important to determine what is at work on the idealist philosopher's discourse unknown to him, the truth which proclaims, very different yet contained within the one he consciously articulates.

As a matter of fact, isn't it curious that Plato, in order to explain the transfer, the access from one place to another and to demonstrate, reveal, and make understood what sort of illusion underlies our direct contact with the real, would imagine or resort to an apparatus that doesn't merely evoke, but quite precisely describes in its mode of operation the cinematographic apparatus and the spectator's place in relation to it.

It is worth re-reading the description of the cave from this perspective.

First, the space: "a kind of cavernous underground chamber with an entrance open to the light" but too small to light it up. As Plato points out farther on: "a dim space." He emphasizes the effect of the surrounding darkness on the philosopher after his sojurn in the outside world. To his companions he will at first appear blind, his eyesight ruined; and his clumsiness will make them laugh. They will not be able to have confidence in him. In the cave, the prisoner-spectators are seated, still, prisoners because immobilized: unable to move—constraint or paralysis? It is true that they are chained, but,freed, they would still refuse to leave the place were they are; and so obstinately would they resist that they might put to death anyone trying to lead them out. In other words, this first constraint, against their will, this deprivation of movement which was imposed on them initially, this motor inhibition which affected so much their future dispositions, conditions them to the point that they prefer to stay where they are and to perpetuate this immobility rather than leave. Initial constraint which seems in this way to turn itself into a kind of spite or at least to inscribe the compulsion to repeat, the return to a former condition. There are things like that in Plato? It is not unnecessary to insist on this point as we re-read the platonic myth from the special perspective of the cinematographic apparatus. Forced immobility is undoubtedly a valuable argument for the demonstration description that Plato makes of the human condition: the coincidence of religious and idealist conceptions; but the initial immobility was not invented by Plato; it can also refer to the forced immobility of the child who is without motor resources at birth, and to the forced immobility of the sleeper who we know repeats the postnatal state and even inter-uterine existence; but this is also the immobility that the visitor to the dim space rediscovers, leaning back into his chair. It might even be added that the spectators immobility is characteristic of the filmic apparatus as a whole. The prisoner's shackles correspond to an actual reality in the individual's evolution, and Plato even draws the conclusion that it could have an influence on his future behavior, and would be a determining factor in the prisoner's resistance to breaking away from their state of illusion. "He might be required once more to deliver his opinion on those shadows, in competition with the prisoners who had never been released...If they could lay hands on the man who was trying to set them free and lead them up, they would kill him." Does he mean that immobility constitutes a necessary if not sufficient condition for the prisoner's credulity, that it constitutes one of the causes of the state of confusion into which they have been thrown and which makes them take images and shadows for the real? I don't want to stretch Plato's argument too far, even if I am trying to make his myth mean more than it actually says. But note: "In this underground chamber they have been from childhood, chained by the leg and also by the neck, so that they cannot move and can see only what is in front of them, because the chains will not let them turn their heads." Thus it is their motor paralysis, their inability to move about that, making the reality test impractical for them, reinforces their error and makes them inclined to take for real that which takes its place, perhaps its figuration or its projection onto the wall-screen of the cavern in front of them and from which they cannot detach their eyes and turn away. They are bound, shackled to the screen, tied and related—relation, extension between it and them due to their inability to move in relation to it, the last sight before falling asleep.

Plato says nothing about the quality of the image: is two-dimensional space suited to the representation of depth produced by the images of objects? Admittedly, they are flat shadows, but their movements crossings over, superimpositions and displacements allow us perhaps to assume that they are moving along different planes. However, Plato calls the projector to mind. He doesn't feel a need for making use of natural light; but it is also important to him to preserve and protect that light from an impure usage: Idealism makes the technician. Plato is satisfied with a fire burning behind them "at some distance higher up." As a necessary precaution, let us examine Plato's accuracy in assembling his apparatus. He is well aware that, placed otherwise, the fire would transmit the reflections of the prisoners themselves most prominently onto the screen. The 'operators,' the 'machinists' are similarly kept out of the prisoners' sight, hidden by "a parapet, like the screen at a puppet-show, which hides the performers while they show their puppets over the top." For, undoubtedly, by associating themselves with the objects that they are moving back and forth before the fire, they would project a heterogeneous image capable of cancelling the real-effect they want to produce: they would awake the prisoner's suspicions; they would awake the prisoners.

Here is the strangest thing about the whole apparatus. Instead of projecting images of natural-real objects, of living people, etc. onto the wall-screen of the cave as it would seem only natural to do for simple shadow plays, Plato feels the need, by creating a kind of conversion in the reference to reality, to show the prisoners not direct images and shadows of reality but, even at this point, a simulacrum of it. One might easily recognize the idealist's prudence, the calculated progress of the philosopher who prefers pushing the real back another notch and multiplying the steps leading to it, lest excessive haste lead his listener to again trust his senses too much. In any case, for this reason (or for another), he is led to place and to suppose between the projector, the fire and the screen, something which is itself a mere prop of reality, which is merely its image, its copy, its simulacrum: "figures of men and animals in wood or stone or other materials" suggestive of studio objects of papier mache decor, were it not for the more striking impression created by their passing in front of the fire like a film.

All that is missing is the sound, in effect much more difficult to reproduce. Not only this: more difficult to copy, to employ like an image in the visible world; as if hearing, as opposed to sight, resisted being caught up in simulacra. Real voices, then, they would emanate from the bearers, the machinists, and the marionette players (a step is skipped in the reference to reality) but nevertheless, given over to the apparatus, integrated with it since it requires a total effect for fear of exposing the illusion. But voice that does not allow representation as do artificial objects—stone and wooden animals, and statues—will still give itself over to the apparatus thanks to its reverberation. "And suppose their prison had an echo from the wall facing them?" When one of the people crossing behind them spoke, they could only suppose that the sound came from the shadow passing before their eyes." If a link is missing in the chain that connects us back to reality, the apparatus corrects this, by taking over the voice's echo, by integrating into itself these excessively real voices. And it is true that in cinema—as in the case of all talking-machines—one does not hear an image of the sounds but the sounds themselves. Even if the procedures for recording the sounds and playing them back deforms them, they are reproduced and not copied. Only their source of emission may partake of illusion; their reality cannot. Hence, no doubt one of the basic reasons for the priviledged status of voice in idealist philosophy and in religion: voice does not lend itself to games of illusion, or confusion, between the real and its figurativity (because voice cannot be represented figuratively) to which sight seems particularly liable. Music and singing differ qualitatively from painting in their relation to reality.

As we have seen, Plato constructs an apparatus very much like sound cinema. But, precisely because he has to resort to sound, he anticipates an ambiguity which was to be characteristic of cinema. This ambiguity has to do with the impression of reality: with the means used to create it, and with the confusion and lack of awareness surrounding its origin; from which result the inventions which mark the history of cinema. Plato effectively helps us to recognize this ambiguity. For, on the one hand, he is careful to emphasize the artificial aspect of reproduced reality. It is the apparatus that creates the illusion, and not the degree of fidelity with the Real: here the prisoners have been chained since childhood, and it will therefore not be the reproduction of this or that specific aspect of that reality, which they do not know, which will lead them to attribute a greater degree of reality to the illusion to which they are subject (and we have seen that Plato was already careful to insert artifice, and that already what was projected was deception). On the other hand, by introducing voice, by reconstructing a talking machine, by complementing the projection with sound, by illustrating as it were the need to affect as many sense faculties as possible, at any rate the two most important, he certainly seems to comply with a necessity to duplicate reality in the most exact manner and to make his artifice as good a likeness as can be made. Plato's myth evidently functions as a metaphor for an analogy on which he himself insists before dealing with the myth: namely that what can be known through the senses is in the same relationship to that which can be known through the intellect as projection in the cave is to experience (that is, to ordinary reality). Besides that, isn't it remarkable that Plato should have been forced to resort to such a procedure and that, in his attempt to explain the position, the locus of that which can be known through the intellect, he was led to take off, so to speak, towards "illusion"; he was led to construct an apparatus which will make it possible, that it is capable of producing a special effect through the impression of reality it communicates to the spectator.

Here I must add something which may be of importance: in the scene taking place inside the cave, voices, words, "[these echoes which] they could only suppose that the sound came from the shadow passing before their eyes," do not have a discursive or conceptual role; they do not communicate a message; they belong to ordinary reality which is as immediate to the prisoners as are images; they cannot be separated from the latter; they are characterized according to the same mode of existence and in effect treated in the same way as words in a dream "fragments of discourse really spoken or heard, *detached from their context*" (my emphasis), and functioning like other kinds of dream representation. But there is another way to state the problem. What desire was aroused, more than two thousand years before the actual invention of cinema, what urge in need of fulfillment would be satisfied by a montage, rationalized into an idealist perspective precisely in order to show that it rests primarily on an impression of reality? The impression of reality is central to Plato's demonstration. That his entire argument is developed in order to prove that this impression is deceptive abundantly demonstrates its existence. As we have already noted, something haunts Plato's text: the prisoners' fascination (how better to convey the condition that keeps them chained up, those fetters that prevent them from moving their heads and necks), their reluctance to leave and even their willingness to resort to violence. But isn't it principally the need to construct another scene apart from the world, underground, in short to construct it as if it existed, or as if this construction also satisfied a desire to objectify a similar scene—an apparatus capable precisely of fabricating an impression of reality. This would appear to satisfy and replace the nostalgia for a lost impression which can be seen as running through the idealist movement and eating away at it from inside, and setting it in motion. That the real in Plato's text is at an equal distance from or in a homologous relationship to the "intelligibly real,"—the world of Ideas—and "reality-subject"—"the impression of reality" produced by the apparatus in the cave should moreover be sufficient to make us aware of the real meaning of the world of Ideas and of the field of desire on which it has been built (a world which, as we know, "exists outside of time," and which, after numerous encounters, the conscious subject can rediscover in himself.)

Cave, grotto, "sort of cavernous chamber underground," people have not failed to see in it a representation of the maternal womb, of the matrix into which we are supposed to wish to return. Granted, but only the place is taken into account by this interpretation and not the apparatus as a whole; and if this apparatus really produces images, it first of all produces an effect of specific subjects—to the extent that a subject is intrinsically part of the apparatus; once the cinema has been technically perfected, it produces this same effect defined by the words "impression of reality" (words that may be confusing but which nevertheless need to be clarified. This impression of reality appears as if—just as if—it were known to Plato. At the very least, it seems that Plato ingeniously attempts and succeeds in fixing up a machine capable of reproducing "something" that he must have known, and that has less to do with its capacity for repeating the real (and this is where the Idealist is of great help to us by sufficiently emphasizing the artifice he employs to make his machine work) than with reproduction and repetition of a particular condition, and the representation of a particular place on which this condition depends.

Of course, from the analytic perspective we have chosen, by asking cinema about the wish it expresses, we are aware of having distorted the allegory of the cave by making it reveal, from a considerable historic distance, the approximate construct of the cinematographic apparatus. In other words, a same apparatus was responsible for the invention of the cinema and was already present in Plato. The text of the cave may well express a desire inherent to a participatory effect deliberately produced, sought for, and expressed by cinema (and the philosopher is first of all a spokesman of desire before becoming its great "channeler," which shows why it is far from useless to bring an analytic ear to bear on him despite or because of his rationalizations, even though he deny it as intolerable suspicion, even and especially though he complain, rightly, from his point of view of our having distorted his text). We can thus propose that the allegory of the cave is the text of a signifier of desire which haunts the invention of cinema and the history of its invention.

You see why historians of cinema, in order to unearth its first ancestor, never leave off dredging a pre-history which is becoming increasingly cluttered. From the magic lantern to the praxisnoscope and the optical theater up to the *camera obscura,* as the booty piles up, the excavations grow: new objects and all kinds of inventions,—one can feel the disarray increasing. But if cinema was really the answer to a desire inherent in our psychical structure, how can we date its first beginnings? Would it be too risky to propose that painting, like theater, for lack of suitable technological and economic conditions, were dry-runs in the approximation not only of the world of representation but of what might result from a certain aspect of its functioning and which only the cinema is in a position to implement? These attempts have obviously produced their own specificity and their own history but their existence has as its origin a psychical source equivalent to the one which stimulated the invention of cinema.

It is very possible that there was never any first invention of cinema. Before being the outcome of technical considerations and of a certain state of society's development (necessary to its realization and to its completion), it was primarily the target of a desire which, moreover, its immediate success as well as the interest which its ancestors had aroused has demonstrated clearly enough. A desire, to be sure, a form of lost satisfaction which its apparatus would be aimed at rediscovering in one way or another (even to the point of simulation) and to which the impression of reality would seem to be the key.

I would now like to look more closely at what the impression of reality and the desire objectified in it entails by surveying certain analytical texts.

And since I have already mentioned the cave, "a kind of cavernous underground chamber," as Plato says, I went back to the *Interpretation of Dreams* and discovered a remark of Freud's that could guide our search. This remark is to be found in the passage dedicated to examples of dream work. Freud examines the kinds of figuration that occur during analysis. After having shown how the treatment gets itself represented, Freud comes to unconscious. "If the unconscious, in so far as it belongs to waking thought, needs to be represented in dreams, it is represented in them in underground places." Freud adds the following which, because of the above, is very interesting: "Outside of analytic treatment, these representations would have symbolized the woman's body or the womb." If the world of Ideas offers numerous concepts which correspond to those which Freud discovered in the Ucs (the permanence of traces, the ignorance of time), that is, if the philosophical edifice can be envisaged as a rationalization of the Ucs's thrust, of its suspected but rejected existence, then we can ask whether it is not the Ucs or certain of its mechanisms that are figured, that represent themselves in the apparatus of the cave. In any case, paraphrasing Fechner, we could propose that the scene of the cave (and of cinema) is perhaps quite different from that of the activity of representation in a state of wakefulness. In order to learn a little more about that other scene, it might be useful to linger a while before the dream-scene.

A parallel between dream and cinema had often been noticed: common sense perceived it right away. The cinematographic projection is reminiscent of dream, would appear to be a kind of dream, really a dream,[1] a parallelism often noticed by the dreamer when, about to describe his dream, he is compelled to say "It was like in a movie..." At this point, it seems useful to follow Freud closely in his metapsychological analysis of dream. Once the role and function of dream as a protector of sleep and as fulfillment of a wish has been recognized as well as its nature and the elaboration of which it is the result, and after the material, the translation of the manifest content into dream-thoughts has been studied, one must still determine the conditions of dream formation, the reasons that give dream a specific qualitative nature in the whole of the psychical life, the specific "dream effect" that it determines. This is the subject of ch. VII of *The Interpretations of Dreams* and the *Supplement to the Theory of Dreams* fifteen years later. In the latter text, Freud at first seems concerned with understanding why dream manifests itself to the dreamer's consciousness in the form of what might be called the "specific mode of dream," a feature of reality which should more properly belong to the perception of the external world. What are the determining factors of a necessarily metapsychological order, i.e. involving the construction and operation of the psychical apparatus, which makes it possible for dream to pass itself off for reality to the dreamer. Freud begins with sleep: dream is the psychical activity of the dreamer. "Sleep," he tells us, from a somatic viewpoint, "is *a revivescence of one's stay in the body of the mother, certain conditions which it recreates: the rest position, warmth and isolation which protects him from excitement.* (emphasis added) This makes possible a first kind of regression in the development of the self back to a primitive narcissim which results in what has been defined as the totally egotistical nature of dream: the person who plays the main part in dream scenes is always the dreamer himself". Sleep favors the appearance of still another type of regression which is extremely important for the manifestation of the dream-effect: by deactivating equally the Cs, Pcs and Ucs systems, i.e., by allowing an easier communication between them, sleep leaves open the regressive path which the cathetic representations will follow as far as perception. Topical regression or temporal regression combine to reach the edge of dream.

I do not want to insist excessively on Freud's analyses. We need only note that the dream wish is formed from daytime residues in the Pcs system which are reinforced by drives emanating from the Ucs. Topical regression first allows the transformation of the dream thoughts into images. It is through the intermediary of regression that word representations belonging to the preconscious system are translated into thing representations which dominate the unconscious system.[2] "Thoughts are transposed into images—mostly visual ones—thus the representations of words are reduced to representations of objects corresponding to them as if, throughout the whole system, considerations of representability overwhelmed the whole process." So much so that a dream wish can be turned into a dream phantasy. Once again, it is regression which gives dream its definitive shape. "The completion of the dream process is also marked by the fact that the content of thought, transformed by regression and reshaped into a phantasy of desire, comes into consciousness as a sensory perception and then undergoes the secondary elaboration which affects any perceptual content. We are saying that the dream wish is hallucinated and finds, in the guise of hallucination a belief in the reality of its fulfillment." Dream is "an hallucinatory psychosis of desire"—i.e. a state in which mental perceptions are taken for perceptions of reality. Moreover, Freud hypothesized that the satisfaction resulting from hallucination is a kind of satisfaction which we knew at the beginning of our psychical life when perception and representation could not be differentiated, when the different systems were confused, i.e. when the system of consciousness-perception had not differentiated itself. The object of desire (the object of need), if it happens to be lacking can at this point be hallucinated. It is precisely the repeated failure offered by this form of satisfaction which results in the differentiation between perception and representation through the creation of the reality test. A perception which can be eliminated by an action is recognized as exterior. The reality test is dependent on motricity. Once motricity has been interrrupted, as during sleep, the reality test can no longer function. The suspension of motricity, its being set apart, would indeed favor regression. But it is also because sleep determines a withdrawal of cathexis in the Cs, Ucs and Pcs systems that the phantasies of the dream wish follow the original path which differentiate them from phantasies produced during the waking state.[3] Like daytime phantasies, they could have become conscious without nevertheless being taken for real or completed; but, having taken the path of regression, not only are they capable of taking over consciousness but, because of the subject's inability to rely upon the reality test, they are marked by the very character of perception and appear as reality. The processes of dream formation succeed well in presenting dream as real.

The transformations accomplished by sleep in the psychical apparatus: withdrawal of cathexis, instability of the different systems, return to narcissism, loss of motricity (because of the impossibility of applying the reality test), contribute to produce features which are specific to dream: its capacity for figuration, translation of thought into images, reality extended to representations. One might even add that we are dealing with a more-than-real in order to differentiate it from the impression of the real which reality produces in the normal waking situation. The more-than-real translating the cohesion of the subject with his perceived representations, the submersion of the subject in his representations, the near-impossibility for him to escape their influence and which is dissimilar if not incompatible with the impression resulting from any direct relation to reality. There appears to be an ambiguity in the words poorly expressing the difference between the relationship of the subject to his representations experienced as perceived and his relation to reality.

Dream, also tells us, is a projection, and, in the context in which he uses the word, projection evokes at once the analytic use of the defense mechanism which consists in referring and attributing to the exterior representations and affects which the subject refuses to acknowledge as his own, and it also evokes a distinctly cinematographic use since it involves images which, once projected, come back to the subject as a real perceived from the outside.

That dream is a projection reminiscent of the cinematographic apparatus, is indeed what seems to come out of Lewin's discovery of the dream-scene, the hypothesis for which was suggested to him by his patients' enigmatic dreams. One young woman's dream, for example: "I had my dream all ready for you, but while I was lying here looking at it, it began to move in circles far from me, wrapped up on itself, again and again, like two acrobats." This dream shows that the screen, which can appear by itself, like a white surface, is not exclusively a representation, a content—in which case it would not be necessary to priviledge it among other elements of the dream content; but, rather, it would present itself in all dreams as the indispensable support for the projection of images. It would seem to pertain to the dream apparatus. "The Dream screen is a surface on which a dream seems to be projected. It is the 'blank background' (empty basic surface) which is present in dream although it is not necessarily seen; the manifest content of dream ordinarily perceived takes place over it, or in front of it." Theoretically it can be a part of the latent content or of the manifest content, but the distinction is academic. The dream-screen is not often noticed by analysts, and, in the practice of dream interpretation, the analyst does not need to deal with it." It is cinema which suggested the term to Lewin because, in the same way as its analog in the cinematographic apparatus, the dream-screen is either ignored by the dreamer (the dreaming spectator) or unrelated to the interest resulting from the images and the action. Lewin adds nevertheless (and this remark reminds us of a modern use of the screen in cinema) that in some circumstances, the screen does play a part of its own and becomes discernible. According to Lewin's hypothesis, the dream-screen is the dream's hallucinatory representation of the mother's breast on which the child used to fall asleep after nursing. In this way, it expresses a state of complete satisfaction while repeating the original condition of the oral phase in which the body did not have limits of its own, but was extended undifferentiated from the breast. Thus, the dream-screen would correspond to the desire to sleep: archetype and prototype of any dream. Lewin adds another hypothesis: the dream itself, the visual representations which are projected upon it would correspond to the desire to be awake. "A visual dream, repeats the child's early impression of being awake. His eyes are open and he sees. For him, to see is to be awake. Actually, Lewin insists on Freud's explanation of the predominance of visual elements in dream: that latent thoughts in a dream are to a large extent shaped by unconscious mnesic traces which can only exist as a visual representation—the repetition of a formal element from the child's earliest experience. It is evident that the dream-screen is a residue from the most archaic mnesic traces. But, additionally, and this is at least as important, one might assume that it provides an opening for understanding the dreamer's "primal scene" which establishes itself during the oral phase. The hallucinatory factor, the lack of distinction between representation and perception—representation taken as perception which makes for our belief in the reality of dream, would correspond to the lack of distinction between active and passive, between acting and suffering experience, undifferentiation between the limits of the body (body/breast), between eating and being eaten, etc. characteristics of the oral phase and borne out by the enveloping the subject within the screen. For the same reasons, we would find ourselves in a position to understand the specific mode in which the dreamer identifies with his dream, a mode which is anterior to the "stade du miroir," to the formation of the self, and therefore founded on a permeability, a fusion of the interior with the exterior. On the other hand, if the dream itself, in its visual content, is likely to represent the desire to stay awake, the combination dream-screen/projected images would manifest a conflict between contradictory motions, a state in effect of un-distinction between an hallucinatory wish, sign of satisfaction and desire for perception, of contact with the real. It is therefore conceivable that something of a desire in dream unifying perception and representation—whether with representation passing itself for perception—in which case we would be closer to hallucination—, or whether perception passes itself for perceived representation, i.e. acquires as perception the mode of existence which is proper to hallucination, would take on the character of specific reality which reality does not impart, but which is provoked by hallucination: a more-than-real that dream precisely considered as apparatus and as the repetition of a particular state which defines the oral phase, would, on its own be able to bring to it. Dream alone?

Lewin's hypothesis which complements and extends Freud's ideas on the formation of dream, in relation to the feeling of reality which is linked to it, presents, in my opinion, the advantage of offering a kind of formation stage, of dream constitution, which might be construed as operative in the cinema-effect. Impression of reality, and that which we have defined as the desire of cinema, as cinema in its general apparatus would recall, mime a form of archaic satisfaction experienced by the subject, by reproducing the scene of it.

Of course, there is no question of identifying mental image, filmic image, mental representation and cinematographic representation. The fact that the same terms are used however does reveal the very workings of desire in cinema i.e. at the same time the desire to rediscover archaic forms of desire which in fact structure any form of desire, and the desire to stage for the subject, to put in representation of form, what might recall its own operation.

In any case, this deviation through the "metapsychological fiction" of dream could enlighten us about the effect specific to cinema, "the impression of reality," which, as is well known, is different from the usual impression which we receive from reality, but which has precisely this characteristic of being more than real which we have detected in dream. Actually, cinema is a simulation apparatus. This much was immediately recognized, but, from the positivist viewpoint of scientific rationality which was predominant at the time of its invention, the interest was directed towards the simulation of reality inherent to the moving image to the unexpected effects which could be derived from it without finding it necessary to examine the implications of the cinematographic apparatus being initially directed towards the subject and simulation's possible application to states or subjects-effects before being directed toward the reproduction of the real. It is nevertheless curious that in spite of the development of analytic theory, the problem should have remained unsolved or barely considered since that period. Almost exclusively, it is the technique and content of film which have retained attention: characteristics of the image, depth of field, off-screen space, shot, single-shot-sequence, montage, etc.; the key to the impression of reality has been sought in the structuring of image and movement, in complete ignorance of the fact that the impression of reality is dependent first of all on a subject-effect and that it might be necessary to examine the position of the subject facing the image in order to determine the need for cinema-effect. Instead of considering cinema as an idealogically neutral apparatus, as has been rather stupidly stated, as an apparatus the impact of which would be entirely determined by the content of the film (a consideration which leaves unsolved the whole question of its persuasive power and of the reason for which it revealed itself to be an instrument particularly well suited to exert ideological influence) in order to explain the cinema-effect, it is necessary to consider it from the viewpoint of the apparatus that it constitutes, apparatus which in its totality includes the subject. And first of all, the subject of the unconscious. The difficulties met by the theoreticians of cinema in their attempt to account for the impression of reality are proportionate to the persisting resistance to really recognizing the unconscious. Although nominally accepted, its existence has nevertheless been left out of the theoretical research. If psychoanalysis has finally permeated the content of certain films, as a complement to the classic psychology of character's action and as a new type of narrative spring, it has remained practically absent from the problematics raised by the relation of the projection to the subject. The problem is nevertheless to determine the extent to which the cinematographic apparatus plays an important part in this subject which Lacan after Freud defines as an apparatus, and the way in which the structuring of the unconscious, the modalities of the subject's development throughout the different strata deposited by the various phases of drives, the differentiation between the Cs, Pcs and Ucs systems and their relations, the distinction between primary and secondary processes make it possible to isolate the effect which is specific to cinema.

Consequently, I will only propose several hypotheses.

First of all, that taking into account the darkness of the movie theater, the relative passivity of the situation, the forced immobility of the cine-subject, and the effects which result from the projection of images, moving images, the cinematographic apparatus brings about a state of artificial regression. It artificially leads back to an interior phase of his development—a phase which is barely hidden, as dream and certain pathological forms of our mental life have shown. It is the desire, unrecognized as such by the subject, to return to this phase, an early state of development with its own forms of satisfaction which may play a determining role in his desire for cinema and the pleasure he finds in it. Return towards a relative narcissism, and even more towards a mode of relating to reality which could be defined as enveloping and in which the separation between one's own body and the exterior world is not well defined. Following this line of reasoning, one may then be able to understand the reasons for the intensity of the subject's attachment to the images and the process of identification created by cinema. A return to a primitive narcissism by the regression of the libido, Freud tells us, noting that the dreamer occupies the entire field of the dream scene; the absence of delimitation of the body; the transfusion of the interior out into the exterior, added Lewin (other works, notably Melanie Klien's could also be mentioned); without excluding other processes of identification which derive from the specular regime of the ego, from its constitution as Imaginary. These do not however strictly pertain to the cinema-effect, although the screen, the focalization produced by the basic apparatus, as I indicated in my earlier paper[4], could effectively produce mirror effects, and cause specular phenomena to intervene directly in the viewing experience. In any case, the usual forms of identification, already supported by the apparatus would be reinforced by a more archaic mode of identification, which has to do with the lack of differentiation between the subject and his environment, a dream-scene model which we find in the baby/breast relationship.

In order to understand the particular status of cinema, it is necessary to underline the partial elimination of the reality test. Undoubtedly, the means of cinematographic projection would keep the reality test intact when compared to dreams and hallucination. The subject has always the choice to close his eyes, to withdraw from the spectacle, or to leave, but no more than in dream does he have means to act in any way upon the object of his perception, change his viewpoint as he would like. There is no doubt that in dealing with images, and the unfolding of images, the rhythm of vision and movement, are imposed on him in the same way as images in dream and hallucination. His relative motor inhibition which brings him closer to the state of the dreamer, in the same way that the particular status of the reality he perceives (a reality made up of images) would seem to favor the simulation of the regressive state, and would play a determining role in the subject-effect of the impression of reality, this more-than-real of the impression of reality, which as we have seen, is characteristic not of the relation of the subject to reality, but precisely of dreams and hallucinations.

One must therefore start to analyze the impression of reality by differentiating between perception and representation. The cinematographic apparatus is unique in that it offers the subject perceptions of a reality whose status seems similar to that of representations experienced as perception. It should also be noted in this connection that if the confusion between representation and perception is characteristic of the primary process which is governed by the pleasure principle, and which is the basic condition for the satisfaction produced by hallucination, the cinematographic apparatus appears to succeed in suspending the secondary process and anything having to do with the principle of reality without eliminating it completely. This would then lead us to propose the following paradoxical formula: the more-than-real, i.e. the specific characteristic (whatever is specific) of what is meant by the expression "impression" of reality, consists in keeping apart (toning down, so that they remain present but as background) the secondary process and the reality principle. Perception of the image passing for perception: one might assume that this is precisely here that one might find the key to the impression of reality, that which would at once approximate and differentiate the cinematographic effect and the dream. Return effect, repetition of a phase of the subject's development during which representation and perception were not yet differentiated, and the desire to return to that state along with the kind of satisfaction associated to it, undoubtedly an archetype for all that which seeks to connect with the multiple paths of the subjects desire. It is indeed desire as such, i.e. desire of desire, the nostalgia for a state in which desire has been satisfied through the transfer of a perception to a formation resembling hallucination which seems to be activated by the cinematographic apparatus. According to Freud: "To desire initially must have been an hallucinatory cathexis of the memory of satisfaction."[5] Survival and insistence of bygone periods, an irrepressible backward movement. Freud never ceased to remind us that in its formal constitution, dream was a vestige of the subject's phylogenetic past, and the expression of a wish to have again the very form of existence associated with this experience. "Dream which fulfills its wish by the short-cut of repression does nothing but conserve a type of primary operation of the psychical apparatus which had been eliminated because of its inefficiency." It is also the same survival and the same wish which are at work in some hallucinatory psychoses. Cinema, like dream, would seem to correspond to a temporary form of regression, but whereas dream, according to Freud, is merely a "normal hallucinatory psychosis," cinema offers an artificial psychosis without offering the dreamer the possibility of exercising any kind of immediate control. What I am really saying is that for such a regression to be possible, it is necessary for anterior phases to survive, but that it be cathected by a wish, as is proven by the existence of dream. This wish is remarkably precise, and consists in obtaining from reality a position, a condition in which what is perceived would no longer be distinguished from representations. It can be assumed that it is this wish which prepares the long history of cinema: the wish to construct a simulation machine capable to offer the subject perceptions which are really representations mistaken for perceptions. Cinema offers a simulation of regressive movement which is characteristic of dream—the transformation of thoughts by means of figuration. The withdrawal of cathexis of all the systems Cs, Pcs, Ucs, during sleep, causes the representations cathected by dream during the dream work to determine a sensory activity; the operation of dream can be crudely represented by the following diagram:

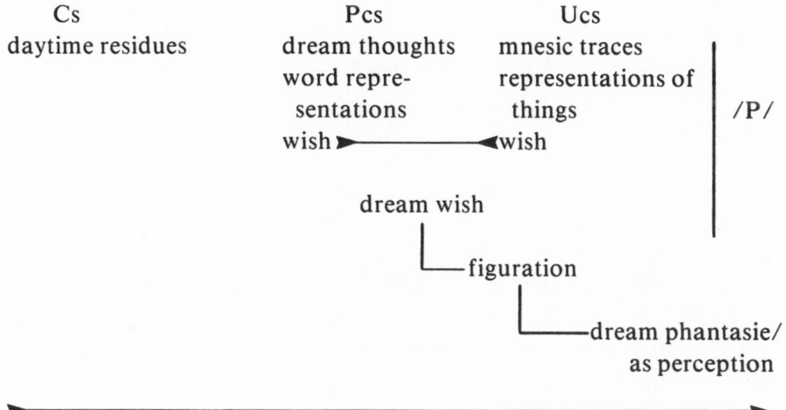

The subject-effect of the cinematographic apparatus would be presented as:

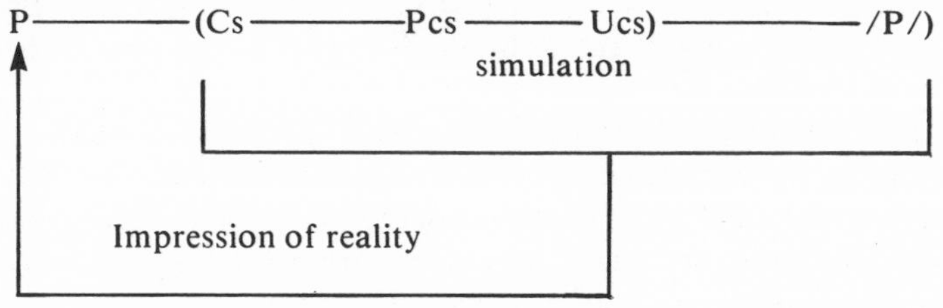

The simulation apparatus therefore consists in transforming a perception into a quasi-hallucination endowed with real-effect which cannot be compared to that which results from ordinary perception. The cinematographic apparatus reproduces the psychical apparatus during sleep: separation from the outside world, inhibition of motricity; in sleep, these conditions causing an overcathexis or representation can penetrate the system of perception as sensory stimuli; in cinema, the images perceived (very likely reinforced by the set up of the psychical apparatus) will be overcathected and thus acquire a status which will be the same as that of the sensory images of dream.

One cannot hesitate to insist on the artificial nature of the cine-subject. It is precisely this artificiality which differentiates it from dream or hallucinations. There is, between cinema and these psychical states, the same distance as between a real object and its simulacrum, with this additional factor that dream and hallucination are already states of simulation (something passing itself off for something else, representation for perception). One might even argue that it is this embedded structure which makes it so difficult to deal with the subject-effect. While, in dreams and hallucinations, representations appear in the guise of perceived reality, a real perception takes place in cinema, if not an ordinary perception of reality. It would appear that it is this slight displacement which has misled the theoreticians of cinema, when analyzing the impression of reality. In dream and hallucination, representations are taken as reality in the absence of perception; in cinema, images are taken for reality but require the mediation of perception. This is why, on the one hand, for the realists, cinema is thought of as a duplicate of reality—and on the other cinema is taken as an equivalent of dream—but the comparison stops there leaving unresolved the problem raised by the impression of reality. It is evident that cinema is not dream: but it reproduces an impression of reality, it unlocks, releases a cinema effect which is comparable to the impression of reality caused by dream. The entire cinematographic apparatus is activated in order to provoke this simulation: it is indeed a simulation of a condition of the subject, a position of the subject, a subject and not of reality.

Desire for a real that would have the status of hallucination or of a representation taken for a perception, one might wonder whether cinema is not doubled by another wish, complementary to the one that is at work in the subject and which we have presumed to be at work in Plato's cave apparatus.

For, if dream really opens on to another scene by way of a repressive track, one might suppose that the existence of an unconscious where the subject's early mode of functioning persists, the unconscious, defined by the primary process, constantly denied, rejected, excluded, never ceases requiring of the subject and proposing to him, by multiple detours (even if only through artistic practice), representations of his own scene. In other words, without his always suspecting it, the subject is induced to produce machines which would not only complement or supplement the workings of the secondary process, but which could represent his own overall functioning to him: he is led to produce mechanisms mimicking, simulating the apparatus which is no other than himself. The presence of the unconscious also makes itself felt through the pressure it exerts in seeking to get itself represented by a subject who is still unaware of the fact that he is representing to himself the very scene of the unconscious where he is.

Translated by Jean Andrews and Bertrand Augst

NOTES

1. A close relationship which has led film-makers to believe that cinema was the instrument finally suited for the representation of dreams. There still remains to understand the failure of their attempt. Is it not that the representation of dreams in cinema would not function like the representation of dreams in dreams, precisely destroying the impression of reality in the same way as the thought that one is dreaming intervenes in dream as a defense mechanism against the 'mashing' desire of dream. The displacement of dream in the projection results unavoidably to send the spectator back to his consciousness; it imposes a distance which denounces the artifice (and is there anything more ridiculous than those soft focus clouds, supposedly dreamlike representations) and to destroy completely the *impression of reality* which precisely also defines dream.

2. In *The Ego and the Id,* Freud adds comments which allow him to assert that "visual thought is closer to the unconscious processes than verbal thought, and older than the latter, from the phylogenetic as well as from the ontogenetic standpoints. Verbal representations all belong to the Pcs, while the unconscious only relies on visual ones."

3. This is why it is not by paying attention to the content of images that one is able to account for the impression of reality, but by questioning the apparatus. The differentiation between phantasies and dream is due to the transformation of the psychical apparatus during the transition from the state of being awake to sleep. Sleep will make necessary the work of figuration the economy of which can be created

by daytime phantasies; in addition, daytime phantasies do not accompany the belief in reality of the fulfillment which characterizes dream. This is why in attempting to understand the cinema-effect—the impression of reality—we have to go through the intermediary of dream and not daytime phantasies.

4. See "Ideological Effects of the Basic Cinematographic Apparatus," *Film Quarterly,* 1974.

5. It may seem peculiar that desire which constituted the cine-effect is rooted in the oral structure of the subject. The conditions of projection do evoke the dialectics internal/external, swallowing/swallowed, eating/being eaten, which is characteristic of what is being structured during the oral phase. But, in the case of the cinematographic situation, the visual orifice has replaced the buccal orifice: the absorption of the subject in the image, prepared, predigested by his very entering in the dark theater. The relationship visual orifice/buccal orifice acts at the same time as analogy and differentiation, but also points to the relation of consecution between oral satisfaction, sleep, white screen of the dream on which dream images will be projected, beginning of the dream. On the importance of sight during the oral phase, see Spitz's remarks in *The Yes and the No.* In the same order of ideas, it may be useful to reintroduce Melanie Klein's hypotheses on the oral phase, her extremely complex dialectics between the inside and the outside which refer to reciprocal forms of development.

REFERENCES

Lewin, Bertram, "Sleep, the Mouth and the Dream Screen," *Psychoanalytic Quarterly,* vol. 15, 1946, 419-443) "Inferences from the Dream Screen," *International Journal of Psychoanalysis,* vol. 29, 1948, 224-431.

"The subject is an apparatus. This apparatus is lacunary, and it is within this lacuna that the subject sets up the function of an object as lost object." Jacques Lacan, *Les Quatres Concepts fondamenteux de la psychanalyse* (Paris, LeSeuil, 1973).

That certain created beings should have the power of foreseeing events in the germ of causes, just as the great inventor perceives an art of science in some natural phenomenon unobserved by the ordinary mind, this is not one of those violent exceptions to the order of things which excite unthinking clamor; it is simply the working of a recognized faculty, and of one which is in some measure the somnambulism of the spirit. This proposition, on which rest all the various methods of deciphering the future, may seem absurd,—but the fact remains. Observe also that to predict the great events of the future is not, for the seer, any greater exhibition of power than that of revealing the secrets of the past. The past and the future are equally unknown in the system of the incredulous. If past events have left their traces, it is reasonable to infer that coming ones have their roots. Whenever a soothsayer tells you, minutely, facts of your past life known to yourself alone, he can surely tell you of events which existing causes will produce. The moral world is cut out, so to speak, on the pattern of the material world; the same effects may be found in it, with the differences proper to their varied environments. Thus, just as the body is actually projected into the atmosphere and leaves in it existing the spectre seized by the daguerreotype which arrested it in its passage; so ideas, real and potential creations, imprint themselves upon what we must call the atmosphere of the spiritual world, produce effects upon it, remain there spectrally,—it is necessary to coin words to express these unknown phenomena,—and hence certain created beings, endowed with rare faculties, can clearly perceive these forms or these traces of thoughts or ideas.

Balzac

Author and Analyzable Subject

Jean-Louis Baudry

A theory of cinema should differentiate itself from the multiple interventions, discourses, and assorted discussions occasioned by cinema. It seemed to me that a certain suspicion, a kind of dissatisfaction, more than a desire for scientificity, would seem to motivate the move towards theory. Somewhat paradoxically, I thought that stupidity, naivete or innocence might be at the source of the urge for theory. Much more than talking about theory (the term defined an object already constituted) I would rather have talked about a move towards theory, a theoretical tendency, a penchant for theory. A theoretician might be defined as someone who would be searching—passionately because his entire well-being is involved—trying to establish points of reference for himself. Generally anyone feels secure on familiar grounds, but the theoretician is not quite certain that he won't get lost; while other people have no difficulty moving around, he gets entangled, having difficulty ignoring a feeling of confusion which he is first inclined to attribute to his own limitations. Actually, his passion may well be less a passion for knowledge (or truth, although he may occasionally find it) than a compulsion to find his bearings. And, because he really does not quite understand what other people are talking about, (that is, for himself, because he is fully capable of following them in their discourses since he can fake it), he would be tempted to remain silent. Or, at least, if he were to rattle on, he would use words in the same way an insect uses his antennae, with small, cautious moves, groping his way, taking incredible chances because of the limitations of his sensory perception. Theoretical strategy may well lead to knowledge; its initial impulse nevertheless appeared to me to be recognition. The desire to know what's what had to precede that of knowing.

That's what I told myself while thinking about the applications for a theory of cinema. I thought that I had found an answer by distinguishing three different things: the product, the producer, and whoever the product is addressed to. The film, the author, and the spectator. Naturally, I had no trouble justifying my theoretical inclination considering my own contribution to the theory of cinema. While I may have contributed to change the concept of spectator, and while I had speculated about the effects of the cinematographic apparatus if only because, as a child, I had already experienced them, these still affected the adult I had become (often annoyed by an excess of emotion which did not seem explainable by the quality of the show). Of course, I didn't forget that the desire to go to the movies preceded the choice of the film. Actually, that's something which ordinary discourse had also noted: we go to the movies before deciding which film we want to see. And cinephiles, among whom I did not count myself, seem just as blind in their passion as those lovers who imagine they love a woman because of her qualities or because of her beauty. They need good movies, but most of all, to rationalize their need for cinema.

Thus, out of these three topics, two had been dealt with by film theory. Film had long been the object of more or less systematic studies amidst the exulting discovery of the surprising possibilities offered by the new art. These studies have been updated during the past ten years, first by Christian Metz's semiological research and then by psychoanalytic studies.[1] The spectator had also become an object of theoretical study.

The time had now come to question the first among these complex objects of a theory of cinema, the author, who should have been called the producer-subject if the term had not already been used to designate the financial producer in the cinematographic enterprise. It would have been better to call the endeavor production, and whoever undertakes such a project, the producer.

Naturally, I knew that the "*auteur* theory" which was characterized conceptually in literature as a theory of the producer-subject in the signifying practice of writing was far from complete and raised multiple problems despite the value, progress, and results which these studies had produced.[2] While many points could be debated, at least concerning the intersection between historical materialism and psychoanalysis a theory of the producer-subject of the literary signifier had emerged thanks to a semiological approach to the text itself, and thanks to an understanding of "poetic language", to use Kristeva's own terms to describe the constituting nucleus of literature. Other art forms, painting, sculpture, music, could have led, I believe, to similar analyses. In all these arts, once the signifying matter of expression is recognized in its historical depth, there is a fairly direct relationship of contact between a producer-subject who is unquestionably individualized and the matter of expression he is working with. This individualization of the producer-subject is matched by an analysis of desire involving, according to the analysts, partial drives.[3] Thus, when I was thinking about the author of films, all my questions also pointed in that direction. Almost naively, I wondered what was the drive which motivated the filmmaker, to what kind of representation or fantasy does the desire to make movies refer? If one end of the basic apparatus (the one related to projection) makes it possible to circumscribe and study the specific effects and define a cine-subject, does the other end, the creative process, make it possible to isolate a *ciné-auteur?* Is cinema a signifying practice like all the others, or does the weight of the basic apparatus make the concept of author debatable or difficult to define?

According to the prevalent cinematographic discourse, there seems to be no doubt about the concept of *auteur.* Film *auteurs* can be differentiated on the basis of their works. If by chance an Eisenstein were to be discovered in some attic, it would be identified without difficulty. The same thing would be true for a Bunuel, a Dreyer, a Bresson. While the entire corpus of films is not made up of auteur films, there is no doubt that an auteur cinema does exist. If it is possible that cinematographic production includes genre films as well as auteur films, going from the object best suited to satisfy the requirement of commercial cinema and the most elaborated art object, the same thing is also possible for other signifying practices whether they be writing, music, or painting.

However, it was a mistake to assimilate cinema to other signifying practices. On the one hand, I had been saying that there was a connection between the manufacturer and his product, and on the other, when it comes to cinema again, the basic apparatus, its conditions of production, introduced an intermediary whose transformations or distortions might legitimately be questioned. Between the author and his product, between the producer-subject and the work, between the hand and the material, multiple strategies inteferred, interventions foreign to the artist emerged, and it was not certain that he would be able to achieve perfect mastery over them.

Some of these interventions may be explained by the costly nature of cinema. Since a film requires substantial investments, cinema must respond to social pressure, social requirements, ideological pressure—whether the latter manifests itself by the need for profitability in capitalist countries or more directly in the necessity to conform to accepted normalcy in the so-called socialist countries. Undoubtedly formulae like "freedom of the artist" are suspect and justifiably so. In every instance where ideology offers expressive concepts (and often to say nothing), it is a good idea to look for the underlying determinations, force fields, manifestations of causality. It is nevertheless true that, depending on the economic and material contingencies which affect these artistic practices, they benefit from greater or lesser facility of expression. To the extent that there is an almost direct transitivity between the writer and language, and that material support plays a relatively small part, society has difficulty controlling and supervising the modalities of writing.[4] It can only intervene at the level of the diffusion of the text, not its production. It costs little to publish, but it costs nothing to write. Whoever writes does not have to account to anyone, to use a revealing common expression. The film-maker, for his part must account, keep accounts, and take things into account, even if he often does not do badly for himself. In the very moment he is producing it, the product does not belong to him. The "contractor" can intervene, veto, cut, add, interrupt, insert. Even the distributor can require modifications determined by the limitations of projection. Upon seeing the film, the spectator or the theoretician has very good reasons to want to know what must be credited to the author and what to the social conditions, which are exterior to him but which he can of course always internalize and make his own.

In addition to these first intrusions into the body of the work, must also be added the difficulties created by the basic apparatus itself. There are first of all those which have to do with the constraints and limitations of the material itself: limitations of the camera, quality of the negative and of the printing, lighting conditions etc. But there is also the author's reliance on his crew, a plurality of subjects each following his own determinations.[6] Directors often talk about the problems they have to deal with during the shooting, what they wanted to do, and insist on the fact that the scenes as they have been shot are but one approximate version of what they had in mind. So much so that the "theoretician" in search of an author becomes increasingly more perplexed. And the more so because of the way in which the conditions of production often dictate a division of labor which makes it difficult to determine what to attribute to whom: script writer, dialoguist, adaptor, director, but also cameraman, stage designer or lightman. There are so many intermediaries that the relationship between the work and the artist, the work and its conception, is no longer related to the concept of signifying practices that I mentioned earlier. The dictionary is perhaps justified in giving composer, painter, sculptor, writer as synonymous with author and putting under types of authors a list going from ampelographist to vaudevillist which omits director, film-maker, or script writer.

It would seem that cinema has a particular status which comes from its double nature, being at once an industrial object and a signifying body. And undoubtedly, like most objects resulting from a signifying practice, film is an ideological-commercial object manufactured to satisfy relatively well defined desires as well as to mold mental attitudes. Being the outcome of an industrial process in that sense, it too, should have characteristics common to any manufactured object.

Both the manufactured object and the work of art must be linked by a common concept which includes the diacritical property implied by the concept of author. It is in relation to that common and differentiating characteristic that cinema can locate itself on an ideal line between the pure industrial object and the work of art.

Indeed, any goods which are produced must include a producer-subject in order to be produced. However, it is the very nature of the producer-subject which is likely to vary, at the two extreme limits expressing producer-subjects irreducible to one another. On the one hand, taking a car as an example, the producer-subject is an unrepresentable collective subject that corresponds to a state of society. On the other hand while the manufactured object may well satisfy the needs and desires of a consumer it does not represent any individualized subject, and no manifestation of desire can be perceived through it. Every individual subject who has contributed to its production has been erased, effaced, neutralized, annulled. No expression of desire, representation, fantasy or drive can be detected in it.

I had quickly realized that by raising the question of authorship in connection with cinema, I had some unformulated earlier model in mind. One model: literature. The relationship between the author and his text is immediately recognizable, obvious. The author is identified by the specific manner in which he uses language. Besides the precise, deliberate intentions of the author, even outside his own literary activity, which is internal to him, there is also something which is struggling to be found and kept, something as indescribably as the quality of a gaze, the intonations of the voice, which can be called an intelligence, a vision of the world, and, better yet, a style. Something that, since Freud, we have better means to understand.

In the case of such artistic practices as literature, painting, sculpture or music, the individual character and the signifying nature of these practices involve a subject, the very subject discovered by Freud when he discovered the unconscious. While in social practices the multiple and unacceptable manifestations of the unconscious are nullified, in artistic practices, these expressions, by their very nature, contribute to form the specific character of the work by the modalities of their production in the function that society assigns to them (display of desire, even and particularly as in the indirect means of religion), the seal which makes it identifiable among all others. Within it a subject can be surmised, and the work refers back to a subject that pertains to his unconscious, to a subject that can be subjected to analysis.[7] This was the diacritical distinction that I had been looking for and which seemed likely to clear up a number of misunderstandings. Everything that belongs to the order of culture (as opposed to the order of nature) has a producer-subject.

Under specific circumstances that very subject is 'analyzable'. As a matter of fact, such objects as a car, a bar of soap, a thimble, an umbrella, point back also to a producer-subject who is identified with an analyzable subject. The producer-subject is completely saturated by the analyzable subject.[8] However, there must also exist intermediate objects in which the social production does not entirely eclipse the analyzable subject who has intervened in their production. Surely society records that phenomenon every time that the name of an actual, physical person is mentioned, since one is pretty much sure that there is also evidence of an analyzable subject.

I thought that high fashion might provide a good example of such intermediate objects which, although commonly used and manufactured by a collective subject, contain, even if only as merely a trace, something which had to do with the analyzable subject. It is not by chance that the personality of Madame Chanel was the object of much curiosity and inspired many commentaries. Between her suits and who she was, people imagined a relationship. It had become evident that the Chanel style did not merely point back to a particular fashion and to the good taste of a distinguished woman. Through Chanel's idea of "woman" which was detectable in the way she dressed there emerged a neurotic structure and the style of an unconscious. Her suits were not merely a privileged and unique expression of fashion that changed every year. Undoubtedly, had Madame Chanel's personality been less well-known, it would have been presumptuous to try to attempt to speculate about the conflicts that tormented her based on an analysis of her suits. However, the signifier was analyzable because it unquestionably referred back to an unconscious.

I could see the objections which could be made. The difference between an industrial product and an art object does not lie in the presence or non-presence of an analyzable subject but rather in their basic matter of expression. The latter is constituted by a signifier, the former is not. Nevertheless, there are productions which, while made up of a signifier, do not contain, at least that's what I thought, an analyzable subject. Neither mathematical discourse in its completed form, nor the civil code, nor the majority of newspaper articles reveal the existence of an analyzable subject. In these instances, the signifier refers either to the subject of knowledge, an ideological subject, a collective subject, in short, it is unanalyzable.[9] This is why I thought that it was necessary to distinguish an analyzable signifier from a signifier, the former being not always constituted in the order of language and recognized sign systems. Nevertheless, it could be assumed that the analyzable subject was likely to enter more readily into objects produced in the order of the signifier.

Undoubtedly it would be a good idea to consider further the nature of the analyzable signifier. Could I say that the signifier is formed by the irreducible trace left by an analyzable subject pointing to whatever is analyzable in this subject. What is it that makes it possible to uncover an analyzable component of this subject? I had imagined it unforeseeable, slipping into a thousand forms, assuming thousands of appearances, capable of permeating the most unexpected object, taking advantage of the material, its grain, its color, its transparency, or unpredictable features. Generally, I had found it invisible, imperceptible but unruly, resisting erasure.

Last summer, at Aix-en-Provence, where we had gone to spend the day without anything specific to do, waiting for evening to attend the theater of the Archeveche, I had occasion to experience the difficulty of getting hold of the analyzable signifier. Along the Mirabeau avenue, now turned into a mall, there was a crafts fair. All kinds of objects were displayed on cards or stands. Bracelets; rings, necklaces, brooches made of welded silver wires, dresses, scarves, vests, made of rustic materials or dyed silk; belts, bags, some in thick leather, others made of skins so supple that they seemed to crumple as easily as tissue paper. Studded wooden shoes, others made in a dark red brown leather, polished shoes, sandals. There were also dolls, crudely made toys like those that three year olds attempt to make with three pieces of wood. Elsewhere sun dials could be admired carved out of a beautiful white stone, decorated with Roman numerals. Of course, every stand displayed different kinds of objects with a different workmanship. It was evident that the people selling them had also made them. Some worked, either in order to show off their skill or simply to occupy themselves. Near the sun dials, the stone cutter was handling the chisel and hammer, long hair, thick eyebrows and a beard filled with chips. One could sense that they, unlike ordinary shopkeepers, could not praise their products. As I was watching them I thought their disinterest somewhat affected. The strollers for their part, the eventual buyers, looked on silently, touched lightly, showing proper respect for these objects. Whenever they consulted each other, it was always at some distance from the stand, and any purchase was preceded by a kind of silent ballet, extended salutation or, a kind of feint towards the display of the object. Isolated in the midst of these stands there were a few flea marketeers selling old metal wares, pewter pots and copper pans, small clocks. The dissonance was immediately striking. People chatted aloud. Comments by the buyers walking by provoked responses from the vender. There were discussions, critical exchanges, bargaining. This fair had first struck me as typical of one of the contemporary forms of defense most frequently used against the overwhelming anonymity of capitalism, exemplary by the pronounced desire for originality betrayed as much by these craftsmen's physical appearance, attitude, clothing, as by the trademarks of their production. As the hours of the day went, we had returned several times to the mall having explored the very proper streets of the old Aix and admired the demure, imposing look of its hotels, I began to perceive a kind of complicity between the craftsman and creations, a familiarity. But I had some difficulty finding words to express what I felt. It could have been said, for example, that there was the same difference between the venders as between the displays, between the individual wares. This is not the same as saying that the product resembled his producer. The respect, the consideration of the passers-by or the potential buyers, showed that they had understood the strength of the bond between the producer and his work. They knew that a criticism of the object would have been as offensive as an opinion about the physical appearance of the vendor. However, terms like identification, narcissistic objectivation, which could have been used to conclude a somewhat hasty analysis, didn't satisfy me. It was evident that these objects' trademark, unlike that of those manufactured industrially, was not primarily aiming to stimulate the consumer's desire. They hadn't been produced for the sole purpose of exciting the consumer and the manner in which they were displayed differred from the loud seduction strategies of ordinary commerce. I was led to conclude that something was being performed, a scene was being played, no doubt for the sake of generating desire. The scene didn't involve the consumer and the object, but the passer-by and the craftsperson through the object. The display of objects, offered to the eye but waiting there rather than trying to grab the passer-by's attention, the distraction of the craftsperson, the slightly calculated indifference—it was now clear to me that all that expressed a request. With each new display the passer-by was solicited by a request, an insistence, the very same one, I would like to think, that results from the bond between all the objects in the same display created by the same hand. That particular insistence seemed to express another insistence. Of course, as the humanist apostles of manual work claim, every object expresses a craftsperson. However, I don't think that these objects expressed it like a reflection, as if a reproduction of a personality had been inserted in it. Unkindly, I thought that these objects were more successful in simulating than in being what the craftsperson would have liked them to be. In any case, it was always the same request that they repeated. I understood the need for the craftsperson to mark the object that he had made with a special characteristic feature, distinction, making it different from the others. It was imperative that the studded clogs or those made of red polished leather be identifiable among all the others. The craftsperson used these details to say that had he bought wooden shoes, or shoes of polished leather, that's the way he would have liked them. These objects concealed not only his work, but also his desire. The irreducible mark that expressed that desire effectively expressed a demand: "Recognize my desire. Love me for what I am." The object would not offer itself to the passer-by's gaze and wallet without, in this game of recognition and seduction, the producer-vendor's reserve, which was necessary in order to compensate for the object's exposure. In buying, the purchaser recognizes and legitimizes this desire.

We were thus in a position to add a complement to Marx's formula. It is not merely labor which is placed in the objects. Desire is also manifest in higher quality products of a certain kind, those which have undergone particular modes of production. This desire played out on the infinitely complex scene of the unconscious was detectable in the merchandise as an *analyzable signifier.*

This was the kind of reading which occupied me during this day spent on the Mirabeau Avenue while waiting to hear *Cosi fan Tutte,* trying to guess what had been deposited in each category of objects, the differential mark that the craftsperson could not help but have inscribed, whether knowingly or not, willingly or not, the mark which was the very trace of his desire as subject. I now realize that walking from one display stand to the next, I was looking for an analyzable signifier.

The examples I just gave testified, or at least I imagined they did, that the discovery and the detection of the analyzable signifier demanded vigilance. If it was the identifiable, actual presence of an analyzable signifier which allowed the affirmation of the effective existence of an analyzable subject, when it was hypothetical, it was imperative to find the means to uncover it. Unfortunately, given the nature of the unconscious and in particular of the characteristics of what Freud describes with the term dynamic (the extreme unstability of signs which are going to express the moving relationships of psychical forces being confronted)—it was probably going to be very difficult to find uncontestable points of reference.

If a specific characteristic must be attributed to the analyzable signifier, that would have to be its unpredictablity. However, while the analyzable signifier—indeed unforeseeable—can slip by the subject's consciousness or his will, it doesn't imply that while not very visible, it will not blind the eyes once recognized. Its manifestations, its anchoring, depend on circumstances, the material affected by the subject's practice and of course, on the subject himself whom the signifier represents. However, the ability to identify the analyzable signifier also depends on the observer. The latter has to be skilled at analytical practice, clever in being able to detect the tricks of the unconscious, the lapse of vigilance, although the analyzable signifier can not in any way be confused with symptoms, or identifiable to a compromise formation. Yet, it would have been just as futile to attempt to establish an exhaustive list of its manifestations as it would have been to suspect all the epiphanies of the analysand's unconscious.

Looking at works of art, I would have identified one such instance in the privileged manifestations of what is called style. Undoubtedly, because it is the unconscious's physiognomy which is at stake, because it is the way the unconscious and the signifier are caught in the same folds, the result is as specific as the contour of a cloth over a body. There is an infallible way to recognize what it is but it is less easy to analyze what it is made of, the characteristics of its individuality which pertain at once to the nature, consistency and dimension of the material; the shape, posture of the body and its way of moving; and finally, the manner in which the cloth has been cut, gathered, sewn on the body.

The kinship between style and the analyzable signifier induced me to think that one of its characteristics, the one most likely to be discovered, lies in an insistence, a reiteration, a capacity for emphasis, perseverance. Since style is only the manner in which a system of signs wrinkles repeatedly under the insistence of an unconscious.

In a similar line of thinking, the criteria used to attribute works came to mind, and especially for painting. We know that the method developed by Morelli did not privilege a painter's so-called characteristic features (Leonardo's depiction of a smile, Raphael's rendering of eyes) which were insignificant details in the eye of the majority of people and perhaps even of the artist himself. In the same way as in a police story one must look for hidden clues, not readily apparent, those where the artist like the criminal leaves his trace, because he is unable to know that he is leaving it there. According to Morelli, the details which make the attribution possible are revealing because on the verge of completing a work, artists let themselves use a quasi-automatic formula and a kind of mechanical writing.[10] The analogy between these terms and the automatic writing technique used by the surrealists in an attempt to summon the unconscious should be noted. Of course, characteristic details are just as revealing as insignificant details, but because it is thought that they are characteristic of a style they can be imitated. The insignificant detail is revealing because it is insignificant and this is why it signifies the presence, the effective intervention, of an author. It is not very surprising that Freud mentions the same Morelli in "Michaelangelo's Moses" and noted the similarity between his method and psychoanalytic investigation.

> He achieved this by insisting that attention should be diverted from the general impression and main features of a picture, and by laying stress on the significance of minor details, of things like the drawing of the fingernails, of the lobe of an ear, of halos and such unconsidered trifles which the copyist neglects to imitate and yet which every artist executes in his own characteristic way...It seems to me that his method of inquiry is closely related to the technique

of psycho-analysis. It, too, is accustomed to divine secret and concealed things from despised or unnoticed features, from the rubbish-heap, as it were, of our observations.

Studies like the essay on Leonardo or Moses presuppose the existence of an analyzable signifier in every art work and Freud states clearly what that could be. It should be noted in connection with this point that in these two texts by Freud the analyzable signifier is not necessarily made up of "the rubbish heap of observation". The Mona Lisa's smile which reappears in the painting of Saint Ann with the Virgin Mary and the Child which Freud dissects as analyzable signifier did not quite remain unnoticed. On the other hand, the composition of the painting (Saint Ann) which seems to impose a double headed body, or Moses' forefinger deep in his beard in Michaelangelo's sculpture are less obvious.

As we progress we meet again an earlier objection: If Freud hadn't had Michaelangelo's or Leonardo's testimony at his disposal (about the vulture fantasm or the disputes with Jules II) would he have been able to identify those analyzable signifiers? The analyzable signifier does not exist without a subject. Is it possible to isolate one (or several) analyzable signifier in a given work if nothing is known about its subject? It can be answered that available testimonies sharpen the observation of analyzable signifiers. However, once recognized the latter facilitate access to motivation unnoticed by the subject. In so doing one moves from the analyzable to analysis. Furthermore, the fact that one may be ignorant of the identity of the analyzable subject does not prevent the differentiation of the analyzable signifier. We find the proof for this in painting in the discovery of anonymous works and the regrouping of several paintings around a name's identity. Although in this case the analyzable signifier may well bear the specific trace left by a subject it continuation of analysis without biographical documentation. One may not move from the analyzable to analysis.

There still remains the case where, in an ordinary product, the analyzable subject is himself problematic. The absence of a perceptible analyzable signifier does not imply that one will not be found later on. While the presence of an analyzable signifier authorizes the postulation of the existence of an analyzable subject, the absence of an analyzable signifier, which may be purely accidental, does not warrant the conclusion that there is no participation of the analyzable subject as such.

What about cinema?

Starting from the concept of author I considered several parameters that rendered the uncritical use of the term "author" difficult. First of all, cinema combines intimately personal initiative and collective work; the fact that it does function on the basis of a model of fabrication comparable to industrial production practice while incorporating individual practices important in themselves (because the various subjects intervening in the different steps of the production process are not equally interchangeable). Furthermore, because of its enormous economic dependency, and as a signifying practice, cinema is affected by the combined pressure of market laws and ideology. At the same time as films must usually satisfy the largest number of people while conforming, with a few exceptions (there must be some) to dominant ideology, cinema must also serve this ideology as a means of transmission and of transformation. Thus, the concept of author does not seem to account for the producer-subject because in cinema, the latter is doubly heterogeneous. Cinema combines the unanalyzable collective subject and the analyzable individual subject; it instills the latter with an ideological subject because it molds its product into the representation desired by the largest number of people.

Finally, the analyzable subject is also plural. Several "hands" can be detected in the cinematographic signifier. The mere juxtaposition of a soundtrack and an image track is already evidence of this heterogeneity. Consequently, the analyzable signifier may well appear in different aspects whenever there are operations which trigger the intervention of an individual subjective influence in a film production. Scenario, decoupage, montage, dialogue, color, decor, direction of actors, gesture and intonation, etc.

For the homogeneous concept of author it is thus preferable to substitute the concept of analyzable subject in the same way as it would seem preferable to call attention to the analyzable subjects as themselves plural and heterogeneous. This assumes that a film will allow a plurality of analyzable subjects to show, and that the analyzable signifiers can thus accumulate, confront and contradict one another, and transform the proclaimed intentions of the single author.

Undoubtedly, cinema is not the only signifying practice which contains this heterogeneity of a producer subject and its analyzable subject. In many frescoes and paintings critics have been able to identify a number of different "hands" thus making it easier to understand the problems that these works presented to connoisseurs. However, I would prefer to compare a film to a church—if not to a cathedral—a monument erected under a strong ideological pressure whose style is influenced by both the technological conditions of the period and its ideological concepts. These churches (I was thinking of the Romanesque churches from Auvergne) confirm the existence of a master planner in the disposition of the pillars and openings, in the relationships among architectural masses, in the choice of stone in the play of light and the movements of shadows during the hours of the day, while the several hands of the sculptors are identified in the carved cornices, with their motifs, their mannerisms, the obsessions that they reveal. This comparison was not as risky as it would seem. Perhaps when the conditions of film projection will change, through technical progresses which promise to allow us to have access at will to films, it may become possible to walk leisurely, to wander, to loaf about, stroll and loiter, as we are accustomed to do when we are visiting a church, noticing details, stopping suddenly around a corner to examine an unexpected figure, delighted to be able to explore the ordered depth of a film, to appreciate a thousand details in a sequence while experiencing the unique character of the whole. It seemed to me that with the possibility of *contemplating* a film, that the concept of author was very likely to change. Besides, hadn't the miracle of cinema consisted as much in the production of movement out of photographic stillness as of making movement stop and thus creating a synthesis of the arts of space and the arts of time, to add to the theater, dance, the opera what they lacked, the advantages of contemplation associated with painting.

Furthermore, I also thought that concepts such as author and analyzable subject, heterogeneity of the producer-subject made it possible to identify a number of laws—or to clarify certain debates.

I wondered for example if ideological effectiveness was not in part a neutralization function of the analyzable subject. Cinema's tendency towards transparency, a neutrality of cinematographic writing (a degree zero which surely must have varied according to periods, mental habits developed by filmgoers) could find an explanation in that. We would thus have a progressive law of exclusion between analyzable subject and ideological subject. Actually cinema is not the only instance of such a law. Murder mysteries, detective stories, sentimental novels, photo-romans, which typically attempt a degree zero of writing, are characterized by the elimination of the analyzable subject, through a rewriting technique used to eliminate the asperities of the analyzable signifier. This is why, paradoxically, the ideological output of films made in a Hollywood "style" is far superior to that of Eisenstein in spite of the latter's intentions. In order to understand this phenomenon, it may be useful to turn back to the apparatus. Whenever the analyzable signifier is excessively characterized, i.e. the visible imprint and the all too noticeable dominance of the cinematographic signifier by an analyzable subject perturb the more than real impression of reality which is at work in the apparatus, somewhat like, due allowance being made, the way the intrusion of the other's fantasmatization can interfere in our own fantasmatic elaboration during sexual intercourse. Neutral writing, on the contrary, enables the apparatus to function at the optimum of its capacity.

One can also notice that the more a film fits a specialized genre, or the more it is designed to satisfy precise organizational drives, the less it must contain of an analyzable signifer. Pornographic films and violent films are fairly representative in their mediocrity of the rarefication of the mark of the individualized subject of desire in the filmic signifier. In this respect, the opposition between pornographic cinema and erotic cinema, and the debate which they triggered, seems to be solvable by using the concept of the analyzable subject. It isn't the content, the crudeness, the obscenity of images, nor formal beauty which constitute its diacritical elements, but the process of production. In one case, the film is turned towards the subject, it responds to the *mise en forme en space* of a subject's representations and has to do more or less directly with his unconscious organization. Its signifier refers back to an analyzable subject. In the other case, it is turned towards and for an indeterminate spectator and the signifier must organize itself as an all-purpose cliche, indiscriminately assimilable. The idea is to create the largest common denominator for the representations of desire, a common denominator corresponding to the zero limit of writing.

I imagined still other uses for these notions. The development of the mass media triggered a wild extension of cinematographic type signifiers. In institutions as constricting as television, an increase in ideological pressure is unavoidable. One may well imagine that it might be possible to measure censorship, its internal and external power, its unknown or explicit control, and its failures also, on the basis of the density of the perceptible analyzable signifier in slices and segments of programs. No more than in novels or plays, the I of the enunciation in cinema provides the proof of the presence of the analyzable subject. Quite the contrary. Since the I is merely the last ruse of a censoring instance intended to fake the existence of a subject of desire where only a pure ideological subject expresses itself.

Finally, I hoped that the concepts of analyzable signifier and analyzable subject would bring a better comprehension of the infinitely complex product that is a film and would provide criticism with finer analytical tools while allowing the continuation of a theoretical development in the field of cinema. In any case, it seemed to me that the pursuit of the signifier and of the analyzable subject in film should stimulate a new kind of attention which should reveal itself as fascinating.

Occasionally, it occured to me that we still haven't learned to watch films, that we haven't had the means at our disposal, except for a few specialists with access to a viewing table, and that if cinema is still a very young art, the reading of films has barely begun. On these occasions, I wasn't far from thinking that a more complete and detailed vision of the producer-subject would inevitably lead to the production of new, original, unprecedented filmic forms.

NOTES

1. It is not possible to be exhaustive. The works of Bellour, Kuntzel, Vernet, should be mentioned. On the signifier of cinema see Christian Metz, whose *Imaginary Signifier,* which appears in 10/18, collected the texts consecrated to this domain. In the *Cahiers du Cinéma* see the texts of Pascal Bonitzer, Jean-Pierre Oudart, Pierre Baudry, and Jean-Louis Comolli.

2. I should mention among these the work of Julia Kristeva because of their systematic character and because of their genuine attempt to exhaust the subject.

3. For example, Marcelin Pleynet's *L'Enséignement de la péinture.* The problem is still whether a particular art form is always associated with the same partial drives in different artists. In my opinion, it would be a mistake to skip without intermediary, as this school of thought leads us to believe, from partial drives to a signifying practice—a tendency towards mechanism. (Freud is quite emphatic on this point: drives never manifest themselves except through *representation,* and that is the basis of the interminable rivalry between the satisfaction of drives and the search for the objects of desire. When one talks about breath, rhythm, drive, undoubtedly because of the influence of Artaud's work, one is under the domination of an organic model which, in the final analysis and among other things is only a representation. I too, have contributed to this error with my criticism of representation in the process of literary creation.

4. There is hardly any need for an institution to learn the technique. Language belongs to everyone and literature benefits from an irregular or mistaken use of language. This is why, among signifying practices, it is the only one which has always been accessible to the oppressed and outcasts, women and madmen.

5. This is for example what Renoir said about *Madame Bovary* in *La Politique des Auteurs.* "Yes, it was very long, and it was much better. As a matter of fact, the film was destroyed when it was shortened; but it wasn't the producers who did it because they fought as much as they could; it was the distributors who didn't have the nerve to release a film which was more than 3 hours long. That wasn't done. That was at a time when double features seemed to be the answer to the crisis in cinema, because there was already a crisis, just like today. Actually, it's the same one. The distributors said: 'We like the film a lot, but we can't, it's not possible...we've got to cut.' So I cut. But strangely enough, once cut, the film was longer, really, morally, than when it wasn't cut. It never seemed to end—you know, I find the film in its current length somewhat boring. When it lasted 3 hours, it wasn't boring at all. I showed it before it was cut...Unfortunately, I think that the original print must have disappeared as soon as we made cuts in the copy, then the negative was burnt and all the outtakes were thrown out."

6. Renoir again: "When I began to make movies, things were still done very conventionally. I'll never forget a conversation with some carpenters, set painters in the first film I worked on. I explained to them that I needed for the sets the common room in a farm in the Southern part of France, and that consequently, given the fact that one finds a lot of walls made out of pebbles, covered irregularly with cement, it would be a good idea to make the wall somewhat uneven and to whitewash the walls. These people were listening to me with some impatience because they found my explanations useless because that type of decor was known and classified. They kept telling me, 'But Mr. Renoir, we know what "rustic" looks like. The rustic style, well, the wall is irregular with apparent beams.' 'Precisely, I don't want the beams to show' 'Oh! But in the rustic style the beam's got to show!'

7. This kind of analyzable determination has to be understood in a restrictive sense. The presence of an analyzable subject in an object does not mean that it is analyzable in the object. The identification of the presence of the unconscious subject and the analysis of the determinations of this unconscious are not of the same order. Psychoanalysis of art has certainly contributed to maintaining a confusion between what is analyzable and the possibility for analysis. This does not mean that the analyzable never makes it possible to link the object back to the subject. However this possibility is relative to works and subject. From the dynamics of the conflicts of the author, their intensity, the forces of oppositions being confronted, the period when the work was created, etc. I just thought that for the moment, it was im-

portant to stress the independence of analyzability from the possibility for analysis and that it did not necessarily lead to interpretation.

8. I thought that the concept of analyzable subject would be useful to clarify some misunderstandings, for I remembered the debate about history. Was history a process without a subject? From an orthodox Maoist viewpoint, the mass-subject created history. Undoubtedly this debate suffered from philosophical overtone. It is not even very clear whether it was not based on the different models which make the Hegelian and the Marxist dialectics. To the extent that it is identified with the very movement of the mind, in the latter, dialectics is conceived through the intermediary of the model of a subject of desire, the best example of which is that of the master/slave relationship which, since Freud, pertains to the concept of the unconscious. On the other hand, for Marx, the subject of history is conceived as a collective subject which emerging industrial production illustrates in a particularly striking way. To the extent that history is constituted and produced out of facts and discourses, to the extent that it is a process, it is difficult to think that it cannot refuse a subject. However, this subject would not be an analyzable subject, unless one recognizes as such the effect of the action of great leaders, which would amount to recognizing the presence of an analyzable subject within an analyzable subject, and for example the thrust and the action of desire within the framework of a world of needs.

9. A piece of clothing, like a car, is not made out of signifiers but can enter into a system of signs and thus become a signifier. See Barthes' *Le Systémè de la mode* or *Mythologies.*

10. See the article Attribution in *Encyclopedia Universalis.* (Paris, 1975)

Film Directors. A Revolution

Dziga Vertov

1

Looking at the pictures that have come to us from the West and from America, and bearing in mind the information we have about the work and experiments abroad and at home, I arrive at this conclusion: The death sentence passed by film-directors in 1919 on every film without exception is effective to this very day.

The most thorough observation reveals not a single picture, not a single experiment directed, as they should be, towards the *emancipation of the film-camera,* which remains wretchedly enslaved, subordinated to the imperfect, undiscerning human eye.

We are not protesting at the *undermining* of literature and the theatre by the cinema, and we fully sympathize with the use of the cinema for all branches of science, but we define these functions of the cinema as sidelines diverging from the main line.

The basic and most important thing is: CINEMA-PERCEPTION OF THE WORLD.

The starting-point is: *use of the film-camera as a cinema-eye, more perfect than the human eye for fathoming the chaos of those visual phenomena which evoke spatial dimension.*

The cinema-eye lives and moves in time and space, apprehends and fixes impressions in quite a different way from that of the human eye. The position of our bodies at the moment of observation, the number of features perceived by us in one or another visual phenomenon in one second of time is not at all binding on the film-camera, which, the more perfect it is, the more and the better it perceives things.

We cannot make our eyes better than they are already made, but we can perfect the film-camera without limit.

Up to today the film-cameraman has many a time suffered rebukes about a running horse which on the screen moved unnaturally slowly (rapid turning of the film-camera handle), or, conversely, about a tractor which ploughed a field too quickly (slow turning of the film-camera handle and so on.

These are accidents, of course, but we are preparing a system, a contrived system of cases like these, a system of *apparent* irregularities which probe into and organise phenomena.

Up to today we *have coerced the film-camera and made it copy the work of our own eyes.* And the better the copying, the more highly was the shot considered.

From today we are liberating the camera and making it work in the opposite direction, furthest away from copying.

All the weaknesses of the human eye are external. We affirm the *cinema-eye, that gropes in the chaos of movements for a resultant force for its own movement, we affirm the cinema-eye with its dimension of time and space, growing in its own strength and its own resources to reach self-affirmation.*

2

...I force the spectator to see in the way most advantageous for me to show this or that visual phenomenon. The eye is subordinated to the will of the film-camera and directed by it onto those consecutive moments of action, which in the briefest and clearest way lead the cinema-phrase to the heights or depths of resolution.

For example: a shot of boxing, not from the point of view of a spectator present at the match, but a shot of the consecutive movements (methods) of the boxers. Or: a shot of a group of dancers—but not from the viewpoint of a spectator sitting in a hall with a ballet on stage in front of him.

It is known that a spectator at a ballet watches haphazardly sometimes the general group of dancers, sometimes separate dancers at random, and sometimes somebody's feet: *a series of incoherent impressions, different for each single spectator.*

We must not present the cinema audience with this. The system of consecutive movements demands shots of the dancers or boxers as an exposition of the tricks presented one after the other, with the *forced* transference of the spectator's eyes onto those successive details which must be seen.

The film-camera drags the eyes of the audience from hands to feet, from feet to eyes, and so on in the best order possible, and organises details into a regular montage-study.

3

You can be walking along the street in Chicago today, in 1923, but I can make you bow to the late comrade Volodarsky, who in 1918 is walking along a street in Petrograd, and he will return your bow.

Another example: the coffins of national heroes are lowered into their tombs (taken in Astrakhan in 1918), the tombs are filled in (Kronstadt, 1921), a gun salute (Petrograd, 1920), eternal remembrance, hats are removed (Moscow 1922)—such things can be fitted together even from thankless material which was not specially filmed (see *Kino-Pravda* No. 13). A further example of this is the montage of the greetings of the crowd and the montage of the salute of the vehicles for comrade Lenin (*Kino-Pravda* No. 14), taken in different places, at different times.

...I am the cinema-eye. I am a constructor.

I have set you down, you who have today been created by me, in a most amazing room, which did not exist up to this moment, also created by me.

In this room are 12 walls filmed by me in various parts of the world.

Putting together the shots of the walls and other details I was able to arrange them in an order which pleases you, and which will correctly construct by intervals the cinema-phrase, which is in fact a room.....

....

I am the cinema-eye. I create a man more perfect than Adam was created, I create thousands of different people from various preliminary sketches and plans.

I am the cinema-eye.

I take from one person the strongest and deftest hands, from another I take the strongest and swiftest legs, from a third the most beautiful and expressive head and I create a new, perfect man in a montage...

4

...I am the cinema-eye. I am a mechanical eye.

I, a machine, can show you the world as only I can see it.

From today I liberate myself for ever from human immobility. *I am in perpetual motion,* I approach and move away from objects, I creep up to them, I climb onto them, I move alongside the muzzle of a running horse, I tear into the crowd at full speed, I run before the fleeing soldiers, I tip over onto my back, I ascend with aeroplanes, I fall and rise together with falling and rising bodies.

Here am I, the camera, rushing about guided by a resultant force, manoeuvring in the chaos of motions, fixing motion from motion in the most complex combinations.

Freed from the obligation of 16-17 frames a second, freed from the limits of time and space, *I can contrast any points in the universe,* wherever I might fix them.

My way leads to the creation of a fresh perception of the world. And this is how I can decipher anew a world unknown to you.

5

...Once again let us settle one thing: the eye and the ear.

The ear does not spy and the eye does not eavesdrop.

A division of functions:

The radio-ear—the montaged "I hear!"

The cinema-eye—the montaged "I see!"

This is for you, citizens, for a start, instead of music, painting, theatre, cinema and other castrated effusions.

Amid the chaos of motions rushing past, rushing away, rushing forward and colliding together—into life there comes simply *the eye.*

The day of visual impressions has passed. How can a day's impressions be constructed into an effective whole in a visual study?

If everything that the eye saw were to be photographed onto a film there would naturally be confusion. If it were artistically assembled, what was photographed would be clearer. If the encumbering rubbish were thrown out, it would be still better. We shall obtain an organised manual of impressions of the *ordinary eye.*

The mechanical eye—the film-camera, refusing to use the human eye as a crib, repelled and attracted by motions, gropes about in the chaos of visual events for the path for its own motion or oscillation, and experiments by stretching time, breaking up its motions, or vice versa, absorbing time into itself, swallowing up the years, thereby schematizing prolonged processes which are inaccessible to the normal eye...

...To the aid of the machine-age comes...the *cineaste-pilot,* who not only controls the motions of the camera but who *trusts* in it during spatial experimentation, and...the *cineaste-engineer,* who controls the cameras at a distance.

The result of this sort of combined action of the liberated and perfected camera, and of the strategic brain of man directing, observing and taking stock of things, is a noticeably fresher, and therefore interesting, presentation of even the most ordinary things...

...How many people are there thirsting for spectacular shows that wear out their trousers in the theatres?

They flee from the daily round, they flee from the prose of life. And yet the theatre is almost always just a wretched counterfeit of that very same life plus a stupid conglomeration of the affectations of ballet, musical squeaks, lighting effects, decorations (from the daubing-type to the constructive-type) and sometimes the excellent work of a literary master, perverted by all the rubbish. Certain masters of the theatres are destroying the theatres from the inside, breaking the old forms and declaring new slogans for work in the theatre; brought in to help this are bio-mechanics (a good exercise in itself), the cinema (glory and honour to it), writers (not bad in themselves), constructions (there are good ones), motor-cars (how can one not respect a motor-car?), and gun-fire (a dangerous and impressive trick in the front rows), but in general not a single feature stands out in it.

Theatre, and nothing more.

Not only not a synthesis, but not even a regular miscellany.

And it cannot be otherwise.

We, the film-makers, are determined opponents of premature synthesis ("to synthesis as the zenith of achievement!"), and realise it is pointless to mix up fragments of achievement: the poor infants immediately perish through overcrowding and disorder. And in general —*the arena is small.*

Please let's get into life.

This is where we work—we, the masters of vision—organisers of visible life, armed with the ever-present cinema-eye.

This is where the masters of words and sounds work, the most skillful montage-makers of audible life. And I venture to slip in with them the ubiquitous mechanical ear and mouth-piece—the radio-telephone.

What does this amount to?

It means *the newsreel film and the radio newsreel.* I intend to stage a parade of film-makers in Red Square on the occasion of the *Futurists'* issuing of the first edition of the montaged radio-newsreel.

Not the "Pathe" newsreel-films nor Gaumont (a newspaper-type "newsreel") and not even *Kino-Pravda* (a political "newsreel"), but a genuine cinema newsreel—*a swift review of VISUAL events deciphered by the film-camera, pieces of REAL energy* (I distinguish this from theatrical energy), *brought together at intervals to form an accumulatory whole by means of highly skilled montage.*

This structure for the cinema allows any theme to be developed, whether comic, tragic, contrived or anything else.

The whole trick lies in this or the juxtapositioning of visual features, the whole trick lies in the intervals.

The unusual flexibility of the montage-construction permits any political, economic, or other motifs be brought into the cinema-study. And that is why

FROM TODAY neither psychological nor detective dramas are needed in the cinema

FROM TODAY theatrical productions taken onto film are not needed

FROM TODAY neither Dostoevsky nor Nat Pinkerton need be scripted

Everything can be included in the new concept of the newsreel film.

These two things now make a decisive entry into the muddle of life:

1) the cinema-eye, which disputes the visual presentation of the world by human eye, and presents its "I see!"
2) the cineaste-montageur, who organises moments of life-construct now seen in *cinema-eye* fashion for the first time.

Translated by Richard Sherwood

An Anagram Of Ideas On Art, Form And Film

Maya Deren

CONTENTS OF ANAGRAM

		A THE NATURE OF FORMS	B THE FORMS OF ART	C THE ART OF FILM
1	THE STATE OF NATURE and THE CHARACTER OF MAN	1A	1B	1C
2	THE MECHANICS OF NATURE and THE METHODS OF MAN	2A	2B	2C
3	THE INSTRUMENT OF DISCOVERY and THE INSTRUMENT OF INVENTION	3A	3B	3C

PREFACE

Any critical statement by an artist which concerns the field of his creative activity is usually taken to be a manifesto or a statement of the theories upon which the creative work is based. Art abounds in works designed to demonstrate principles and manifesto, and these are, almost without exception, inferior to those works from which the principles were derived.

In my case I have found it necessary, each time, to ignore any of my previous statements. After the first film was completed, when someone asked me to define the principle which it embodied, I answered that the function of film, like that of other art forms, was to create experience—in this case a semi-psychological reality. But the actual creation of the second film caused me to subsequently answer a similar question with an entirely different emphasis. This time, that reality must exploit the capacity of film to manipulate Time and Space. By the end of the third film, I had again shifted the emphasis—insisting this time on a filmically visual integrity, which would create a dramatic necessity of itself, rather than be dependent upon or derive from an underlying dramatic development. Now, on the basis of the fourth, I feel that all the other elements must be retained, but that special attention must be given to the creative possibilities of Time, and that the form as a whole should be ritualistic (as I define this later in the essay). I believe, of course, that some kind of development has taken place; and I feel that one symptom of the continuation of such a development would be that the actual creation of each film would not so much illustrate previous conclusions as it would necessitate new ones—and thus the theory would remain dynamic and volatile.

This is not, therefore, to be taken as a manifesto. It is an organization of ideas in an anagramatic complex instead of in the linear logic to which we are accustomed.

An anagram is a combination of letters in such a relationship that each and every one is simultaneously an element in more than one linear series. This simultaneity is real, and independent of the fact that it is usually perceived in succession. Each element of an anagram is so related to the whole that no one of them may be changed without effecting its series and so effecting the whole. And, conversely, the whole is so related to every part that whether one reads horizontally, vertically, diagonally or even in reverse, the logic of the whole is not disrupted, but remains intact.

In this essay the element is not a single letter, but an idea concerned with the subject matter of its position in the anagram; that is, 2B, for instance, deals with the forms of art in reference to the mechanics of nature and the methods of man. In every other respect the principles governing an anagram hold. As printed, it proceeds from the general to the specific. Those who prefer the inductive method may read the elements in reverse order. Or one may slice through on the diagonal, picking up the sides afterwards.

I recommend this form to anyone who has faced the problem of compressing into a linear organization an idea which was stimulating precisely because it extended into two or three different, but not contradictory directions at once.

It has seemed especially useful to me in this essay. In the effort to apply the currently accepted esthetic theories to the first new art form in centuries, I have found it necessary to re-examine and re-evaluate principles which had become so "understood" a quality of other arts as to have constituted, for the past century, the unquestioned premises of creative action. And so I have found myself involved in fields and considerations which seem far from my original concern with film. But I believe that these are not as irrelevant as they may, off-hand, seem.

Modern specialization has discouraged the idea of the whole man. One is timid to invade or refer to territories which are not, strictly speaking, one's own. In the need to do so, nevertheless—for to arrive at principles requires comparative analysis—it is possible that I have been inaccurate in various details. And in seeking for the principles of various concepts of art form, I have examined not those talents whose genius is to transcend all principles, but those lesser lights who, in failing to transcend them, illustrate them best. This may give, at times, the impression of a wholesale under-estimation of modern art; and for this impression, which does not reflect my real evaluation, I must apologize. Whatever the errors of generalization or the weaknesses of critical omission, they are committed in the interest of showing film (in such a relatively short space) not as a localized, specialized craft but as an art form, sharing with other art forms a profound relationship to man, the history of his relation to reality, and the basic problems of form.

In an anagram all the elements exist in a simultaneous relationship. Consequently, within it, nothing is first and nothing is last; nothing is future and nothing is past; nothing is old and nothing is new. . .except, perhaps, the anagram itself.

1A

At the moment, it has become fashionable among all the self-appointed mentors of public conscience, to bemoan the inertia of the people towards the atom bomb, and to chastize this complacency with elaborate attitudes of righteous indignation, or pompous didacticism, or despair and silence. But inertia is, precisely, not a reaction—wrong or right;—it is the sheer persistence of an attitude already firmly habitual. The almost casual acceptance of the use of atomic energy is, if anything, testimony to man's complete adjustment to science; for him, it is merely the most recent in a long series of achievements, some of which, like electricity and the radio, have had far more the quality of miracle.

The anxiety of the scientists is based upon an intimate awareness of the destructive potential of the *method* which has been achieved. But ever since the curtains of specialization descended upon the methodology of science, men have humbly accepted their inability to comprehend the detailed processes of such miracles, and have limited themselves to evaluating only the final results, which they have agreed to accept at their own risk. The gas piped through every kitchen simplifies the act of suicide; electricity can cause a strange death; cars can collide; airplanes can crash; tanks can explode. But man had come to terms with scientific disaster long ago, and remains consistent in his attitude.

What amazes him most, in the spectacle of current anxiety, is that the miracle-makers themselves, at this late date, seem to be attempting to reopen the first of all questions: to bite or not to bite of the forbidden fruit. Is not the public justified in its reluctance to become seriously involved in what is so obviously an academic discussion? And it is even possible that, pondering the force which can be contained in a fistful of matter, man might find poetic justice in an atomic bomb formed in the shape of an apple.

The distress of the scientists is, on the other hand, also justified. The occidental culture of the 17th century, where they began their specialized labors, had been homogeneous. All nature and reality, including man, had been previously accepted as a manifestation of the will of a central, absolute consciousness. In transposing that consciousness from the central position in the metaphysical cosmos to a location in man's own brain, the principle of conscious control and creative manipulation was, if anything, reasserted in science. It was logical to expect that this was true, as well, of all the other fields of activity.

But today the scientist emerges from the laboratory to discover himself part of a schizoid culture. The rationalism upon which he has predicated himself is an insular entity in a sociological structure which operates in terms of the most primitive motivations and non-rational procedures. And this ambivalence is most strikingly evident in the existence of art forms which, claiming the scientific attitude toward reality as their source of inspiration, result in romantic or realistic exaltations of nature, and develop finally into the ecstasies of a surrealism whose triumphant achievement consists in eliminating altogether the functions of consciousness and intelligence.

Presumably, man had enjoyed an age of reason in the 18th century. Yet today the concept of "reason" is as ambiguous as it had been during the 17th century, when ambiguity served to dis-simulate the actual revolution which was taking place. According to medieval concepts of absolute consciousness, the reason why a stone fell was because God willed that it do so. Reason was a function of the will of an inscrutable, immutable deity. Modern thought began with a most timid and subtle re-definition. When astronomical observations revealed the consistency of cosmic movement, it became necessary to account for this as a part of the nature with which the universe had been divinely endowed, which could henceforth function independently, (subject, of course, to divine intervention at will). In this way the divine will became a creator of laws, instead of functioning according to laws, as its consistency would have implied. The reason why a stone fell, now, was because such action was of its divine nature.

The following development was equally subtle. Reason was made a logical function, without a sacrifice of its metaphysical authority, by the simple device of attributing to the divine consciousness a rational character. When Milton wrote that it was more "reasonable" for the earth to revolve in the heavens than for the immense heavens to revolve their bulk around the earth, he was implying to deity the values of economy and efficiency—values relevant actually to the needs and conditions of man. From these "reasonable" terms to the "logical" terms of scientific cause and effect was but the last step in the achievement of a most critical intellectual revolution.

In the course of displacing deity-consciousness as the motive power of reality, by a concept of logical causation, man inevitably re-located himself in terms of the new scheme. He consciously distinguished himself from the nature which had now ceased to be divine, and proceeded to discover in himself, and within the scope of his manipulations, all the powers which he had previously attributed exclusively to deity. By the development of instruments of observation and discovery, such as the telescope, he achieved a measure of omnipresence. Through mathematical computations, he was able to extend his knowledge even beyond the reach of his instruments. From a careful analysis of causation and incidence, he developed the powers of prediction. And finally, not content to merely analyze an existent reality, he undertook to activate the principles which he had discovered, to manipulate reality, and to bring togehter into new relationships the elements which he was able to isolate. He was able to create forms according to his own intelligence. Thus he succeeded in usurping even the main attribute of divinity. . .fecundity. And although he was careful not to claim this, he had become himself God, to all intents and purposes, by virtue of the unique possession, among all natural phenomena, of creative consciousness.

I do not mean to imply that the exercise of consciousness originated in the 17th century. Previously, when man had considered himself a manifestation of divine consciousness, it was precisely through the exercise of consciousness that he could reaffirm his relationship with deity. The concerns of that relationship were moral, and up until the 17th century his activities—especially those of a philosophic and esthetic nature—consisted of moral (or ethical) ideas articulated in consciously creative and controlled forms.

Only when he relinquished his concept of divine consciousness did he confront the choice of either developing his own and accepting all the moral responsibilities previously dispensated by divinity, or of merging with inconscient nature and enjoying the luxurious irresponsibility of being one of its more complex phenomena. He resolved this problem by the simple expediency of choosing both; the forms of our modern culture are an accurate manifestation of this ambivalence. Man himself is a natural phenomenon and his activities may be either an extension and an exploitation of himself as a natural phenomenon, or he can dedicate himself to the creative manipulation and transfiguration of all nature, including himself, through the exercise of his conscious, rational powers.

Wherever he functions as a spontaneous natural phenomenon, he gives rise to forms typical of nature; wherever he functions as an analytical and creative intelligence, he achieves forms of an entirely different character. Nature, being unconscious, functions by an infinite process of inviolable cause and effect whose result are inevitabilities. But the forms of man are the results of a manipulation controlled according to motivation and intention. The forms of nature, springing from anterior causation, are often ambiguous both in their "natural" function and towards man. A mountain, created by the cooling of the earth's crust, is ambiguous in the first sense, since its incidence may or may not "serve" some purpose to the rest of the nature around it. A tree is ambiguous in its relation to man, in that its form and character are not intentionally designed, by nature, to serve any of the purposes to which man may put it. The forms of man, furthermore, are much more explicitly and economically determined by the function for which they are intended, even to the point of being limited, in their use, by that intention.

In these distinctions are implicit the moral attitudes which are respectively appropriate. The forms of nature, being inevitable, are amoral, and even at their most destructive, as in disease, cannot be considered morally responsible. The forms of man are, on the contrary, subject to moral evaluations in terms of the conscious intentions which they incorporate and they are not a priori exonerated from such judgment by their mere existence or even persistent survival.

All these basic distinctions, applied to the forms prevalent in modern culture, reveal its schizoid character. The achievements of science and industry are constituted of the forms and methods of man. The manifestations of much of our art (with which I am here specifically concerned) reveal, by and large, an effort to achieve the forms of nature.

Man's mind, his consciousness, is the greatest triumph of nature, the product of aeons of evolutionary processes, of infinite mutations, of merciless elimination. Now, in the 20th century, there are many among us who seek the long way back. In an essay on the relationship between art and the intellect, Charles Duits has given his commentary on sur-realism a profound humor by referring to it in a terminology drawn from the medieval period. In the sense that the sur-realist esthetic reflects a state of mind which antecedes the 17th century, he is not only correct, but, if anything, too lenient. Their "art" is dedicated to the manifestations of an organism which antecedes all consciousness. It is not even merely primitive; it is primeval. But even in this effort, man the scientist has, through the exercise of rational faculties, become more competent than the modern artist. That which the sur-realists labor and sweat to achieve, and end by only simulating, can be accomplished in full reality, by the atom bomb.

2A

Total amnesia, although less spectacular than many other forms of mental disorder, has always seemed to me the most terrifying. A man so reduced to immediate perception only, has lost, in losing experience, all ability to evaluate, to understand, to solve and to create—in short, all that which makes him human. Moreover, in the process of evolving conscious memory man has had to forfeit those complex instinctual patterns which substitute, or rather, antecede, memory in animals. The infant kitten, out of itself—by a process of "vertical" inevitabilities—and through its own immediate experience of reality, will become a complete cat. But a human infant, out of itself, will not develop into its proper adulthood. It must learn beyond its instincts, and often in opposition to them, by imitation, observation, experimentation, reflection—in sum, by the complex "horizontal" processes of memory.

By "horizontal" I mean that the memory of man is not committed to the natural chronology of his experience—whether of an extended period, a single event, or a compulsive reaction. On the contrary, he has access to all his experience simultaneously. He can compare the beginning of a process to the end of it, without accepting it as a homogeneous totality; he can compare similar portions of events widely disparate in time and place, and so recognize both the constancy of elements and their variable functions in one context or another; and he is able to perceive that a natural, chronological whole is not immutable, but that it is a dynamic relationship of functioning parts.

So he is able to understand fire separate from the pain of his own burns.

For an animal, all experience remains immediately personal. Man's first step, accomplished through reflective recollection, is to depersonalize, to abstract from his personal experience.

Nowhere is the method more clearly epitomized than in mathematics. In order even to measure, it has first to abstract from the experience of space to a number. The concept of subjectivity, to which esthetic criteria have such frequent reference today, originated not in reference to art but, precisely, to science.

When man undertook to analyze the causes and effects of nature, on the basis of his observation, he became aware of the distorting window-glass of his subjectivity. At first he devoted himself to the development of instruments designed to "correct" his vision and to compensate for the limitations of his subjective perceptions—the sundial, the stable weight, the microscope, the telescope.

But even this was not enough. He became eventually aware of his subjective position. He understood that when, across a large distance, or in a reverse wind, the sound followed long after the image of an action—that this discrepancy was not due to an inaccuracy of observation because of a failure of his senses, but that it was a condition of his subjective position, one which would exist regardless of the presence of minds or senses to perceive it.

The theory of relativity is the latest triumph in the development of theoretical computations designed to overcome and compensate for the inalienability of subjective position. And if science has found it necessary to arrive at all these instruments and calculations in order to analyze reality realistically, how can the artist "realist" presume to cover the same ground on the basis of his personal powers of perception? Is not the relative poverty of contemporary art at least partly due to the fact that, in taking realism (which is not at all the same as objectivity) as its ambition it has basically denied the existence of art and substituted science?

The realist describes his experience of reality. He denies the value of the original, *artificial* reality created by the rigours and disciplines of the art instrument. But he is unwilling, also, to submit to the rigours and disciplines of the scientific instrument in objectively analyzing the existent reality. And so he moves among the optical illusions of that which really is, and the shadowy dreams of that which, by art, might be. He is tortured both by the anxieties of "truth," and the demands of that most precious of man's qualities—the vanity of the creative ego.

For man it has never been enough to merely understand the dynamics of a reality which would continue, in any case, to exist independently of his analysis. If all men had agreed, with the realists and the romantics, to describe, exalt, and extend the "natural condition" there would be no such thing as science, philosophy or art.

Even in science—or rather, above all in science, the pivotal characteristic of man's method is a violation of natural integrity. He has dedicated himself to the effort to intervene upon it, to dissemble the ostensibly inviolate whole, to emancipate the element from the context in which it "naturally" occurs, and to manipulate it in the creation of a new contextual whole—a new, original state of matter and reality—which is specifically the product of his intervention.

Once a natural integrity has been so violated, by the selection of elements from the original context, all subsequent integrations are no longer natural or inevitable. The task of creating forms as dynamic as the relationships in natural phenomena, is the central problem of both the scientist and the artist.

The most simple and primitive of artificial wholes is the arithmetical whole, which is the sum of its parts. The next step is the construction of a whole which consists of the sum of its parts in a certain arrangement, either in space or in time. A machine is such a whole, and standardization is possible because the parts are interchangeable with their equivalents. That is, a bolt or wheel may be replaced by similar bolts or wheels; a like organization of bolts, wheels, pulleys, etc., will result in a like machine. In such constructions the parts remain themselves; and although they may be designed to function in a certain manner, they are not transformed in the process of functioning. Consequently, such wholes are initially predictable from a knowledge of their parts.

But man's great dream is to achieve a whole whose character is far more mysterious and miraculous—that dynamic, living whole in which the inter-action of the parts produces more than their sum total in any sense. This relationship may be simple—as when water emerges from the interaction of hydrogen and oxygen. But let a third element be added, which transfigures both; and a fourth, which transforms the three—and the difficulties of analysis and creation become incalculable.

The entire alphabet is insufficient to describe the infinite complex of variables which the theoretical formula of life or great art would involve. For the inter-action of the parts so transforms them into function that there are no longer parts, but a simple, homogeneous whole which defies dissectional analysis, and in so sublimating the complex history of its development, seems an instantaneous miracle.

All of living nature is constituted of such forms, and the nature in man may occasionally fuse all his resources into a moment of such miracle. Yet in creating man's consciousness—the capacity for conscious memory—nature created an impatience which will not wait the necessary aeons until a million conditions coincide to produce a miraculous mutation.

Memory makes possible imagination, which is the ability to so accelerate real, natural processes that they become unreal and abstract. It can telescope into a moment's thought an evolution which might take centuries and fail to occur altogether. It can arrange desirable conditions which, in nature, would have to occur as rare coincidence. Invisibly, and without the critical failures of actuality, man, in his mind, shuffles and re-shuffles the elements of his total experience—sensations, ideas, desires, fears—into a million combinations. In works of fantasy we can see the process as it occurs: the curious and often fascinating energy of a mind at work.

But should that triumphant moment—when the elements of a man's experience suddenly fuse into a homogeneous whole which transcends and so transfigures them—be left to the rarities of natural coincidence? Or should the artist, like the scientist, exercise his imaginative intelligence—the command and control of memory—to consciously try, test, modify, destroy, estimate probabilities, and try again. . . always in terms of the instrument by which the fusion will be realized.

3A

In a world so intimately overwhelmed by scientific discovery, revelation and invention—where even the most desolate island becomes a fueling station for the globe-circling airplane—it is impossible to justify a neglect or ignorance of its realities. Yet the schizophrenic solution is precisely this: to dispute nothing, to resolve no conflicts; to admit to everything and to disguise, under the homogeneity of this unassailable tolerance, the most insiduous contradictions. The popularized notion of Dr. Jekyll and Mr. Hyde fails to comprehend that very element which makes the actuality possible: that the face of the man and the beast are one and the same.

Today the ostensible aspect of all man's endeavors is a scientific justification and the midnight hour when the true flesh becomes distinguished from the skillful mask has not yet been proclaimed. The "realist" presumes as the scientific observer. The sur-realist, disguised as the "sub-conscious" itself, demands the moral clemency which man has always graciously extended to that which cannot help itself (albeit from a superior position and with an undertone of condescension).

Such borrowng of scientific terms serves to create the illusion that the actual informations of that field are being put to a creative use. The work of art is thereby graced with the authority granted the science; and the principled procedure of the former escapes investigation since the specialized procedure of the latter is beyond popular comprehension. Unfortunately, it is not always that the art gains, as that the science loses, eventually, its popular prestige. The sur-realist exploitation of the confessional for its own sake has served to minimize the therapeutic intentions of disciplined, responsible psychiatry and has inspired the notion that anyone can be an analyst, particularly in art criticism. Yet such labors most often display an abysmal ignorance of both psychiatry and art.

One of the most revealing borrowings from science is the term "primitive," from anthropology. An age like ours, obsessed with a sense of evil, guilty failure, will seek redemption in devious ways. Although anthropology would be the last to support such a notion, it has pleased certain critics to imagine that the moral character of primitive societies is innocence; and so it pleases them the more to imagine that they discover, in the professional ignorance of the "modern primitive" painter, some archeological moral fragment, well preserved, of that idyllic time. Even if they are not dismayed by such a confusion between an intellectual and a moral quality, how can they imagine it desirable for men to think as if the discoveries and inventions of the past centuries had not intervened—to effect, even if it were possible, a total cultural amnesia at will?

I am certain that thoughtful critics do not use the term "primitive" without definition and modification. But its general usage, and as a category title for exhibits, reveals a comparative ideal based on the superficial similarity between the *skilled simplicity* of artists whose culture is limited in informations and crude in equipment; and the *crude simplifications* of artists whose culture is rich in information and refined in its equipment.

The artist of a primitive society was far from its most ignorant and isolated member. On the contrary, since his function was to represent, towards the community, the "advanced" principles of the highest moral, political and practical authorities—both human and divine—he had almost to be best informed of all.

He had to create masks, garments, patterns of dance movement—*real forms which would have super-natural authority,* a most difficult accomplishment. The "lucky" symbol on the war-weapon must transcend, through form, the mortality of the natural source from which it was drawn. The tapestries and wall paintings must be the comforting presence of protective powers in the home. He must compose a chant seductive enough to invoke the favor of one god, or threatening enough to exorcise the evil spirit. He stood half in the human world and half in the world of the super-natural powers; much was demanded of him by both; he could not afford the luxury of ignorance or impressions.

That that mythology is, today, an imaginative exercise for us, should not obscure the reality it had for those who lived by it. And since the greater part of the knowledge of primitive societies was a mythological knowledge, the art was an art of knowledge. But today, the distinction of the "modern primitive" is that he is unhampered by the facts which so often inhibit the imagination of his contemporaries, and so is freer to pursue the utterly imaginative concept.

It is not only in the discrepency of intellectual attitude that the real primitive and the "modern primitive" differ, but also, and necessarily, in the forms of the art.

Two-dimensionalism, and similar conventions, on the basis of which "modern primitives" are so called, does not, in the art of primitive societies, derive from an inability to comprehend or to realize the three-dimensional perspective. Various theories have been advanced for the consistent use of abstracted and simplified form in primitive art. T.E. Hulme suggests that when man is in conflict with a nature which he finds dangerously uncontrollable, he attempts to order and control it, vicariously, by doing so in his art; whereas when he has an aimable, confident relationship to nature he is pleased to repeat such sympathetic forms. It is an interesting and perhaps valid theory.

In any case, an absolutism of art forms seems highly appropriate to societies which, subject to natural disaster, rigidly localized by geographic and material restrictions, must place the unity of the tribe above all else and thus evolve an absolutism of political, moral and economic authority and an absolutistic concept of time and space.

Thus the art works of primitive cultures comprehend and realize a whole system of ideas within their forms. For this reason they have always an authoritative and sober aspect, and even at their most delicate and refined, they seem somehow weighted with dimensions of destiny and meaning. However mysterious the complexities and configurations may be, they never are fanciful or fantastic (except to the fanciful and fantastic). Certainly its intent is never casual, personal or decorative. The shield which was originally conceived primarily to protect, by material and magical means, is today of value on the basis of its sheer beauty, alone. Can anything testify better to the skill with which the primitive artist was able to fuse all functions (mythological, material and esthetic) into a single form? But does the "modern primitive" even aspire, much less achieve such fullness of dimension?

At its most sincere, as with Rousseau, contemporary primitive painting is a style of personal expression, a curiously naive and individual system of ideas. Sometimes, as in such creative talents, it can be sustained in the face of the informations of modern culture. But this is not often the case.

Creativity consists in a logical, imaginative extension of a known reality. The more limited the information, the more inevitable the necessity of its imaginative extension. The masks of primitive ritual extend the fierce grimace of the uncontrolled animal; the astronomical literary voyages of the 17th and 18th centuries extended the suggestions of the telescope. The contemporary "primitive" may achieve some extraordinary effects by imaginatively extending some immediate, simple knowledge. But imagine his embarrassment at suddenly confronting fields of knowledge whose real discoveries make redundant his extensions, and are often even more astounding and miraculous. His knowledge is invalidated and ceases to serve as a springboard for creative action. Adjusted to the stable, absolute concepts of his own small world he cannot, in a moment, readjust his imagination to extend the new, miraculous realities of the airplane, the telephone, the radio. Nor can he make the philosophical and psychological adjustment necessary to relocate himself in the strange relativisms of time and space which these instruments introduce into his life.

As the art dealers know very well, the "modern primitive" must be a zealously guarded recluse. But if this is so, he differs from the true primitive not only in being less informed of his own culture (in meaning if not in actual fact) and in creating forms irrelevant to its informations, but in creating them also in isolation, rather than in functional relation to that culture. Failing of a mythological authority for his ideas, his point of view on reality, however charming, must stand comparison with our knowledge of reality. All this conspires to make of the "modern primitive" a singular curiosity which must, at best, be evaluated not by the pseudo-scientific approach implied in the word "primitive," but as a personal style which stands or falls, as all art does, by the creative genius of the artist.

I hope that in using the exaggerations of the special category of the "modern primitive" I have not weakened my essential point. In its ambiguous implications, and in the possibility of contrasting it to its namesake, it afforded a convenient opportunity to point out a common failure of modern thought to understand that *art must at least comprehend the large facts of its total culture, and, at best, extend them imaginatively.*

As I suggest elsewhere, the distinctions between the romantic, the realist and the sur-realist are not as great as each of them would like to believe. To invade (as they all do) the province of science—the analysis of the nature of reality—with the minimal instruments of personal perception is surely not the same as to benefit by the discoveries arrived at by refined, scientific methods. To be a deliberately primitive scientist is today, of all ambitions, the most senseless. And to substitute such redundant, exploratory activity for that of creating an art reality is to fail entirely to add to the variety and richness of one's culture.

Art is the dynamic result of the relationship of three elements; the reality to which a man has access—directly and through the researches of all other men; the crucible of his own imagination and intellect; and the art instrument by which he realizes, through skillful exercise and control, his imaginative manipulations. To limit, deliberately or through neglect, any of these functions, is to limit the potential of the work of art itself.

The reality from which man draws his knowledge and the elements of his manipulation has been amplified not only by the development of analytical instruments; it has, increasingly, *become itself a reality created by the manipulation of instruments.* The reality which we must today extend—the large fact which we must comprehend, just as the primitive artist comprehended and extended his own reality—is the relativism which the airplane, the radio and the new physics has made a reality of our lives.

We cannot shirk this responsibility by using, as a point of departure, the knowledge and state of mind of some precedent period of history. My repeated insistence upon the distinctive function of form in art—my insistence that *the distinction of art is that it is neither simply an expression, of pain, for example, nor an impression of pain but is itself a form which creates pain* (or whatever its emotional intent)—might seem to point to a classicism. If so, I must remind the reader that I have elsewhere characterized the "ritualistic" form (in which I have included classicism) as an exercise, above all, of consciousness. The reality which such consciousness would today comprehend is not that of any other period. In this, and in the invention of new art instruments, lies the potential originality of the art of our time.

1B

Accustomed as we are to the idea of a work of art as an "expression" of the artist, it is perhaps difficult to imagine what other possible function it could perform. But once the question is posed, the deep recesses of our cultural memory release a procession of indistinct figures wearing the masks of Africa, or the Orient, the hoods of the chorus, or the innocence of the child-virgin . . . the faces always concealed, or veiled by stylization—moving in formal patterns of ritual and destiny. And we recognize that an artist might, conceivably, create beyond and outside all the personal compulsions of individual distress.

The evidence accumulates, and presses, in the occident, towards the 17th century. And it becomes important to discover how and why man renounced the mask and started to move towards the feverish narcissism which today crowds the book-stores, the galleries, and the stage.

The change was subtle. The relationship of thought and art on the one hand and discovery and invention on the other, is not a settled marriage, grown steady with agreement and adjustment. It is more like a passionate flirtation, full of defiance, reluctance, anticipation and neglect. It is true that in his treatment of personality Shakespeare anticipates that amalgam of romanticism and realism which reached its peak in the 19th century and has not yet spent its force. But the formal whole in which the characters of his dramas expounded their personal emotions, was as stringent a destiny as that of classicism. Perhaps the secret of his art lies, precisely, in the impact of the intensely romantic personality upon a universe still absolute in structure.

In the 17th century man, along with nature, ceased to be a manifestation of the absolute divine will, and accepted, in the first pride of his newfound, individual consciousness, the moral responsibilities which he had, until then left to the dispensation of the deity. All this was reflected in the classicism of the early 18th century, and it seems to me evident that if a period of classicism could occur in the full flush of this exhilarating belief that man was, to all intents and purpose, the dominant figure of the universe, then it must be *a form predicated not upon absolutism, but upon the idea of consciousness.* Whether this consciousness is a manifestation of deity in man, or whether it is of man's own nature becomes important only at the moment that its powers are put to a test and found wanting. It was exactly such a failure which the violences, confusions, and reversals which followed seemed to indicate.

For man, in his political and social activities, did not pause to develop instruments and methods equivalent to those which the scientist, in his province, labored to perfect. Nor did he stop to realize that invention anywhere could successfully follow only upon cautious preparations and analyses. His repeated failure to invent a social organization which would be immediately successful and appropriate to his new concept of the universe was a critical blow to his newly acquired self esteem and seemed to be a failure of consciousness itself. Nor was he experienced enough a scientist to be consoled by the long history of failure which, in scientific experiment, precedes any achievement. Even if he were aware of this, his central position in the universe endowed his problems, pains and disappointments with an importance to which the impersonal, experimental failures of science could not presume to compare. He could not now endure those troubles which, as a more modest element of the universe, he had previously accepted in the firm conviction that even misfortune contained some benediction according to the inscrutable will of God.

His adjustment to this complex of conditions was most dextrous. As a realist, conversant with scientific causation, he relinquished the principle of control and "acknowledged" the forces of reality as beyond the scope of his individual, moral responsibility. But as a romantic, he retained his exalted position in center of the universe and so was entitled to give full expression to his individual concerns and agonies. In this way he could be both nature and deity, except that, as part of nature, he could not be held responsible as a divine will. Once this principle was established, it was simple to accomplish, eventually the shift of emphasis from self-expression to self-exaltation as a phenomenon of nature whose actions and reactions, being inevitable, were, like nature, outside the law of moral responsibility; and, finally, encouraged by the dignified benediction of psycho-analysis, as a science, he could indulge in the ecstasies of sur-realist confessional. Since to confess to some banality is to lose the advantage of confessional, even those artists who are reasonably happy find it necessary to pretend to horrors in the effort to present a "truth which is stranger than fiction."

The romantic and the sur-realist differ only in the degree of their naturalism. But between naturalism and the formal character of primitive, oriental and Greek art there is a vast ideological distance. For want of a better term which can refer to the quality which the art forms of various civilizations have in common, I suggest the word ritualistic. I am profoundly aware of the dangers in the use of this term, and of the misunderstandings which may arise, but I fail, at the moment, to find a better word. Its primary weakness is that, in strictly anthropological usage, it refers to an activity of a primitive society which has certain specific conditions: a ritual is anonymously evolved;

it functions as an obligatory tradition; and finally, it has a specific magical purpose. None of these three conditions apply, for example, to Greek tragedy. On the other hand, they are, in a sense, exterior to the ritual form itself, since they refer to its origin, its preservation and its function. Moreover, it is hardly beside the point that all art forms were originally a part of such rituals and that the form itself, within itself, has remained strikingly intact in general outline, in spite of the changes in these exterior conditions. It is to these constant elements, which seem to me of major importance since they exist simultaneously in unrelated cultures, to which I have reference.

Even when it is not the anonymous primitive ritual, the ritualistic form is not the expression of the individual nature of the artist; it is the result of the application of his individual talent to the moral problems which have been the concern of man's relationship with deity, and the evidence of that privileged communication. It is never an effort to reveal a reality which, in the face of divine omniscience and power, man could not presume to know.

The ritualistic form reflects also the conviction that such ideas are best advanced when they are abstracted from the immediate conditions of reality and incorporated into a contrived, created whole, stylized in terms of the utmost effectiveness. It creates fear, for example, by creating an imaginative, often mythological experience which, by containing its own logic within itself, has no reference to any specific time or place, and is forever valid for all time and place. How different is the customary modern method, which induces fear by employing some real contemporary figure which, in reality, inspires it; or reconstructs some situation which might be typical of the contemporary experience of some cultural majority. Such a method may be temporarily effective, but the conditions of life, and so the "real" experience of men, changes with a rapidity which can date such "realism" in a few years. That which was frightening today is no longer frightening tomorrow.

Above all, the ritualistic form treats the human being not as the source of the dramatic action, but as a somewhat depersonalized element in a dramatic whole. The intent of such depersonalization is not the destruction of the individual; on the contrary, it enlarges him beyond the personal dimension and frees him from the specializations and confines of personality. He becomes part of a dynamic whole which, like all such creative relationships, in turn, endows its parts with a measure of its larger meaning.

If it can be said that, in romanticism, the tragedy results from the destructive, tragic nature of its central figure, then it must be said, by contrast, that in ritualistic form the tragedy confers often upon an unsuspecting person, the heroic stature of the tragic figure.

In its method—*a conscious manipulation designed to create effect,* in contrast to the spontaneous compulsions of expression—and in its results—*the new, man-made reality,* in contrast to the revelation or recapitulation of one which exists—the ritualistic form is much more the art equivalent of modern science than the naturalism which claims to be so based.

Today it would decline to concern itself with a revelation of reality not because man is incapable, but because science is more capable than art in that capacity. And it would be predicated upon the exercise of consciousness, not as the instrument by which divine will is apprehended, but as the human instrument which makes possible a comprehension and a manipulation of the universe in which man must somehow locate himself.

2B

The impulse behind my insistent concern with the triumphant achievements of science is most elemental: I believe simply that an analysis of any of man's achievements may reveal basic principles of methodology which, properly adjusted to the immediate conditions of other problems, may lead to similar triumphs. I do not claim this to be an original attitude, for naturalism is presumably just such a transcription from the methods of science to those of art. My argument is that if such a procedure is to have any value, then it must be based on a thorough observation of the whole method, and not a tangential development of some portion of it. If the complex specialization of science in the 18th and 19th centuries obscured the basic design of its method, then it might even have been better to follow, as example, some other field of achievement altogether.

Just as the varying use of the word reason reflected the development of the concept of reason in the 17th century, so the current use of the word consciousness reveals the underlying concept of its function. In art, today a state of consciousness is understood as synonymous with a capacity for observation. This capacity may range, in degree, from the most simple sensory perception to the most complex analysis or the acute, associational insight. These are then recorded in a style of notation which may range from the defiantly awkward (proof of the fact that the original impression of a truth has not been tampered with) to the decoratively graceful (the flirtatious pirouette of the artist around his subject).

In such a concept of art, the role of the artist has degenerated into a basic passivity. He functions as an often inaccurate barometer, scaled in emotional degrees, whose nervous fluctuations are recorded by a frequently defective mechanism, in a code whose key is often inconstant and sometimes even unknown. His achievement, if any, consists in a titilating reproduction of a reality which can be enjoyed in air-conditioned comfort by an audience too comatose to take the exercise of a direct experience of life.

The essential irony of such a concept is that, in undertaking to reveal the nature of reality, the artist enters the province of science, lacking the very weapons, skills and strategems with which the scientist has carefully equipped himself; and worst of all, he has no concept for the function of his discoveries, except to stuff, mount and exhibit the more impressive and presentable portions (or, with the sur-realists, the more gruesome and shocking) on the walls of his house, as proof of his capacity for extravagant emotional adventure.

In science, the findings, no matter how painfully accumulated, are but the raw materials of an ultimate creative action. The first step of creative action is the violation of the "natural" integrity of an original context. But much of the art of our time, and of the period immediately preceding it, has, as its avowed purpose, the representation or projection of some natural integrity in terms of its own exaltedly "inalienable" logic of inevitabilities. This is equally true of the various "schools" who imagine themselves in fundamental opposition. Nor should the basic method be obscured by those singular talents who, in the process of creating, transcend all theoretical principles.

The "realists," critical of the esoteric aspects of sur-realism, propose an art form constituted of "common, recognizable emotions" occurring in a "common, realistic" frame of reference, and presented in the "common language of every day speech." They regard this as a guarantee of communicability and "mass appeal." Yet the precedents of our cultural history do not support such a theory. On the contrary, the most popular theaters—the Elizabethan and the Greek—dealt with emotions universal only by generalization, but extraordinary in their immediate quality (Hamlet and Oedipus), resulting from extraordinary circumstances, and articulated in a most uncommon, highly stylized speech.

It is at least to the credit of the sur-realists that once they accepted the forms of nature as model, they were relentless and uncompromising in the logical pursuit of this principle. In atomizing the human being, they even anticipated, in a sense, a scientific destiny. Many of their paintings, if they were not presented as works of the imagination, might easily pass for emotionally heightened reportorial sketches of Hiroshima (of the kind which Life Magazine reproduces): the nightmare of oozing blood, the horror of degenerative death from invisible, inner radiations, the razed landscapes reduced to its primeval elements, the solitary, crazed survivors. But even if one were not to find such a point of exterior reference, the sur-realists are self-avowedly dedicated to externalizing an inner reality whose original integrity has been devotedly preserved.

Both the "realists" and the "sur-realists" have a very righteous contempt for the group loosely characterized as the "romantics." The realists criticize them for "escaping" from reality, whereas the sur-realists criticize them for the sentimentality with which they idealize reality. But one consistent motivation of the creative act is the conviction of one's originality; the entire personal justification of whatever effort is required is that the result does not duplicate (at least in its particular aspects) the achievements of another artist. Taken in terms of the representation or the expression of natural reality, the originality of achievement becomes, then, an originality of discovery, a pursuit of the exotic, novel condition, exterior or interior, the search for the "truth which is stranger than fiction."

Thus the argument between the "realists," the "sur-realists" and the "romantic escapists" is not one of form, nor even of the method of art, but merely a disagreement as to which landscape is of most consequence: the familiar, drug-store around the corner, the inner chamber of horrors, or the island utopias of either an inner or outer geography.

Before psychiatry, as a science, began its investigation of emotional realities, or photography its immaculate observation of material reality, the artist was often concerned with either or both of these. But he did not always indulge in the simple expediency of representation as he does today. That which was, in reality, a result of natural, inevitable processes had to emerge, in the work of art, as the effect of a controlled, artificial manipulation. The configurations and colors of a landscape are a part of an infinite complex of climatic, chemical, botanical, and other elements. In a painting of such a landscape, the harmony, brilliancy, etc., had to be achieved through the manipulation of paint, line, color, shape, size. The least requirement of such a transcription was professional skill and an understanding of one's chosen medium.

The art world today is overwhelmed by the products of arrogant amateurs and dilletantes who refuse to respect their "profession" by even so much as a dedication to its skills and techniques. The emphasis is upon spontaneity in the act of creation, although this is the last possible means by which inevitability can be created in the work itself. It is revealing that the exercise of skill—professionalism in its highest sense—is at an apparent all-time low in art. The prevalent feeling is that you, too, can be an artist in three easy lessons, providing you are "sensitive" or "observant," and so can discover, in the world outside or in the microcosmos of your own tortures, some bit of reality which has not already been exploited. The central problem is to represent it with a fair degree of fidelity.

But why would one exalt the integrity of nature or any part of it, in its own terms, or seek to fashion an art form out of its "intrinsic values" and inalienable logics, when our age has arrived at the ultimate recognition of relative relationships in the discovery that all matter is energy? If the achievements of science are the result of a violation of natural integrity, in order to emancipate its elements and re-relate them, how can an artist be content to do no more than to perceive, analyze and, at most, recreate these ostensibly inviolable wholes of nature?

To renounce the natural frame of reference—the natural logic and integrity of an existent reality—is not, as is popularly assumed, an escape from the labor of truth. On the contrary, it places upon the artist the entire responsibility for creating a logic as dynamic, integrated and compelling as those in which nature abounds. To create a form of life is, in the final analysis, much more demanding than to render one which is ready-made.

The intent to create a new set of relationships effects, first of all, the selection of elements. In a naturalistic form, an element is selected in terms of a presumed "intrinsic" value; actually, this value is not intrinsic but is conferred upon it by the context in which it "naturally" occurs. In creating a new form, the elements must be selected according to their ability to function in the new, "un-natural" context. A gesture which may have been very effective in the course of some natural, spontaneous conversation, may fail to have impact in a dance or film; whereas one which may have passed unnoticed may be intensely moving if it lends itself to a climactic position in art context.

On the face of it, such considerations may seem obvious. Yet much of naturalistic art relies precisely on the "intrinsic" value of the element. Here it is not the context of the work which endows the element with value, but the associational process by which the audience refers that element to its own experience of reality. To rely upon such reference is to limit communicability to an audience which shares, with the artist, a common ground of experience.

Such "timely" art stands in great contrast to, for instance, the Greek drama, which has survived precisely because the elements which it employed had only a coincidental reference to the reality of the period in which it was created. Actually, these elements were emancipated from all immediately recognizable contexts, and so were never dependent upon being confirmed by personalized references of the audience. Their value derives from the integrated whole of which they are a part, and this whole is not a familiar, but a new experience. Being new, it illuminates emotions and ideas which may have escaped our attention in the distracting profusions of reality, and so becomes educational (in the finest sense of the word). The lavish fecundity of nature, without which it could not survive all material disasters, gives way, in art, to a concept of economy. Out of the wealth of remembered experience, the elements are selected with discrimination, according to their compatibility with the other elements of the intended whole.

In speaking of the relationships which are created in scientific forms, I listed those wholes which are the sum total of parts, and those which are the sum total of parts in a certain arrangement (as in a machine), and finally that "emergent whole" (I borrow the term from Gestalt psychology), in which the parts are so dynamically related as to produce something new which is unpredictable from a knowledge of the parts. It is this process which makes possible the idea of economy in art, for the whole which here emerges transcends, in meaning, the sum total of the parts. The effort of the artist is towards the creation of a logic in which two and two may make five, or, preferably, fifteen; when this is achieved, two can no longer be understood as simply two. This five, or this fifteen—the resultant idea or emotion—is therefore *a function of the total relationships, the form of the work* (which is independent of the form of reality by which it may have been inspired). It is this which Flaubert had reference to in stating that "L'idee n'existe qu'en vertu de sa forme."

One of the most unfortunate aspects of the dominance of the naturalist tradition in art today is the existence of an audience unaccustomed to the idea of the objective form of art. Instead, accustomed to a work of art as a reference to nature, they anticipate a re-creation of their own experience. They take issue with any experience which does not conform with their own, and characterize it as a personalized distortion. On the other hand, they may, coincidentally, concur with that observation, in which case it is not a distortion, but an "acute insight into reality." The development and decline of the vogue for surrealism is almost a graph of the fluctuation of such coincidences.

Yet, as I have pointed out elsewhere, the most enduring works of art create a mythical reality, which cannot refer to one's own personal observations.

Even antiquity does not always protect such works from dismemberment by the subjective audience. But in contemporary art, and especially when the elements are drawn from reality, the audience is certain to approach the work as if it were altogether a natural phenomenon. They isolate from it those elements which they find most personally evocative, and interpret them according to their personal context of experience. Such an individualism implies a complete refusal to recognize the intention of the artist in creating a specific context, and the meaning which is conferred upon the elements by this context. It results in the incredible platitude, intended always as a compliment, that in the great works of art every one can read his own personal meaning. Or, as I treat in detail elsewhere, the dismemberment may be achieved by the instrument of an alien system, such as Freudianism.

A work of art is an emotional and intellectual complex whose logic is its whole form. Just as the separate actions of a man in love will be misunderstood, or even thought "insane," from the logic of non-love, so the parts of a work of art lose their true meaning when removed from their context and evaluated by some alien logical system. And just as an analysis of the reasons for love may follow upon the experience, but do not explain or induce it, so a dis-sectional analysis of a work of art fails, in the act of dismemberment, to comprehend the very inter-active dynamics which give it life. Such an analysis cannot substitute, and may even inhibit, the experience itself, which only an unprejudiced receptivity, free of personal requirements and preconceptions, can invite.

In the effort to protect their art from dismemberment, many painters have become abstractionists. By eliminating recognizable form, they hoped to eliminate exterior reference. It is my impression that music, being by nature abstract, is less subject to such dismemberment, although I have heard the most gruesome tales of what has been done even to Mozart. But language is, by its own nature, recognizable. For this reason we have developed, in connection with poetry, a phenomenal quantity of interpretative literature. Many writers compose more creatively in their commentaries upon other writers than they do in their art proper. Poetry has suffered most at the hands of the subjective reader, for each word can be pried from its context and used as a springboard for creative action in terms of some personal frame of reference and in all art, the more integrated the whole, the more critically it is effected by even the most minute change.

When Marcel Duchamp drew a mustache on the Mona Lisa, he accepted the painting as a ready-made reality out of which, by the addition of a few well-placed lines, he created a Duchamp, which he thereafter exhibited under his own name. And the subjective spectator who adds his personal mustaches to works of art should have the courage and the integrity to thereafter assume responsibility for his creative action under his own name.

As in science, the process of creative art is two-fold: the experience of reality by the artist on one side, and his manipulation of that experience into an art reality on the other. In his person he is an instrument of discovery; in his art he exercises the art-instrument of invention.

Contemporary art is especially characterized by an emphasis upon the artist as himself instrument of discovery and the role of the art instrument has, for the most part, degenerated into a mere means of conveying those discoveries. In other words, the emphasis is upon reality as it exists, obvious or obscured, simple or complex.

The incidence of naturalism in art is in almost direct proportion to the extent to which the elements of reality (the experience of the artist) can serve also as the elements of the work of art; and to the extent to which the natural, contextual logic in which they occur can be simulated or reconstructed in the art work. Thus, naturalism has been most of all manifest in the plastic forms, where the art elements—lines, colors, masses, perspectives, etc.—can be immediately derived from reality.

Language, on the other hand, consists of elements which are themselves un-natural and invented. Here it is possible to be naturalistic in reference to a language reality: that is, a conversation, being already a transcription of ideas and emotions into verbal patterns, can be itself reproduced as an intact reality in literature. One has only to compare the dialogues of classic literature to the conversations of naturalistic novels and dramas, or, further, to the word-doodling of some sur-realist "poetry," to see the difference in the approach to language.

Even in naturalism, a departure from ready-made conversational reality, or from word-ideas, may inspire a creative exercise on the part of the writer. A verbal description, however accurate, is not the reality itself of a chair, for instance, since the chair exists in spatial terms; just as a painting becomes "literary" when it is based upon an effort to illustrate, in spatial terms, ideas which are essentially verbal.

Flaubert is thought of as a prime example of an artist dedicated to the accurate description of reality. Yet his linguistic diligence indicates that he thought, actually, of creating, in verbal terms, the equivalent of the experience which he had of spatial reality. He succeeded in creating a verbal reality whose validity is not at all dependent upon the degree of accuracy which it achieves in reference to the reality by which it was inspired. In Flaubert it is completely irrelevant whether there ever existed, in reality, the chair which exists in the novel. But in many of those writers which claim to his tradition it is, on the contrary, important for the reader to decide: are these things really true in the world?

The chair which Flaubert creates by the exercise of his art instrument—language—is not a visual image, it is a verbal image. Moreover, it is, prescisely, an independent verbal image and not a symbol. (I elaborate on this distinction, in another respect, elsewhere.) For if it were a symbol, its meaning would reside outside the work, in whatever reality—object or event—it represented as substitute or had reference to. I stress this independence of an image created by the work of art itself because there is a tendency, today, to regard all images as symbols: to insist that nothing is what it is but that it must "stand for" something else.

In view of the currently loose, casual usage of the word "symbol," it would seem important to re-ascertain its more explicit meaning. In speaking of the direct, immediate meaning of an "image," I do not intend to exclude the process of generalization. On the contrary, the individual moment or image is valuable only insofar as its ripples spread out and encompass the richness of many moments; and certainly this is true of the work of art as a whole. But to generalize from a specific image is not the same as to understand it as a symbol for that general concept. When an image induces a generalization and gives rise to an emotion or idea, it bears towards that emotion or idea the same relationship which an exemplary demonstration bears to some chemical principle; and this is entirely different from the relationship between that principle and the written chemical formula by which it is symbolized. *In the first case the principle functions actively; in the second case its action is symbolically described, in lieu of the action itself.* An understanding of this distinction seems to me to be of primary importance.

All works employing figures of mythology are especially proposed as evidence of the "symbolic" method. Yet to say this is to imply that a Greek tragedy would fail to convey its values to one ignorant of the complex genealogy and intricate activities of the pantheon.

It may be argued that the references which would, today, be ascertained only by scholarly research were, at the time of the creation of the work, a matter of common knowledge. But I have pointed out elsewhere, and it is relevant here, that an integrated whole emerges not from some intrinsic value of its elements, but from their function in dynamic relationship to all the others. Consequently, even when an object may have also some exterior symbolic reference, it functions accordingly in the whole, and so is redefined by its own immediate context. Zeus is a great power in the mythological pantheon. But Zeus also functions as a great power whenever he is introduced as a dramatic element in a theatrical creation—to the extent that the author believed in the mythology. Consequently we can know his power from the work of art where it is re-created by the art instrument, without knowing anything else. In this way it is possible for an image to "mean" much directly, and not by virtue of an indirect, symbolic representation.

It may be possible that some esoteric research into the domestic complications of the pantheon would reveal some second level of meaning, as symbolic reference. But it is a question as to whether appreciation is ever intensified by such effort. And I doubt that such works of art, dedicated to the creation of an experience which should illuminate certain ethical or moral principles, would entrust their primary ideas to a second or third level of diagnosis.

For similar reasons, I cannot see what is to be gained by the current tendency to regard all the images of a work in terms of Freudian symbolic reference. A competent artist, intent on conveying some sexual reference, will find a thousand ways to evade censorship and make his meaning irrevocably clear. Even the incompetants of Hollywood daily achieve this; should we deny at least a similar skill in our more serious artists?

My contention is that whenever an image is endowed with a certain meaning-function by the context of the work of art—the product of an art instrument itself—then that is the value proper of the image in reference to the specific work. When an author is delicate in reference to love or sex, it very well may be that he intends it as a delicate experience (as contrast and deliberate counter-point to other experiences in the work); or, as artist, he may prefer to leave such lyric, exalted experience to the imagination of the audience, rather than confine and limit it by the crudities of his technique. And what right have we then to shout out that which he intended to have the qualities of a whisper; or destroy his counter-points; or to define that which he, in considered humility, found, himself, undefinable? To do so would be to destroy the integrity which he has carefully created—to destroy the work of art itself.

One could, perhaps, psycho-analyze the artist as a personality... why does he think love to be a delicate and magical experience? But to the extent that the artist manipulates and creates consciously according to his instrument, the instrument acts as a censor upon the free expression which psycho-analysis requires, for he selects, from his associational stream of images, those which are appropriate to and compatible with the other elements.

Psycho-analysis, while valid as a therapy for mal-adjusted personality, defeats its own purpose as a method of art criticism, for it implies that the artist does not create out of the nature of his instrument, but that it is used merely to convey some reality independent of all art. It implies that there is no such thing as art at all, but merely more or less accurate self-expression. In an essay on La Fontaine's

"Adonis," Paul Valery makes some very penetrating observations on the difference between the personal dream and the impersonal work of art, which are very relevant to this whole discussion.

It is customary today to refer to the sensitivity or perception of an artist as a primary value; and to the extent that the artist seeks to reveal the nature of reality, it is entirely appropriate to consider him, by inference, an instrument of discovery. But if such is his function, then he cannot protest a comparison with the other instruments of discovery, such as the telescope or the microscope, and, in the provinces of his frequent concerns, the instruments and methods of the sociologist and the psychologist. Nor can he protest an evaluation of the "truths" at which he arrives, not only in comparison to our own personal impressions as audience, but also according to the extent that these "truths" conform to the revelations of specialists who devote themselves to the same material. We tend to approach a work of art with a certain sentimental reverence, but if we are able to avoid this prejudice in comparing, for example, one of the "psychological" novels to the meticulous observations of a well-documented case history, I, for one, find the latter to be by far a more stimulating, revealing experience of reality.

Such psychological novels (I except, obviously, such masters as Dostoevsky, James, etc.) often fail not only in the accuracy of their observation, but, in their determined efforts to analyze the personality, frequently contradict the fundamental principle of effectiveness in art: they fail to so present their observations as to make a certain conclusion inevitable to the reader, and they substitute, instead, a statement of their own conclusion. All is understood for us, and we are deprived of the stimulating privilege of ourselves understanding.

The decorative "artistic" periphery of such "analytical" works of art fails to disguise their essentially uncreative nature and serves, most frequently, to simply obscure that very truth which the artist undertakes to reveal. There are also other disadvantages to art as scientific observation. Gertrude Stein has somewhere stated that "the realism of today seems new because the realism of the past is no longer real." And if the validity of a work depends upon either the accuracy of its revelations or the novelty of its discoveries it is subject to the failure here implied, of becoming, one day, duly past. If the importance of "Paradise Lost" had been predicated upon the "truth" of its medieval cosmography, the astronomical discoveries of the 17th century would have invalidated the entire work.

Unlike the inventions of science, which are valuable only until another invention serves the purpose better, the inventions of art, being experiences of emotional and intellectual nature, are, as such, valid for all time. And unlike discoveries, which are confined by the fixed limits of human perception, or advanced in a different manner by scientific instruments and knowledge, the collaboration between imagination and art instrument can still, after all these centuries, result in marvelous new art inventions.

1c

My extended analysis and criticism of the naturalistic method in art is inspired by my intimate awareness of how much the very nature of photography, more than any other art form, may seduce the artist (and spectator) into such an esthetic.

The most immediate distinction of film is the capacity of the camera to represent a given reality in its own terms, to the extent that it is accepted as a substitute proper for that reality. A photograph will serve as proof of the "truth" of some phenomenon where either a painting or a verbal testimony would fail to carry weight. In other art forms, the artist is the intermediary between reality and the instrument by which he creates his work of art. But in photography, the reality passes directly through the lens of the camera to be immediately recorded on film, and this relationship may, at times, dispense with all but the most manual services of a human being, and even, under certain conditions, produce film almost "untouched by human hands." The position of the camera in reference to reality can be either a source of strength, as when the "realism" of photography is used to create an imaginative reality; or it can seduce the photographer into relying upon the mechanism itself to the extent that his conscious manipulations are reduced to a minimum.

The impartiality and clarity of the lens—its precise fidelity to the aspect and texture of physical matter—is the first contribution of the camera. Sometimes, because of the physical and functional similarity between the eye and the lens, there is a most curious tendency to confuse their respective contributions. By some strange process of ambiguous association (which most photographers are only too willing to leave uncorrected) the perceptiveness and precision of a photograph is somehow understood to be an expression of the perceptiveness of the eyes of the photographer. This transcription of attributes is more common than one might imagine. When the primary validity of a photograph consists in its clarity or its candidness (and these are by far the most common criteria) it should be signed by those who ground the lens, who constructed the fast, easily manipulated camera, who sweated over the chemistry of emulsions which would be both sensitive and fine-grained, who engineered the optical principles of both camera and enlarger—in short, by all those who made photography possible, and least of all by the one who pushed the button. As Kodak has so long advertised: "You push the button. IT does the rest!"

The ease of photographic realism does not, however, invalidate the documentarist's criticism of the "arty" efforts (characteristic of a certain period of film development) to deliberately muffle the lens in imitation of the myopic, undetailed and even impressionistic effects of painting where, precisely, the limitations of human vision played a creative role in simplifyng and idealizing reality.

On another level, the realists are critical, and again justifiably so, of the commercial exploitation of film as a means of reproducing theater and illustrating novels. . .almost as a printing press reproduces an original manuscript in great quantity. Out of respect for the unique power of film to be itself a reality, they are impatient with the painted backdrops, the "furnished stages," and all the other devices which were developed as part of the artifice of theater and drama. If it is possible, they say, to move the camera about, to capture the fleeting, "natural" expression of a face, the inimitable vistas of nature, or the unstageable phenomenon of social realities, then such is the concern of film to be exploited, as distinct from other forms.

Such a concept of film is true to its very origins. The immediate precursor of movies was Mary's photographic series of the successive stages of a horse running. Between this first record of a natural phenomenon, and the more recent scientific films of insect life, plant life, chemical processes, etc., lies a period of increasing technical invention and competency, without any basic change in concept.

In the meantime, however, a concern with social reality had branched off as a specific field of film activity. The first newsreels of important historical events, such as the coronation, difffer from the newsreels of today only in terms again of a refined technique, but from them came the documentary film, a curious amalgamation of scientific and social concerns. It is not a coincidence that Robert Flaherty, who is considered the father of the documentary film, was first an explorer, and that his motivation in carrying a camera with him was part anthropological, part social, and part romantic. He had discovered a world which was beyond the horizon of most men. He was moved both by its pictorial and its human values; and his achievement consists of recording it with sympathetic, and relative accuracy. The documentary of discovery—whether it records a natural, a social, or a scientific phenomenon—can be of inestimable value. It can bring within the reach of even the most sedentary individual a wealth of experience which would otherwise come only to the curious, the painstaking, and the heroic.

But whenever the value of a film depends, for the most part, upon the character of its subject, it is obvious that the more startling realities will have a respectively greater interest for the audience. War, as a social and political phenomenon, results in realities which surpass the most violent anticipations of human imagination. Because it also played an immediate role in our lives, we were obsessed with a need to comprehend them. And so, since the reality itself was more than enough to hold the interest of the audience (and so required least the imaginative contributions of the film maker) the war documentaries contain passages which carry naturalism to its farthest point.

I should like to refer to two examples which are strikingly memorable but essentially representative. In a newsreel which circulated during wartime, there was a sequence in which a Japanese soldier was forced from his hideout by flame throwers and ran off, burning like a torch. In the documentary "Fighting Lady" there is an exciting sequence in which the plane which carries the camera swoops down and strafes some enemy planes on the ground. This latter footage was achieved by connecting the shutter of the camera with the machine gun so that when the gun was fired the camera would automatically begin registering.

An analysis of these examples can serve to illuminate the essential confusion, implicit in the very beginnings of the idea of the natural form in art, between the provinces and purposes of art and those of science, as well as the distinctions between those art forms which depend upon or extend reality, and those which themselves create a reality. The footage of the burning soldier points up the reliance upon the accidents of reality (so prevalent in photography) as contrasted to the inevitabilities, consciously created, of art. The essential amorality and ambiguity of a "natural" form is also apparent here; for were we not prepared by previous knowledge,—by an outside frame of reference—we would undoubtedly have deep compassion for the burning soldier and a violent hatred for the flame thrower.

In the case of the camera which is synchronized with the machine gun, the dissociation between man and instrument, and the independent relationship between reality and camera, is carried to an unanticipated degree. If this film can be said to reflect any intention, it must be that of death, for such was the function of the gun. In any case, the reality of the conflict is itself entirely independent of the action of the camera, rather than a creation of it, as is true of the experience of an art form.

Nor is it irrelevant to point out here that the war documentaries were achieved with an anonymity which even science, the most objective of professions, would find impossible. These films are the product of hundreds, even thousands, of unidentified cameramen. This is not another deliberate effort of the "top brass" to minimize the soldier-cameraman. It is a reflection upon a method which, unrestricted by budgetary considerations of film or personnel, could be carried to its logical conclusion. These cameramen were first instructed carefully in the mechanics of photography—(not in the form of film)—and were sent out to catch whatever they could of the war, to get it on photographic record. The film was then gathered together, assorted according to chronology or specific subject, and put at the disposal of the film editors. If the material of one cameraman could be distinguished from another, it was in terms of sheer technical competence; or, perhaps, occasionally a consistent abundance of dramatic material which might testify to an unusual alertness and a heroic willingness to risk one's life in order to "capture" on film some extraordinary moment.

This whole process is certainly more analogous to the principle of fecundity in nature than to that of the economical selectivity of art. Of all this incalculably immense footage, no more than a tiny percentage will ever be put to function in a documentary or any other filmic form.

Let me make it clear that I do not intend to minimize either the immediate interest or the historical importance of such a use of the motion-picture medium. To do so would require, by logical analogy, that I dismiss all written history, especially since it is a much less accurate form of record than the film, and value only the creative, poetic use of language. *But precisely because film, like language, serves a wide variety of needs, the triumphs which it achieves in one capacity must not be permitted to obscure its failures in another.*

The war years were marked by a great interest in the documentary, just as they were characterized by the overwhelming lionization of foreign correspondents, and for the same reason. But such reportage did not become confused in the public mind with the poem as a form, simply because they both employed language. In spite of the popularity and great immediate interest in journalism, the poem still holds its position (or at least such is my fervent hope) as a distinguished form of equal, if not superior, importance in man's culture; and although it may, in certain periods, be neglected, there is never an implication that, as a form, it can be replaced by any other, however pertinent, popular, or refined in its own terms.

I am distressed, for this reason, by the current tendency to exalt the documentary as the supreme achievement of film, which places it, by implication, in the category of an art form. Although an explicit statement of this is carefully avoided, the implication is supported by an emphasis upon those documentaries which are significant not for their scientific accuracy, but for an undertone of lyricism or a use of dramatic devices—values generally associated with art form. Thus the campaign serves not so much to point up the real values of a documentary—*the objective, impartial rendition of an otherwise obscure or remote reality*—but to cast suspicion upon the extent to which it actually retains those documentary functions. A work of art is primarily concerned with the effective creation of *an idea* (even when that may require a sacrifice of the factual material upon which the idea is based), *and involves a conscious manipulation of its material from an intensely motivated point of view.* By inference, the unconsidered and unmodified praise which has recently attended the documentarist requires of him, again by inference, that he function also in these latter terms.

In this effort he has not failed altogether. When the reality which he seeks to convey consist largely of human and emotional values, the perception of these and their rendition may require of the documentarist a transcription similar to that which I discuss elsewhere, when the art reality becomes independent of the reality by which it was inspired. "Song of Ceylon" (Basil Wright and John Taylor), sections of "Forgotten Village" (Steinbeck, Hackenschmied and Klein), "Rien Que Les Heures" (Cavalcanti), 'Berlin" (Ruttman), the Russian "Turksib" and the early work of Dziga Vertov are among those documentaries which create an intensity of experience, and so have validity quite irrespective of their accuracy. They are the counter-part, in literature, of those travel-journals which inform as much of the subtleties of vision as of the things viewed or of those impassioned reportages which convince as much by the sincere emotion of the reporter as by the fact reported.

But the documentary film maker is not permitted the emotional freedom of other artists, or the full access to the means and techniques of this form. Since the subjective attitude is, at least, theoretically discouraged as an impediment to unbiased observation, he is not justified in examining the extent of his personal interest in the subject matter. And so he finds himself occupied, to an enervating degree, with material which does not inspire him. He is further limited by a set of conventions which originate in the methods of the scientific film. He must photograph "on the scene" (often a very primitive one) even when material circumstances may hamper his techniques, and force him to select the accessible rather than the significant fact. He must use the "real" people, even if they are camera-shy or resentful of him as an alien intruder, and so do not behave as "realistically" as would a competent professional actor. If I were to believe in many of the documentaries which I have seen, I would deduce that most "natives" are either predominantly hostile, taciturn or simply ill-humored, and capable of mainly two facial expressions: a blank stupidity punctuated by periods of carnival hysteria. Even in our urban, sophisticated society, the portrait photographer inspires an uneasy rigidity. It would be a rare native indeed who, confronted by the impressive and even ominous mechanism of the camera and its accoutrements (and that in the hands of a suspect stranger), could maintain a normally relaxed, spontaneous behavior. These are but some of the exterior conditions rigidly imposed upon the documentary film maker, in addition to the creative problems within the form itself.

Yet the products created under these conditions are made subject, by the undefined enthusiasms of their main "appreciators," to an evaluation in terms usually reserved for the most creative achievements of other art forms. And so the documentarist is driven to the effort of satisfying two separate demands, which are in conflict. He fails, in the end, to completely satisfy either one or the other.

I am sure that few, if any, of the so-called documentaries would be acceptable as sufficiently objective and accurate data for either anthropologists, sociologists or psychologists. On the other hand, few, if any, are comparable in stature, authority, or profundity, to the great achievements of the other arts.

The documentarist cannot long remain oblivious of his ambiguous position. The greater his understanding of truly creative form, the more acute is his embarrassment at finding his labors evaluated in terms which he was not initially permitted or presumed to function. Whereas, formerly, he might have been able to maintain some middle ground, the insistence of the current campaign precipitates the basic conflicts, and forces upon him the necessity of a decision. It will succeed, in the end, in driving the more creative workers, embarrassed by the exaggerated, misdirected appreciation, out of the field. And it will be left in the hands of skilled technicians where, perhaps, it rightfully belongs.

Since these ideas are in opposition to the current wave of documentary enthusiasm, and would, perhaps, be ascribed to the prejudice of my own distance from that form, I should like to quote from an article by Alexander Hammid. He has been recognized as an outstanding talent in documentary film for 18 years, both here and abroad. He is the director of the "Hymn of the Nations" (the film about Toscanini) and other films for the OWI, and (as Alexander Hackenschmied) photographed and co-directed "Forgotten Village," "Lights Out in Europe," "Crisis," and a multitude of documentaries which have been circulated only in Europe. It therefore must be admitted that he would be at least "conversant" with the problems of his field.

It is revealing that Mr. Hammid devotes considerable space to the fact that, in order to achieve a "realism" of effect, it is often necessary to be imaginative in method:

"In their (the early documentarists) drive towards objectivity, they brushed aside the fact that the camera records only in the manner in which the man behind it chooses to direct it. I believe that the necessity of subjective choice is one of the fundamentals of any creation. In other words, we must have command of our instrument. If we leave the choice to our instrument, then we rely upon the accident of reality which, in itself, is not reality. The necessity of choice and elimination which eo ipso are a denial of objectivity, continues throughout the entire process of film making; ...Many people believe that if there is no arrangement or staging of a scene, they will obtain an unadulterated, objective picture of reality...But even if we put the camera in front of a section of real life, upon which we do not intrude so much as to even blow off a speck of dust, we still arrange: by selecting the angle, which may emphasize one thing and conceal another, or distort an otherwise familiar perspective; by selecting a lens which will concentrate our attention on a single face or one which will reveal the entire landscape and other people; by the selection of a filter and an exposure...which determine whether the tone will be brilliant or gloomy, harsh or soft...This is why, in films, it becomes possible to put one and the same reality to the service of democratic, socialist or totalitarian ideologies, and in each case make it seem realistic. To take the camera out of the studio, and to photograph real life on the spot becomes merely one style of making films, but it is not a guarantee of truth, objectivity, beauty or any other moral or esthetic virtue. As a maker of documentary films I am aware of how many scenes I have contrived, rearranged or simply staged...These films have been presented in good faith and accepted as a "remarkably true picture of life." I do not feel that I have deceived anyone, because all these arrangements have been made in harmony with the spirit of that life, and were designed to present its character, moods, hidden meanings, beauties and contrasts...We have not reproduced reality but have created an illusion of reality."

And Mr. Hammid pursues his observations with relentless logic—right out of the documentary field, as it is generally understood:

"I believe that this reality, which lives only in the darkness of the movie theater, is the thing that counts. And it lives only if it is convincing, and that does not depend upon the fact that someone went to the great trouble of taking the camera to unusual places to photograph unusual events, or whether it contained professional actors or native inhabitants. It lies rather in the feeling and creative force with which the man behind the camera is able to project his visions."

If we accept the proposition that even the selected placing of the camera is an exercise of conscious creativity, then there is no such thing as a documentary film, in the sense of an objective rendition of reality. Not even the camera in synchronization with the gun remains, for it could be argued that such an arrangement was itself a creative action. And, many documentarists, confronting in the principle of objectivity an implication of their personal, individual uselessness, salvage their ego and importance by a desperate reversal. They attempt to establish, as the lowest common denominator of creative action, the exercise of even the most miniscule discrimination.

If such a low denominator is not acceptable, does it become so according to the degree and frequency of selectivity? Such a gradation can be enormous, as Mr. Hammid's reference to angles, lenses, filters, lighting, suggests. In the final analysis, is creative action at all related to elements and the act of selection from them? For would not such a concept make creativity commensurate with the accessibility of elements, so that a man of broad experience would have a high artistic potential, whereas the shy, retiring individual would not? Or does it begin, as Mr. Hammid last implies, on a level different entirely, where the elements are re-combined, not in an imitation of their original and natural integrity, but into a new whole to thus create a new reality.

2c

For the serious artist the esthetic problem of form is, essentially, and simultaneously, a moral problem. Nothing can account for the devoted dedication of the giants of human history to art form save the understanding that, for them, the moral and esthetic problems were one and the same: that the form of a work of art is the physical manifestation of its moral structure.

So organic is this relationship that it obtains even without a conscious recognition of its existence. The vulgarity and cynicism, or the pompousness and self-conscious "impressiveness" of so many of the films of the commercial industry—these "formal" qualities are their moral qualities as well. Our sole defense against, for example, the "June-moon" rhymes and the empty melodies of Tin Pan Alley lies in the recognition that the "love" there created has nothing in common with that profound experience, known by the same name, to which artists have so desperately labored to give adequate, commensurate form.

And if the idea of art form comprehends, as it were, the idea of moral form, no one who presumes to treat of profound human values is exonerated from a moral responsibility for the negative action of failure, as well as the positive action of error.

Least of all are the documentarists exonerated from such judgment, for in full consciousness they have advanced, as the major plank of their platform, not an esthetic conviction but a moral one. They have accepted the burden of concerning themselves with important human values, particularly in view of the failure of the commercial industry to do so adequately. They stand on moral grounds which are ostensibly impregnable.

Yet it is my belief, and I think that I am not alone in this, that the documentaries of World War II illuminate precisely how much a failure of form is a failure of morals, even when it results from nothing more intentionally destructive than incompetency, or the creative lethargy of the "achieved" professional craftsman.

Surely the human tragedy of the war requires of those who presume to commemorate it—film-maker, writer, painter—a personal creative effort somehow commensurate in profundity and stature. Surely the vacant eyes and the desolated bodies of starved children, deserve and require, in the moral sense, something more than the maudlin cliches of the tourist camera or the skillful manipulations of a craftsman who brings to them the techniques developed for and suitable to the entertaining demonstration of the manufacture of a Ford car. Is it possible not to be violently offended to discover that all these inarticulate animal sounds of human misery, all the desperate and final silences can find no transcription more inspired and exalted than the professional fluency of a well-fed voice and commentary. And how can we agree that the heroism of a single soldier is in the least celebrated by the two-dimensional record of his falling body; or that the meaning of his death is even remotely comprehended by whoever is capable of exploiting the ready-made horror of his mangled face, which he can no longer protect from the cynical intimacy, the mechanical sight of the camera.

Whether there will ever appear a spiritual giant, of the stature of a Da Vinci, who can create, out of his individual resources, the form of such gigantic tragedy is a question. Short of such achievement, the least requirement is a profound humility, and a truly immense, dedicated, creative effort which would begin with the conviction that any skill or technique which has served a lesser purpose is a priori inadequate for this one. Where even such considerations are absent—and they are absent from all the war documentaries which I have seen—the result is nothing less than a profanity in a profoundly moral sense.

During the war, the documentarists interpreted the great public interest as a triumph for their form. But after the photographs of skeletonized children, the horrors of Dachau, the burning Japanese soldier, the plunge into the very heart of fire—after all the violences of war—even the best intentioned reportages of matters perhaps equally important but less dramatic and sensational cannot but seem anticlimactic and dull.

On the other hand, the extension of realism into sur-realism, as a spontaneous projection of the inner reality of the artist—intact in its natural integrity—is impossible. Since it is the camera which actually confronts reality, one can theoretically achieve, at most, a spontaneity of the camera in recording, without conscious control or discrimination, the area that it is fixed upon. This naturalism is preserved only if the pieces of film are conscientiously re-combined into the relationship of the reality itself, as in documentaries. Moreover, since the camera records according to its own capacity, even the most personalized editing of this material cannot be taken as a free expression of the artist. Thus, while film may record a sur-realist expression in another medium, "film spontaneity" is impossible.

The Hollywood industry, its shrewdness undiverted by esthetic or ethic idealisms, knew (even before the war had ended) that only the imaginatively contrived horror or the fantastically artificial scene could capture the attention of a public grown inured to the realities of war.

To these ends, Hollywood had been itself primarily responsible for increasing the catalogue of elements which film has at its disposal for creative manipulation. In the spatial dimension it had access to the source material of the plastic arts. In the temporal dimension it had access to all movement, which could also be used to round out a two dimensional shape so that it functioned as a three-dimensional element. When sound was added, the linguistic elements upon which literature is founded, and also natural sound and music, were made available. Now, with the rapid development of color processes, still another dimension of elements is being proffered film.

My insistence upon the creative attitude, and the "un-natural" forms to which it gives rise, might seem to comprehend Hollywood films, which are obviously artificial in form. But film has access not only to the elements of reality but also, and as part of reality, to the ready made forms of other arts. And Hollywood is as realistic in reference to these art realities—literature, drama, dance, etc.,—and as faithful to their original integrities, as the documentary is in reference to social reality. This is, moreover, a tendency which has grown with time.

The film producer, responsible for the success of a project in which increasingly enormous sums are usually invested, avails himself of material, methods and personnel which are already "tested and approved." Consequently, most films make use of the elements of reality not according to the film instrument, but as elements already part of an integrated art form.

As the film industry became secure and also subject to the scrutiny of French, British and German cultural criteria, it became culturally defensive, and interested in achieving "class" on an intellectual level.

In typical "nouveau-riche" fashion, the studios began to buy some of the more "intellectual" writers almost in the way that a piano, prominently displayed, is widely used to lend an aspect of refinement to a home. And just as piano lessons are rarely pursued to the point of any real musical accomplishment or understanding, so I doubt that there has ever been any real intention to make use of the real capacities of the best writers. The Hollywood writer cannot be blamed for a reluctance to recognize or admit the humiliating, decorative purpose for which he receives his irresistible salaries and so is angry and bewildered at being forced to function in films on a level far below that which ostensibly induced the original bargain. There are times when this situation creates an impression of Hollywood as no less than a Dantesque purgatory from which rise, incessantly, the hysterical protest of violated virgins.

Nevertheless, the literary approach, encouraged by the use of verbal expression in sound, has set the pattern of film criteria in much the same way that token music lessons set the pattern of musical taste and account for the notion that the "light classic" composition is the "good music." It might have been better for films if the industry was never able to afford the cultural pretension of employing writers or buying literary works but were forced to continue in the direction of some early silent films. These emphasized visual elements and even sometimes, as in the comedies of Buster Keaton, displayed a remarkable, intuitive grasp of filmic form.

I do not intend to minimize the importance of literature or drama or of any of the art forms which film records; nor even to minimize the value of such records. On the contrary, just as I am deeply grateful to some documentaries for showing me a world which I may have been otherwise denied, so I am grateful to those films which make it possible for me to see plays which I could not have attended or the performances of actors now retired or dead.

But just as I do not consider documentary realism a substitute for the creative form of film proper, neither do I feel that this is accomplished by an extension of the recording method to cover the forms of any or all the other arts. The form proper of film is, for me, accomplished only when the elements, whatever their original context, are related according to the special character of the instrument of film itself—the camera and the editing—so that the reality which emerges is a new one—one which only film can achieve and which could not be accomplished by the exercize of any other instrument. (If, on the face of it, this seems a stringent, purist or limiting requirement, then I can only point out that, far from inhibiting the other art forms, such a principle, in terms of their respective instruments, is most manifest in the greatest of their achievements.

This critical relationship between form and instrument is the special concern of the section dealing with instruments; but it is impossible to make clear how a fiction film remains, even on film, a literary form, without reference to the manner in which instruments operate in creating a form.

In discussing the formal emergent whole of a work of art, I pointed out that the elements, or parts, lose their original individual value and assume those conferred upon them by their function in this specific whole.

Such redefined elements are then pre-disposed towards functioning in the respective form from which they derive. Consequently, even when a Hollywood writer aspires to film as a distinct medium, he usually begins with the literary and verbal elements to which he has been previously devoted. These encourage, if not actually impose, the creation of the very literary form which he has ostensibly refuted, as a principle, in film. For this reason it is usually impossible to distinguish whether film is an "original" (conceived specifically for filming) or an "adaptation" of a novel, or a novel preserved more or less intact.

The special character of the novel form is that it can deal in interior emotions and ideas—invisible conflicts, reflections, etc. The visual arts—and film is, above all, a visual experience—deal, on the contrary, in visible states of being or action. When a fictional character, whose meaning has been created by the development of his interior feelings and ideas, is to be put into a film, the first problem is: what should he do to show visibly what he thinks or feels—what is the activity best symptomatic of his feelings? This "enactment" must not take an undue length of time, and so certain "symptom-action" cliches are established. We have come to accept a kiss as a symptom-action of love, or a gesture of the hands thrown back as a symptom-action of an inner fear, etc.

Thus the Hollywood fiction film has created a kind of visual short-hand of cliches with which we have become so familiar that we are not even aware of the effort of transcription. As we watch the screen we continually "understand" this gesture to stand for this state of mind, or that grimace to represent that emotion. Although the emotional impact derives not from what we see, but from the verbal complex which the image represents, the facility with which we bridge the gap and achieve this transcription deceives us, and we imagine that we enjoy a visual experience. Actually, this has nothing in common with the directness with which we would experience a truly visual reality, such as falling, whose "symptomatic sensations" would have to represent it in a literary form.

The visual cliche acts, therefore, as a symbol, in the way that the cross is a symbol for the whole complex of ideas contained in the crucifixion. When we react emotionally to a cross, it is not to the visual character of the cross proper but to the crucifixion, to which the cross leads as a bridge of reference. It is true that symbols have been used in many works of art, but they have been drawn, always, from a firmly established mythology. Moreover, the artist rarely relies upon such an exterior frame of reference. He is usually careful to reaffirm, in the immediate context of his work of art, those values which the object, as symbol, might have in exterior reference. It is impossible to maintain, for instance, that a good painting of the Madonna would fail to convey its devotional, exalted emotion even to someone ignorant of the symbolism employed.

The rapidity with which so many Hollywood films cease to make sense or carry emotional weight is an indication of their failure to create meaning in the direct visual terms of their own immediate frame of reference. The shorthand cliches which they employ, to bridge back to the literary terms in which the film is actually conceived, are drawn not from a recognized mythology but from superficial mannerisms which are transitory and soon lose their referential value. If the great works of art have succeeded in retaining their value even long after their symbols have lost their referential power it is precisely because their meaning was not entrusted, in the first place, to the frail bridges of the symbolic reference.

It is also a common belief that when a literary work contains many "images" it is especially well suited to being filmed. On the contrary, the better the writer, the more verbal his images...in the sense that the impact derives not from the object or events described, but from the verbal manner of their description. I take, at random, the opening paragraph of "The Trial" by Franz Kafka.

"Someone must have been telling lies about Joseph K. for without having done anything wrong he was arrested one fine morning. His landlady's cook, who always brought him his breakfast at eight o'clock, failed to appear on this occasion. That had never happened before. K. waited for a while longer, watching from his pillow the old lady opposite, who seemed to be peering at him with a curiosity unusual even for her, but then, feeling both put out and hungry, he rang the bell. At once there was knock on the door and a man entered whom he had never seen before in the house."

In this paragraph the words are themselves simple; concrete; they describe a physical event in which both real actions and real objects are included. Yet I challenge anyone to create, in visual terms, the meaning which is here contained in no more than a moment's reading time.

In literature, when an image or an event is modified by the negative, as "failed to appear" or "had never seen before" they are endowed with a meaning impossible to achieve in visual terms by mere absence. Yet it is precisely this negative reference which is important in the paragraph quoted. In visual terms the time which would be required to first establish an expectation in order to disappoint it, would be so long and the action so contrived, as to contradict the very virtue of economy which is here achieved, and to unbalance, by the emphasis which time always brings to an event, the subtle structure of the work. Not only by the pathos and disappointment of negative modification, but by a thousand other verbal and syntactical manipulations, good literature remains verbal in its impact no matter how much it seems to deal with concrete situations and images. I would even go so far as to say that only that literature which fails to make creative use of its verbal instrument, could be made into a good film. And I would like to place this entire consideration before those writers who imagine that their constant use of imagery in short stories and poetry would indicate an inhibited talent for film.

The comparative economy with which an emotion can be established in verbal or in visual terms is, as a matter of fact, a good indication of whether it is a verbal or a visual image for there are, on the other hand, visual moments, which contain such a rich complex of meanings, implications, over- and under-tones, etc., that only a labored and lengthy verbal description could begin to convey their impact. The immense difference between an accurate description of an experience and the experience itself must not be minimized.

In many films such indirection—the visual description of non-visual experiences—is concealed by a rococo of photographic "effects." For example a static sequence will be photographed from a dozen different angles, even when such a shifty point of view is not, emotionally or logically, justified. But all the photographic virtuosity in the world cannot make a visual form out of a literary concept.

Theater, unlike literature, is concerned with an exterior physical situation in which a verbal activity takes place; and the sound film is able to retain theater intact in its original terms. Similarly, dance retains its stage logics in film, music is composed in concert terms and remains unrelated to the other sounds of film except in an "accompanist," theatrical fashion. I think I have, perhaps, made my point which is, in any case, amplified in the section dealing with the film instrument.

And it seems to me that the development of a distinctive film form consists not in eliminating any of the elements—whether of nature, reality, or the artifices of other arts—to which it has access, but in relating all these according to the special capacity of film: the manipulations made possible by the fact that it is both a space art and a time art.

By a manipulation of time and space I do not mean such established filmic technique as flash-backs, parallel actions, etc. Parallel actions for instance—as in a sequence when we see, alternately, the hero who rushes to the rescue and the heroine, whose situation becomes increasingly critical—is an omni-presence on the part of the camera as a witness of action, not as a creator of it. Here Time, by remaining actually constant, is no more than a dimension in which a spatial activity can occur. But the celluloid memory of the camera can function, as our memory, not merely to reconstruct or to measure an original chronology. It can place together, in immediate temporal sequence, events actually distant, and achieve, through such relationship, a peculiarly filmic reality. This is just one of the possiblities, and I suggest many others in a discussion of the instrument of film itself.

But it would be impossible to understand or appreciate a filmic film if we brought to it all the critical and visual habits which we may have developed, to advantage, in reference to the other art forms. On the other hand, since a film makes much use of natural reality, we may be inclined, by habit, to approach it as if it were, truly, a natural phenomenon, and proceed to select from it elements which we interpret according to some personal context, rather than the context which the film has carefully evolved. Or, accustomed to film as a record of another art form, we anticipate a literary-symbolic logic. Just as, in waiting anxiously for a specific friend, we fail to recognize or even see the other faces in a crowd, so, in watching for some familiar pattern of relationship in a film we may fail to perceive the reality which is there created.

Another habit is the current tendency to psycho-analyze anything which deals in an imaginative reality. The special conditions of film production, where it is the camera which perceives and records, according to its capacity, introduces a non-psychological censor. The spontaneous associational logics of the artist cannot be retained intact by an instrument which eliminates certain elements by virtue of its mechanical limitations and introduces other elements by virtue of its refined optics, its ability to remember details which the sub-conscious might not have considered significant, its dependence upon weather conditions, its use of human beings in their own physical terms, etc. As a matter of fact, the less the artist collaborates with the instrument, with full consideration to its capacities, the more he will get, as a result, film which expresses mechanics of the camera, and not his own intentions.

It is not only the film artist who must struggle to discover the esthetic principles of the first new art form in centuries; it is the audience, too, which must develop a receptive attitude designed specifically for film and free of the critical criteria which have been evolved for all the older art forms.

3c

Everything which I have said in criticism of film may create an image of severe austerity and asceticism. On the contrary, you may find me many evenings in the motion-picture theater, sharing with the other sleepers (for nothing so resembles sleep), the selected dream without responsibilities. The less the film pretends to profundity—the less it is involved in a mediocre compromise of ideas and emotions which might be otherwise important—and the more casually circus-like it is, the more it fills the role of an extremely economical, accessible divertissement; or, as with the documentary, a satisfaction of our curiosity about the world.

But in so well exploiting the reproductive potential of film, the makers have for the most part permitted this function to supplant and substitute for a development of film-form proper. The failure of film has been a failure of omission—a neglect of the many more miraculous potentials of the art instrument.

In directing my critical remarks at the Hollywood industry, I have made convenient use of familiar points of reference; but I do not concur in that naive snobbishness which places the European industries so far above it. It must never be forgotten that only the better foreign films are imported, and that we are therefore inclined to generalize from these, neglecting that the French neighborhood double-feature is on a much lower level. And because we see few foreign films, at long intervals, the acting and the camerawork seem exotically interesting and fresh. Actually, in terms of their own native soil, these films are often as cliche and conventionalized as ours, which incidently, seem fresh and exotic to Europeans. It is true that French films, for instance, sometimes create a more subtle, introverted intensity, particularly in romantic relationships, than ours do; but I feel that this is not so much an expressly filmic virtue as a filmic fidelity to a reality both of French life and art, just as a healthy buoyancy is characteristic of many American expressions.

Above all it must never be forgotten that film owes at least as much to D. W. Griffith and Mack Sennett as to Murnau and Pabst of Germany, Melies and Delluc of France, Stiller of Sweden and Eisenstein of Russia. It is not my intention to enter, here, upon a discussion of the various styles of film-making. There are already many historical volumes on the subject. In all of them the Russian films occupy an important position, one which has created, again on the basis of a mere handful of selected achievements, a legendary notion of the Russian film industry as a whole. Although Eisenstein and his compatriots must be credited with an intensely creative extension of "montage" and other conventions (for these originally inspired methods have fallen into conventionalized usage) it must be remembered that they were so inspired by its more casual, prior use by Griffith (to whom they themselves give due credit).

Even with montage, the all-over concept of the form as a whole of the Russian films is that of the literary narrative. And at the risk of seeming heretical, I feel that although "Potemkin" has sequences which are extremely impressive (Eisenstein is nothing if not impressive, usually ponderously so), for sheer profundity of emotional impact and for an intensely poetic concept of film, I find nothing there to equal various sequences in the much less publicized works of Dovzhenko, such as "Frontier" or "Ivan."

It is disappointing to find, even in the "experimental" field, that the infinite tolerance of the camera—its capacity to record whatever is put before it under many modifying conditions, is too great a temptation. The painter who has an earnest interest in spatial manipulations often continues, as a film-maker, to function according to his original plastic concepts. Using chiffon and other devices he may conscientiously restore to the laboriously perfected optics of the lens all the limitations which characterize human vision, so that he can then proceed to create again as a painter. He may compose his frame as one does a convas, in the logics of simplified masses, lines and, as substitute for color, an arrangement of blacks, white, and all possible gradations of gray. The results are, of course, inferior to painting. Many of the gradations which are intended as color are lost in the process of multiple reproduction—a problem which painters do not face.

Moreover, since after all this is a motion picture, he arrives eventually at that unpleasant moment when the image, finally, must move and will disarrange its studied composition. Still photographers, for instance, have learned how to translate time into spatial terms. But in film, the problem is inverted. Space must be given meaning over time. A careful attention to some of the "art" films photographed by still photographers reveals an actual discomfort with time, and movement is most frequently merely an uneasy moment of transition, accomplished as rapidly as possible, between two static spatial compositions.

The abstract film is also derived from painting, both in principal and in the person of its pioneers. Such films are, it seems to me, not so much films as animated paintings, for the creative abstraction itself takes place on the spatial, plastic plane—the plane of painting—and is then registered, as any other reality, upon the film. To abstract in filmic terms would require an abstraction in time, as well as in space; but in abstract films time is not itself manipulated. It functions, in the usual way, as a vacuum which becomes visible only as it is filled by spatial activities; but it does not itself create any condition which could be thought of as its own manifestation. For an action to take place in time is not at all the same as for an action to be created by the exercise of time. This may become clearer later when I discuss the camera as an instrument of invention in temporal terms.

Like the rest of his work, the film of Marcel Duchamp occupies a unique position. Although it uses geometric forms, it is not an abstract film, but perhaps the only "optical pun" in existence. The time which he causes one of his spirals to revolve on the screen effects an optical metamorphosis: the cone appears first concave, then convex, and, in the more complicated spirals, both concave and convex and then inversed. It is Time, therefore, which creates these optical puns which are the visual equivalents, in "Anemic Cinema," for instance, of the inserted phrases which also revolve and, in doing so, disclose the verbal pun.

My main criticism of the concept behind the usual abstract film is that it denies the special capacity of film to manipulate real elements as realities, and substitutes, exclusively, the elements of artifice (the method of painting). It may be easier to make an abstract film by recording the movements of colored squares by ordinary photographic process; but even this is usually done one frame at a time, like a series of miniature canvasses. And it is possible to paint upon successive frames a successively larger or smaller square or circle which, when projected, will appear to approach or recede according to the plastic principles of painting. Many abstract films are painted directly on the celluloid. Any concept of film which can in theory and practice dispense with the use of both camera and editing does not seem to me to be, properly speaking, a film, although it may be a highly entertaining, exciting or even profound experience.

Realism and the artifices of other arts can be combined by photographing an imaginatively conceived action related to an obviously real location. For when the tree in the picture is obviously real, it is also understood as true, and it can lend its aura of reality to an event created by artifice beneath it. Such a delicate manipulation between the really real and the unreally real is, I believe, one of the major principles of film form.

Nothing can be achieved in the art of film until its form is understood to be the product of a completely unique complex: the exercise of an instrument which can function, simultaneously, both in terms of discovery and of invention. Peculiar also to film is the fact that this instrument is composed of two separate but interdependent parts, which flank the artist on either side. Between him and reality stands the camera...with its variable lenses, speeds, emulsions, etc. On the other side is the strip of film which must be subjected to the mechanisms and processes of editing (a relating of all the separate images), before a motion picture comes into existence.

The camera provides the elements of the form, and, although it does not always do so, can either discover them or create them, or discover and create them simultaneously. Upon the mechanics and processes of "editing" falls the burden of relating all these elements into a dynamic whole.

Most film-makers rely upon the automatically explorative action of the camera to add richness to their material. For the direct contact between camera and reality results in a quality of observation which is quite different from that of the human being. For example the field of vision of the human eye is comparable to that of a wide-angle lens. But the focus of the eye is relatively selective, and, directed by the interests or anxieties of the human being, will concentrate upon some small part of the entire area and will fail to observe or to remember objects or actions which lie outside its circle of concentration, even though these are still physically within the field of vision.

The lens, on the other hand, can be focused upon a plane (at right angles to the camera) within the depth of that field and, everything in that plane of focus, will be observed and recorded with impartial clarity. Under favorable light conditions, the depth of that plane can be enormously extended, so that the camera can record, in a single frame a greater richness of reality than the human eye would ever be aware of in a glance. The camera thus contributes a dimension of observation to photography by compensating for a prejudice of human vision. It does not discover, however, in the sense of revealing more than the most perfect or leisurely human vision could perceive.

It is shocking to realize how little the camera, as an instrument of discovery, has been exploited outside of scientific investigation, where the results remain in the hands of scientists as part of their data. Yet, to my mind, the sheer visual excitement of photographs taken through a microscope, for instance, transcend by far—in beauty of design, delicacy of detail, and a kind of miraculous perfection—most of the accidental or laboriously composed still lifes of vases, strings, and such objects. I refer anyone who wishes to spend an exciting afternoon to the photographs of ocean organisms, plant sections, cancerous growths, etc., which are on file at the Museum of Natural History in New York. I exclude from my criticism the handful of photographers who have, in the use of extreme enlargements, and similar techniques, shown a creative grasp of such possibilities.

The motion-picture camera, in introducing the dimension of time into photography, opened to exploration the vast province of movement. The treasures here are almost limitless, and I can suggest only a few of them. There is, for example, the photographic acceleration of a movement which, in reality, may be so slow as to be indiscernable. The climbing of a vine, or the orientation of a plant towards the sun are thus revealed to possess fascinating characteristics, qualities, and even a curiously "intelligent" integrity of movement which only the most patient and observant botanist could have previously suspected.

My own attention has been especially captured by the explorations of slow-motion photography. Slow-motion is the microscope of time. One of the most lyric sequences I have ever seen was the slow-motion footage of the flight of birds photographed by an orinthologist interested in their varied aerodynamics. But apart from such scientific uses, slow-motion can be brought to the most casual activities to reveal in them a texture of emotional and psychological complexes. For example, the course of a conversation is normally characterized by indecisions, defiances, hesitations, distractions, anxieties, and other emotional undertones. In reality these are so fugitive as to be invisible. But the explorations by slow-motion photography, the agony of its analysis, reveals, in such an ostensibly casual situation, a profound human complex.

The complexity of the camera creates, at times, the illusion of being almost itself a living intelligence which can inspire its manipulation on the explorative and creative level simultaneously. (I have just received from France a book entitled "L'Intelligence d'une Machine" by Jean Epstein. I have not yet read it, but the approach implied in the title and the poetic, inspired tone of the style in which Mr. Epstein writes of a subject usually treated in pedestrian, historical terms leads me to believe that it is at least interesting reading for those who share, with me, a profound respect for the magical complexities of the film instrument.) A running leap has, with slight variations, a given tempo; slow-motion photography creates of it a reality which is totally unnatural. But a use of slow-motion in reference to a movement which can, in parts, be performed at a variable tempo, can be even more creative. That is, one can shake one's head from side to side at almost any rate of speed. When a fast turning is reduced, by slow-motion, it still looks natural, and merely as if it were being performed more slowly; the hair, however, moving slowly in the lifted, horizontal shape possible only to rapid tempos, is unnatural in quality. Thus one creates a movement in one tempo which has the qualities of a movement of another tempo, and it is the dynamics of the relationship between these qualities which creates a certain special effectiveness, a reality which can only be achieved through the temporal manipulation of natural elements by the camera as an art instrument. In this sense, such a shot is a new element which is created by the camera for a function in the larger whole of the entire film. Another example of a uniquely filmic element is the movement created by the reversal of a motion which is not, in reality, reversible. By simply holding the camera up-side-down (I cannot stop to explain the logic by which this occurs), one can photograph the waves of the ocean and they will, in projection, travel in reverse. Such film footage not only reveals a new quality in the motion of the waves, but, creates to put it mildly, a most revolutionary reality.

Such an approach is a far cry from what is usually understood by the cliche that the province of motion pictures is movement. Film-makers seem to forget that movement, as such, is already used very thoroughly in dance, and to a lesser degree, in theater. If film is to make any contribution to the realm of movement, if it is to stake out a claim in an immeasurably rich territory, then it must be in the province of film-motion, as a new dimension altogether of movement.

I have not, myself, had the opportunity of experimenting with sound, but I am convinced that an explorative attitude, brought to the techniques of recording, mixing, amplifying, etc., could create a wealth of original film-sound elements. Even in the process of developing film emulsion itself, lives the negative image, where the inversion of all values reveals the astonishing details and constructions which fail of visual consequence in the familiar values of the positive image.

The burden of my argument is that it constitutes a gross, if not criminal esthetic negligence to ignore the immense wealth of new elements which the camera proffers in exchange for relatively minute effort. Such elements, constituted already of a filmic dynamic of space and time relationships, (related to all other accessible elements), are the elements proper of the larger dynamic of the film as a whole.

I have already pointed out that the reproduction, on film, of the other art forms does not constitute the creation of a filmic integrity and logic. Just as the verbal logics of a poem are composed of the relationships established through syntax, assonance, rhyme, and other such verbal methods, so in film there are processes of filmic relationships which derive from the instrument and the elements of its manipulations.

As a matter of fact, the very methods which result in a failure of the other art forms in film may be the basis of creative action in film itself, once the effort to carry over the values of one to the other is abandoned. Such inversion is possible largely because film is a time-space complex of a unique kind.

Film has been criticized, from the point of view of dramaturgy, as lacking the integrity and immediacy of fine theater. It is pointed out that the limitations of the stage impose upon the playwright an economy of movement, an emphasis upon the construction and development of character and situation, and a creative attention to the verbal statement upon which the immediate burden of projection rests. The very mobility of the camera, it is said, encourages a lazy reliance on an essentially decorative use of scenery and realistic detail. A plot so dull that it would not hold the attention of the theater audience for more than a moment, borrows a superficial excitement from a frequent change of location, angles and similar movements of the camera. These also permit a neglect of verbal integrity and achievement. The insistent artificiality of the processes of film-making—the complicated and intense lighting, the unresponsive machinery, the interruptions of the action—make it virtually impossible for the performer to maintain the intensity and integrity of conviction which is so central to theater, or to achieve the vitality which results from his direct contact with his human audience.

I agree. I agree absolutely that film, as theater, is less satisfying an experience than theater as theater. But, on the other hand, the sly tendency of theater to, at times, imitate the methods (however unexploited) of film by a "realism" of setting, frequent changes of scene, and a panoramic idea of construction is neither good theater nor acceptable film.

(In my criticism of the panoramic construction I do not intend to include vaudeville variety shows, musicals or that supremely triumphant example of such construction: "Around the World in Eighty Days." These are part of a form completely separate from drama and are in the tradition of the "word battles" and the other contests of skills already developed to a high level (often higher than ours) in the tribal cultures of Africa, the Pacific, etc., where they also function as a socially adjusted exercise of individual exhibitionism.)

Moreover, it seems to me that many of the "technical" difficulties are at least compensated for by such advantages as the opportunity to repeat an action until its most perfect delivery is recorded for all time. It is true that theater does often function on a higher level than film-theater, but this is due not to technical qualifications but rather to the fact that, for theatrical presentation, plays do not gear themselves to a prescribed level guaranteed to return the amounts invested in a film. In addition and as a consequence, performers who are genuinely concerned with the profundity of their roles prefer to remain in the theater. These are the real reasons behind the loss of stature which plays so frequently suffer in being rendered into films.

This is a comparatively recent development. In the early days, the film industry was in complete disrepute: theatrical professionals considered it, for the most part, a vulgarity, and it had not yet proven its commercial possibilities sufficiently to become seductive to them. It could not afford to buy rights, hire playwrights or trained actors, or indulge in a vast personnel and a division of labor. It had, consequently, to rely upon and develop its own resources.

The most frequent practice was to work with a very limited crew, most of whom had no previous professional standing to lose, and would therefore try anything. It was not uncommon, for example, to use almost everyone except the camera-man for extras in group scenes; or for the actress to design her own costume; or for the camera-man to suggest a preferable action; or for the director to take over the camera; etc. In this way, the films became a collaborative effort of the crew, rather than the current assembly-line product of a hierarchical, myopic division of labor. Above all, for sheer lack of writers who would deign to concern themselves with movies, the films were often "written" on the spot by the camera, according to a very skeletal, vague story plot. The masterpieces of Mack Sennett and Chaplin derive precisely from this procedure.

It was also responsible for the development of a peculiarly filmic concept,—the personality film—as in the Pickford films or the vamp films. Although probably suggested by the vehicle plays of theater, it was actually, for a period, extended into a qualitatively different form. The special techniques of film—the concentrated close-up—and the special qualities of film projection—the overwhelming, intimate experience of a face as the sole, living reality in a total darkness—made possible an unprecedented exploitation of the very personality of an actress, from which the action of the plot itself emanated. Although it has now fallen into an unimaginative, pedestrian usage—as in the Grable films which must be propped up with songs, jokes, etc.,—it also led to such achievements as "Joan of Arc" (Karl Dreyer). In keeping with a false concept of "refinement," the "better" films are now reverting to plays, playwrights, and play-actresses.

But I am sure that I am not alone in my deep affection for those films which raised personalities to almost a super-natural stature and created, briefly, a mythology of gods of the first magnitude whose mere presence lent to the most undistinguished events a divine grandeur and intensity—Theda Bara, Mary Pickford, Lillian Gish, Rudolph Valentino, Douglas Fairbanks, and the early Greta Garbo, Marlene Dietrich, Jean Harlow and Joan Crawford. (For another point of view on these figures, I recommend "The Hollywood Hallucination" by Parker Tyler.)

Moreover—to return to the dramaturgic criticisms—suppose that the fact that a camera can stop, wait indefinitely, and then start again, was used, not as substitute for the intermissions during which the stage scenery is shifted, but as a technique for the metamorphosis (implying uninterrupted continuity of time) in spatial dimension?

In the film dance which I have made, the dancer begins a large movement—the lowering of his extended leg—in a forest. This shot is interrupted at the moment when the leg has reached waist-level, and is immediately followed by a close-up shot of the leg in a continuation of its movement—with the location now the interior of a house. The integrity of the time element—the fact that the tempo of the movement is continuous and that the two shots are, in editing, spliced to follow one another without interruption—holds together spatial areas which are not, in reality, so related. Instead of being destructive to a dramatic integrity, the mobility of the camera and the interruption and resumption of action, here creates an integrity as compelling as that of the theater, but of a totally different quality.

There are many uniquely filmic time-space relationships which can be achieved. I can point, at random, to a sequence from another film, "At Land." A girl enters and crosses the frame at a diagonal. She disappears behind a sand dune in the foreground at the edge of the frame, and the camera, at this moment, actually stops operating. The girl walks away a considerable distance and takes her place behind a farther dune away. The camera then resumes its shooting and immediately begins to turn (in a panoramic movement) in the direction in which the girl just left the frame. Since it starts registering at the identical position at which it stopped, some five minutes before, there is no spatial indication of the time which has transpired, and consequently we expect to find the girl emerging the dune which had just concealed her. Instead, she emerges from the dune much more distant, and so the alienation of the girl, from the camera, exceeds the actual time which would have presumably been necessary. In this case, a continuity of space has integrated periods of time which were not, in reality, in such immediate relationship; just as in the previous example, time and space were inversely related, according to a similar principle.

To the form as a whole, such techniques contribute an economy of statement comparable to poetry, where the inspired juxtaposition of a few words can create a complex which far transcends them. One of the finest films I have seen, "Sang d'un Poet" (Blood of A Poet) comes from Jean Cocteau who, as a poet, has had long training in the economy of statement. It is a film which has, incidently, suffered immensely at the hands of "critics" for in its condensation it contains enough springboards for the personal, creative interpretations of a convention of "analysts." And its meaning depends upon a good many immediately visual images and realities which the literary symbolists ignore either through choice or limited capacity.

It is possible for me to go on for pages, citing one example after another, where a dynamic manipulation of the relationships between film-time and film-space (and potentially, film-sound) can create that special integrated complex: film form. But descriptions of such filmic methods are obviously awkward in verbal terms. I hope that these explicit examples suffice to clarify the principle. Above all, I sense myself upon the mere threshold of an indefinitely large, if not infinite, range of potentialities in which, eventually, there will be revealed principles beside which my concepts may seem exceedingly primitive.

Such revelations will, in their time, be as appropriate to the state of the culture—its perception of reality, the methods and achievements of its manipulations, and the complex of emotional and intellectual attitudes which attend all of these—as the problems with which I have here concerned myself, seem now to be.

The theory of relativity can no longer be indulgently dismissed as an abstract statement, true or false, of a remote cosmography whose pragmatic action remains, in any case, constant. Since the 17th century the heavens—with God and His will—and the earth—with man and his desires—have rapidly approached each other. The phenomena which were once the manifestations of a transcendent deity are now the ordinary activities of man. A voice penetrates our midnight privacy over vast distance—via radio. The heavens are crowded with swift messengers. It is even possible to bring the world to an end. From the source of power must emanate also the morals and the mercies. And so, ready or not, willing or not, we must come to comprehend, with full responsibility, the world which we have now created.

The history of art is the history of man and of his universe and of the moral relationship between them. Whatever the instrument, the artist sought to re-create the abstract, invisible forces and relationships of the cosmos, in the intimate, immediate forms of his art, where the problems might be experienced and perhaps be resolved in miniature. It is not presumptuous to suggest that cinema, as an art instrument especially capable of recreating relativistic relationships on a plane of intimate experience, is of profound importance. It stands, today, in the great need of the creative contributions of whomsoever respects the fabulous potentialities of its destiny.

A Work Journal of the Straub/Huillet Film 'Moses and Aaron'

Gregory Woods

Notes on Gregory's Work Journal

Danièle Huillet

(Gregory Woods' work journal is on the left-hand pages and Danièle Huillet's notes are on the right-hand pages.)

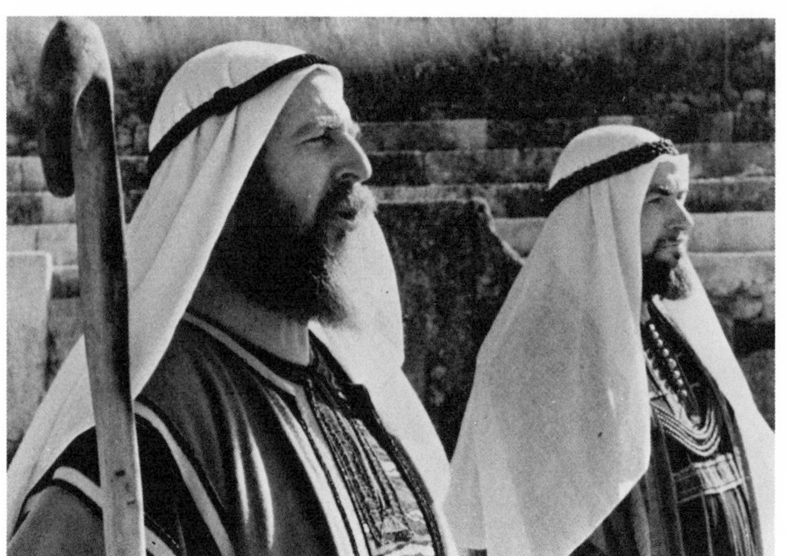

Wednesday, August 14th, in the early morning, at opening time, we were at Cinecitta with the Ford-Transit to load the Fisher giraffe which we had had such trouble in getting. A giraffe is to the microphone what the crane is to the camera and is a help in making things a bit simpler for the sound engineer not because it permits movements of the mike to accompany those of the camera; we will hardly use it at all for this (camera movements almost never occurring to accompany actors, but to relate or oppose the groupings, hence the sound has no reason to change place); but this giraffe permits, thanks to its very extended arm, setting up the mike, above the frame, even in a very open framed shot, at the end of this horizontal arm, far from the foot of the giraffe closer to the singers' positions, without the microphone or its shadow being in the field of vision. But when we began to look for a giraffe in Rome, an instrument only used here, if ever, in studio, saying that we would need it for at least three weeks of exteriors, there was panic. We were looking for the Mole-Richardson giraffe whose arm reaches to 8 metres. The only one there was we found a part of, the famous arm, being used as a barrier for cars (considering its length, evidently very practical) at the studio of SAFA; as no one ever used it, it had been taken apart and destroyed. So we had to set our hooks out for the Fisher, whose arm is but 4.50 m and whose three existing samples were in Cinecitta. They began by telling us that they didn't know if they would be available, but that, since there were three of them, there was a chance that one at least...In fact there were all three of them tidily in storage and we had only to choose, pack up and load. Our perchman, Georges Vaglio, will take loving charge of it, put it back every evening into the hut behind the amphitheatre and handle it artfully during the filming. In addition, Louis Hochet, the sound engineer, brought a perch specially made by him which mounted reached to 8 m, and his normal perch, the one he used for the *Chronicle of Anna Magdalena Bach,* of 4m. From Cinecitta we go to the A.T.C./E.C.E. behind the Villa Doria-Pamphilij (*ex*-Villa Pamphilij, expropriated after *Othon,* at present it belongs to the city) to load all the material [Mitchell B.N.C. camera, rails, carriage, *torrette* (adjustable platforms), boards, reflectors, etc.] into the Ford-Transit where the giraffe is already, and in a second one rented to us by the E.C.E. The three Pisan propmen/electricians and Paolo Benvenuti and Jean-Marie set to work on loading and packing and fastening the material, carefully checked on the preceding days with the cameraman Saverio Diamanti and his assistant Gianni Canfarelli, so that nothing is damaged during transport.

In the preceding weeks, we had already transported to the church at Alba Fucense, thanks to the Ford-Transit that Paolo had got on loan free from a small theatre company in Florence, a big electric copper

cable of 300 metres, the calf, gold-leafed at Cinecitta and weighing 90 kilos, the separate pieces which, assembled, will make up the altar and the steps before and around it, and, from Avezzano, the boards of different lengths, widths, and thicknesses which will be used all during the filming, and the security batteries to assure us of electric current even in case of a breakdown of the mains supply.

Wednesday, August 14th, in the afternoon, the three propmen/electricians and Paolo arrive at Alba Fucense with the two Ford-Transits, and will work up till the arrival of the rest of the crew on Saturday on setting up the big electric cable which will permit us to branch on to the mains inside the amphitheatre where there is no electricity, at a frequency of 50 cycles, whose regularity is constantly checked during the filming giving a security nearly absolute for the synchronism between the camera and the Nagra tape-recorder which records the sound live on one side, and the two other Nagras which have to be synchronised with this first one and have to be in synchrony with each other as well. In addition, they have to install gas lamps in the corridor which runs along a half of the amphitheatre and will serve us for a bit of shade, protect us from the rain, and store the material; to construct a sort of hut in a space outside the amphitheatre to shield the choristers from the sun and, if be the case, from the rain, and set up the chairs there loaned us by the city of Avezzano; to install the electricity in the church where the costumes are to be arranged and ironed and where our 'Keepers of the Treasure' are to sleep, to build the costume racks in wood for 120 costumes.

On **Friday the 16th** the sound engineer Louis Hochet and Jeti Grigioni, his second assistant, arrive with the Renault transport truck in which all the sound equipment is installed, coming from Paris and passing through Switzerland, where they made a last check with Kudelski, the maker of the Nagras. From Nice, by car with wife and daughter comes Georges Vaglio, with whom we haven't yet worked and who will prove to be, as Louis had told us, a very good technician, very well disposed and dedicated.

5254 and not 32-35 is the number of the Eastmancolor negative we used; probably the last film shot in Italy with this negative. During the time we were filming there the new 5247 negative was already out which the Kodak specialists advised us against using for a film so hazardous, so *risqué*, the laboratories not yet knowing how to handle it well.

Should I perhaps orient myself to a temporary phenomenon like the American film market which within two decades with a rapacious culture has succeeded in destroying a thing that was good? When I think about film I think of future films which must necessarily be artistic films. And for these films my music can be useful.

Arnold Schoenberg, discussion on the Berliner Radio, 30th March 1931.

Saturday, 17th August 1974

7 a.m. Arrive at Piazza della Rovere in front of the Straub's with Georg Brintrup in his Deux Chevaus Commercial transport which is to carry the seven boxes of Kodak 32-35 film material to the film site. Each box contains ten rolls of a thousand feet each, 70,000 feet or 21,000 metres in all (90 ft. = 1 min.). The general rule in calculating the quantity of film to buy is according to a one to eight ratio. When we went to pick up the order of film material at Kodak Jean-Marie explained that he was planning on a one to ten ratio. Gabriélè Soncini comes in his Renault R4 soon after us. Into it we pack the remaining props, earthen jars and other equipment not already transported to the church at Alba Fucense which is being used as our warehouse during the film. Gabriélè drives with me and Leo Mingrone to the house of Renata Morroni, the *costumista,* while J.-M. and Daniele wait for the other cars together with which they will leave for Avezzano. At Renata's we meet Paolo Benvenuti and load the six crates of costumes for the chorus and the soloists into the Ford transport truck he is driving. After making us coffee, Renata gets her things together and we leave Via Tiburtina for the Autostrada leading east, up from the summer heat of Rome, to the Abruzzi.

After an hour we come in sight of Monte Velino, 2487 metres high, which marks the entry to the ancient region of Marsica. The local Italic peoples who lived here were destroyed by the Roman army in the fourth century B.C. On the ruins of one of the local settlements Rome built Alba Fucens which grew to importance during the Empire as a regional centre and a residence for captured or uncooperative rulers. Turning south on the highway we arrive at Avezzano, pop. 30,000, the present regional centre where Daniele has reserved rooms for the crew and the cast. In one of our six hotels we drop Renata off and then take the road leading 8 km north to Alba Fucense. On the way we meet up with J.-M. and Georg and drive together up to the *paese* by the ruins of the ancient city inhabited by a farming community of 165. J.-M. stops to get the keys for the church and to greet the people he has come to know here during his visits since 1969. A dirt road leads past

We are going to use this new negative, but in 16 mm — 7274 — with the film next year, testing if there is progress over the preceding one and what is lost to win this progress; or if, indeed, it serves Kodak mainly as an industrial progress, i.e. a film which is more quickly developed permitting the laboratories to work faster, hence more, in using therefore more Kodak negative...

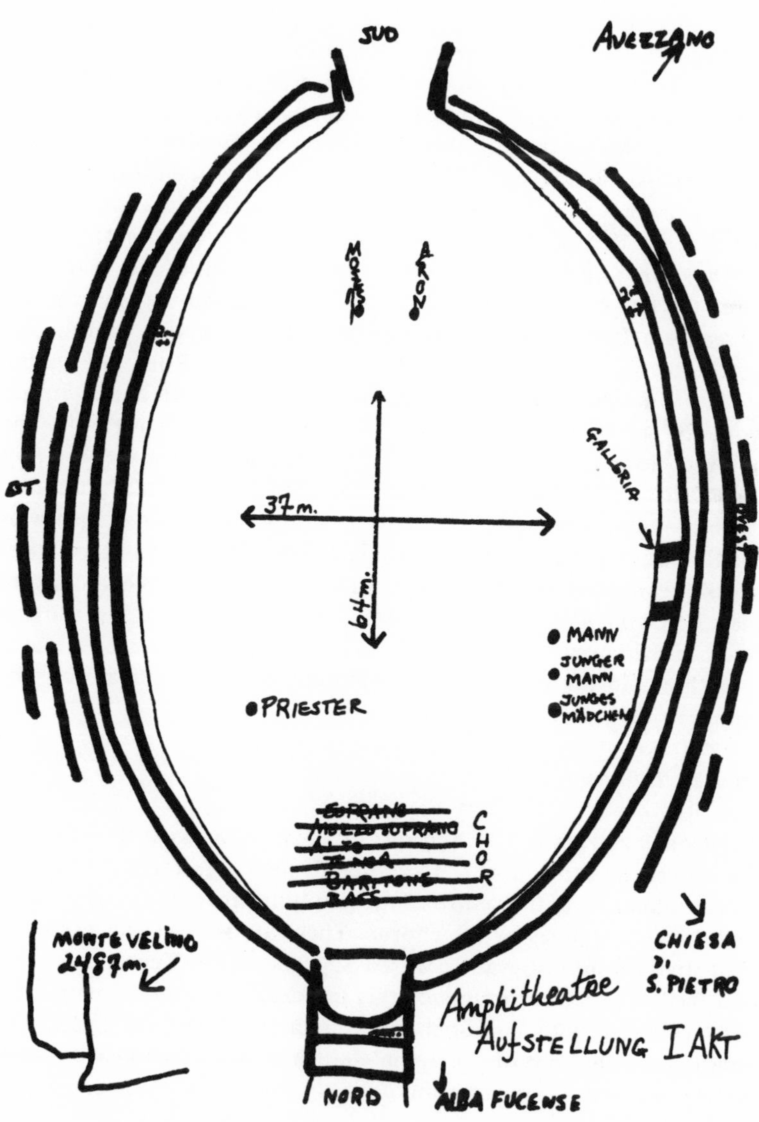

the single street up to the twelfth-century Romanesque Basilica of San Pietro. It is in this stone building, restored in 1957 after its destruction in an earthquake in 1915 which claimed the lives of hundreds of villagers, that we unpack what is to be used in the amphitheatre below. Daniele instructs us to set the props in the crypt underneath the altar, the costume crates in the sanctuary space set up for costumes and changing, and the film boxes on the steps of the marble pulpit. The church is locked and we arrange to meet in the amphitheatre after lunch.

The amphitheatre is a space 100 metres (330 ft.) by 79 metres (260 ft.) dug into the hill on top of which San Pietro, ancient site of a temple of Apollo, stands. Its oval arena measures 64 metres by 37 metres. After journeying 11,000 kilometres around Italy in 1969, the Straubs decided on this as the site they would use for filming Schoenberg's opera, 'Moses und Aron'. This was ten years after their original decision to make a film of the opera. Jean-Marie first saw 'Moses und Aron' at the Berliner Oper in 1959, two years after the first staging of the work in Zurich and eight years after the composer's death. He wired to Daniele who came from Paris to see it, and they determined to realise a film of the opera. The German *Drehbuch* (screenplay) which they made of it is dated: Berlin, end of '59—Rome, beginning of '70. When we meet in the amphitheatre in the afternoon, Straub works on setting up the main axis which will divide the arena for the opposing forces which encounter each other in the first act. We also spend time cleaning up the arena of pieces of broken glass and cigarette butts, tourism's tribute to antiquity. Georg Brintrup leaves for Rome to stay at the Straub's apartment where he will look after Misti, pregnant and hungry feline. In the evening the others return to their hotels in Avezzano. Hans-Peter Boffgen and I set up a living space in the corner of the church. We will stay here to keep a watch over things in the church and the amphitheatre at night during the month's time we will spend shooting the film here.

Sunday, 18th August

The troupe arrives at 9:30 and sets to work on marking the places of the soloists and the chorus. J.-M. stands on a *torretta* (platform) set on the main axis in the centre of the amphitheatre and has us stand in place to set the lines of the chorus. There are six rows according to their division into Soprano, Mezzo-Soprano, Alto, Tenor, Baritone, and Bass. The corner points of this trapezoid are marked with large nails wrapped with coloured masking-tape around the head. The chorus is set in front of the arena's north portal which bears a stone inscription commemorating the donation of the amphitheatre by Q.

Naevius Cordus Sutorius Macro to his native city. Macro, Pretorian Prefect under Tiberius and, therefore, predecessor in this post to the Lacus played by Jubarite Semaran in straub's *Othon,* was forced to suicide by Nero after a career of ruthless cruelty which is recounted in the 'Annals' of Tacitus. These stones lay on the ground in pieces when the Straubs first came five years ago in their film-site search for a plateau in a mountainous region. Their discovery during the course for recent excavations permit archaeologists to date the construction of this amphitheatre to the south of the then populous city of Alba Fucens *ca.* A.D. 40. Opposite the chorus in front of the south entry the positions of Moses and Aaron are nailed down. On either side of the chorus the opposing forces of the Priest and the Man, Young Man and Young Girl are set, the Priest to the east on their left and the three soloists to their right on the west hillside of the amphitheatre. We use the underground tunnel *(galleria)* under the hillside steps to store the equipment not in use, and to keep our tanks of water in the cool.

In the afternoon Louis Hochet begins to test out the sound equipment within the acoustics of the amphitheatre.

In this search we covered 11,000 km on paved and unpaved roads during five weeks, profiting from my mother's vacation and, hence, from her small Citroen. We 'discovered' Alba Fucense almost at the beginning of our trip, but as we didn't yet know exactly what we were looking for (we left with the idea of a plateau and a mountain — it was left for us to discover as the voyage went along that a plateau wasn't protected from the wind nor from the noises that rise from the valley, and that the 'theatre' action as well as the singing risked being dispersed there, and that we did indeed need a plateau, but one with a hole in it, and that this amphitheatre was not only the hole in the plateau in a mountain setting, but what's more the theatrical space which would concentrate the action instead of dispersing it, and all that in a geologically volcanic countryside. I was less enthusiastic than Jean-Marie who had already fallen in love with its magnificent shape of an ellipse and the extraordinary acoustic, for it was June 7th and it was raining in streams which bade no good for the future...From curiosity as well as from 'professional conscience' and because we hadn't in any case decided as yet to shoot the first two acts in the same place and we were therefore looking for two or three other places for the first act, the amphitheatre was at that point for the second act, we consequently continued our search for about another 10,900 km as far as Sicily. We saw other sites, in Sicily as well, but none as logical and attractive and with 'that love at first sight'. Slowly I was coming around to the idea (to film the whole thing at the same site) which Jean-Marie had had (it is always harder for me than him to break away from naturalism, and as it is already a problem for him, it takes us some time to get used to our own ideas...). On the way back (we had eliminated Sardinia for geological reasons, but also because of the distance, for to transport the technical crew, material, but, above all, singers and chorus so far to where the means of transport for return were unsure and that with people who were tied to concert dates or recording schedules in the four corners of the culture industry would have been madness) we passed once more by Alba Fucense and it was at that point that we decided definitively—for the site. The decision to film all but the third act there we took slowly during the course of the following year, gradually as we made our trips to the amphitheatre and learned to know the surrounding countryside. It was also during the course of this first trip that we 'discovered' the Lake of Matese, where we filmed the third act, and there as well, the impression made on the first glance

Monday, 19th August

The 66 members of the ORF-Chor (Austrian Radio Chorus) begin to arrive. Most of them have flown from Vienna to Rome and will arrive later today, but some have come in their cars. In the church Renata and the two other *costumiste,* Augusta and Maria Teresa, have been ironing the costumes and assembling the veils and slippers for each member. The singers try on their costumes in the dressing space that Daniele has arranged for them. In the amphitheatre Ugo Piccone, Director or Photography, works with Saverio Diamanti, cameraman, and Gianni Canfarelli, assistant cameraman on the pan the camera does tomorrow in Shot 19 so that it is out of the range of the microphones which are set above the soloists and on the ground resisted all the other lakes that we were consequently able to see, the last temptation to change having been the Lake of Campotosto, a year before filming—and even with the apprehension experienced in finding one day in August that there was practically no more water in the lake....But the idea of a lake had already been substituted for that of the sea, the idea which we had at first in writing the filmscript, above all because the sound of the waves would blur the text. We consequently gave up the idea, the lake being simpler, less charged symbolically, and more realistic geologically and geographically.

And why from the beginning had we wanted Italy? Because Schoenberg was Viennese, his music eminently European, even if there are constantly intuitions of an astonishing realism which one discovers in going to the Orient—to Africa (for us, Egypt), and so we wanted a European country which would be a bridge between Europe and Asia/Africa. Spain and Greece, out of the question. And Italy, in addition to its geology, geography, its climate, its political situation, had the advantage (?) of a cinematic industrial machine which doesn't work in its entirety, but certain of whose parts, on the condition that one has plenty of energy, bullheadedness, and time, are usable still.

Louis had already had time to test the acoustics of the amphitheatre a year beforehand, when we had had him come from Paris to see and hear our amphitheatre—for we were greatly apprehensive: having taken Renato Berta and Jeti Grigioni after the filming of *History Lessons* to Alba Fucense to have an opinion, Jet had made a very long face and seemed to think that we were crazy....The ellipse form and the stone ground as well as the large stones surrounding sent the sound back in multiple echoes. Louis asked if we would envisage filming elsewhere: 'No', we told him. 'Well then,' he said, 'we'll have to solve the difficulties as they come along. And the acoustic is so beautiful that it's worth the effort and we mustn't put in wood panelling or things of that sort for they would only augment the dangers and destroy something.' After which I don't know if he slept in peace for the following year, but in any case, we slept much better!

No; a third only arrive by plane, the other two-thirds in cars from Vienna or Salzburg, often with husband or wife. Straub and I are apprehensive, for what's more there is the returning traffic of *Ferragosto,* the mid-August feast, and the biggest Italian holiday...Sunday evening, I will make the rounds of all the hotels of Avezzano several times to check that all our group is safely arrived. All goes well, no accidents, no delays. To take this whole troupe to the amphitheatre we rented a large bus and a small bus at Avezzano, and we added one of our Ford-Transits with the seats back in place which

before the chorus. Hochet tests out the sound for the soloists and sets up the microphones with his assistant, Georges Vaglio.

There is a test run-through of Shot 18 with the three soloists.

Paolo Benvenuti drives. For we didn't want them all to come into the village with their cars, which would have frightened and upset the peasants and their animals accustomed to not seeing more than a few tourists for but a month during the year. To all the technicians who came by car, and to some singers from the chorus and Aaron, for whom we made exceptions permitting them to come by car, we made some recommendations: prudence, slow speed, look out for animals, no noise. All will go without hitches, there won't be the tiniest chicken run over, and our relations with the villagers will remain normal and calm up to our departure.

As for the costumes, we chose them from among the 3,000 costumes of this type from the house of Cantini (one of those parts of the Italian industry which functions rather better than elsewhere—on condition that one avoids the decorative traps preferred by the Italian talent, J.-M. detests to have new costumes made, we much prefer to choose among those which already exist). We carried them home, laid them out on the floor, assembled them (colours of the robes, the mantles, the veils, the shoes sorted out according to the measurement cards sent by the chorus representative, Mrs. Kapek), cleaned them up a bit, patched and ironed them. Then during our third trip to Vienna, in winter 1973, with Louis Hochet come from Paris to control with us the technical conditions in the recording studio, to discuss our requirements with the Viennese technicians, to persuade Prof. Preinfalk to make his chorus sing in six rows and not in four as had been the custom since 1934—four rows, that would have made it necessary, in order to frame it, to film in cinemascope! During this trip from Rome we carried with us five suitcases filled with the costumes of all the women in the chorus which we tried on in Vienna, pinning up the adjustments to be made, changing the colours or the material when they weren't right. Having taken them back to Rome, I do a part of the adjustments myself (those which I know will be poorly done or not at all by the house that rents the costumes), then we return the costumes so that they can be cleaned, etc. When we go to Vienna for the rehearsals and the recording of the music in March we carry along a second load, heavier still; all the men's costumes for the same procedure. Meanwhile, we had either carried a choice of possible costumes to the soloists during our rehearsals with them (Moses, Aaron, Man, Young Man), or taken advantage of their arrival in Rome for a concert (Priest, Young Girl) to have them try on their costumes. This will permit the costume seamstresses to make all the final preparations in a half day the day before shooting.

Shot 19 and Shot 22 are those which fix *les regles du jeu,* those from which will flow all the other shots and the framing of the first act: whence the necessity to fix exactly the places of the protagonists

(chorus, group of three—Young Girl, Young Man, Man—the Priest, and, finally, Moses and Aaron) in relation to the centre of the ellipse, each group in relation to the other, each soloist in relation to his neighbour or neighbors in the cases of Moses and Aaron or of the three youths: the Young Girl must be far enough away at the same time from the chorus and from the Young Man, her neighbour, so that it be possible in Shot 22 with a lens-objective of 50 to film her first alone, without having the arm of her neighbour or the nose of a chorister of the extreme left in the field. But she must also be close enough to her neighbour, the Young Man, and he to his neighbour, the Man, so that it be possible in Shot 19 to have all three of them together in the field with a 40; but also with this 50 lens, in the case of Shot 22 or the 40, in the case of Shot 19, one should be able to 'trap' the entire chorus when one pans on it, and not only the entire group, but even the air or the ground about them, for Jean-Marie never wants to 'cut out' the group, rather to film it with some space above and below, to the left and to the right. Likewise, the position of the Priest had to be such that one might frame him without having the nose of a chorister in the field, but also such that it be logical in its distance from the other groups. Finally one had to find the proper heights for the different framings on the chorus, and imagine the variations on the same axis, since we will not jump this axis until Shot 31 passing on to the left profile of the priest (whom we have up to then always seen in profile) when he revolts: 'Thy staff compels us, yet it does not compel Pharaoh to let us free!', to stay on this other side of the axis up to the end of the first act. As well, for Shot 22, we had to find and fix the proper distance, at the same time, to the chorus for the end of Shot 24 and of the two partners between themselves for this Shot 24 but also for all the other shots where we will only see one of the two partners. This proper distance having to be at the same time right for the staging of the action (theatrical), for the confrontations or for the complicity, and at the least, for the psychology of the actors between each other. Finally, last problem for us to be resolved from the beginning (since afterwards, the rules of the game laid down, we could no longer escape them except by the rules of a game of chequers, so that we did not break them, as much as for economic reasons—not to keep the chorus there all the time of the shooting, but to group together the shots of the chorus, then those of the soloists, to end up without singers—Jean-Marie couldn't shoot 'in order', which made the acrobatics still more break-neck) was the problem of the conductor, of Gielen, who had to conduct the chorus and the soloists, hence be seen by them in the best conditions, evidently not be in the field of the shot, even in the case of a pan which in the end covers 300 degrees of the ellipse as in Shot 24, and be in relation to the camera in such a

When this is finished, Gianni packs the parts of the camera into their cases and the three Pisan *macchinisti* (propment), Cecco, Nanni, and Ninni, drive it to the small hotel in the village where they sleep and where they store the Mitchell after work. The Golden Calf, Guistiniano, as the Straubs call him, is also stored there until we start shooting the second act orgy scene.

Tuesday, 20th August **Shot 19,20**

The first day of shooting. The whole ORF chorus arrives at the church by 8:30 with cars and a chartered bus from Avezzano. When they have changed into costume, there is a general rehearsal of today's music in the resonant hollow of the bare stone church. Dr. Preinfalk, the chorus director, tunes them up with scales on the piano that the Straubs have had shipped here from Rome. Afterwards, they make their way downhill to the amphitheatre. In the meantime the Straubs are setting up for Shot 19. The Mitchell is set up at the height of three platform levels on a *toretta* to the left of centre. When the chorus comes down, and the mikes are set up, Danièle sends the assistants to the posts which we are to keep during the shooting time for the filming in the amphitheatre. Paolo Benvenuti stands out on the roadway entrance to Alba Fucense to stop traffic from disturbing the recording. Sebastian Schadhauser stands at the entry to the dirt road that leads up to the church and to the amphitheatre from the *paese*. They are both in communication with Danièle by means of walkie-talkies. At the north entrance to the amphitheatre stand Leo Mingrone and Gabriele Soncini and on the south Hans-Peter Boffgen. My post is 50 metres above on the hilltop of the amphitheatre overlooking the shooting. Our main job during the shooting is to guard that outsiders horizontal *and* vertical (height) position that the singers (chorus or soloists) look at him without having the regard which they should have for the group with which they are in contact be 'false' but rather only slightly diverted, so that one feels a third pole, but that it only be felt, so that this distraction doesn't kill the dramatic relationships also. For this reason we played surveyor, dividing the terrain, marking the centre, measuring the heights, from Sunday, two days before the 'real' beginning of the shooting. All this work rebounding consequently upon that of the sound engineers who had, in their turn, to solve their problems or present them to us when they couldn't solve them alone—which happened rarely....

Nini and not Ninni—for Gainfranco = Gianni = Nini, Nanni for Alvaro *Nanni*cini, Cecco for Francesco.

Giustiniano: we had named him so in Paris when we had been there in October '73 with the Ford-Transit, on loan (already!) from the Florentines to that Pisan of a Benvenuti, to get it from the moulding workshop of the Louvre (where, incidentally, the worker/artisans are almost all Italians!) and to carry it to Cinecitta and have it covered with gold leaf: struck on seeing it no longer in granite as in the Louvre, but reproduced in plaster, by its resemblance to the small bull of *The General Line*. But, said we, it isn't *The General Line*, but *the just line*, and so we named it Justinian—Giustiniano.

don't upset the activity on set as it requires the uninterrupted concentration amongst the Straubs, the crew and the musicians. When everyone is in place Jean-Marie calls out for 'Silence' and *absolute Ruhe.* Previous to this the sound-men have adjusted the sound-level in the tiny earphones that transmit the orchestral score for the shot to the four soloists and to Michael Gielen, the conductor, who stands on a platform before the musicians, but out of the sweep of the camera pan, with the score before him, one ear in the headphones for the recorded orchestral part and one free for the singers. During the recording session in Vienna in April and May two sets of tapes were made. One complete recording of the opera which is to be released by Philips later in the year, and one of the orchestra without the singers for the recording during the film. The music is divided into the measures *(Takte)* which constitute each shot.

The tapes that Hochet is using in his sound truck begin with three beeps at the beginning of the music. On them the orchestral part of the opera is transmitted to the soloists and the chorus which has a low frequency speaker set in its midst. Beside the sound truck sit Jeti Grigioni with the Nagra recorder that now tapes the voices of the singers, and Bernard Rubenstein, the assistant conductor, with the score before him to check the reading of the voices that are being recorded live in his earphones against the notes written in the music score. In this shot the camera pans left from MLS (medium long shot or the German *Halbtotale)* on the Priest to the three soloists, MLS, opposite him past the chorus and then, right, back on the chorus, MLS which stands between them. After further adjustments of the sound-level the shooting begins. It is an intensely hot sun. Some of the members of the chorus feel sick. Between the takes they go into the shade underneath the north portal. J.-M. wants to be sure to have at least two good takes and one usable spare before the shot is *gestorben* (killed). After each take, *ripresa,* is done Danièle writes down the length in feet of the shot which is recorded on the Mitchell, the objective of the lens used, and the notation B *(buono)* for good, R *(riserva)* for usable spare, and S *(scarta)* for incomplete or unusable take. After nine *ciak* (clappers) Straub is satisfied.

This whole explanation of the recording is, I find, not very clear, and at times even, quite frankly, wrong. Let's see if I can do better:

(a) the chorus of the Vienna radio had rehearsed all the choral parts of the opera for four months with its director Prof. Preinfalk in the disposition and formation decided by us and which it would have for the film; each one on his own account, the soloists did likewise; we had worked with Gielen, with Aaron and Gielen, and alone with Aaron, with Moses for the third act—each time making the trip, either to Brussels for Aaron and Gielen, or to Austria for Gielen and Aaron, or to Stuttgart for Moses;

(b) from March 29th '74 to Easter, two weeks, we are in Vienna where we are present at the rehearsals of the orchestra with Gielen, Keuchnig (a conductor of Vienna who helps to prepare the orchestra), and the 'official' assistant, Bernard Rubenstein, expressly come from Illinois. The week before Easter Louis Hochet arrives: we prepare with him the material which afterwards will be used in the transposal. There are the first rehearsals of the complete chorus and orchestra together. Louis begins to be able to judge the difficulty of the music which until then, he had only heard in bits from the record by Rosbaud which we had made him hear. Together we spend the Easter days at the house of Gielen on the Mondsee (lake of the moon!), and look over the latest problems...

From Easter Tuesday until mid-May, rehearsals and recording, block by block—each 'block' corresponding to a shot of the film, from measure *x* to measure *y*, or even from one note of music in such measure to another note—of all the blocks, that is, of all the shots, that is, of the whole score. Working difficulty: the chorus, which is not composed of 'singing professionals', but of people who have a job and sing 'extra' in the chorus, from personal interest and in certain cases to earn some extra money, above their salaries, can only sing after 5 p.m. This meant that we had to establish a work plan where all the blocks including the chorus would be recorded in the evening, and in the morning all those without the chorus, with the orchestra alone or with the soloists (which, for the soloists who didn't like to sing in the morning, did not proceed unproblematically!).

Each block had to be recorded twice: a first time, orchestra and singers together, normally; then a second time, only the orchestra, *without* the singers, which was very difficult for the musicians and for Gielen, not having the support of the singers. This second recording, dry, without echo, and mono, made on a 4-track machine, was re-recorded by Louis each afternoon, during the pause after the morning recording session and before the one at 5.30, on narrow tapes simultaneously on two synchronised Nagra IVs, with three *mille* (beep-beep-beep) at the beginning of each block.

In certain cases there was a first mixing with Gielen who was there anyway at each 'transposing' session, for him to check his work while listening to it with a measure of distance. These two synchronised Nagras were 'piloted', 'piloting' being an electrical system, equivalent to the perforations of the magnetic tapes of 35mm (or 16 mm!), which permits having an invariable length each time one re-records the sound—hence a definitive length and a guaranteed synchronisation;

(c) during the shooting, in August-September '74, Louis had two Nagras in his sound truck: one stereo Nagra IV—that is, with two tracks on one tape which permitted him to record, for example, the chorus on one track and the soloists on the other, or one soloist on one track and the soloists on the other, and so to have later, at the definitive mixing, a supplementary possibility to equilibrate the voices. This stereo Nagra normally started first, as for every film where one takes the sound live: then the camera started, the clapper-board was done which gave the synchronous sign between the image and the live sound recorded at the same time by the camera and the stereo Nagra; then Louis made the second Nagra in his sound truck start, a Nagra III (the one used for recording the *Chronicle* in Germany!) on which passed one of the two tapes which he had transposed in Vienna and piloted the orchestra alone which corresponded to the shot which we were rolling. (The other tape, exactly identical to this one, made at the same time in Vienna, we jealously guarded in our hotel room in Avezzano and, brand new, was the one which we transposed afterwards on to the perforated 35 mm magnetic tape to be used in montage.) Thus, it sent the orchestra block corresponding to the shot we were filming, preceded by the three beeps which carried on to the tape which was turning on the stereo Nagra: these three beeps were the synchronising signal between the two sound tapes. To prevent the orchestra from being carried over on to the stereo Nagra tape, Louis switched

Saverio then takes the *provino* for publicity stills. We break for lunch at one.

The chorus is sunburnt and ill-humored. There are loud voices in German and Italian to be heard during the confusion of distributing the *cestino* (package lunch) to the choristers after their morning under the sun. In the afternoon clouds come up interrupting the shooting of Shot 22 with the short summer rainshower called a *temporale*. The camera starts on the Young Girl who sings: 'He will free us!', pans right on the chorus, LS/MLS, 'See Moses and Aaron!', and then at the end pans fast to the right around to the south on Moses and Aaron, LS/MLS, opposite the chorus, whose arrival the chorus has described. Straub cuts after 13 takes, but more will have to be done tomorrow.

it off immediately after the third beep; he missed his mark but once out of about a thousand! It is this tape of the Nagra III, evidently, which the soloists heard by means of a receiver hidden in one of their ears (the other ear for them to hear themselves to be able to sing), the chorus heard by means of a small speaker (two, in some cases) hidden in their midst or out of the frame on the edge of the field, and Gielen by means of a headphone which covered both his ears, preventing him from hearing what those he was conducting were singing.

Finally, outside the truck, a third Nagra, Jeti's Nagra IV, recorded the two tapes of the orchestra and the live sound (the singers and the other noises) retransmitted from the Nagra III and the stereo Nagra and roughly mixed to permit a judgement, mainly about the synchronism of the singers with the orchestra. This was the mixing which Bernard Rubenstein, Gielen's assistant listened to with his headphones; in uncertain cases, Gielen could listen to this mixing over immediately and judge for himself, to make corrections, if need be. In the evening, at the hotel, from after dinner often until midnight, we listened to the day's takes, Gielen, Straub, Jeti and I (sometimes with a singer not already sleeping...) on this Nagra to check for a last time, the choices 'still warm' made after shooting. In addition, every day after each shot, I listened with Louis in his truck to the takes kept of the live sound to check them and be sure that there hadn't been any unnoticed accidents which perhaps might not have been heard in the evening on Jeti's 'mixed' tape.

A *provino* is a metre, a metre-and-a-half of film taken after a shot which is judged to be good, with the clapper-board on which *provino* is written in the frame, which the laboratory uses to test the density of the negative before developing it, and later to make samples of before printing the take. It has nothing to do with *Standphotos* or publicity stills. During the shooting we only allow work photos to be made; the stills of the film we have made from photograms taken from the discarded takes or from bits of the montage negative from the beginning or the end of a shot, once the montage negative is finished with and the first copy printed.

Wednesday, 21st August **Shot 22,21,23**

In the morning, takes 13-27 of Shot 22. At midday we shoot Shot 21, frontal long shot on the chorus: 'a lovable God!'. Eleven takes. Another explosion at the *cestino* about the distribution of the food. Paolo decides to let the musicians take care of it themselves in the church, while the crew will eat down in the amphitheatre. 2.15, Shot 23, another frontal long shot, high-angle view, on the chorus: 'Do you bring hearing, message of the new God?'. During a pause, while Saverio and Gianni check the camera for dust and hairs, *controllare la macchina,* which J.-M. has them do at the end of every reel, the chorus sits together in the shade underneath the archway of the north portal and sings Austrian Landler to relax from singing Schoenberg's complicated music before filming equipment in the blaze of the sun. Finished after 6 takes. The assistants return from their posts and store the equipment in the trucks and in the *galleria.* The chorus changes out of costume up at the church and leaves at five.

Thursday, 22nd August **Shot 20, 24**

7.50 a.m. Daniele arrives at San Pietro. The first Shot, 20, is without chorus, so she wants the whole chorus to stay inside the church until it is done so that they won't make any noise to interfere with the recording. The camera is set in high-angle view on a three storey *toretta,*

From experience we know that the first three days of shooting are always difficult: people who don't know each other having to get used to working together. From experience, we also know that the difficulties or ill-humour disappear quickly. In fact, after the fourth day the relations with the chorus got better, despite differences of language, and they all made a great effort to do their part in a job of work that was hard for everybody; many came to tell us how sorry they were to leave and how interesting they had found the work; the chorus took up a collection to give a sum of money to the costume ladies and the hairdresser, who they had treated poorly the first two days, as a going-away present. Our only lasting problem was that of the 'comfort stations': the trailer toilet, aside from the fact that it costs a great deal to rent, and that it is absurd, is a solution, perhaps, for a star or two. But for a hundred people it is completely useless and unusable! The technicians, the soloists and their families, Gielen, Bernard took care of their problems without speaking to us about them; as for the chorus members I had made an agreement with the farmers next to the church to let the emergency cases come there, against a remuneration...Unfortunately, on the first two days, our scarcely organised choristers, hardly out of the buses which took them to the church, headed *en masse,* men and women, for the farmer's—who closed his door on the third day to everyone and did not accept, except on my pressing insistence, to revoke his decision and then only for feminine necessities. Prof. Preinfalk suggested to me 'to do as we did in the *Wehrmacht* and tell the three propmen to dig trenches, one for the men and one for the women, surrounded by branches'. This proposal which I went to propose to the three Pisans to ask their advice provoked a mad outburst of laughter—until Cecco had an idea of genius: the whole zone being 'registered' and under the protection of the Ministry of Fine Arts, it wasn't permitted for us to dig holes there! I let two days go by and went to relay the message to Prof. Preinfalk and his wife. It was repeated to the choristers, taken absolutely for serious, and there wasn't in consequence the least allusion to the subject, everyone, it seems, having taken care of this general problem individually.

MCS/MLS on the Priest. Then it pans right around the empty arena to the Man, Young Man, and Young Girl, MLS, who sing in excited expectation of the 'adorable God' that Moses is bringing. 25 takes.

The chorus comes down at noon. We set up the circular tracks in a semi-circle in front of Moses And Aaron for Shot 24. This is the entry of Moses and Aaron before the people. Moses, Gunter Reich, speaks in the *Sprechstimme* (spoken voice) which Schoenberg devised for his part, announcing 'The Unique, Eternal, Almighty, Omnipresent, Invisible...', until Aaron, Louis Devos, interrupts him, singing 'He has chosen you before all peoples'. Thus Schoenberg indicates at their very arrival the unreconcilable difference of understanding between the prophet of the inexpressible Idea and the Minister of the graspable Word. While the camera is on the two protagonists the music that the chorus sings is not recorded now. They will use the tapes already done in Vienna for most of the parts that are 'off'. At the end the chorus sings being taken live after the camera pans to it: 'Then are we all lost, for we see him not! Ha ha ha ha!'. After the lunch-break at 2.30 the weather becomes overcast and rainy. So we must wait for a while to recommence. After 3.30 it begins to clear and the sun is out for the last hour of shooting. 12 takes. After the chorus leaves J.-M. starts planning for Shot 31 on the Priest. He leaves with the crew at seven.

The first twelve days of shooting were hard for the technicians. I had explained to each of them that we had to shoot without a day off all the time we had the chorus, for, if it were to begin to rain (it happens often in Italy that in mid-August the weather is spoiled by storms, and one must wait until September for it to change; and in this mountain region, when it rains, it is often several days in a row without interruption, unlike in Rome, where there are bad turns that don't last; we couldn't set the shooting for July which is the surest month, for the chorus wasn't free: concerts at Salzburg, etc.; and 1974 was an exceptionally dry year, not a drop of rain since the start of May! If the rain began, then it might well last for several weeks...) and we were unable to shoot for one or two weeks while the chorus was there, which represented an expense of 30,000 marks a day, we would have to interrupt the film...and interrupting meant never being able to finish it, for, even if we (by what miracle?) found the money to finish it later, the singers and Gielen were engaged for 1,2,3 years...concerts in the four corners of the earth, opera, radio, records: the culture industry is one of the most flourishing in capitalist society. So it was absolutely necessary not to lose a day while the weather permitted us to go on and shoot with the chorus. All the technicians had agreed to shooting without a day off for the first 12 days and to recoup the missing day off later, when the chorus would have left. But the fatigue, after the first eight days, began to make itself felt and everyone

Friday, 23rd August **Shot 30,25,31**

Shot 30. 'A wonder fills us with terror'. The camera, at eye-level, to the left of centre MLS on the chorus pans left to the three soloists, MLS, and up to the Bush as the Voice is heard 'off'. J.-M. tells me to move back out of view as my post stands just above this part of the hillside. Eleven takes.

At eleven we set the camera on a *toretta* in high-angle view LS on the chorus for Shot 25: 'Stay far from us with thy God, with the Almighty!' The conductor, Michael Gielen, explained to me that it was musically too diffcult a chorus to put at the end of Shot 24 as it was in the original screenplay decoupage, since even without it Shot 24 is nearly five minutes long. So J.-M. stopped after measure 565 in the score and made measures 566-620 a separate shot. The weather becomes bad, so after ten takes we break for lunch and then do six more at three.

Shot 31 in light high-angle view CS on the Priest, in right profile. Cecco holds a board of white polystyrene against his face to reflect more of the fading afternoon light. Werner Mann, majestic in his black and white sacerdotal robes, cautions the chorus against the enthusiasm of the soloists, after the miracle of the serpent: 'Thy staff compels us, yet it does not compel Pharaoh to let us free!' Afterwards, when we come down after the shot is killed, J.-M. prepares for tomorrow's Shots. Gabriele and I stand in place for Moses and Aaron. The Straubs drive with today's material to the studios of Luciano Vittori in Rome to see the rushes of the film that Gabriélè has already brought there during the week.

Saturday, 24th August **Shot 36,37**

8 a.m. Daniele arrives at the church while J.-M. has gone down to the amphitheatre. She says the rushes were fairly good but there were some calcium deposits on the prints which were screened. We carry some props down to the amphitheatre where J.-M. is to be seen picking up cigarette butts. He wears a white sun-hat he bought when in Egypt in May to film the two shots of the Nile which will end Act I. After helping Renata get Reich and Devos into costume in the church, I go to my post 30 metres away. Shot 36. The camera pans left from LS/MLS on the chorus past the three soloists to Moses and Aaron, who shows Moses' healthy hand. There are many test takes for the

became more nervous, especially on the days of big heat! But everyone held up: Gielen, who was very afraid of the shooting, for technical reasons (no one had yet attempted what he did, with a music so difficult, and which has not yet entered into our cultural habits) but also for psychological ones, recounted in the end, his wife Helga told us, that these three weeks had been the happiest of his life, that he had discovered collective work...

We had been to Egypt once before, Christmas 1972, Jean-Marie and I, alone, without camera or photographic equipment...Roland Delcour, whom Jean-Marie had known as correspondent of 'Le Monde' at Bonn, was at that time in Cairo, and we had been invited to sound. There is always a general sound run-through of the music before the actual filming. Today it takes several to get the tone in Aaron's earphones neither too loud nor too weak. By fixing the positions of the different groups set against each other in the first act, Straub has underlined the formal, agonal quality, at once primitive and classical, of Attic drama. Here the only moving part is the eye of the camera. This fixed quality on the set is in total contrast to the constant mutability of the weather. The light can change every half hour here. It will be interesting to see how this human immobility in contrast to the constant flux of nature reflects in the film.

visit him. We stayed in Egypt for three weeks, half the time in Cairo, the other half travelling through the Egyptian countryside in train, by boat, in plane, by car, and on bike all along the Nile from Cairo to Alexandria to see the delta, and from Cairo to Aswan passing by Luxor. It was then that we fixed on the sites that we wanted to film (the single shot planned for in the filmscript then transforming itself into two shots), and that we made friends at Luxor with the young peasant, who later, when we did the shooting, went with us on the mountain to the site which we had chosen, allowing us to escape the curiosity seekers...We wanted not only to find the site (sites!) where to film our shots but also to see how the people live, the objects, the gestures, the costumes—to bring back the objects which were indispensable for us and which we knew, rented in Rome from 'specialists', would be of a striking ugliness and falsity; the earthenware jar from which Aaron pours the water and the blood we bought from a temple guardian. He asked us 250 liras for it, just what it cost him to buy a new one! In English, the only language which permits one to communicate a little if, as a good European, one doesn't speak a word of Arabic, we told him, giving him 400 liras, that it was a souvenir from us to him, this small bit of extra money. He explained to us that his jar was good, that it held water well, which was true, as we had observed beforehand. For hours afterwards Jean-Marie had scruples asking himself if the man would find one as good, if it was good to have taken it from him....A peasant of Luxor sold us the saddle of a dromedary for 10,000 liras, all that was left, since he had had to sell the dromedary some months earlier, and didn't know if one day he would have the money to buy another. There our Egyptian friend helped us, for he knew a little French from having worked on the digs of the French archaeologists (who, at Luxor, as at Alba Fucense, except that here the archaeologists are Belgians and the peasants are ItalianS, hire peasants for one or two months to dig and unearth; when the archaeologists don't come, there as well as here—here 30,000 people leave the Abruzzi each year to go in search of work to the north or in foreign countries—it is a catastrophe, for it is the disappearance of a source of ready money, this ready money being almost as rare for the peasants of Alba Fucense as for those of Luxor); he also helped by taking us to the artisans who shaped and polished, by hand, the alabaster cups which we brought back and used for the wine, in the night, poured from the goat-skin (Shot 62) and for the blood of the virgins (Shot 64). (A German music critic who, let us hope, hears better than he sees, thought, when the priest pours the blood from a cup of white alabaster into the hole of the altar, he saw a plastic basin....) From a merchant water-salesman of Cairo we bought the black goatskins for 2,000 liras, with, there again, an uneasy conscience, for if for

him it was a lot of ready money at the moment, what was he then to do to sell his water with only the two skins he had left? Even there we would have given up buying them from him, resigning ourselves to having them made new in Italy, if we hadn't seen that in refusing to buy them from him after he got the impression that we were interested in them, his disappointment was too great... We took the two oldest ones leaving him the newer ones. He must have thought that we really didn't understand a thing about it!

The kindness of the Egyptians (those whom we saw, for we met no bourgeois: the Egyptian bourgeois, even 'friends' of the Delcours, no longer came to see them for fear of being compromised, and it isn't by going around the streets of Cairo on foot, where everyone who is not poor travels by taxi, that one sees the middle-class!) is immense, even in the wretched neighbourhoods of Cairo where no European ever goes—except just passing through in a cab!—where they would have every reason to be hostile to us quite simply because neither Jean-Marie nor I had the pallor of centuries of undernourishment. But this kindness hit us still harder for the discovery, arriving at Cairo by plane, of a city almost like the Calcutta which we had seen in the only film of Louis Malle which ever interested us. In the country the poverty is often extreme, it is visible because the people are so worn out and tired that they don't take the slightest care of their animals, but, despite the disease bilharzia, despite the harvests, one after another without respite, profiting not those who make them but their exploiters, there is still the appearance of equilibrium of an agrarian civilisation (the people who go into town in the morning at dawn to sell vegetables, fruits, animals, the husbandry of the riverside, the artisans' ingenuity, the complement of the weariness due to undernourishment which is a calm, a slowness, a tempo of living which are also, in spite of everything, riches which we have forgotten); in Cairo on the contrary, with its seven million inhabitants ceaselessly increasing, there is the misery of the city, desperate even if one tells oneself that it is there that revolt foments. After this first trip, what we hadn't as yet clearly decided about was clear: we wouldn't go to Israel after having been in Egypt.

In May 1973 we returned with Ciccio (Renato Berta) and a 16 mm Beaulieu camera and some Kodak reversible film to make our two shots—under cover, for we couldn't demand authorisation saying it was for *Moses and Aaron,* and we didn't want to lie. Everything went without obstacles, except that Jean-Marie, who had cut his finger on a snow-plough when we had run into a snow-storm at Campotosto in the beginning of May as we were going to see the lake again to take the definitive decision to shoot not at Compotosto, but at Matese, was travelling by bicycle on the roads of Luxor with his left hand in the air

During lunch Basti reports that a man came this morning to announce that the amphitheatre was his property. The Straubs have a permit to use the amphitheatre from the Sopraintendenza alle Antichita e Belli Arti di Abruzzo-Molise which has supervised the recent reconstructions here. This will not be the first time they will have to do with an expropriated *padrone*, as they had to deal similarly with the owners of the Villa Pamphilij in Rome for shooting the fourth act of *Othon*. We discuss the matter, but decide the work at hand is more interesting.

to stop the pain caused by the rush of blood to his finger's wound and under an already well-heated sun while he was stuffed with antibiotics, with Ciccio, his wife Ombretta, and me behind him in case he should collapse, for the Italian doctors had told us that it was very dangerous to go into the sun with antibiotics in the body(?); and also, except for the fact that the same Ciccio who persisted, despite our advice, and as a good Swiss unaware of why the locals covered themselves from head to foot, in doing the shot in the mountain of Luxor, for three hours (we did it over a dozen times, for the movement with an amateur camera tripod, was very difficult, as well as the speed), with naked chest, took so much sun that the following night he slept nude because of the heat and caught some kind of bronchial pneumonia: the three days in Cairo on return, while Ombretta visited the city, he spent in bed at the hotel, was sick in the plane and didn't feel better until setting foot in Rome!

I will go with Leo within a few days to see the said proprietor who is in fact a woman, the man who came being her major-domo: she did not pretend to have ownership of the amphitheatre, having in fact been expropriated by the Ministry of Fine Arts, but of the pathway that leads down to the amphitheatre, single entryway, the only one connecting the road to the church. After discussing the matter, explaining that we aren't the Americans (Huston had shot the exteriors of his *Bible* at some 100 km from there, on the other incline of the Abruzzi, and the rumour must have spread that one could get some money out of it, once a film was being shot) but that given that actually we do use this pathway to have the sound truck, Gabriélè's car, the camera truck and one or two private cars pass through, we are prepared to make remuneration, on condition that it be reasonable....We make an agreement for 60,000 liras in two payments, one right away of 30,000 liras, and the second at the end of shooting. No one otherwise tried to blackmail us, except the curate of the church which we use for the costumes, the material, etc., and where Gregory or Hans-Peter sleep. This one at first claimed that the fact of not being able to celebrate marriages in his church (which is not the village church, but a 'classified' monument, where the rich or snobbish come to get married from time to time) for a period of 5

Shot 37 at first CS on Aaron, the camera pans left by Moses and by the Priest onto the chorus in a long shot. 'Through Aaron Moses lets us see, how he himself has beheld his God.' From its position south of centre by Moses and Aaron the pan of the camera takes in the very top of the storage shack standing outside the amphitheatre in the direction of Monte Velino, so we cover the roof over with bits of shrubbery. The weather changes from cloudy to rainy and then starts to clear up. After five the chorus gets impatient to finish. The 24th take is good, so we wrap it up. With the feet and inches tapes measure from the Mitchell, 'West Hollywood', we take the outline of the chorus position and mark it out in the centre of the arena before the *toretta* for Shot 48. At night it is very tranquil here. There is a clear silver light, even without the moon which makes dark blue silhouettes. The Ursa Major (Big Dipper), Leopardi's 'Vaghe stelle dell' Orsa', is set just above the outline of Monte Velino as if about to dip on its snowless peak some of the Milky Way.

weeks was making him lose 300,000 liras....Jean-Marie and I went to see him: he ended up admitting to us that it certainly wasn't that much, but that he had bought a small house for his family (his sister and brother-in-law and their numerous children) and that he, having to pay by instalments, figured that a film..., that if he was paid 300,000 liras as a lump sum that would cut down the payments by that much! We made a settlement for 100,000 liras then again in two payments, one at the beginning and one at the end of shooting. For the permit to shoot in the amphitheatre, the Fine Arts Ministry of Chieti was quite correct, thanks to a young intendant who has since been named to Perugia: no complications, free authorisation, because, as he said to us, 'in a democracy these sites should be freely at the service of the public, under the sole condition that there be no deterioration to them'.

On the other hand, the Superintendence of Monuments of Aquila was—sole exception—most incorrect: We had had authorisation to use the church by means of a 'rental fee' of 50,000 liras and a 'deposit' of 100,000 which was to be returned to us after the shooting. In addition, we gave 10,000 liras to the old woman, the church guardian, when we returned the keys after shooting was over. When we asked for our deposit back, after having checked, Straub and I, that nothing, absolutely nothing had been damaged in the church, and ourselves conscientiously cleaned the church from top to bottom so that the old woman would not have to do it, the Superintendence refused to return our deposit on the pretext of damages which were, evidently, never enumerated to us. We let it drop, being too busy, with the film finished, with other problems, but I still wonder today what *maffiosa* operation is behind it and especially, why this dishonesty and these lies for a sum so small!

Shot 18. The opening of the third section of the first act. The title, white on blackfilm, 'Moses and Aaron announce to the people the message of God' is Shot 17, measures 244 to 252. The Young Girl, Eva Csapo, the Young Man, Roger Lucas, and the other Man, Richard Salter, recount the passage of Aaron on his way to meet Moses in the desert. The camera in a light low-angle view is medium close shot on Eva and pans left from her to Roger and then to Richard. This is their last Shot to be sung and the first in which they appear in the opera. Eva and Richard are finished after this, and Roger comes back in a week to sing in Shot 60. It is very hot and the flies cause a problem for the microphones and keep flying around Eva. Daniele tries using some insect repellent. They do 26 takes.

The chorus, mute and looking ahead, stands in place for Shot 33 while Aaron works the miracle of Moses' leprous hand. The camera in light high-angle view takes them in a medium long shot from the left. During the lunch break we set the camera on the top of a three-storey *toretta.* In Shot 48, the only appearance of the chorus in the second act, the chorus stands below, south of the *toretta* within the lines we marked off yesterday. In this sharp high-angle view, compactly filled with the angry *Volk,* the chorus moves its gaze from Aaron on its left, ahead to the Elders: 'Slaughter them, burn them, the priests of this false God!' This is the last shot of the chorus as a whole. Louis Hochet sets up the microphones in the direction of the south entry and J.-M. takes the chorus out and has them walk into the amphitheatre to record the sounds of their entry, for the 'Noise from the distance, quickly closer' at the end of Shot 45. They march in three times. With that the shooting schedule with the chorus is completed, J.-M. thanks them and bids them farewell until the radio concert of the Opera which is to be performed in Salzburg on the 21st of October.

Then we take the camera down and set it in low-angle view, close up for a 3/4 profile of the Priest. Shot 38. The chorus off calls for freedom and he bursts forth in admonishment: 'Madmen! Whereof shall the desert nourish you?' After this J.-M. sets up the tracks for a tracking in on Aaron in Shot 39. I stand in place for Aaron while J.-M. discusses the camera angle and lens objective with Ugo and Saverio. He wants to start with Moses and Aaron cut *americano* (3/4) and track to a close shot of Aaron and then have Aaron walk out of the frame to the left for the miracle of the Nile water turned into blood.

After packing up, we leave Hans-Peter at the church and I go into Avezzano to eat with Leo. Jean-Marie and Daniele come to the restaurant and eat with us. Daniéle is busy filling out the pay vouchers that the crew is paid for daily expenses every ten days. J.-M. explains

Before the start of shooting, Paolo had had a man with a blowing machine come to spread, it seems, anti-fly insecticide, which the communes sometimes rent. But Straub refuses to have this operation repeated, as he considers it too dangerous: these insecticides, he says, are a violent poison, the animals could come to eat the grass on the sides of the amphitheatre and that passes into their milk, etc. I side with his opinion: so we will combat the flies with a product that campers use, which we apply delicately with a paper napkin on the actor's faces and on the stem or the surface of the mikes...

some aspects of financing the film through agreements with the Austrian ORF for the musicians and the participation of the German, French, and Italian television. Most of the people in the restaurant are working on the film and there is a general feeling of relief to have finished with this first stage of the filming. **The beauty of watching the film being made is seeing it as a documentary on the fifteen years of work and preparation that have brought the Straubs to the simplicity of a well-informed concept in each Shot where everything has already been planned, recorded, and rehearsed, thus leaving the act of filming itself free to be a document on the work that has preceded it.**
Letter of Schoenberg to Alban Berg, 8th August 1931:
Peculiarly enough I work in the very same manner: the text is only during the composition definitively finished, even sometimes only afterwards. This proves itself extraordinarily. Naturally, and you have surely done it as well, it is only possible, when one has before all else a very exact conception, and the artistry consists indeed there, not only to keep this vision constantly alive, but rather by the working out of the details still to reinforce, enrich, and expand it!

Monday, 26th August **Shot 39,40**

We spend the whole morning on Shot 39. Moses responds to the Priest: 'In the desert the purity of thought will nourish you...' and then Aaron interrupts him changing his words into the enchantment of wonder. The camera MCS on them tracks to CS on Aaron who stands in the foreground against the south entry and at the end walks left out of the frame. The shot is *gestorben* at one.

Shot 40. The Nile water turned into blood. CS on the jug and on Aaron's hands from his left side. Everything is rehearsed thoroughly before the blood, which Paolo has brought from a local slaughter-house, is actually put in the jug. Aaron takes a forceful grip of the handle and inclines it down at the word 'blood' till it flows out. He sings: 'No, you are not mistaken: what you now see is blood!' Meantime the weather has become grey and rainy. After two takes Aaron changes position to another place and the camera is set up again as the ground was already blood-stained below him. Gunter Reich, who is now free, comes up to my post and we talk while they are setting up again. He has a pleasant British manner in English. Born in Silesia, he had to leave because of the Nazis, so he grew up in Israel. He started out singing as a tenor, but when he came to Germany to study, his teacher opened his voice to bass-baritone. He sings with the Stuttgart opera. I asked him how he feels about having a role where he only sings seven measures in the whole opera (Shot 16) against the extraordinary tenor part of Aaron. He says that Schoenbergs *Sprechstimme* is marked in the score with a particular cross mark on the staff for every

syllable and that he is just as responsible to Gielen's direction and Bernard Rubenstein's comments as Louis Devos. Finished at five after 4 takes.

Tuesday, 27th August **Shot 41,32,35,34**

Shot 41. This time Aaron pours out 'The clear water of the Nile'. This is the last of Aarons's *Wunder.* The camera CS on Aaron in left profile. He sings: 'Yet the Almighty frees you and your blood.' The chorus off sings'Chosen! Chosen!' which will be taken from the Vienna tapes and mixed later with the band of Aaron's voice. This is the last scene of the first act to be filmed since the final chorus, 'Eternal God, we consecrate to Thee our offerings and our love' is to be the two pans over the Nile at Luxor and at Aswan that J.-M. shot in May (Shot 42 and 43). The two-minute-thirty-second Interlude, 42 measures, 'Where is Moses?' is blackfilm with the title 'Before the Mountain of Revelation' in white (Shot 44).

12.30, Shot 32 in low-angle view. The camera on the chorus pans left MCS/MLS to Moses and Aaron. Aaron shows Moses' healthy hand, and Moses leads it to his heart. Shot 35. CS on Aaron in left profile. Camera in light 'frog perspective' (low-angled view). 'Know yourselves therein: without courage, sick, despised, enslaved, persecuted!' Shot 34, a silent shot CS on Moses' leprous hand. The chorus 'off' sings during this shot. Nevertheless, Hochet takes ambiance so J.-M. insists on *absolute Ruhe* during shooting time. From five to eight the *contadini* (farm people) come to the church to try on their costumes for Shot 58. The simplicity of these costumes accentuates the primitive beauty of the faces of these hard-working people. Some of the women decide not to go through with it, so Paolo asks the *contadino* who lives next to the church and his wife and mother, and they accept.

Wednesday, 28th August **Shot 46,49**

Shot 46. MLS on the Elders. The men of the chorus are ranged in three rows with the Priest in the front on the right of the frame. Jean-Marie has them stand in place and we drive in nails to mark their position. The Mitchell is set on top of a two-storey *toretta* and directed down on them frontally. J.-M. uses the view-finder to decide on the objective. He and Daniele discuss it with Ugo and Saverio. The Elders sing 'Hear! Hear! Too late!' looking slightly to the right to indicate Aaron, and then they look straight ahead to indicate the approach of the chorus. Shot 49. At first on the Edlers as in Shot 46. 'Aaron, help us! Give in!' The camera pans left on Aaron in right profile turned towards the people. He sings: 'People of Israel! Thy Gods I give back to thee, and thee to them, as is thy desire.' After the run-through shooting starts at 2.20. Devos is not feeling well, so we cut at five.

‘...on the chorus pans left’ is wrong: there was no panning shot and the choir had already left.

We go up to the church and carry the four pieces of polystryrene set on a wood frame that make up the altar and the pedestal for the Golden Calf down to the arena. J.-M. digs the space for the pedestal himself and we place it down, weigh it with rocks and fasten it for its burden. Before it we assemble the three pieces of the platform which fit together as a base with four steps for the cube centered on top which serves as the altar. The whole is painted a brown identical to the colour of the mixture of baked earth and straw used by the Hebrews to make bricks and which the Straubs found still in use in Alexandria. The altar which was made in Cinecitta has been stored in the church until now. After it is set in place, the steps are covered with boards to protect their surface. We then cover it with large sheets of plastic to protect it against the wind and fasten them against the wind. From now on Hans-Peter and I will divide the charge of keeping watch down here at night. Daniele gives us the old camping tent which belongs to them since '54 to use. I help Hans-Peter set it up. He chooses to stay down here for the first night. I sleep in the church. Jean-Marie asks him to watch at what time the moon comes over the amphitheatre.

We owe Aaron much grateful recognition: certainly, if he caught cold it is his fault, because, despite our biddings, he persisted with one take done, in getting half undressed to go to practise for the next one in the *galleria* which runs under one half of the amphitheatre and which is as cold inside as it is hot outside: the result could be expected. But, that day, he knew that we were doing the last shot with the 17 choristers and him, and that if we could finish the shot that day, we had no more to shoot with them but a shot without him, Shot 58, with the village people, and that we could then send them back to Vienna (the choristers always stayed on to wait at Avezzano, for two days after the last day of shooting with them, and the soloists and Gielen as well, until we had seen the rushes at the lab, to be sure that they could leave, that there had been no catastrophe at the lab, and nothing needed reshooting).

On the other hand, if we hadn't been able to finish on that day with him and them, we would have had to wait until he could sing again with our chorus members and to pay them during this time: hence he made a great effort, and while no one else thought it was possible, he made it: the last entire take of this shot, the twentieth, the one we have in the film, this moment when Aaron 'betrays', relents, is also the one where one most feels the effort and the pain of the singer. This 'mishap' was of use for us, for we would never have obtained, nor thought to obtain, this voice on the point of breaking, without this illness and without the courage and the will of Devos. The twentieth take done, the chorus spontaneously applauded Aaron; he wanted to try again, for he hopes to be able to 'do better': we try three more times, but each time his voice breaks, each time more quickly. So then it is finished, we take him to the hotel right away. Gielen, Reich, Straub and I cut a funny figure, for we know that the risk exists that after this effort he might not be able to sing for months....

No, not at Alexandria: Alexandria is a city of the Mediterranean, close to an Italian city, poorer, more populous, also with traces of fascist-style architecture. We saw these bricks and brought one back for the Cine-Ars (!) of Cinecitta which was to make our altar in polystyrene (which we almost didn't get: fortunately we had ordered it 18 months before the shooting, for with the petrol crisis having broken out, this by-product of petrol was no longer to be found; and when it began to arrive again from America the price was five times increased!), we saw them by the Nile, between Aswan and Luxor, drying in the sun, as thousands of years ago: a small 'industry' (factory) on the edge of a village.

Thursday, 29th August **Shot 58,57**

Early morning. Cecco, Nanni and Ninni put the Golden Calf in a delivery wagon and transport it into the arena. Daniélè is nervous about the Calf as the gold finish done in Cinecitta chips off easily and is difficult to retouch well. With great care we lift it up on top of the pedestal and fasten it inside with wire to the frame of the pedestal. J.-M. reports that the doctor has ordered Devos to rest for at least three days. He has a slight fever and won't be able to sing until he is well. This upsets the shooting schedule and is no happy prospect for the film. We must wait and see after three days. About 11 a.m. Shot 58 is ready. The *contadini* come down from the church in their costumes.

The necessity of bringing forward shots which were to have been filmed later and of pushing back those which called for Aaron's presence worries me, not only because I must quickly find the best decision for organisation and economy trying not to forget any of the factors, but, most of all, because I know (and I am alone to know, except for perhaps Louis because, since he has been on the film for two years with us, he knows a part of the difficulties involved, Jeti because he has a rapid sensibility, and Gabriele because he was with us for all the pre-shooting preparations; the others, Saverio and Gielen included, are so used to seeing Jean-Marie 'function' as Brecht would say that they don't even envisage that the machine all of a sudden might get derailed!) what nervous tension it represents for Straub to have to set his wires up another way, to not make an error in judgement, not to be overcome; I hope that his nerves will hold. The possibility that Aaron may not be able to sing at all, that we must push aside to think only about the daily work—tell ourselves to climb one mountain at a time. When I have periods of discouragement, when I am not sure of being strong enough or tough enough to get through to the end, I tell myself that if Mao and his peasants got that immense country going, it would be dismal if we couldn't get to the end of a film. And it works, I begin to get moving again. At night when we go to bed at one or two in the morning (sometimes three if it is an evening when we had to go to Rome to see the rushes), I fall asleep like a rock—to get up without fail at five and spend the time until six or six-thirty on the balcony of the hotel room examining the sky to see where the clouds are going, if the weather will be good...5 o'clock, that's the time on the other hand when J.-M. goes to sleep worn out from having thought over what he has to shoot; two hours later it's time to wake him up....Fortunately, we have the luxury of being able to take a good hot bath to wake us up, and the Italian coffee is effective!

It is without question to wait without shooting until Aaron is again in condition to sing, for Gielen has to conduct the Gurrelieder and his rehearsals begin two days after the end of the shooting scheduled for

J.-M. directs the men and women beggars to pass from right to left in front of the altar. He tells them not to look at the *cosa nera* (the camera) as they go by. The camera is on tracks set diagonally to the left of the altar. It starts on the procession. The beggarmen lay their cloaks on the altar and the beggarwomen lay fruit and bread on it. After they pass the camera tracks back for the entry of the aged men from the right towards the altar. For these two groups the music is already taped. As the aged men move towards the altar they will be heard to sing: 'The last moments, which we have yet to live, take them as offering.' After this the camera pans left to the Elders by the altar who sing live: 'They have killed themselves!'

During the *cestino* I hear Daniele discussing 'le Gregory' with Jean-Marie. Ninni and I are to carry the litter on which lies the sick woman in Shot 57. The camera in light high-angle view on her as she sings and raises herself in the direction of the Calf. Gielen is set up on the side of the altar so that the sick woman, Elfriede Obrowsky, can follow him and still look up in the direction of the 'image of the Gods'. When she has sung we carry her left out of the frame and the camera tracks slowly in on the front part of the altar. J.-M. directs us to continue carrying her until the track is finished because he wants Vaglio to record the sound of our exit. After a while my hands start to hurt from carrying the litter. I try to concentrate on the sinuous melody that my passenger sings. We finish after 16 takes. Mario, the son of Sig. Pancrazio, *custode* of the amphitheatre, helps me to set up the tent. As soon as I am in my sleeping bag I fall asleep.

Friday, 30th August **Shot 10**

8 a.m. I wake up when the Straubs arrive at the amphitheatre. Because of Aaron's indisposition, they have had to change the shooting schedule until he can sing. The camera is set on a one-level *toretta* close up on Moses for Shot 10. J.-M. discusses the camera movement for this nine-minute shot with Saverio. It remains on Moses, here

him. In the case of a catastrophe he would give up the Gurrelieder, but we want to spare him that and the legal, economic, and career difficulties that that would pose for him; aside from his anxiousness, of course, to conduct the Gurrelieder right after *M & A*. We had asked everyone to keep a few days in reserve for us beyond the last day of scheduled shooting, but, after the experience of Vienna where everything was finished without delays (at the price, at times, of what nervous tension!) with an immense optimism and a complete lack of conscience of the possible atmospheric breakdowns (even in Italy! especially in Italy, where everything is unstable and open to risk, the weather, the land, the people), they arranged their time without keeping this reserve for us!

Before directing anything whatsoever, Jean-Marie asks for chairs and sets them up so that the group of peasant men and women on one side, and that of the old men on the other, can sit down outside of the field of the frame between each take. They are all very courteous, very calm, and all is finished by midday. I pay out the 8,000 liras promised (for several days beforehand I was raking in bills of a thousand and five thousand everywhere, and I had asked Leo to pass by the bank to change some bills of ten thousand to have all the accounts ready for each); I didn't have them sign, an operation which I detest (except with the technicians, who have it as a habit, but who are always amazed, even those who have already worked with us, that I pay them at the beginning of the week, hence in advance, and not at the end of the week after the work is furnished...Since I don't see why people be asked to anticipate their work; and besides, I am quite content to dispose of this money without carrying it around with me any longer or keeping it at the hotel). They are content because we had told them that it might be that it would last all day and they were finished in two hours. We are content for we had told Friedl Obrowsky that if all went well, we might perhaps be able to do the shooting with her in the afternoon, that she should 'get into voice' and rehearse with Bernard in the morning; she didn't come for nothing, we are able to do the shooting.

without a veil, until the end of his dialogue with the Voice from the Thornbush. After he declares, ‘My tongue is awkward: I can think, but not speak’, the camera pans up to the thornbush and slowly left around the whole amphitheatre, during which the Voice sings of its chosen people, over to the mountain on which it then stays fixed. The pan is about 300 degrees around, passing along the line between the top of the amphitheatre and the sky until it stops on the figure of Monte Velino in the distance. Because of its length, over nine-hundred feet of film, each take uses an entire reel of material. Shooting starts in the sun at 10.30 but after three takes the clouds over Monte Velino have completely covered it from view. At noon we stop and wait for the clouds to lift. In the afternoon Velino becomes visible again, so shooting recommences. Killed after eight takes. The beginning of this scene, measures 1 to 5, is blackfilm with the title ‘The Calling of Moses’ (Shot 9).

Saturday, 31st August

Nothing to shoot today. We are attendant on Devos’ good health. In the afternoon we practice Shot 60. Midnight the Straubs come into the amphitheatre to look at the moon for a later Shot, but it is very cloudy.

No; it was what had been foreseen in the filmscript: in montage, we said that it was dumb, that it was much better to see Moses from the first note, as he slowly raises his hands into the frame: to accomplish such a movement is difficult for an actor, why cut out the beginning of it? And this kind of hesitation, why destroy it? So Shot 10 begins with the first note of the opera.

What Gregory doesn't know, for he was on guard in the amphitheatre, is that after having rehearsed Shot 60 with the three men on the camera and the three propmen, one of the most difficult to set up, with Cecco, Gabriele and Dietmar Schings, come to see us from Frankfurt, and Leo, we had been to look over the entry to the path which is the sole passageway to arrive at the site where we wanted to shoot with the horses. Hochet and Vaglio follow us to have a look for themselves at the entry to the path for the next morning. It is a hill facing the hill fo the amphitheatre, on the other side of the main road from Avezzano. An unpaved road leads off the paved road: it is this one that, apart from some tractors, the garbage-trucks take on their way to empty their garbage a bit farther on....For the path which leads from this unpaved road to the quarry which is at the foot of the hill where we wanted to shoot with the horsemen the next day, but also later, at night, with the man who runs by burning, this path leaves from the centre of the garbage-dump of the city of Avezzano....The entry to this path, which we had still seen and checked three days before with Gabriélè, we were no longer able to find. Going back and forth we finally understood why: the garbage had been turned over, more exactly construction rubble, on top of the entry of the path....It is late, the offices are closed, no question of finding anyone from the city to help us; and tomorrow is Sunday! We send Louis off, tell him that we will inspect, for him to go and rest; Cecco leaves as well to get Nanni and Nini and some shovels from the village. We stay there waiting until I work myself into a rage ('Let's see if men can't work

Sunday, 1st September **Shot 59,60**

Shot 59. On a nearby hill the twelve Tribal Princes and the Ephraimite ride down a path on horses, pass by the camera on the curve of the path and go farther to the left out of the frame. The camera pans with them as they ride by and stays for a second on the mountain, still the Velino in the distance. At midday they arrive at the amphitheatre. The Tribal Princes come with their horses from a riding academy in Tagliacozzo near by.

Shot 60. The camera is set on tracks on the right of the altar. At first CU of the Ephraimite, in low-angle view, who sings 'Princes of the tribes, pay hommage with me, to this image of regulated powers!' Then the camera tracks back to MLS on the Tribal Princes who are kneeling before the altar. They rise at the approach of the Young Man, who menacing with a bar goes to the first step of the altar and sings 'Smashed be this image of the temporal! Pure be the outlook on eternity!' The Ephraimite, Ladislav Illavsky, walks right, grabs him around the neck, throws him to the ground, and goes left out of the frame followed by the twelve Tribal Princes. *Gestorben* around three. J.-M. prepares the tracking shot in Shot 26 for tomorrow.

Monday, 2nd September **Shot 26,27,29,69**

Shot 26. The camera at first CS on Moses. He says 'Almighty, my power is at an end, my idea is impotent in Aaron's word!' The camera then tracks back to cut them both *americano* MCS. Aaron threatens:

their way through this too') and start clearing off the junk with my hands;) it is still day, at night we couldn't get much done. J.-M., Gabriele, Leo, Dietmar Schings do likewise: Leo and I even have slight wounds on our hands from the ends of some cutting metal. At the end of two hours Cecco has not yet returned but we have cleared off sufficiently enough for the cars to pass; Gabriele with his new 4CV Renault (which I suspect him having bought to replace the old one he had, to be sure not to have a car which would let us down in the middle of shooting, but he never wanted to admit it), passes over it again and again to flatten out the ground at the risk of ruining his beautiful new car; 'A car is made to be used', he says....When Cecco, Nanni and Nini arrive it is the black of night, but the work is practically finished: by the light of the headlights they fill in the last holes. The next morning none of the rest of the crew will notice a thing. We ask Dietmar what he thinks about the *metier* of a cineaste-garbage cleaner; that, when they ask him what he saw of the shooting of *M & A* on his return to the television at Frankfurt, he recount this evening.

We go to wash and eat and then Jean-Marie and I return in Gabriélè's auto to examine the positions of the moon in the amphitheatre. It is indeed very cloudy!

The night between Saturday and Sunday: the clouds continue to gather; about one o'clock the rain begins; at five when I wake up, it is raining in streams and the clouds continue to arrive....We are supposed to be on the hill for the horses at eight. At 6.30 it is still raining: I let Jean-Marie sleep and go from one balcony to another observing the progress of the clouds....I don't know what to decide: there is no improvement in view, but on the other hand to give up shooting with the horsemen today is a catastrophe: one part works and couldn't be free tomorrow, it risks snowballing disorganisation of the whole work schedule, since Aaron is feeling better and thinks he'll be able to sing tomorrow. In the course of a trip from one balcony to another, I meet Vaglio in the corridor: he goes with me on to the other balcony and tells me in his singing accent: 'Where we live in Nice when the weather is like this in the morning, at ten o'clock the weather is fine. You'll see, at ten o'clock the weather will be fine, we should go.' Well, the decision is made, I am only half convinced but I decide to change nothing. I wake up Jean-Marie who says it is madness but he decides anyway to get up. We get to the hill at 8.30, everyone arrives slowly, but not the least horseman or horse in sight. I am not worried for I know all these swagglers and I was sure that they would be late; they are no peasants, but the sons of comfort. The rain has stopped but the sky is still completely overcast. Even so we take the camera out and begin to get ready. Cecco, our great prophet as to the weather tells us

'Be silent! The word am I and the deed!' and snatches away Moses' staff. Moses, in consternation, turns to him in right profile.

Lode, as Devos is called to distinguish him from Louis Hochet, is recovered from his fever. He is in good voice today. Though he speaks in French with us, Devos, a Belgian, has little difficulty with the German text. There are 6 takes between 11.30 and 12.30. Shot 27 CS on Aaron who stands right side in the frame turned to the chorus. He throws the staff to the ground and sings: 'This staff leads you: see the serpent!' After the *cestino*, Shot 29. The camera on the left MCS on Moses and Aaron in low-angle view. Aaron holding the staff sings: 'Know the might that this staff imparts to the leader!' He steps over to the right to restore it to Moses and returns to his place on Moses' left. At four Cecco, Nanni, and Ninni set up the Mitchell just outside the south entry of the amphitheatre and hook it up by cable to the generator. I sit by it on guard until they come back in the evening to take film of the moon rising over the hill to the east where Shot 59 was filmed yesterday.

that on this hill he is less sure of himself than in the amphitheatre where the peasants had taught him to 'read' the light or the clouds on Monte Velino....At 9.30 we are ready, but still no shadow of a horse to be seen. I ask Gabriele to go to Avezzano, where the horses were brought from Tagliacozzo, about 30 km distant, the evening before by the owner of the ring, precisely so that they wouldn't have to part at dawn this morning to be on time for the shooting, to see what is going on. Renata and Rino have prepared all the costumes down in the quarry, the clouds break, the azure appears. It is as yet no more than a tiny bit of sky but Vaglio triumphs. 10 o'clock Gabriele returns: the horses had been left in a field in the open sky and this morning they were completely drenched! The horsemen had had to rub them down, let them dry and rub them down again, for a humid horse cannot be saddled, under pain of wounding him by splitting his skin....Only now they are arriving. In a quarter of an hour the first ones arrive, at eleven everyone is dressed and ready. The first take (we will do three) is still with a cloudy sky, the third has no more than a tiny little cloud which quickly crossed the field to the right....

In the afternoon the sky becomes dark and menacing; our horsemen have to kneel down, get up and kneel down again eleven times. For the pampered sons that they are, they act well: the only one to complain of his knees hurting is the owner of the ring. We ask one of the horsemen what the said owner is giving them from the 500,000 liras that we pay him for horses and horsemen: 'Nothing, a meal. And then he knows that we like riding and this time, to go back to Tagliacozzo this evening, we can ride free.'

Lode is Louis in Flemish; Devos is a Flemish Belgian, the reason he speaks German well. What's more, Straub worked with him particularly on the pronunciation of the texts, first during the rehearsals at Brussels or at the Mondsee with Gielen, then at Vienna during the recording: all the points that were still weak were circled or underlined in red, and Lode worked over them again on his own, between May and August, such that the progress between the text recorded at Vienna and that recorded at Alba Fucense is great.

While sitting there I work on my translation of the libretto into English that will serve as a basis for the subtitles which we will do in January. Little Mario keeps me company. He asks me if I am a *tedesco* like the other people here. I draw him a map of North America to show him where New York is. About seven Saverio arrives and the others after him. The full moon comes up at 20.10. J.-M. says this Shot 69 is a tribute to the composer of 'Pierrot Lunaire'! Gianni says that we should take advantage of this occasion without Hochet to make a lot of noise while shooting as they usually do in Italian films. They roll 1,400 feet, 20 minutes' worth of the film. We pack up the equipment and they leave by nine. The amphitheatre is bathed in moonlight. The Golden Calf wrapped in plastic looks like a veiled bride. A cat runs through the bushes.

Tuesday, 3rd September **Shot 45,47,51**

Shot 45. The camera in light high-angle view CS on Aaron in front view. He stands before the west side of the arena. Firstly he directs his eyes to his left to indicate the Elders who sing off 'Forty days! How long still?' When he sings in answer to them he bends his head down, then looks to his right to indicate the entry of the irate chorus, whose sound Hochet has recorded. Jean-Marie encourages the natural theatricality in Devos' expression. He never tells him to make an expression, but leads him to create one. Shot 47. Aaron stands as before, but the camera is now in sharper high-angle view atop a three-storey *toretta.* As Aaron's treachery increases, so does the distance of the camera. When Aaron sings, 'on this height' he gestures to his left in the direction of the mountain. Bernard Rubenstein is sometimes not as satisfied with the correctness of the singing as is Gielen. J.-M. at times uses this as a reason for further takes. He asks Bernie if the taping followed the score. Bernie replies 'O.K.', but without enthusiasm, and then J.-M. announces one more take for Bernie. 3 p.m. Shot 51. Aaron stands before the Golden Calf after he has relented to the people. The camera in low-angle view on the Golden Calf and CS on Aaron who stands left in front of it. He sings: 'This image witnesses that in everything that is, a God lives!' and points up to the Calf, concluding 'Revere yourselves in this symbol!' The chorus: 'Their physical visibility', Shot 50, which precedes this, will be whitefilm.

After this come the orgy scenes of the second act, Shots 52 to 71. 5 p.m. It rains heavily so we quickly cover up the altar and Guistiniano. After it clears J.-M. and Danièlè work on the positions of Moses and Aaron before the altar in Shots 73-79. We nail Moses' place before the altar and Aaron ahead to his left. Daniele holds the *Drehbuch* for J.-M. while he looks through the view-finder to judge the distance between them. J.-M. who doesn't know how to wink, must use his hand to keep one eye shut when he looks through the *Sucher* (view-finder).

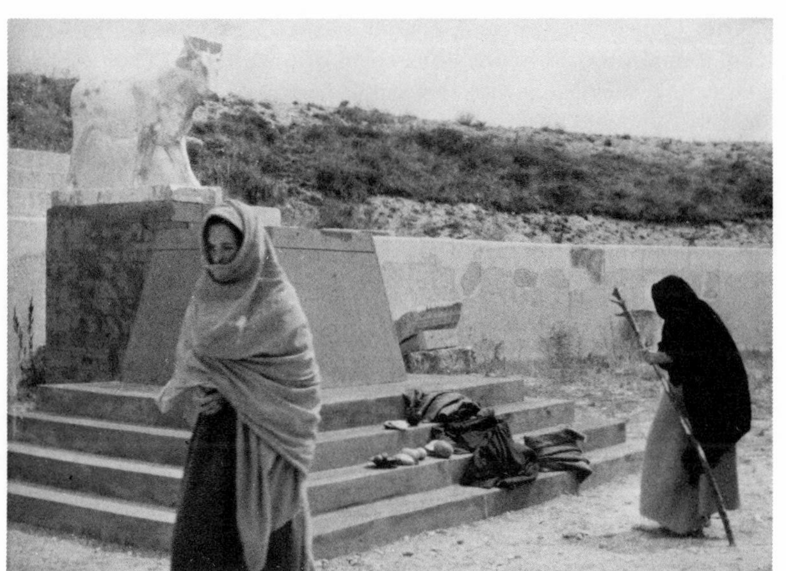

After dinner at Carmelo's, a good inexpensive restaurant in Avezzano, Leo and I pass by the hotel room of the Straubs. Each evening after eating, they listen with Jeti and Gielen to the day's tapings to be sure the sound and the music are good.

Wednesday, 4th September

Day of rest. I stay in the amphitheatre. J.-M. and Daniele are gone to Rome to see the rushes. They buy three boxes more film material and more Agfa tapes for the Nagra recording.

There is only one way to connect directly to the past and to tradition: to begin everything over again, as if all that had gone before were false; to grapple once again with the essence of the thing most exactly, instead of reducing oneself to developing the technique of a pre-existent material.

Arnold Schoenberg, 'Aphorisms, Anecdotes, Sayings', 1932/49.

Thursday, 5th September **Shot 72,74,75,76,73**

7 a.m. Shot 72 in the early morning. Gielen comes down dressed in a leather costume with a helmet to play the Watchman. Jean-Marie sets him up on top of the north-east side of the amphitheatre to the right of the mountain. Lens objective 50 takes in the expanse of the mountain in the early light. The camera is set on the *ruotolette* (six-wheel dolly) that the Straubs brought back from Rome yesterday. Saverio lets me look through the eye of the Mitchell to see how much the lens takes in. Custom in Italy is that anyone not directly working on the camera who looks through the camera has to buy drinks for the whole crew. Gielen looks in the direction of the mountain, then turns and cries: 'Moses is going down from the mountain!'

10.30, Shot 74. Moses: 'Aaron, what has thou done?' Aaron: 'Nothing new!'. Moses stands before the altar with the tables of the law. Aaron on his left and in front of him. The camera set in light high-angle view on their right in the space that separates Moses on the left and Aaron on the right. Aaron stands in right profile, Moses 3/4 frontal view, each looking ahead, avoiding each other's glance. Shot 75. Close-up on Aaron in right profile: 'As always: I heard the voice within me.' Moses (off): 'I have not spoken.' Aaron: 'Nonetheless I have understood.' The tables which Moses carries are marble. One set is inscribed with an old Hebrew text of the Decalogue chiselled by a stone-mason who works for the Cimitero Israelitico in Rome. The other three pairs are blank. They are rather heavy so Nanni helps Gunter to hold them between takes. During *cestino* I wonder if there will be a *temporale* as often happens in the afternoon. J.-M. says, *Le temps, comme l'histoire, ne se répete pas.* 2.30, Shot 76. MCS in high-

Vaglio, on the giraffe, records this dialogue with a single mike (the Neumann U87) panning slightly from Moses to Aaron and from Aaron to Moses; I am worried, for Georges doesn't know a word of German, so he has no marking points to know when to pass from one to the other, and the least retardation on his part can produce a detestable 'fading' which would oblige us to start this very long, and, for the singers, very difficult take, all over again (for the synch, but also for Aaron who is still vocally worn by his illness). I ask Georges if he is quite sure of himself; he says, 'It's O.K.' So I don't interfere. And, in fact, he succeeds perfectly at each take in his recording.

angle view on Moses who with the tables on his right side turns to Aaron: 'The imperishable, say it like these tables, perishably, in the speech of thy mouth!'

4 p.m. Shot 73. The camera in light low-angle view close-up on the Golden Calf. Moses (off) says: 'Begone, thou image of the inability to grasp the boundless in an image!' Hochet takes Moses' voice direct. After, during the already taped chorus 'off': 'All pleasure, all joy, all hope is gone!', the Calf disappears through a fade-in.

Friday, 6th September **Shot 77,78**

Shot 77. The camera on a *toretta* in high-angle view CS on Aaron in right profile. The heart of the combat between Aaron's arguments for life in the world: 'I love this people, I live for it and want to preserve it', and Moses: 'I love my idea and live for it!' Almost three minutes long. After much practice shooting starts at eleven. Aaron looks straight ahead throughout turning slightly towards Moses during their dialogue.

Afternoon, Shot 78. The camera, still in high-angle view, CU on Moses in front view. Moses has the tables raised above his head: 'Then I smash these tables, and will pray God that he recall me from this office!' Then he throws them to the ground to his right. This is the last discourse between the protagonists in this act. Moses does 4 takes, breaking two pairs of tables.

Sleeping in the tent, I am awoken by the wind at midnight. It feels like a storm. I go and fasten the plastic around the altar and the Calf and secure the tent. Nonetheless the wind soon blows down the tent and I get wet and tangled within. At 2 a.m. Hans-Peter comes down with a flash-light and helps me to take my things to the church.

Saturday, 7th September **Shot 80,79,12**

I get up early and go down to the amphitheatre. Lay out the tent to dry and take the plastic off the altar. The puddles of last night are gone. Jean-Marie and Daniele are relieved to find nothing damaged. We set up for Shot 80, the last of the second act. Camera in high-angle view MCS/MLS on Moses now on his knees. During practice Renata is concerned about Moses' veil when he bends over. She wants to pin it, but J.-M. says to let it flow as it will. At the end, Moses: 'O word, thou word, that I lack!' grabs his head in his hands and sinks, despairing, to the ground. 11 o'clock, shot 79. A pan from left to right of the thornbush on the hillside of the amphitheatre to run against the chorus's reacceptance of Moses' God, even though through the words of Aaron.

Afternoon, Act I, scene 2, 'Moses encounters Aaron in the desert', title white on blackfilm for Shot 11, measures 98-123. Shot 12. The

Slightly? The first time Aaron turns towards Moses not slightly but in an extended, already menacing manner while saying to him 'So mache dich dem Volk verstandlich, *auf ihm angemessne Art'* (So make thyself understandable to the people, *in a manner suited to it).* The second time, at the end of the shot, the last time one sees Aaron in the film before finding him bound on the ground again in the third act, Aaron turns violently towards Moses, with a closed fist, saying to him: 'Die auch nur ein Bild, ein Teil des Gedankens sind' (That are also only an image, a part of the idea).

camera in high-angle view, LS, on Moses with his staff in his right hand and the veil that he is not wearing in Shot 10, faces Aaron who stands opposite him to the right in the frame. The drama of confrontation distanced like a show-down in a western. It's a windy afternoon. Aaron's veil flies around a lot. In this opening music Schoenberg introduces the four sets of twelve tones on which the rest of the opera is structured in Aaron's vocal line. Moses counters these operative flights with the reflective weight of his *Sprechstimme.* Aaron: 'Thou, son of my fathers, does the great God send thee to me?' Moses: 'Thou, son of my father, brother of the spirit, from whom the Unique shall speak forth: perceive me and him and say what thou understandest.'

Sunday, 8th September **Shot 13,14,15**

Louis Devos tunes up his voice on the piano in the church while we set up for Shot 13. Camera in high-angle view as in Shot 12. Aaron comes down at 10.45. CS on him in left profile. Moses stands facing him off. Hochet sets up mikes for their verbal duel. To begin shooting Jean-Marie checks first to see if Hochet is ready with the tape. Then he checks with Saverio for the camera. Then he says 'Vas-y, Louis!' and Hochet starts the orchestra tape which begins with three beeps for the measures of each Shot. Gielen standing visible to them with the working score in front of him cues them in and conducts. Aaron sings: 'Imagination of the highest fantasy, how it thanks thee for that thou dost excite it to form images!' Gnostic theorisation versus the theistic idea. Moses (off): 'No image can give thee an image of the Unrepresentable.'

12.30, Shot 14. Moses: 'Unrepresentable, because invisible, because immeasurable, because unending, because eternal, because omnipresent, because almighty. Only one is almighty.' The camera in high-angle view on Moses in front view. The set-up of the camera cuts Aaron off from Gielen. So Bernard Rubenstein conducts him in singing 'Unrepresentable God.' (At lunchtime Georg Brintrup arrives from Rome with news that Misti had four kittens.) Afternoon, Shot 15. High -angle view CS on Aaron, this time in right profile. *Gestorben* at three. During shooting a discarded cigarette burns three large holes in the sleeve of the canvas coat Jean-Marie has had for 25 years. Renata is going to see if she can patch it up.

It was hard to find the distance for this shot: Straub wanted the two 'antagonists' to be removed one from the other, at the same time for realistic reasons (in the desert where the space is without limits, two men who meet and call each other back and forth have no reason to do it while mincing their steps) and for theatrical reasons, but neither did he want this distancing to bother the two actors, who had to hear each other, technically nor psychologically (at least not too much!). So he began by asking Gunter and Lode to find the distance which seemed right themselves; Gunter wanted to be rather close to Lode, too close for the taste of J.-M. who said nothing. Luckily Lode for himself wanted to be far away from Moses, at a distance which corresponded to what J.-M. had in mind: Gunter, who is good-natured, let himself be persuaded....

In the evening of **September 15th** after having seen the rushes, we go to the house to see the kittens: they are just eight days old, and all four of them greet us puffing out menaces—until they realise that their mother is feasting our homecoming; then they calm down. We will give them their names, for the two males, Liebknecht *(amabile servo)* and Aronne (because he has a black spot on one eye and the air of a pirate, like Devos for several weeks during rehearsals because he had done underwater fishing and had seriously infected one eye—he had to have cortisone injections and wore a black patch; J.-M. had gotten used to the idea of having an Aaron with an eye-patch and was almost disappointed at the disappearance of the patch already at Vienna!); for the two females, Elba, because the father was a cat from the Isle of

Monday, 9th September **Shot 16,14**

Shot 16. Last shot for Moses and Aaron before they come back to do the third act on the 19th of September. The camera atop a three-storey *torretta* in high-angle view MCS frontal on Moses. He sings: 'Purify thy thinking, loose it from what is worthless, consecrate it to the true', the only seven measures of the music sung by Moses. Danièle wasn't satisfied with the music in Shot 14 yesterday. Aaron sang 'Unrepresentable God' too low. So they do a retake. After this Gielen and Rubenstein are finished as the remaining music for Act II is taped already. The *macchinisti* leave for Rome to get the lights at Cinecitta for the night scenes in Act II.

Tuesday, 10th September

Day of Rest. I work on translating Act III. About 6 o'clock five dancers of the New Dance Forum of Cologne arrive to look at the amphitheatre and try on their costumes for tomorrow. It begins to rain heavily for two hours. Everyone goes up to the church where it is damp and uncomfortable. We left pools of water in the arena. Danièle is concerned, for the dancers are scheduled to dance in the morning.

Elba, red and black, which, the mother being black and white, produces two tricolour daughters, and Kapek, from the name of the chorus delegate with whom for months I discussed the hotel rooms to be booked for the chorus members, the means of travel, the modalities of payment—the Austrian chorus members wanted absolutely to be paid in marks for they had no confidence in the lira, but certain members wanted to spend their vacation holidays in Italy after the shooting and so wanted liras...etc.—she too was russet coloured. The two males stayed together at the house of friends in Rome who have a terrace, Elba is at Monte Porzio Catone with Renata's sister, who has a garden, and Kapek in Paris....We brought her there when we went to do the mixing of the film in Paris, Louis not trusting the Italian installations, and we, in any case, wanting to do the optical sound in Paris where they do better work as well with the 35 mm optical sound as (and here, absolutely) with the 16 mm optical sound! With Gabriele and his Renault and about fifty cans of film (working copy, sound, etc.), and the stereo Nagra that Louis left with us after the re-recording in case we had other re-recordings to do, for in the Rome studios there was no stereo Nagra to be found, and with Kapek then hidden under a road-map we pass through customs, for none of all of this, neither film, nor Nagra nor cat had been declared. On return, for the passage of the Italian frontier, it was the same thing, except that Kapek had stayed behind with my mother where she still is.

Wednesday, 11th September **Shot 55,54,56**

Morning. The amphitheatre is already dry. The pools left ridges of weeds in lines marking the arena's surface. The dancers come down in costume and Rino, the make-up man, does up their faces after a copy of the masks in Malraux's 'Le Musée imaginaire de la sculpture: la statuaire'.

At nine the truck arrives from the slaughterhouse carrying the newly killed beast to be set beside the altar for Shot 55. It is set along the side of the altar on the right.

This shot must be done with care and rapidity for the cattle must be brought back to the slaughterhouse by noon to be refrigerated or the meat will start to go bad, and instead of paying the morning's rental for its use, Straub will have to pay for the beast. Along with it they have brought the head and shank of another animal to set on the altar as an offering. The camera is set in high-angle view before the altar. By the beast are two real butchers who have come with the truck, dressed in skins like the dancers. One holds the cattle's front leg back while the other begins to cut it underneath. The camera then pans to the left on the altar where the beast's head and shank are set in offering before the Golden Calf. At my post I sit copying out the camera changes Daniele has made in the revised *Drehbuch* which belongs to Bernie Rubenstein, who is leaving to fly to America today.

After the truck leaves with the animal, we set up for Shot 54 with the dancers. Each one has a butcher's knife which the Straubs brought back with them from Egypt. They dance with them in front of the offerings on the altar. The camera in high-angle view on a *torretta* to the left of the altar and farther back than before. Afterwards, the cattle

From illustrations of African masks he took the inspiration in painting the faces of the dancers. In the 12 months preceding the shooting we had been four times to Cologne to set up the dances with Jochen Ulrich and his dancers. These dances especially displeased the German music critics—doubtless because they are incapable of recognising people who know how to do their profession when this professional work is not present in academic fashion. Jochen is the only one to be treated as poorly as we are, and we are pained about it. What always astounds me is that bourgeois critics allow themselves to be provoked so easily!

Gabriele and Leo went to look for our two young men at the slaughterhouse, for they were supposed to arrive with the freezer truck at eight, but I am sceptical; and I was right for they weren't there: Gabriele and Leo had to go looking for them at Avezzano, which is why they arrive an hour late. When I point out to them that twenty people were kept waiting for their arrival, one of them rapidly runs off a story to me of one of their friends who was to have died this very morning, etc. A story of pure invention which makes me burst out laughing. The truth is that after the rain of the night before they had figured that we wouldn't be shooting this morning and had stayed in bed!

Not only because we would have to pay for it: above all because it would have been an animal killed in vain, if it can't even be eaten afterwards as a result. We didn't want under any conditions to have an animal slaughtered especially for the film so we found this solution with the director of the slaughterhouse.

parts are wrapped up in plastic and put in the cool shade of the *galleria* for the lunch break.

The rails are set up for a track forward in Shot 56. The rails are sprinkled with talc so as not to make noise against the rubber wheels of the dolly wagon. The dancers rehearse the two parts of their dance. Nanni practises the movement of the track-in with Saverio and the camera on the car at the end of the second dance. Hochet plays the music for them while Vaglio picks up the sound of their movements with a directional mike. Finished at 4.30.

Thursday, 12th September **Shot 28,63,64,70,71**

The camera on top of a *torretta* to the right of the altar for Shot 28. A shot of the serpent after Aaron throws Moses' staff to the ground. A professional animal dealer for the cinema arrives in a station-wagon with a cobra. The camera is directed on an empty patch of the arena through which the cobra is to move from bottom to top. The owner carries it in a little box and handles it with a forked stick. In his left hand he has a shield of protective glass. The intense heat of the sun makes the snake lethargic and uncooperative. It doesn't move very much. The prop-men try coaxing it towards them by attracting it to the black cloth they flash before it. But it doesn't get excited. The owner gets a little excited, though. Jean-Marie informs him that he doesn't work with the careless method of the normal Italian cinema and that they will keep shooting until they get some usable footage. The cobra does move a bit but usually to the shade by the altar. They run five reels of film on it.

The imbecile who brought the cobra didn't have the slightest notion about the psychology of his animal. Every time that the cobra, after a moment of calm, was about to do something interesting, he would hit it on the tail, in consequence making it part in the other direction. He called it without noticing that the sound bounced around the ellipse of the amphitheatre and that the cobra heard it from the opposite direction to the one which this idiot wanted to make it go. Unless, as Saverio had it, the poor animal had been so terrorised by his 'tamer' that it would systematically head in the other direction on hearing him! After some time he proposed drawing it along with a nylon thread saying that the whole of *The Bible* of Huston (Noah's Ark) had been done with nylon threads for the animals (or electric shocks for the lions to make them move). When J.-M. and I had gone to discuss the contract with this fellow who rents animals to film productions and who, it seems, had made a television series entitled 'The Friend of Animals' (in Africa, etc.), I had said to Jean-Marie that this fellow actually detested animals. I was not mistaken.

3 p.m. rehearsals for Shots 63/64. Four Priests stand on the first step of the altar with four maidens, each carrying a bowl and a butcher's knife. In front of them are the four virgins to be sacrificed, their backs to the camera. In the church Renata dresses the *contadini* in their costumes for the shots tomorrow night, to check that they fit.

After eight, when it gets dark, Ugo Piccone starts directing the disposition of the lighting for Shot 63. The camera in light low-angle view, MLS, directly in front of the altar at about 5 metres distance. When the lights are set up we take our posts. The amphitheatre is completely surrounded with the assistants on guard. The local boys have found out that tonight we are shooting with naked virgins, so we spend considerable time chasing them away. When all is ready, Daniele and Rino remove the cloaks from the four Virgins who stand in front of the Priests with their backs to the camera. They raise their arms in a gesture coordinated with the music sung off: 'O Gods, exalt your priests, exalt us, to the first and last pleasure.' The Priests then embrace them in their left arms, the maidens move to their sides and the priests take a *Schlachtmesser* in their right hand and raise it high to strike. J.-M. takes three *Aufnahmen* (takes). Shot 64, CS on the altar. The hands of a Priest pour blood out of a vessel.

At ten we set up the lighting outside the south entry for Shot 70. The camera is below on the left side of the path leading down into the arena. It is directed in low-angle view, MLS, to the level ground above. A naked youth, Enzo Ungari, comes into the frame on the left, rips the clothes from the body of a girl, Bianca Florelli, who stands on the right, lifts her up and carries her running out of the frame past the camera towards the altar. Shot 71 high-angle view, MCS, on the youth before the altar who carries the naked girl at first on one knee and then left still carrying her out of the frame. The camera pans up to the altar where a fire is burning. Against this, the last chorus of the orgy scenes: 'Gods, who gave the soul...' will be heard off. Vaglio takes the sound of the burning twigs in the silence of the night air. They wrap it up and leave at two.

After this, he proposed that we put the camera in the other direction. At that point Jean-Marie gets angry and tells him that he isn't making an Italian film. Naturally, the other man gets annoyed. Ugo, Saverio, Gianni, and Cecco break in and tell him that J.-M. is right, that he doesn't know anything about his animal. Then he wants to discuss the matter for he thinks we won't want to pay him later. I tell him not to fear, that I will pay the sum agreed on, but for him to do me the pleasure of leaving the amphitheatre and go and wait in the church or somewhere else. After he leaves, we can finally shoot in peace with our serpent, and wait until it finds its way of doing what we want it to do. No more noise, no more screaming, it begins to move...

The four priests (Marco Melani, Adriano Apra, Walter Grassi, Husam Aldin M. Ali), the four nude girls (Marina, Silvia, Carla, Gioia) and the four who carry the knives and the cups (Pia, Leonora, Karin, Sidonie) are all friends or friends of friends: J.-M. didn't want to have film extras who, especially in Italy, pass from one 'nudist' film to another, but people whom we knew and whom it doesn't disturb to be shown nude. And he wanted four girls who wouldn't be the thin sticks in fashion, but girls built a bit like those Renoir painted as his countrywomen. He asked each girl to choose the 'priest' who would kiss her; to some it made no difference. Others preferred one to another.

Equally for the couple at the end of the night: Enzo and Bianca live together, it was a pleasure for them to shoot it and for us to shoot it with them.

It is the white alabaster bowl that a blind and completely conditioned critic took for plastic....We only do two takes, for Jean-Marie, who has chosen Husam to do this gesture, is amazed by the immediate rightness of what he does. 'No European', he says, 'would be capable at first attempt of a gesture so realistic, so 'everyday', and at the same time so liturgical'.

Enzo is entitled to all our compliments: four times he carries Bianca running out of the frame for Shot 70, eight times he makes the effort to raise himself to carry Bianca out of the frame for Shot 71, without a murmur, despite his being tired, and the lateness in the night, and without departing from his good spirits. Once we have to interrupt a take, and Jean-Marie who sees that Enzo is becoming exhausted, gets furiously mad with Ugo guilty of the noise which forced us to cut. Ugo, contrite, makes his excuses. Indeed this shooting at night is very wearing for everyone: we begin to prepare at about four in the after-

Friday, 13th September **Shot 65,61,62**

At 5 p.m. Daniele arrives to prepare for tonight's shooting. Gabriele fetches two *damigiani* of red wine, each one containing 24 litres, in the *paese* and we carry them to the grotto where we will be filming later on tonight. The crew begins to work setting up the cable-lines for the camera by the remains of the Roman theatre north-east of the amphitheatre and close by the main forum of the excavations of Alba Fucense. The Mitchell and sound equipment are taken to the site and set in place for Shot 65 in low-angle view towards to middle of the hollow of the theatre. Meantime jars, earthenware, and other breakables are taken to the top of the hill into which the theatre is dug, including a wooden cart bought from a local farmer. When it is night the lights are set up. By 8.30 everything is ready and in one magnificent take everything possible is hurled down from the top. They shoot 150 feet of film, over a minute long of demolition.

After this the slow process of transporting the equipment to the grottos begins. The generator truck goes first, then the cables are laid and the sound truck and camera hooked up. The people from Alba Fucense who have agreed to participate get into costume in the church. The lighting is set up inside the grotto for Shot 61. The noon, and we will stop on the last night at six in the morning; meantime we have to change sites three or four times, transport all the heavy material, the projectors, transformer, camera, etc. Especially for Cecco, Nanni, and Nini, even if we all help them, it is too much. If we were to have to do such a thing over again, I will have learned that it is better not to plan more than one change of place in one night, even if the places are close to each other, so as not to wear out the people too much.

Ugo, on the contrary, was at that point the single dynamo for he was finally able to be an operator *sul serio,* set up the 35 kilowatts of lighting, come and ask Jean-Marie if he was content, explain to him why he had done such and such a thing. We had spoken together about the night lighting before the shooting, when we had taken him to see the amphitheatre; J.-M. sometimes asks for a few corrections of detail, but we have no more problems with Ugo since the shooting of the *Chronicle,* where the very first days were dreadful, but where, after a week's time, Ugo came to offer his excuses and swear us eternal friendship. As Saverio says he's a spoiled child, son of a wealthy family (of the Abruzzi, incidentally!), but ready to take risks in his profession, gifted with a great sensibility for lighting, and who has learned with us what it means to shoot a film with live sound and to respect the work of the sound engineers, that the image does not have priority over the sound, but the same importance, no more, no less!

camera, MCS, on a young man, Mario Pancrazio, standing at the entrance to the grotto, who inspects a sabre given him by an old man. It then pans right on two women, MCS, inside the grotto who exchange presents of fabrics and then continues on to a young man who places a necklace on a girl. The people are quiet and tired and the young people are sleepy by the time the shot is killed at 1 a.m.

Once again the equipment is moved and set up near by in front of the ancient stone wall of the grotto in low-angle view on two men, Paolo Benvenuti and Signor Pancrazio, MCS, who drink wine together. The camera pans left and down CS where six pairs of hands (of the assistants) with bowls have wine poured into them one after another. Then the camera pans up again to the left on to a burning torch which is set in the stone wall. Against this the chorus 'off' 'Blissful is the people' will be played, celebrating the enthusiasm and the exaltation of the people.

We finish shooting at 5 a.m. as Venus *il pianet ch'ad amar conforta* is in bright company with the moon. After the cables are wound and the equipment packed up, we leave at daybreak and drive to our several beds.

Saturday, 14th September **Shot 67,68,66**

I pass a tranquil afternoon in the amphitheatre. At four Danièle comes and we drive to the site by the ruins of the medieval Castello Orsini at the entrance to the village where Shot 68 is to be taken. She and J.-M. have been up since eight this morning after two hours sleep. I do a practice jump from the rock from which the assistants will leap to suicide tonight. The rock cuts down about 1 metre (5 ft.) to the ground. It doesn't seem bad except for the nettles on the ground which I suggest be covered with blankets. We then drive to the site on the hill where the Tribal Princes rode by and begin to carry up the cables to set up the equipment and lighting for Shot 67. A special effects man comes from Rome to be the man who runs by burning. He has on an asbestos suit which is covered by his costume. The camera is directed in light low-angle view to take him *halbtotal* (MLS) as he runs in from left and out to the right with his back to the camera. After practising the run the first take begins. The back of his cloak which is soaked in inflammable gas is ignited and starts burning as he runs for 10 metres by the camera. At the end of his run he dives to the ground and is covered with blankets which extinguish the fire at his back.

After 6 takes it is *gestroben* and we pack up to move to Castello Orsini for Shot 68. It takes two hours to get the cables hooked up and the lighting and camera carried up to the rock. Jeti, Leo, Paolo, Basti, Gabriele and I change into our costumes. We do a few practice jumps. One after another the six of us go up to the edge of the rock and jump

off. The camera is in low-angle view below on the right, directed MCS/MLS on the edge of the rock. We do a first take. J.-M. says it's a rather routine interpretation of a *salto mortale*. When we are in line before the rock to do the second take, I think the thoughts of a suicide before life and death. They are not unfamiliar. When my turn comes to jump it is hard to see ahead because of the light shining in my eyes, but falling I see Basti below me and shift to try to avoid falling on him. On touching ground there is a dreadful pain in my left ankle which makes me squint to keep silence until the end of the shot. My left ankle starts to swell, so Harald Bogel, the production assistant, takes me to the hospital in Avezzano. After I leave they do 4 more takes and then start transporting again to the south entry of the amphitheatre by which a man, Cecco, falls on his sword in Shot 66, the camera MLS/MCS on the man sitting under a tree who falls on his sword.

Sunday, 15th September

Day off for the crew. I spend my first day in a hospital. The people are very friendly. The old men reminisce about the campaign in Ethiopia and the visitors tell me of their relatives in the States. I read Chandler's 'Red Wind' and try to sleep. In the evening the Straubs visit.

Monday, 16th September **Shot 52,53**

In the morning I am taken for an X-ray. At ten they tell me I have a small fracture in my left tibia. My leg is wrapped in cotton and set in plaster. The technician says I can leave when the plaster is dry. I must wear it for thirty days. At six Hans-Peter arrives with his friend Anna to take me from the hospital. During the day they filmed the two shots which begin the orgy scenes with the animals in the amphitheatre. Shot 52, LS in light low-angle view on the animals, a camel, two cattle, etc., who stand in front of the altar.

Only three, one was cut right away. At montage we kept the one where Gregory jumps and goes to break his leg, not only because it was in the end the best one, but also because we thought we owed it to Gregory!

Cecco doesn't fall on a sword in the film, he stabs himself. He is magnificent, our greatest actor: he kills himself with the art and the culture of someone who has seen the major part of the Italian operas (at Pisa, when he doesn't work on a film, since the Tirrenia studios have closed up shop, he is electrician at the opera-theatre, and he sees a host of performances). It is funny and moving at the same time. Fortunately, for it is the last shot of the night and we are all exhausted: some are sleeping under the trees, Jean-Marie works with the lucidity of a sleepwalker, I don't sit down so as not to risk falling asleep. Cecco's talent gives us back energy.

The asses and the cows come from the village; the white camel is brought to us from Pisa ('That's why she walks bent over', Saverio says) by truck, and her trainer this time is very kind; the camel is charming, very sweet and pretty; she is very fond of her trainer; but she

Shot 53, the camera stands left next to the north portal in high-angle view LS on the amphitheatre through which animals of all kinds are led past the altar from the south entry.

has never worn a saddle, and doesn't want to let it be put on her back. J.-M. tells the keeper not to insist, she mustn't be upset, we will put the saddle on the ground beside her. He made her sit down in front of the altar. We put the saddle near her: at first she looks at it distrustfully, then, when she is sure that no one is going to put it on her by surprise, she begins to chew the little tufts of grass around her. The asses and the cows look at her with curiosity. We will shoot three very long takes, for, for such a shot one must film and allow life to carry on its own flow. Georges takes the sound, for we hold out for the breathing and the noises of the harness or of the cart—very beautiful.

At first we had envisaged, evidently, a passage of a herd as in a western—to discover, speaking to the peasants during the preparation of the film, that it wasn't realistic there where we were shooting, and doubtless, neither for the Hebrews with their herds! Each family has one, two, five cows but which are never together into a herd. Each peasant must come with his cow or cows. In addition to all the peasants of Alba Fucense who are willing to come with their animals we find in two neighbouring spots two more important herds, one of 15, one of 12 animals. They bring them to us for midday. The sheep come from Alba Fucense as well. For the goats it is more complicated: the year before there had still been some at Forme. But a few months before shooting they disappeared: the *Forestale* (Water and Forests) obliges the peasants to keep their goats enclosed on the pretext that they ravage the countryside (a farce, when one knows how and on what scale the speculators ravage, pillage and destroy Italy!). The peasants say rightly that goats are not animals that can be kept enclosed. So they sell them. We must find goats a bit farther on, and higher up, at Santa Iona, discuss their transport, come to agreement on 100,000 liras (everything included, truck for transport, petrol, shepherds) and promise the peasants—nothing was signed with them, but they kept their word as did we—that, should an accident happen to a goat (for example, if a goat is scared entering the truck and tries to jump off it might break a limb: and that is irreparable, different for a sheep for which one can put its limb in a plaster-cast; it must be slaughtered), we would pay the price of the animal. At midday as planned, goats and sheep are punctually there.

But Paolo arrives saying that there is a problem: the peasants of the village who were to bring their animals for 5,000 liras each plus 5,000 for the leader over and above that for the animals, try, he says, to blackmail him saying they won't come for less than 8,000 or 10,000 liras per animal and man. I tell him to tell them from me that I am sorry but that my budget cannot be extended at will and that if it is so that we will shoot without them, with only the two herds of 27 animals, the sheep and the goats. Paolo brings the message and then

Tuesday, 17th September

Pack things up at the church. The Straubs take a room for me in their hotel. Walking with my plaster cast is strange but not painful.

Wednesday, 18th September

8 a.m. We leave Avezzano in a caravan of 3 trucks and 3 cars for the 180 km journey south to Lago Matese. Arrive about 2.30. We all check in for the night at the hotel by the lake. Then we drive down to see the site in the dried-up basin of the lake where they are shooting tomorrow. At dinner Gunter Reich and Louis Devos arrive. We all sit at a long table for this last supper. After dinner at the bar, we play *calcetto* and *flipper* and play all the loud rock 'n' roll numbers on the juke-box.

Thursday, 19th September **Shot 82**

We drive to the lake-side in the morning mist. Lake Matese is situated in the centre of the Monti del Matese so that the sun takes a few hours to clear the humidity which settles over the lake during the night. Meantime the camera is set up down in the lake-bed on rails for a track forwards in Shot 82. This dialogue between Moses now in power and Aaron, his prisoner in chains, is the text of the third act of the opera which Schoenberg never set to music. In the manuscript of the score on the last sheet of the second act is written *End of the second* comes to tell me that they are all getting dressed in the church and that there are even more than had been planned, if he should send them back. I tell him no, to take everybody.

We have the keeper of the camel get dressed as well, which hadn't been planned either, but because we like him a lot and we tell him that he will close the procession on foot holding the camel by the reins. Gabriele, Paolo, and Leo are on the outside of the amphitheatre to organise the procession, under orders from Jeti who, since we no longer need his Nagra and the sound is simpler to record, has become an efficient assistant: he gets along well with the peasants, never screams. The first take is not very good, the start is magnificent with the sheep jumping over the goats, but there is a big space left because the cows' departure is not well synchronised as yet. We start again a second time: it is better, the rhythm picks up. The third time is good, we don't want to tire or upset the animals uselessly, we stop. The next day we make sure that there were not accidents with the goats. The peasants go to change their dress, then come to take their money: I have a long list with their names and the number of animals. Not the least discussion. But there is a drama going on in front of the church: the camel refuses to get back into her truck, she is sitting down on the ground and moans. With the freedom all of a sudden, the asses, the sand—she doesn't want to leave any more to go to her zoo. She has to be hauled by force into the truck, and this revolt, which I learn about in its aftermath, the payments finished, strangles my heart.

act/Barcelona/10.III. 1932/Arnold Schoenberg. In '33 he had to leave Berlin, passing from New York to Hollywood. Schoenberg mentions beginning work again on the third act in his letters during his years in America: *But I have already conceived to a great extent the music for the third act, and believe that I would be able to write it in only a few months* (1949), but it remained in fragment, and in the year of his death he wrote: *Agreed that the third act may simply be spoken, in case I cannot complete the composition* (1951). Jean-Marie has rehearsed the text with Reich and Devos so that their recitation follows the rhythmic patterns he intends. The camera at first LS on Moses, Aaron, and two warriors, Hans-Peter Boffgen and Harold Vogel. Moses, without veil as in the first opening shot, stands left in the frame with his back to the camera and turned to the lake. Aaron on the edge of the water lies right with his head on the ground, bound. On his right stand the two warriors. The camera tracks forwards to MCS on Aaron in high-angle view: 'Never did thy word come unexplained to the people!' Moses: 'To serve, to serve the idea of God, is the freedom for which this people is chosen.' The camera pans upwards left CS on Moses still with his back to it in low-angle view. Moses ends with an address to his chosen people: 'But in the desert you are insuperable and will reach the goal: united with God!' This long dialogue is difficult and several takes are cut before the end of the full four-and-a-half minutes it takes because of the trouble in reciting it correctly. In the one good take of the morning before we break for the *cestino,* an aeroplane flies overhead. Then it begins to rain hard for over an hour so they can't get started again until 3.30. The waterline is about 5 metres closer than in the morning and Aaron's place is now set in the mud. They do two good takes so that the shot is killed at five. J.-M. seems content that it is done. The crew returns to the hotel where we begin to break up. Some leave for Rome. I go to Avezzano with Paolo, Hans-Peter and Anna.

Friday, 20th September
Paolo goes to Alba Fucense to pack up the rest of the equipment. At night we eat at Carmelo's. Jean-Marie writes on my plaster-cast: *Je le ferais encore, si j'avais a le faire?!/Pierre Corneille.*

Saturday, 21st September
The Straubs go to Alba Fucense to finish up packing and to say goodbye to the people in the *paese* who have worked with them. At four we depart from Avezzano and drive to Rome.

Here again we owe our deepest tribute to Aaron: when, after the storm, faced with the water which has risen, we hesitate to ask Aaron, whom we know has had a sort of relapse and arrived with a bit of fever for which he has taken antibiotics, to lie down in the mud to continue, and say to ourselves that since we have the two days in reserve as planned, it would be wiser to wait for the next day to begin again because although we no longer need his voice, he still does!) he comes on his own to find us and says that he is ready to try. Afterwards, he will tell us that bedded in the mud for the whole of the second part of the third act, where only Moses is left in the frame, he prayed that Moses succeed in finishing without making a mistake, without a 'loss of voltage'!

So we finish shooting that very afternoon. In the evening it began to rain, it rained the whole night, all the next day, and the days following almost for a month without letting up: The meteorological 'rupture' which we were worried about since the beginning had arrived!

1
2
3
4
5
R.V. LANZONE DIS.

Le Défilement: A View In Close Up

Thierry Kuntzel

FILM: 'Strip of film used in a movie camera', 'film projected in a movie theater.'[1] It is the relationship between thcse two *films* which will be discussed here on the basis of problems raised in an analysis of an animated film by Peter Foldes, *Appétit d'oiseau (Appetite of a Bird).*[2]

From the film ('the strip of film') to the film ('the projected film'), 'a continuous and moving image is substituted for a series of still and separate perceptions': the *code of movement* 'intervenes in the cinematographic apparatus at the exact moment when the photogram flicks from stillness to its negation; this negation is its end, its specific work.'[3]

Photography, Significance

The relationship stillness-separation/continuity-mobility will not be approached from the viewpoint of Roland Barthes[4] and Sylvie Pierre[5] in their work on the photogram: the search for the way in which film accedes to significance. In the examples they discuss, this significance is intimately linked to the *photographic* nature of the filmic image: the effect of presence, the effect of opaqueness of the unprofessional actor's face and body in the silent films' 'typage', or the parodic over-expressiveness of the professional actor in Eisenstein's sound films, all derive from analogy. In (and against) this analogy we also find the formlessness and non-sense which, according to Sylvie Pierre, constitute 'pure significance': 'On this illegible photogram only *'the trace of the absence of time'* remains inscribed in the immobility of the image. It would seem that cinema does not have two bodies, one a-temporal, the discontinuous chain of still photograms, the other temporal, the unrolling of the images: cinema has only one body, the one in which time is inscribed.'[6]

Drawing, Obviation

The animated film differs from the film made up of photographic images in two ways: image and movement. Because it is drawn, the effects specifically determined by the photographic process are eliminated: 'to describe a drawing' is 'to describe a structure which is already organized in relation to a coded signification.'[7] The photogrammatic text of an animated film excludes such dialogisms as 'effect of presence', or 'over-expressiveness' (which would be the result of an excess of photographic representation, but nevertheless would be necessarily anchored in it). Photography lends itself to an obtuse meaning, the drawing is the locus of obvious meaning.[8] As *animated* drawing, it is created (classically) image by image: its 'shooting unit' is the photogram, while in photographic film, it is the shot which constitutes such a 'unit'. Which is to say that in animated films, there is no photogrammatic 'illegibility'; it is functional, coded like any of the other elements. It still partakes of the obvious meaning—everything in it is shaped, everything produces meaning (everything in it is designed *to make sense*). In photographic films, the camera assumes the responsibility for the code of movement which, in the seeming neutrality of technique, appears to *reproduce* a 'real' movement as 'naturally' as photography reproduces a 'real' fixed object. Because in animated films the space of the film-strip is conceived from the outset in relation to the film-projection, movement does not appear as the reproduction of a pseudo-real but as a *production,* in the same way as the image presents itself as a *production* which parades its codes, its signifying processes, without the support of any analogical transfer.[9]

From Film to Film

To stop the moving image of an animated film is not to subvert meaning in the same way as Roland Barthes and Sylvie Pierre understand it:[10] i.e. the fracturing of the communication-signification order. But to freeze the image, is *to subvert* (literally: to reverse) *meaning* (here, direction) of this order which has been conceived in terms of its end—from a place of origin to a place of projection. This subversion is the turning of one's back to the screen, the place assigned to the spectator, in order to get hold of the film-strip, the place of signifying production whose access is usually restricted to the senders. The animator conceives the film-strip (each photogram, the articulation between the photograms) in relation to the film-projection and in relation to a meaning which movement will actually bring about. The analyst proceeds in the opposite direction.[11] He starts from the film-projection which, in its moving globality produces an effect, in order to *dis-animate* the photograms and to pinpoint where the effect is produced. The proposition to conduct the analysis from the effect back to the production is paraphrastically the same as Freud's in 'The Moses of Michelangelo.'[12] With the work of art, Freud proceeds in exactly the same way as in analyzing dreams, by means of the concept of unbinding.[13] He decomposes, fragments, differentiates; where meaning seems compact, he constructs signifying chains; where the object seems to have to be taken in its entirety, he takes it apart and underlines the importance of the 'insignificant' detail: 'It cannot be denied that there is something extraordinarily attractive about attempts at interpretation of [this] kind. This is because they do not stop short at the general effect of the figure, but are based on separate features in it; these we usually fail to notice, being overcome by the total impression of the statue and as it were paralyzed by it.' (S.E., p. 219)

The Eraser

Appetite of a Bird has been the object of several so-called 'experiments in reading the image' at the Research Division of the French Radio and Television Office (ORTF). Instead of 'eliciting' verbal responses from the spectator, each time the film was shown it irremediably blocked them (only disconnected comments or a few timid formal remarks were offered). This blockage did not indicate a lack of interest in the film but rather the impossibility of detecting what actually provoked the *affect* that so many spectators claimed to have experienced, the impossibility of verbalizing the imag(inary). It was as if all the comments were suspended on the mode of 'but...', precisely where Roland Barthes detects the 'traumatic units' in cinema.[14]

The problems of verbalization could be attributed, generally speaking, to the iconic nature of the message (spoken language is eliminated in *Appetite of a Bird*), to the problematic overcoming of 'the distance between the place where "I" speak, reason, understand, and the place where something which is in excess of my words functions: something which is more-than-speech, a meaning-plus-space-plus color.'[15] But iconicity constitutes a minor problem in comparison to the extraordinary 'motion-ness' (*mouvance*) which manifests itself in the entire film: everything is constantly transformed in an uninterrupted graphic production; barely formed, each drawing is deformed into a new one and so on.

The analysis of movement, in this particular instance, could be approached in two ways: the first, a psycho-physiological one, would make it possible, on the basis of a single transformation of an image, to differentiate the elements which are perceived from those which are not (although they are visible when they are not moving) in normal viewing conditions; the second, more semiological, would seek to determine, at the level of the entire film, the logic(s) which control(s) the different transformations. From the viewpoint of the relationship between the film-strip and the film-projection, these two approaches would be complementary: the investigation of the visible (and what seems to disappear in movement), and the analysis of the operations of visible elements in the filmic chain (to what extent does the spectator, subjected to a syntagmatic unfolding of images whose speed is pre-regulated by the machine—24 frames per second—have access to the system by any other means than the laws of unconscious operations?). Between the space of the film-strip and the time of the projections, the film *rubs out*: movement erases its signifying process, and eventually, conceals some of the images which pass by too rapidly to be 'seen', without, nevertheless, failing to produce a subliminal effect (illicit advertising slipping, for the time of a photogram, into the body of a film, it is a particularly crude but revealing example of this effect).

The Field of Transformations

In *Appetite of a Bird,* what is it that is transformed? The characters, to the extent that the drawing allows us to recognize them, initially a man and a woman, whose avatars make up the film. Besides the metamorphoses which affect the global structure of the object—and which each time call for a re-naming—the man becomes a lion; the woman is transformed into a bird, etc.—some elements are transformed within the given figure (without necessitating the re-naming of the object): the man's head inflates, his legs are shortened, areas of the body are displaced, establishing connections like eye-mouth-genitals, etc. These two types of transformations may occur concurrently, a partial transformation often initiating a global transformation. A third type of transformation must be added, one which no longer concerns the codes of iconic designation,[16] but only the *graphic materiality* itself. From one photogram to the next, a given shape may remain 'identical', but here it may be sharp, there it is 'scribbled', as if drawn by a child, elsewhere it is etched out, or filled in, etc.

The example analyzed here is situated on the level of partial transformations (the variations produced within the shape of the bird). The other two levels are nevertheless also articulated there: the level of global transformations to the extent that this transformation reveals, in an abbreviated form, the principles of the entire narrative organization; the level of the transformation of the 'treatment' of the drawing itself. These variations (additions or eliminations of color) from one photogram to the next, while less spectacular than in other parts of the film are nonetheless determinative for its signification.

Decomposition of a Movement

What are the elements of the narrative? A woman—who becomes a bird—is chased by a man—who turns into a lion. Several times, the latter attempts to kill the bird with his paw, but each time, the bird comes back to life (*se re-anime*) until finally it flies away and then swoops down on the lion, devouring it in a second. The narrative logic could be satisfied with this reversal of power positions, the reversal of this gag (if we take the film as a pun), of this conceit (very frequent in Spanish baroque poetry). The bird, however, fat and clumsy, takes off on the left-hand side of the screen, and makes a last pass, a last display, an ultimate 'parade' for the sake of the spectator (whereas until this point all its transformations were within narrative conventions, 'displayed' for the benefit of the lion-man). It is this last ostentatious flight which will be decomposed here.

Twenty one 'phases' have been identified in the photogrammatic text. Phase 11 constitutes the 'cleavage' of this segment, phase 12 repeats phase 10, phase 13 repeats phase 9, and so on, until the return to the bird's original shape in phase 21 (phases 12-21 will not be described again in the analysis). The uneven numbers correspond to the lowered positions of the wings, and to a relative neutrality in the operations of transformation; even numbers mark the raised positions of the wings and the strong up-beat of their metamorphosis—the various sexual (trans)figurations (see figure 1).

The Work of Condensation

At the level of global transformations, the woman's change into a bird and the man's into a lion function to displace the question of sexual difference onto a difference of power. By stressing the power difference, this change makes it possible to transform at the same time the relation of desire into a relationship of violence: *Appetite of a Bird* stages *'a sadistic view of coition'*[17] and archaic phantasies of devouring—and in a larger sense, phantasies of incorporation. In blurring sexual difference, this change leaves open the possibility of bisexuality for the two 'characters' involved, or more precisely, the possibility of the woman, too, having a penis. This infantile phantasy of the phallic mother, legible in filigree in the narrative logic, is actually visualized at several points in the film (in particular during the bird's seduction dance before the lion and in its 'resurrections'—'res-erections' —between the claws of its agressor), but never as clearly as during the final flight. Coming after the narrative point of the bird devouring the lion, this final flight is the point of convergence of the phantasmatic logic set up by *Appetite of a Bird* because the figurations, sometimes feminine, sometimes masculine, which until that point were identified with the bird in this segment, are first alternated (phase 8), then mixed (phase 10).

Phase 8 might well be equivalent to an unsuccessful condensation: 'If the objects which are to be condensed into a single unity are much too incongruous, the dream-work is often content with creating a composite structure with a comparatively distinct nucleus, accompanied by a number of less distinct features. In that case the process of unification into a single image may be said to have failed. The two representations are superimposed and produce something in the nature of a contest between the two visual images.'[18] To the image of the bird, 'a comparatively distinct nucleus', less distinct attributes have been associated: masculinity (a-a') *or* femininity (b-b'), the transformations of the wings and the body taking the shape of the male sexual organ in the first instance, and in the second, exploiting a redundancy of the features of the female genitals. 'The contest between the two visual images', to use Freud's words, requires us, to begin with, to substitute an *and* in the place of the *or:* 'If, however, in reproducing a dream, its narrator feels inclined to make use of an 'either—or'—e.g., "it was either a garden or a sitting-room" ', this does not mean that the dream-thought offered an alternative; that was an "and": a simple addition.'[19] In phase 10, as in 8, there is a succession of two sub-phases, but by means of a simple permutation from a' and b', the two figures are no longer the one masculine, the other feminine, but both, masculine *and* feminine. Perfect condensation, phantasmatic formation,[20] 'transgression of the Antithesis, crossing the wall of opposites, elimination of the difference,'[21] the picture makes it possible to render co-present here, in the same body, the two sexes, to transform the phantasy into an ob-ject—placed in front of, displayed to the eye, in the manner of representations of the Egyptian goddess Mut:'

'...this vulture-headed mother goddess was usually represented by the Egyptians with a phallus; her body was female, as the breasts indicated, but it also had a male organ in a state of erection.'[22]

The Cleavage of the Film

The sub-phase a' and b' of phases 8 and 10 are maintained, for the space of two photograms, exactly as they are described in the above 'decomposition'. The remainder of the photogrammatic text of phases 8 and 10 serves as a transition to insure, when the film is set in motion, the continuity, the flux, the *'défilement'. Défilement* lends itself to the same operation as 'erasing' because it means, in the vocabulary of cinema, 'progression, the sliding of the film-strip through the gate of a projector'[23] and, in military art, the use of the terrain's accidents or of artificial constructions to conceal one's movements from the enemy. In the unrolling of the film, the photograms which concern us 'pass through', hidden from sight: what the spectator retains is only the movement within which they insert themselves and, from the bird's variations, only the shape maintained throughout the entire segment: feminine figuration represented by the synecdoche of the breasts.[24]

'In the process of condensation, on the other hand, every psychical interconnection is transformed into an *intensification* of its ideational content. The case is the same as when, in preparing a book for the press, I have some word which is of special importance for understanding the text printed in spaced or heavy type; or in speech I should pronounce the same word loudly and slowly and with special emphasis.'[25] The hypothesis advanced here concerning the operation of the sub-phase a-a' and b-b' is that those elements which are not seen consciously have an unconscious effect . Their effect is the stronger here because it obeys one of the essential modes of unconscious operation (a mode particularly insistent, Freud says—condensation) and is the more so because the belief that these elements 'stage' (the phallic woman) is at the origin of the disavowal of reality: I *know* that the woman has no penis, *but even so,* she has one which I hallucinate.[26]

In the same way as the psychotic's ego (who hallucinates the phallus) or the fetishist's ego (who maintains his original belief by transferring the value of the phallus to another part of the body), *film seems split* between the film-strip, the place where the fantasy is maintained (where woman is phallic), and the film-projection (where woman appears deprived of a penis). It would seem that the plane of expression of *Appetite of a Bird* re-presents its plane of content, in a dazzling reflection on the articulation of seeing and non-seeing accomplished through the process of movement.

L'Emouvoir

The 'sender'—the animator—and the analyst—the disanimator alone know that *one* (the film) *is divided into two.* In the segment analyzed here, the hypothesis is the limit-possibility of the autonomy of the photogrammatic text and of the film in motion which, as the seen and the unseen, recognition and disavowal, 'continue to exist side by side (...) without influencing one another.'[27] In *Appetite of a Bird,* the cleavage constitutes a general structuring principle which is articulated particulary in the interaction between stillness and motion (*mouvance*). The cleavage becomes apparent only at the conclusion of an expanded textual analysis which no longer tries to turn the film into a picture, to determine its structure, but attempts this time to conceive simultaneously this structure (in this particular case, the photogrammatic text) and the filmic process, the syntagmatic unravelling of the film.[28]

The spectator, who only sees the film-projection and does not examine the film strip, cannot have access to the system of the film, because the latter depends partially on the relation between the two films. He believes (because cinema sustains this belief) that there is only one film, the one he sees on the screen, the film in motion. Consequently, the photogram is seen only as a piece of film *deprived* of movement; already, it is no longer film. It is therefore necessary to correct the connection drawn earlier between the effect produced by the film and the display of cleavage in the segment. The spectator does not see the film as film-strip; therefore, if the relation between the two films is conceived—textually—as cleavage, it seems necessary, in order to analyze the normal viewing conditions—the spectacle—to reconsider the relation in terms of *repression.* The photogrammatic text is not read parallel to the moving film, but the phantasmatic elements are identified; in, under, across (the precise wording is difficult) the projected film. It is this 'marking' which constitutes the specific 'impression' produced by *Appetite of a Bird,* that which could be called, with reference to movement and to the effect: *l'émouvoir.* 'As far as aesthetic pleasure is concerned, it is necessary that there be at the same time a repression of desire (...) and a removal of the inhibition. It is necessary for the spectator to experience both recognition and disavowal. What makes the removal of inhibition possible, thanks to the cathectic energy which is saved up is the formal work of the artist....Form, which has on the surface no relationship to the tendency which is to be invested, is intended to distract the spectator's attention and therefore make possible the discharge of energy.'[29] On the plane of content, the rate of speed of movement (Foldes called another of his films *Plus vite (Faster))* is the condition which enables the spectator to find pleasure in seeing his repressed archaic phantasies represented. But, on the plane of expression, it is the film-projection which, by means of movement, represses the film-strip, barring access to the signifying process which underlies it. *L'émouvoir* is therefore mixed: 'bonus of seduction' guaranteed by motion—the graphic and chromatic 'delirium' which manifests itself in it— and *uncanny,* by leading, in adulthood, to the repressed material of an earlier period: 'a childhood fear', 'a childhood desire', or more simply even (...), 'a childhood belief.'[30]

Filmic Analysis

'The meaning effect no longer merely depends on the content of images' but on the material processes by means of which an illusory continuity which takes into account the persistence of vision is reinstated by the means of discontinuous elements—these elements, film images, containing, between those which precede and those which follow, differences. These differences are indispensable in order to create the illusion of continuity, of continuous movement, the illusion of something running through (time, movement). But there is one condition to this, it is that as differences these differences be erased.'[31] *Appetite of a Bird* makes the most of the possibility of erasing the difference by means of *l'émouvoir:* it makes sense, but which sense? in which parts of the film? according to what logic? It is here that *Appetite of a Bird* calls attention to the specificity of filmic analysis. When Metz defines the means by which the semiologist proceeds in his analysis as 'ideally parallel to that followed by the film-spectator' ('the semiologist seeks to unrevel this trajectory in all its phases, while the spectator skips over all of them at once without any of it being made explicit'), and the 'semiologist's reading' as 'a meta-reading, an analytic reading, contrasted with the spectator's "naive" reading', he conceives the two trajectories, the two readings (the spectator's and the semiologist's) as two separate readings of *the same film. The film in motion* however (*since this is the real topic of the discussion*) *can only yield readings which are more or less 'naive'*, to use Metz's words, i.e. approaches which remain on the side of the *meaning produced,* and not on that of the *production of meaning.* Thus, no matter how accurate a 'view in long shot' may be, Eisenstein puts it in the category of the medium shot;[32] both bear on the filmic signified, the former without any critical perspective, the latter taking a critical stance in relation to the signified. But, it is only with 'the view in close up' that the signifier is taken into account: 'There is a third way to examine a film. Not only is it *possible* to have a third way of reading a film, but it is necessary. It is the analysis of the film *in close up,* through the prism of a tight analysis; the analysis decomposes the film into its parts, resolves its elements in order to study its totality exactly in the same manner as engineers and specialists study a new type of construction in their technologyical field.'[33] If 'to understand how a film is understood,'[34] is for Metz the purpose of analysis, *Appetite of a Bird* insists in an exemplary manner on the fact that the analyst's understanding of *the way the spectator understands cannot be achieved with an analysis of the film which is still:* the operation of the filmic machine (*l'émouvoir*) is inscribed in the film-strip: locus of the work of signification, the effects resulting from the *défilement* have already been assessed in it; the constitution of the differential (discontinuous) network takes place in relation to the undifferentiation of the continuous. The *filmic* which will be the object of the filmic analysis therefore will be found neither on the side of motion nor on the side of stillness, but *between* them,[35] in the generation of the projected film by the film-strip, in the negation of this film-strip by the projected film, by the erasing work (itself erased) of the work of signification.

Translated by Bertrand Augst

NOTES

1. *Grand Larousse Encyclopédique*, vol. V, p. 10.
2. *Appetite of a Bird* is distributed in this country by Films Inc. in Los Angeles.
3. Christian Metz, *Langage et cinéma*, Paris, Larousse, 1971, p. 145.
4. Roland Barthes, 'The Third Meaning: Notes on Some of Eisenstein's Stills,' Translated by Richard Howard; *Artforum*, vol. XI, no. 5, Jan. 1973; originally published in *Les Cahiers du Cinéma*, no. 222, July 1970.
5. Sylvie Pierre, 'Eléments pour une théorie du photogramme,' *Les Cahiers du Cinéma*, no. 226-227, Jan.-Feb. 1971.
6. Sylvie Pierre, *op. cit.*, p. 77.
7. Roland Barthes, 'Le Méssage photographique,' *Communications*, no. 1, 1961.
8. '...it is a meaning which seeks me out—me, the recipient of the message, subject of the reading—a meaning which proceeds from Eisenstein and moves ahead of *me.* It is evident, of course (as the other meaning is, too), but evident in a closed sense, participating in a complete system of intention. I propose to call this meaning the *obvious meaning/le sens obvie/, 'The Third Meaning,'* p. 46.
9. In the case of Walt Disney, the problem should be re-examined because his animated films are an attempt to reproduce the photographic analogy (if only because of the multiplane camera and the use of 'real' movement—as it is analyzed by the camera: 'Walt had only one recourse: shoot his films with live actors, then transfer their movements on celluloid barely distorting their features, which is the method he is using for *Cinderella, Alice* and *Peter Pan.'* Robert Benayoun, *Le Déssin animé;* Paris, J.J. Pauvert, 1961.
10. 'The violently subversive power of the photogrammatic text is...even much more radical than had been sensed by Roland Barthes (analyzing a photogrammatic text dealing with ceremonial, hierarchized, in the unravelling of which points of the greatest legibility possible, of the most solemn form, have been privileged) because it is the very meaning of the image, its whole meaning, which can be subverted by the photogram.' Sylvie Pierre, *op. cit.*, p. 77.
11. 'The signifier and its organization remain the "property"/the prerogative/of the graphic artist...in cinema, the signified offers itself spontaneously to the receiver while the signifier requires an initiation...' Michel Gheude, *Cinéthique*, no. 7-8, p. 64.
12. Sigmund Freud, 'The Moses of Michelangelo,' vol. XIII of the Standard Edition, London, Hogarth Press, 1953. Henceforth referred to as S.E.

13. André Green, 'La deliaison,' *Littérature*, no. 3, October 1971. /The term un-binding is adapted from W.R. Bion, *Elements of Psycho-Analysis*, New York, Basic Books, 1963. (Translator)
14. Roland Barthes, 'Les Unités traumatiques au cinema,' *Revue Internationale de Filmologie*, vol. X, no. 34, July-Sept. 1960.
15. Julia Kristeva, 'L'Espace Giotto,' Peinture, *Cahiers théoriques*, no. 2-3, p. 35.
16. Umberto Eco, *La Structure absente*, Paris, Mercure de France, 1971 (see in particular, ch. 1 in section B: 'The Visual Codes.')
17. Sigmund Freud, 'The Sexual Theories of Children,' S.E., vol. IX, p. 220.
18. Sigmund Freud, *The Interpretation of Dreams*. New York, Avon, 1965, p. 359f.
19. *Ibid.*, p. 352.
20. *Ibid.*, p. 359.
21. Roland Barthes, *S/Z*. Paris, Le Seuil, 1970, p. 221.
22. Sigmund Freud, 'Leonardo da Vinci and a Memory of his Childhood,' S.E., vol. XI, p. 94.
23. Maurice Bessy and Jean-Louis Chardans, *Dictionnaire du cinéma et de la télévision*, Paris, J.J. Pauvert, 1966.
24. This assertion is true in normal viewing conditions, when the film is projected once without any preamble or commentary. When the segment which is analyzed in this article is projected several times successively, at the normal sound speed, and when the spectators have been warned ahead of time of what to look for, the masculine representations are recognized, but never, except with the use of freeze frames, the more bisexual representations of phase 10.
25. Sigmund Freud, *The Interpretation of Dreams, op cit.*, p. 634.
26. O. Manoni, *'Je sais bien, mais quand même...*, 'in *Clefs pour L'Imaginaire* ou *L'Autre Scène*. Paris, Le Seuil, 1969; Manoni's essay refers to a case described by Freud in 'Psycho-Analysis and Telepathy,' S.E. vol. XVIII, pp. 181-185. The English translation of the French rendition *'Je sais being mais quand même...'* reads as 'No doubt it has not come true, but...' p. 183 (Translator)
27. Sigmund Freud, 'An Outline of Psycho-Analysis,' S.E., vol. XXIII, p. 202.
28. This type of textual analysis might provide a solution to the problem of hiatus 'between genesis and structure, process and picture,' which Barthes finds particularly difficult for semiology of cinema. (See ' 'Les "Unités traumatiques" au cinema,' *op. cit.*, p. 14.
29. Sarah Kofman, *L'Enfance de l'art*. Paris, Payot, 1970, p. 149.
30. Sigmund Freud, 'The "Uncanny",' S.E., vol. XVII, p. 233.
31. Jean-Louis Baudry, 'Cinéma: éffets ideologiques produits par l'appareil de base,' *Cinéthique*, no. 7-8; translated in English by Alan

Williams and published in *Film Quarterly,* vol. XXVII, no. 2, Winter 1974-75, 39-47.

32. Christian Metz, *op. cit.,* p. 56.

33. S.M. Eisenstein, 'A View in Close Up,' *Les Cahiers du cinema,* no. 226-227, Jan.-Feb. 1976, p. 14. The view in *general shot* is 'the perception of the film as a whole: of its thematic necessity' of its actuality, of the way it relates to the immediate needs, of its accurate ideological presentation of the problems it deals with, of the way it is accessible to the masses, of its usefulness, of its impact to carry out the struggle, etc.' In the *View in Medium Shot,* 'the spectator is moved by the live display of emotions...gripped by the story and the circumstances...He is immersed by the emotions of music, and he is often unaware that he is listening to music as a sound background to the dialogue which captivates him.'

34. Christian Metz, *op. cit.,* p. 56.

35. While on the side of the obtuse meaning, this definition of the *filmic* is similar to Roland Barthes' in 'The Third Meaning,' *op. cit.,* p. 46: 'Yet, if the authentically filmic (the filmic of the future) is not in movement, but in a third meaning, an inarticulate meaning which neither the simple photograph nor figurative painting can assume because they lack the diegetic horizon, the possibility of configuration which has been discussed...' note 2: 'The innovation represented by the still in relation to these other stills would be that the filmic (which it constitutes) would be doubled in another text: the film' *Op. cit.,* p. 50.

NOTE: Two additional references in conjunction with *Le Défilement* are the preface of *Revue d'Esthétique* No. 234, 1973 and *A Note Upon the Filmic Apparatus* in the *Quarterly Review of Film Studies* Vol. 1 No. 3, August 1976.

BIRD
(black figure on a white background)

1	Wings	Body
2	Wings	Breasts
3	Wings	Breasts (outside edges red)
4	Wings (almost meeting)	Breasts (see #3)
5	Wings (edged in blue and red)	Breasts (see #3 and #)
6	Wings-Vagina (the wings touch each other, the central area remains open in the shape of a vagina; the red goes from the outside edge of the wing to the inside—the figuration of female genitalia)	Breasts (lose their red contour: only the nipple remains colored)
7	Wings (see #5)	Breasts (see #6)
8.	a) Wings-Penis. (the wings come together all the way, forming a penis)	a') Testicles. (for the duration of the penis figuration the nipples disappear)
	b) Wings-Vagina. (the wings)	b') Breasts. (the nipples reappear as in 6)
9	Wings-Vagina (see #7)	Breasts (see #7)
10.	a) Wings-Penis. (see #8a)	a') Breasts. (see #8b')
	b) Wings-Vagina (see #8b)	b') Testicles (see #8a')
11	Wings (see #7 and 9)	Breasts (see #7 and 9)

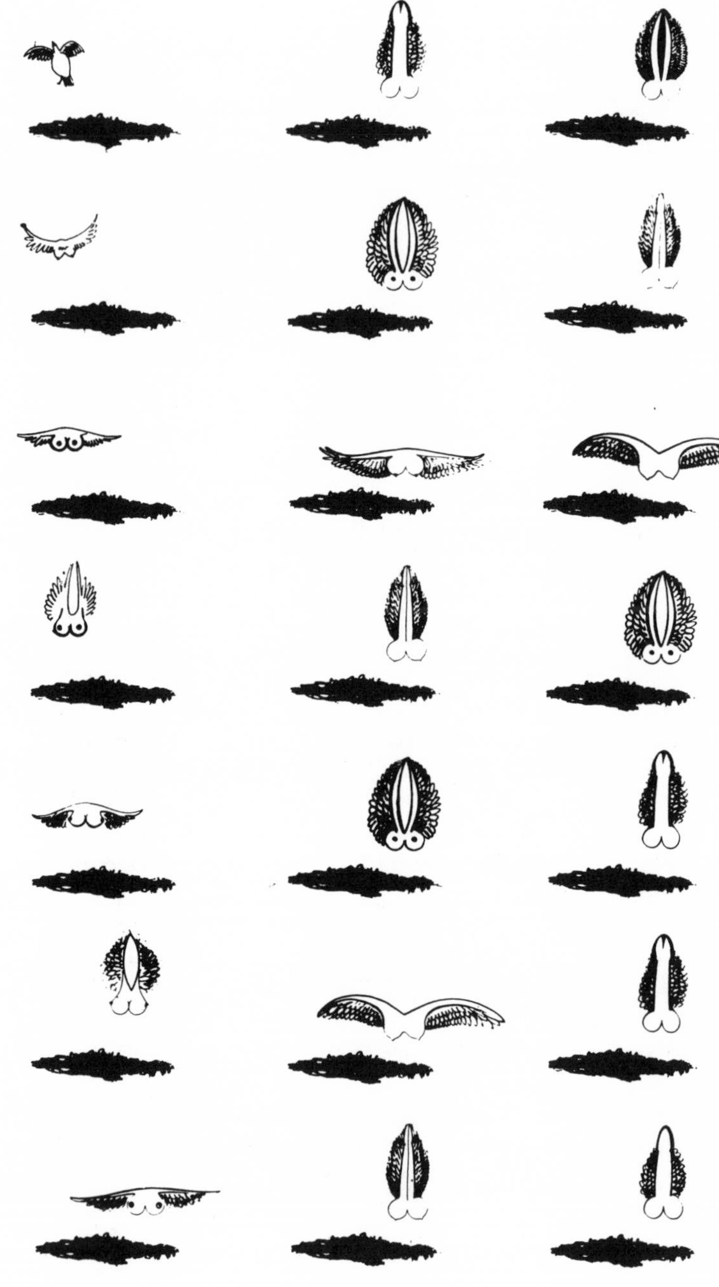

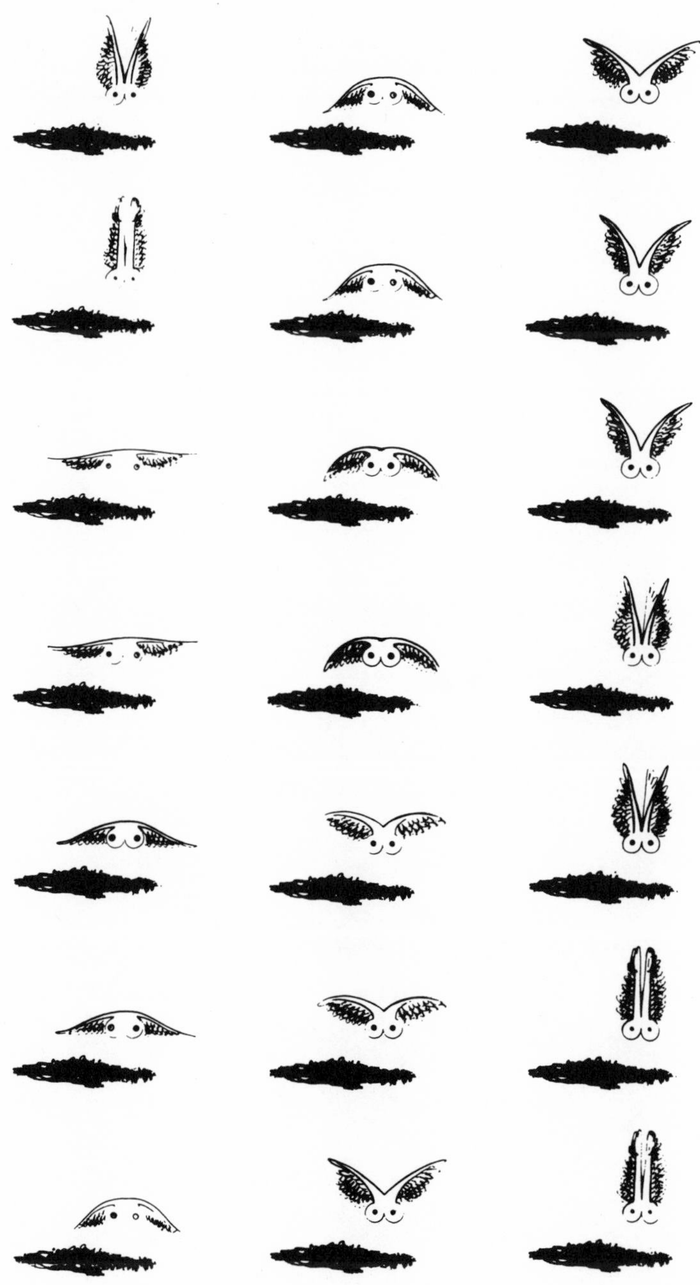

The *Défilement* Into the Look...

Bertrand Augst

Thierry Kuntzel's[1] close scrutiny of the effect produced by the *défilement* of a series of still images passing through the gates of a projector, and Raymond Bellour's[2] analysis of the inflection of the film-text resulting from the director's intervention in the dialectics of the look in the diegesis of the film, and between the characters and the spectators, delineate a new space of investigation for film theory. Both studies deal with what is perhaps the most inaccessible, 'unattainable' among the numerous operations which interact in the production of the cinema-effect, what Kuntzel also calls, 'the filmic': that delicate balance between stillness and movement, whereby 'the film-projection is generated by the film-strip in the denial of this same film-strip by the film-projection in the rubbing out of the work of signification.' A text which also is unattainable, in the sense first used by Bellour of 'introuvable,' by being literally and figuratively unquotable, everlastingly slipping through in the instance of being identified, seized for closer scrutiny. 'Between the space of the film-strip and the time of the projection, the film is rubbed out: movement erases its signifying process, and eventually, conceals some of the images which pass too rapidly to be 'seen' without nevertheless producing a subliminal effect...' In both instances, their analysis reveals the intrinsic duplicity of the cinematographic apparatus, at once stimulating and repressing the spectator's desire for that which must be denied to him in order to manifest itself. The 'film-strip' can only turn into 'film-projection' where the 'unreal' of the image is materialized if, in the instant that the film-strip begins to file past the projector's gate, someone intervenes in the filmic operation in order to inscribe in it the position of an enunciator.

The merit of Kuntzel's article is to combine a precise and detailed analysis of a film-text, 'a view in close-up,'[3] and the broad theoretical implications that it supports. Slowing down the progression of the film-strip, as if viewed on the screen of an editing bench, Kuntzel strips bare the elaborate film-work which conceals the machination of the apparatus.

Pursuing his study of the cinematographic apparatus undertaken in several other studies with reference to the Freudian model, this analysis of the signifying process in Foldes' *Appetite of a Bird* reveals one of the most important effects of the *défilement* in the elaboration of the film-work. Kuntzel calls this effect, *l'émouvoir,* a word untranslatable in English, but which condenses very happily in French, the idea of movement, that of the film's (as film-strip into film-projection), and that of the spectator's, moved visually, psychologically and unconsciously; in *émouvoir,* to move and to *be* moved are uniquely fused to render that startling effect produced by the perception of images which must be repressed in order to be seen. *L'émouvoir* is indeed a key concept which, very astutely, Kuntzel articulates on the mutation of the film-strip into film-projection. The fact that *Appetite of a Bird* is an animated film and not a photographic film, and that, on the plane of content, it displays the spectator's 'repressed archaic phantasies,' provides Kuntzel with a highly exceptional instance of what he called *l'émouvoir* because in photographic films, the *défilement* conceals even more completely the complex operations of the film-work which it sustains. In *Appetite of a Bird,* the effect of *l'émouvoir* is double: it combines the 'calligraphic and chromatic delirium, of animation with the 'uncanny', by means of which the adult spectator accedes to infantile fears, desires, or beliefs, repressed at a primitive stage of his development. All films, and many of their multiple cinematographic operations depend directly on the *défilement,* from the impression of reality to vast operations of the narrative systems. In photographic films however, and Kuntzel emphasizes the importance of this difference at the beginning of his article, it is the camera which takes charge of the codes of movement. In animated films, movement is not the result of a re-production of a pseudo-real; both the iconic representation and movement are conceived as a production. The effect produced by the *défilement* in photographic films is therefore, and by definition, different from *l'émouvoir.*

While it is difficult to duplicate Kuntzel's analysis with the same clarity and simplicity applied to a photographic film, the implications of his demonstration are far reaching because the effect of *l'émouvoir* is not confined to *Appetite of a Bird* or to animated films; it is the very base of the cinematographic apparatus. So much so that without the *défilement* there cannot be a cinema-effect, if we understand by that the effect produced by the passing of the film through the gate of the projector at 24 frames per second, i.e. under the *ideal* conditions of the operation of the basic cinematographic apparatus. This is not to say that the *défilement* does not produce an effect when the film projection is running slower or faster than 24 frames per second; from the early days of cinema to the most radical films of contemporary experimental cinema, the history of cinema shows precisely the opposite. But the effect produced is different. As the projection speed is altered, slower or faster, the presence of the apparatus and its specific operations intrude with greater or lesser insistence in the work of *défile-*

ment. A speed variation of a few frames per second is enough to reveal the ever threatening presence of machination in cinema.

In the course of his discussion of special effects and cinema, Christian Metz remarked, several years ago, that cinema was nothing more than a vast system of deception.[4] The duplicity of the filmic process is nowhere more in evidence than in the way special effects are used, sometimes aggressively displayed as special effects; and sometimes so completely invisible that the spectator is truly deceived. Or, yet still, they are invisible but perceptible, teasing the credulity of the spectator, who is always too eager to play along with the filmmaker's attempt to seduce him by performing 'magical tricks' for him.

Special effects are only a small part of the many devices which constitute the basic cinematographic apparatus. In the film-work, these special effects combine with the many invisible markers of enunciation which regulate the production of the film-text. Perpetually oscillating between visibility and invisibility, special effects, from the doubling of an actor, to the editor's splices, not to mention lighting effects or corny atmospheric musical scores, conspire to reinforce the machination of cinema. It is the artfulness with which this machination is managed which will determine the quality of the spectator's identification, and which may be used to titillate even the analyst's curiosity, pulling him away from his fetishistic desire into the regressive pleasure shared by the rest of the 'naive' spectators.

Cinematographic 'tricks' which are used to produce special effects may be explicit or so finely tuned that they become invisible and imperceptible. The coarser they are, as in the case of superimpressions or demarcation signifiers (fades and lap-dissolves), the more the enunciation apparatus will be in evidence. In the broader context of special effects which are used to prop up the spectator's belief, and to maintain the precarious balance necessary for his disavowal, there is precisely the effect of the film-strip passing through the projector gate. The *defilement* is also one of those 'special effects'—and if one goes back far enough in the history of cinematographic codes, all were at some point perceived as such before they came to be stabilized in the socialization of the cinematographic institution. As Kuntzel's article shows, the *defilement* is at the very center of the filmic machine. It is the operation which sutures the two bodies of the film (the film-strip and the film-projection) into a film-text. By definition, *l'émouvoir* can only be produced if the *defilement* operation retains its optimal conditions of invisibility, so that the differences registered in the material support are effaced (rubbed out) in the projection which creates the illusion of continuous movement. *Défilement,* as we have seen, is also, above all, the effect which, bolstered by iconicity, sutures the basic cinematographic apparatus and the psychical apparatus.

It is evident that the apparatus produces an effect which is different in photographic films from that produced by animated films. What needs to be emphasized is not so much the radical difference in the signifying processes of these two types of films as their similarity. Describing the process whereby some of the photograms in *Appetite of a Bird* dissimulate themselves (literally in French, 'se défilent'), so that only some of the bird's movements are seen, those which denote female sexuality, Kuntzel quotes a passage from *The Interpretation of Dreams* in which Freud calls attention to the transfer of psychic energy in the process of condensation: '...every psychical interconnection is transformed into an *intensification* of its ideational content.' Kuntzel's hypothesis is that the photograms which are not seen in the sub-phases a-a' and b-b'—the images which show the bird's wings forming into the shape of a penis—produce an effect which is unconscious. The effect is all the stronger for the fact that 1. it ' "obeys" one of the essential modes [of operation] of the unconscious, ... condensation,' and 2. the 'belief that these elements "set the stage" '; thus, in this particular instance, it is 'the phallic woman' which is hallucinated. Kuntzel is making an analogy between the cleavage of the film-strip ('where the woman is phallic') and the film-projection ('where the woman appears deprived of a penis') and the ego of the psychotic who hallucinates the penis, or that of the fetishist 'who maintains his original belief by transferring it to another part of the body.' It is however, this same mechanism of 'disavowal' which controls multiple operations of the cinematographic process. At this point, we rejoin the larger problems of the metapsychology of cinema which have been discussed extensively by Christian Metz.[5] There is therefore no need to insist on the importance of this mechanism in cinema, or in the theater for that matter, as Octave Mannoni[6] has shown. I want only to underline the fact that it is the same mechanism which supports the effect of *l'émouvoir* as described by Kuntzel, and the many operations of cinema from the primary disavowal which sustains the spectator's perception of the moving image—the series of still images are no more visible than the penis hidden in the bird's wings—to the complex structuring operations of disavowal inscribed in the 'imaginary signifier.'

It is understood that the audience is not duped by the diegetic illusion, it "knows" that the screen presents no more than a fiction. And yet, it is of vital importance for the correct unfolding of the spectacle that this make-believe be scrupulously respected (or else the fiction film is declared 'poorly made'), that everything is set to work to make the deception effective and to give it an air of truth (this is the problem of *verisimilitude*). Any spectator will tell you that he 'doesn't believe in it', but everything happens as if there were nonetheless someone to be deceived, someone who really will 'believe in it'. (I shall say that behind any fiction there is a second fiction: the diegetic events are fictional, that is the first; but everyone pretends to believe they are true, and that is the second). In other words, asks Mannoni, since it is 'accepted' that the audience is incredulous, who is it who is credulous and must be maintained in his credulousness by the perfect organization of the machine (of the machination)? This credulous person is, of course, another part of ourselves, he is still seated *beneath* the incredulous one, or in his heart, it is he who continues to believe, who disavows what he knows (he for whom all human beings are still endowed with penises). By a symmetrical and simultaneous movement, the incredulous disavows the credulous: no one will admit that he is duped by the "plot".[7]

Thus the *défilement* is but one of the various sub-codes whereby disavowal is inscribed in the film apparatus. As Metz indicates in the same essay, there are many others situated at different points in the signifying process. *L'émouvoir* too is inscribed in the regime of disavowal, and in a sense, doubly so since it is ordered by the basic apparatus but also re-duplicated, so to speak, through the work of condensation at the level of the production of the text. In a larger sense too, the effect of the *défilement* is double. On one level, it transforms the filmscript into film-projection by concealing the work of the cinematographic machination. In the same process however, it redoubles its power over the spectator in order to secure the belief of that other spectator 'seated *beneath* the incredulous one.' 'What is concealed in the manifest text of the dream is primarily the work of dissimulation, the aim of which is to make the dream appear as superfluous, useless and unreadable.' In the same way, the film-projection dissimulates the work of the *défilement* in order to make the film-strip appear 'superfluous, useless and unreadable.'

There is another aspect of Kuntzel's analysis of *Appetite of a Bird* which deserves mention. In several of his papers, he has used the concept of condensation and displacement to describe various complex operations in the figuration of the film-text. However, condensation as used to describe the work of dissimulation in the film-text provides yet another instance of the usefulness of this concept applied to textual analysis. By placing himself firmly on the side of the production of meaning, and not on the side of the 'meaning produced', Kuntzel points out a new approach to the analysis of the film-text. At the end of his study of 'the imaginary referent,'[8] Metz argues that there are instances when the relationship between units of the signified and units of the signifier is such that when 'there are changes in the referent which cannot be assimilated by the code, these changes can no longer make it evolve and thus subvert a small part of its domain', and therefore distort it. This occurs when the forms of displacement and condensation are so strong that 'they directly affect the signifier.' Traditionally, metaphor and metonymy have been conceived as referential operations. Thus, while obviously, any such operation does 'affect' the signifier, it is mostly in terms of the referents mobilized by the trope that they have been studied. According to Metz, Jakobson's more recent reformulation of the theory of metaphor does not alter this attitude since he relies essentially on semantic similarity and contiguity to describe the mechanism of metaphor, saying very little about the signifier. Metz points out that traditional rhetoric was not totally unaware of the possibility for the metaphorical process 'to engage the signifier directly,' but these devices, like alliteration and apophony, have never been directly related to metaphor and metonymy because they 'remained indifferent' to the referent while metaphor and metonymy are defined directly in relation to it. Thus, the more condensation and displacement demark themselves from metaphor and metonymy, the more they intervene directly upon the signifier. This does not mean that the manifestations which directly affect the signifier do not continue to relate to the signified; they extend the range of metaphor and metonymy, *'elles le deborde'* in Metz's words. He points out that in cinematographic texts, too, such movements of displacement and condensation extend their action to coded units. For instance, experimental cinema offers many examples of such action since one of its aims is 'to subvert and enrich perception to make it communicate more extensively with the unconscious, to de-censor it to the maximum.' Metz mentions Kuntzel's article as an analysis of one such instance when 'the action of condensation and displacement bears on the identity of the objects represented and on the manner in which the codes of iconic designation are affected.'[9] Undoubtedly, the referent is affected in *Appetite of a Bird,* but perhaps, what is most significant in Kuntzel's analysis, is that it also illustrates how the signifer is made to actualize the direct 'distortion' brought to bear upon it by the primary process. In this specific instance, the basic apparatus conspires to produce the effect which actually distorts the signifier by means of the *défilement.* The *défilement* which actualizes the distortion of the material of expression is itself inseparable from it. Can there be any better argument to demonstrate the need for the textual analysis of film-texts to incorporate semio-psychoanalysis? Kuntzel's analysis, demonstrates graphically, literally speaking, that neither the linguistic nor the rhetorical model offers a critical and methodological apparatus which is powerful enough to be of much value for the study of the more complex figurations of the film-text. This is also the implication of Metz's recent important study of metaphor and metonymy.

There is finally another dimension of Kuntzel's essay which should be briefly considered. As the juxtaposition of Kuntzel and Bellour's articles perhaps suggests, there is yet another way in which the *défilement* can be perceived as the central operation in the cinematographic process if we relate it to that instant when sight, glance, turns into *fascinum*. Asked to clarify the nature of the 'suture, the pseudo-identification' effected in the articulation between 'the end point of a gesture' and 'the dialectics of identificatory haste,' Lacan stated that they did overlap, but that in no way was it to be construed that they should be considered identical, since the one did precede the other, Lacan's text is important, and since Bellour refers to it in his essay on *Marnie*, I believe that it is useful to quote it fully.

'This moment of the look which ends a gesture, I link very closely to what I have said about the evil eye. By itself, the look not only tends to terminate movement, but it freezes it. Look at these dances I was talking about a moment ago/dances in the Peking Opera/; they are always punctuated by a series of pauses/literally, dead moments/in which the actors stop moving in an attitude which is blocked. What is the stumbling point, this moment in which movement is stopped? It is nothing more than the fascinatory effect in the necessity there is to exorcize the evil eye. It is that which results from stopping movement and which literally kills life. At the instant when the subject suspends his gestures, he is mortified. The anti-life function, the anti-movement, of this end point, this is the *fascinum*, and it is precisely one of the dimensions where the look exercizes its power directly. The instant in which one sees can only intervene as a suture, a junction between the imaginary and the symbolic, repeated in a dialectic, the kind of temporal progression which is called haste, the forward movement, which ends with the *fascinum*.

What I want to emphasize is the absolute separation between the scopic register in relation to the invoking field, vocatory, vocational. In the scopic field, on the contrary, the subject is not essentially undetermined. The subject is actually determined by the very separation which determines the split of the *a*, i.e. the fascinatory part in what the look introduces.'[10]

It would seem that one of the most important consequences of the effect produced by the *défilement* is to duplicate this suture, another instance of the uncanny affinities between the cinematographic and psychical apparatuses. If the economy of the look regulates the operations of the narrative in the classical cinema, as Bellour argues in his paper, it is only because in cinema, the *défilement* sutures the glance and the evil eye to reinstate the domination of the look, its fascination but also its seduction. *L'émouvoir* thus sustains the displacement of the glance into the look.

Bellour's careful examination of the dialectics of the look as it operates in the beginning of Hitchcock's *Marnie* complements, and in a sense, continues Kuntzel's analysis of *L'émouvoir*. The moment in which the film-strip turns into film-projection, when the real of an unreal is materialized in the form of an image, a circuit is turned on, another link in 'the series of mirror-effects organised in a chain,' which constitute the signifier in cinema.

The import of Bellour's contribution is perhaps best perceived when it is placed in the context of the theory of enunciation in cinema. Within the theoretical framework defined by Metz in 'History/Discourse' and in 'The Imaginary Signifier,' Bellour succeeds in demonstrating with great precision just how one of the most elusive modes of operation of enunciation actually functions in a specific text. His argument, as much as his methodology, have far reaching implications for future research in film criticism because, for the first time, it provides a clear model for the study of an area in film studies which has heretofore remained practically untouched. To date, the study of enunciation in cinema has been almost completely dominated by the linguistic and the literary models inspired by the work of Benveniste, Barthes, Todorov and Genette. What renders the study of enunciation in cinema so problematic is the fact that, as in so many other instances in the constitution of the signifier in cinema, the film-text dissimulates the work of enunciation. At the risk of oversimplifying this complex problem, the work of enunciation in cinema might be defined as a discourse which displays itself as 'language', i.e. precisely the opposite of what it is. What distinguishes filmic discourse from other types of discourse is that it constitutes itself as a type of discourse in which the markers of the subject of enunciation have been supressed or concealed. It is a discourse which presents itself as history.

Bellour pursues the implication of this theoretical sketch by separating one of the central enunciative functions from the other operations embedded in the articulation of the film-work. This enunciation function is the look, not just any look, but that look which the American cinema has best inscribed in the body of the classic narrative films, the look determined by the double edged fascination of the image of woman. In order to unravel that specific enunciative function with sufficient clarity, Bellour ingeniously centers his demonstration on what at first sight might seem paradoxical, if not the very opposite of what he is trying to isolate: Hitchcock's intervention in the filmic apparatus. However, it is only to the extent that this intervention is perceptible that it becomes possible to assess the degree to which this intervention dialectically affects the spectator's identification with the image. By pointing to Hitchcock's own 'perverse' participation in this process, and the intensification which results from the insertion of his own look within the diegesis of the film, Bellour also reveals the complex interplays between the spectator's and the character's look, and of course, Hitchcock's doubling back to the spectator through the intermediary of the same characters. Hitchcock's films are not only a perfectly controlled economy of pleasure in the process of generating the 'artificial psychosis' which is the necessary condition of the cinema-effect, he also has best succeeded in articulating the textual systems of a great many of his films around the dialectics of pleasure as ordered by the look. What differentiates his films from those of other directors is not that the look plays an important role in them but that it represents the limit-point whereby pleasure and desire are inscribed in the machination of cinema. Thus, for Bellour, it is 'the body' of the film which is itself the subject and the means through which the director's and the spectator's pleasure—their first and foremost *raison d'être*—are magnified. For Bellour, 'a certain cinema of representation' accentuates 'the image value of the apparatus' by creating 'the extreme condensation of sexuality in the woman's body image' which 'intensifies man's awareness of the irreducible difference of woman's sexuality, and in the same process it diminishes it by means of the representation as a mirror image of woman's sexuality.' It is the intensified image which further increases the fascination 'so as to intensify this same fascination.' Bellour's analysis of the beginning of *Marnie* provides us with a new theoretical operator which not only illuminates Hitchcock's strategies in his appropriation of the cinematographic apparatus in order to assert his position as enunciator but it also delineates the operation model of the enunciative apparatus as constituted by the regime of the look. The work of enunciation exemplified by Hitchcock's inscription of his own desire through the intermediary of his 'fictional delegates' in the diegesis of the film is perhaps unusually refined, but it is also why it reveals more clearly than in other films the intricate structure of this apparatus which, consciously or not, each director must assume, the central demand of fiction in the film-work.[11]

However, for the enunciative function described by Bellour to be fully operative, and for Hitchcock to experience the full gratification he expects from his management of pleasure, it is also essential that other enunciative functions affecting different levels of the filmic discourse also contribute to produce and reinforce the fascination of the image value generated by the film-text. Among these, as we have seen, the *défilement* plays a major role in insuring the effect of *l'émouvoir* which *beneath* the look is displaced from one space to the next, from one character to the next. Only then will the full array of enunciative functions be fully operative. Thus, one might say that the *défilement* is that operation which, in sustaining the cinema-effect, does, in the most invisible and imperceptible way, support the work of enunciation. In fact, it is the necessary condition of enunciation. It is therefore not surprising that when it is exposed, as in the films of Vertov or those of contemporary experimental film-makers, the enunciation is displaced from the regime of the scopic drive (look) to that of the film-object, a displacement of the object of desire which results from the partial jamming of the *défilement*.

NOTES

1. Thierry Kuntzel is also the author of 'Le travail du film,' *Communications,* no. 19, 1972, 25-39, a study of the first segment of Fritz Lang's *M*; 'Le travail du film, 2,' *Communications,* no. 23, 1975, 136-189, a study of the film-work in *The Most Dangerous game*; 'Savoir, pouvoir, voir,' *Ça,* no. 7/8, May 1975, 85-97, a study of 29 shots of the hunt in *The Most Dangerous game.* Several unpublished studies (*La Jetée, The Man with a Movie Camera, King Kong*) will be added to these in a forthcoming book. 'A Note Upon the Filmic Apparatus,' was published in the *Quarterly Review of Film Studies,* vol. 1, no. 3, August 1976, 266-275.

2. Raymond Bellour has written extensively on cinema over the last fifteen years, especially on Lang, Hitchcock and on the American cinema. He has edited numerous film periodicals and books on cinema. Among these, *Le Western* (Paris, 10/18, 1966, new printing 1976), *Dictionnaire du cinéma* (Paris, Editions Universitaires, 1966) and *Le Cinéma américain* (Paris, Flammarion, forthcoming). Among his most recent articles on the American cinema: 'Les Oiseaux: analyse d'une sequence,' *Les Cahiers du cinéma,* no. 217 Sept. 1968 available in English translation from the BFI in London; 'L'Evidence et le code,' *La Revue d'esthétique,* no. 2-3-4, 1973; an analysis of 12 shots from *The Big Sleep,* published in *Screen,* vol. 15, no. 4, 1974; 'Le Blocage symbolique,' *Communications,* no. 23, 1975, 235-350, a close analysis of segment 14 in *North by Northwest*; 'To Analyze/to Segment,' *Quarterly Review of Film Studies,* vol. 1, no. 3, August 1976, 331-353, a study of the segmentation system in *Gigi*; 'Le Texte introuvable,' *Ca,* no. 7/8, May 1975, 77-84, published in *Screen,* vol. 16, no. 3, 1975. Of special interest also are his interview with Christian Metz, *Sémiotica,* 1971, reprinted in his book *Le Livre des Autres* (Paris, l'Herne, 1971), and a chronology of cinema, published in *l'Année 1913* (Paris, Klincksieck, 1971), which also includes an essay entitled: '1913: pourquoi écrire, poete?' Raymond Bellour has also done extensive work on the Bronte sisters, and he has edited collections of essays on Henri Michaux, Jules Verne and Claude Lévi-Straus.

3. This expression is borrowed from an essay by Eisenstein (see the end of Kuntzel's article). The article title in French did not include 'A view in close up.' The addition of this expression to the English translation is intended to call attention to Kuntzel's methodology which constitutes an important part of the article. Just as there are two kinds of spectators, there are two kinds of film critics, and if anything, Kuntzel's article shows that, by definition, one cannot analyze the film-work from the position of the 'naive' spectator.

4. Christian Metz, 'Trucage et cinéma,' in *Essais sur la signification au cinéma,* vol. II, Paris, Klincksieck, 1972; to be reprinted by the Editions Albatros.

5. Christian Metz, 'The Imaginary Signifier,' *Screen,* vol. 16, no. 2, 1975, 14-75; 'The Fiction Film and its Spectator,' *New Literary History,* Autumn, 1976, 75-105.

6. Octave Mannoni, *Cléfs pour l'imaginaire,* Paris, Le Seuil, 1969. See in particular 'Je sais bien, mais quand même...,' 9-33, and 'L'illusion comique ou le théâtre du point de vue de l'imaginaire,' 161-183.

7. 'The Imaginary Signifier,' *op. cit.,* p. 70.

8. 'Métaphore/Métonymie, ou le référent imaginaire,' in *Le Signifiant imaginaire: Cinéma et Psychanalyse* Paris, 10/18, 1977, see especially ch. XIV.

9. For an interesting discussion of such an instance of the 'perturbation of the iconic signifier by the trajectories of the primary process,' see Jacques Dubois et al., 'La chafetière est sur la table,' *Communication et langages,* no. 29, 1976, 36-49.

10. Jacques Lacan, *Le seminaire,* XI, *Quatre concepts fondamentaux de la psychanalyse.* Paris, Le Seuil, p. 107f.

11. Christian Metz, 'History/Discourse,' *Edinburgh 1976 Magazine,* no. 1, 21-25.

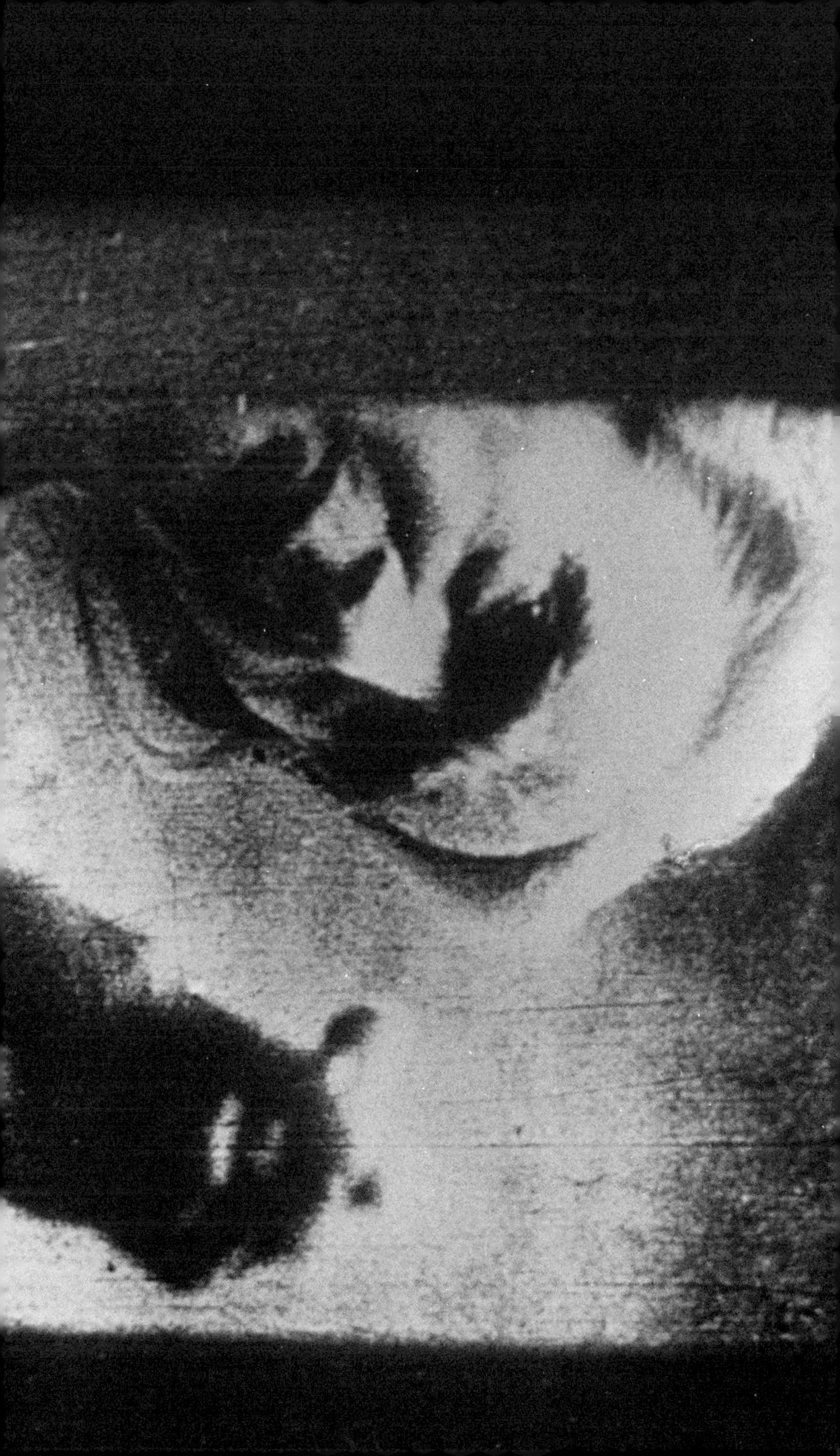

COMMENTAIRE

noir

COMMENT

TAIRE

blanc

COMME

COMMENT

COMMENT TAIRE

TEAR

ECRAN

SUR

ECRAN

blancheur

COMMENTARY

AS, LIKE

HOW

blanchir

HOW TO

SILENCE

blanchiment

TO TEAR

noirceur

SCREEN

ON SCREEN

WENT

PAST

MINUTE

OR

MOMENT

ARILY.

blanchissement

COMMENT

TAIRE

MINUTE

BY

MINUTE

TO

MINUTE

OR

TWO

HOLD

TONGUE

HOLD

noircir

TO

ONE

MORE

noircissure

AND MORE

TIME

TAKES

TO

HUSH

COMMENTAIRE
Theresa Hak Kyung Cha

Photographs:
Stills from VAMPYR by Carl Theodore Dreyer
Reese Williams
Richard Barnes

Every Revolution Is a Throw of the Dice

Danièle Huillet and Jean-Marie Straub

The Typography of the *Coup De Dés*

An original page from Stéphane Mallarmé's *Coup de dés* (whose ninth folio is reproduced below) can serve as a starting-point for a demonstration of the parallel construction of Jean-Marie Straub's latest short (color, 35 mm, 11 min.)

The film is a staging of the typographical work of spatial scansion on whose text Mallarmé worked directly for ten years. Straub constructs a correspondence between the performers and the nine different typefaces of the poem, which determines the duration, the succession, and even the shooting axis of each frame; masculine voices correspond to upper-case letters, feminine to lower-case.

For each frame we indicate the focal length of the lens used (which, corresponding to the holding of a constant width of field, produces a diagrammatic articulation [un articolarsi disgrammatico] of depth) and the times, expressed in seconds, taken from the perforation numbers of the film. The position of the camera, after the first frame, remains fixed within the semicircle of performers, and therefore every tilting of the axis is related to the slope of the terrain. We give a diagram of the positions of the performers relative to the camera and, following it, a legend showing their correspondence to the typefaces of the original text.

In transcribing Mallarmé's poem we have tried to indicate the different levels of spacing by using more leading between lines and by marking with a slash the portions of the text which appear on the right-hand pages (Mallarmé's text, as can be seen from the reproduction, is spread continuously over facing pages).

C'ÉTAIT

issu stellaire

CE SERAIT

pire

non

davantage ni moins

indifféremment mais autant

LE NOMBRE

EXISTÂT-IL
autrement qu'hallucination éparse d'agonie

COMMENÇÂT-IL ET CESSAT-IL
sourdant que nié et clos quant apparu
enfin
par quelque profusion répandue en raretee
SE CHIFFRÂT-IL

évidence de la somme pour peu qu'une
ILLUMINÂT-IL

LE HASARD

Choit
la plume
rythmique suspens du sinistre
s'ensevelir
aux écumes originelles
naguères d'où sursauta son delire jusqu à une cime
flétrie
par la neutralité identique du gouffre

1. Toute révolution est un coup de dés
Jules Michelet
(title - white on black)
2. pour..........
(dedication - red, green, blue on white)

*pour
Frans van de Staak
Jean Narboni
Jacques Rivette
et quelques autres
J-M.S. mai 77

3. panorama of trees, sky, a working-class house, the wall of Père Lachaise cemetery, the memorial Aux Morts de la Commune -25/28 May 1871, ending with a group of nine performer-reciters [recitanti] seated on the grass.
(obb. 32-60 sec.)

4. Helmut Faerber, I — UN COUP DE DÉS
(obb. 18,5 - 5'') — /JAMAIS

5. Michel Delahaye, V — /QUAND BIEN MEME LANCÉ DANS DES CIRCONSTANCES ÉTERNELLES
(obb. 75 - 8'')

/DU FOND D'UN NAUFRAGE

6. Georges Goldfayn, IV — SOIT
(obb. 50 - 3'')

7. Danièle Huillet, 1 — que
(obb. 75 - 40'')

l'Abîme

blanchi
étale
furieux
sous une inclinaison
plane désepérément

d'aile

la sienne
par/
/avance retombée d'un mal à dresser
[le vol

et couvrant les jaillissements
coupant au ras les bonds

/très à l'intérieur résume

/l'ombre enfouie dans la profondeur
[par cette voile alternative
/jusqu'adapter
a l'envergure

/sa béante profondeur en tant que la
[coque
/d'un bâtiment

/penché de l'un ou l'autre bord

8. Georges Goldfayn, IV (obb. 50 - 5'') LE MAÎTRE

9. Danièle Huillet, 1 (obb. 75 - 122'')

/hors d'anciens calculs
où la manoeuvre avec l'âge oubliée

surgi
inférant/
/jadis il empoignait la barre

de cette conflagration/
/à ses pieds
de l'horizon unanime

que se/
/prépare
s'agite et mêle
au poing qui l'étreindrait
comme on menace/
/un destin et les vents

l'unique Nombre qui ne peut pas/
/être un autre
/Esprit
pour le jeter
dans la tempête
en reployer la division et passer fier

hésite
cadavre par le bras/
/écarté du secret qu'il détient
plutôt
que de jouer

en maniaque chenu
la partie
au nom des flots
un/
/envahit le chef
    coule en barbe soumise

naufrage cela/
/direct de l'homme
/sans nef
    n'importe
    où vaine

ancestralement à n'ouvrir pas la main
crispée
par delà l'inutile tête

legs en la disparation

à quelqu'un
ambigu

l'ultérieur démon immémorial

ayant
de contrées nulles
induit
le vieillard vers cette conjonction
                [suprême avec la probabilité
celui
son ombre puérile
caressée et polie et rendue et lavée
assouplie par la vague et soustraite
aux durs os perdus entre les ais
né

d'un ébat
la mer par l'aieul tentant ou l'aieul
                [contre la mer

une chance oiseuse

Fiançailles
dont
le voile d'illusion rejailli leur hantise
ainsi que le fantôme d'un geste

chancellera
s'affalera

folie

10. Helmut Faerber, 1 /N'ABOLIRA
(obb. 18,5 - 1'')

11. Manfred Blank, III COMME SI
(obb. 40 - 2'')

12. Marilù Parolini, 2 Une insinuation/
(obb. 50 - 30'') /simple

au silence/
/enroulée avec ironie
ou le mystère
précipité

hurlé

dans quelque proche/
/tourbillon d'hilarite et d'horreur

voltige/
/autour du gouffre
sans le joncher
ni fuir

/et en berce le vierge indice

13. Manfred Blank, III /COMME SI
(obb. 40 - 1''½)

14. Marilù Parolini, 2
(obb. 50 - 60'') plume solitaire éperdue

sauf/
/que la rencontre ou l'effleure une
[toque de minuit

et immobilise
au velours chiffonné par un
[esclaffement sombre

/cette blancheur rigide

/dérisoire
en opposition au ciel
trop
pour ne pas marquer
exigument
quiconque

/prince amer de l'écueil
/s'en coiffe comme de l'héroıque
irresistible mais contenu
par sa petite raison virile
en foudre
soucieux
expiatoire et pubère
muet/
/rire
/que

15. Aksar Khaled, (obb. 25 - 2''½) ıı /SI

16. Marilù Parolini, (obb. 50 - 37'') 2 La lucide et seigneuriale aigrette/
/de vertige
scintille

puis ombrage
une stature mignonne ténébreuse/
/debout
en sa torsion de sirene
/le temps
de souffleter
par d'impatientes squames ultimes/

/bifurquées

/un roc

/faux manoir
  tout de suite
  évaporé en brumes

/qui imposa
  une borne à l'infini

17. Aksar Khaled, II C'ÉTAIT
(obb. 25 - 2'')

18. Andrea Spingler, 3 issu stellaire
(obb. 40 - 2'')

19. Askar Khaled, II /LE NOMBRE
(obb. 25 - 1''½)

20. Michel Delahaye, V /EXISTÂT-IL
(obb. 75 - 1''½)

21. Dominique Villain, 4 /autrement qu'hallucination éparse
[d'agonie
(obb. 25 - 4'')

22. Michel Delahaye, V /COMMENÇÂT-IL ET CESSÂT-IL
(obb. 75 - 2''½)

23. Dominique Villain, 4 /sourdant que nié et clos quant apparu
enfin
par quelque profusion répandue en
[rareté
(obb. 25 - 8'')

24. Michel Delahaye, V /SE CHIFFRÂT-IL
(obb. 25 - 3''½)

25. Dominique Villain, 4 /évidence de la somme pour peu
[qu'une
(obb. 25 - 3''½)

26. Michel Delahaye, V /ILLUMINÂT-IL
(obb. 75 - 1''½)

27. Aksar Khaled, JJ CE SERAIT
(obb. 25 - 1''½)

28. Andrea Spingler, 3 pire
(obb. 40 - 8'') non
davantage ni moins
indifféremment mais autant

29. Helmut Faerber, 1 /LE HASARD
(obb. 18,5 - 3'')

30. Marilù Parolini, 2 /Choit
(obb. 50 - 19'') la plume
rythmique suspens du sinsitre
s'ensevelir
aux écumes originelles

naguère d'où sursauta son délire
[jusqu'à une cime
flétrie
par la neutralité identique du gouffre

31. Georges Goldfayn, IV RIEN
(obb. 50 - 2'')

32. Danièle Huillet, 1 de la mémorable crise
(obb. 75 - 9'') ou se fût
l'évènement/
/accompli en vue de tout résultat nul
humain

33. Georges Goldfayn, IV /N'AURA EU LIEU
(obb. 50 - 1''½)

34. Danièle Huillet, 1 /une élévation ordinaire verse l'absence
(obb. 75 - 4'')

35. Georges Goldfayn, IV /QUE LE LIEU
(obb. 50 - 2''½)

36. Danièle Huillet, 1 /inférieur clapotis quelconque comme
(obb. 75 - 22'') [pour disperser l'acte vide
abruptement qui sinon
par son mensonge
eût fondé
la perdition

/dans ces parages
du vague
en quoi toute réalité se dissout

37. Georges Goldfayn, IV — EXCEPTÉ
(obb. 50 - 1'')

38. Danièle Huillet, 1 — à l'altitude
(obb. 75 - 4'')

39. Georges Goldfayn, IV — PEUT-ÊTRE
(obb. 50 - 1''½)

40. Danièle Huillet, 1 — aussi loin qu'un endroit/
(obb. 75 - 14'') — /fusionne avec au delà

/hors l'intérêt
quant à lui signalé
en général
selon telle obliquité par telle declivité
de feux

/vers
ce doit être
le Septentrion aussi Nord.

41. Georges Goldfayn, IV — /UNE CONSTELLATION
(obb. 50 - 2'')

42. Danièle Huillet, 1 — /froide d'oubli et de désuétude
(obb. 75 - 30'') — pas tant
qu'elle n'énumère
sur quelque surface vacante
et supérieure
le heurt successif
sidéralement
d'un compte total en formation

/veillant
doutant
roulant

brillant et méditant
/avant de s'arrêter
à quelque point dernier qui le sacre

/Toute Pensée émet un Coup de Dés

43. Paris, beyond the wall of Père Lachaise, working-class quarter;
stationary shot;
(obb. 25 - 46'')

44. (end titles - white on black)
-photography:
Willy Lubtchansky
Dominique Chapuis

-sound:
Louis Hocet
Alain Donavy

-poem
of
Stéphane Mallarmé

-photograph of Mallarmé
in his study

-(re) citants:
Helmut Faerber
Michel Delahaye
Georges Goldfayn
Danièle Huillet
Marilù Parolini
Manfred Blank
Askar Khaled
Andrea Springler
Dominique Villain

Graphic representation of the positions of the performer-reciters.

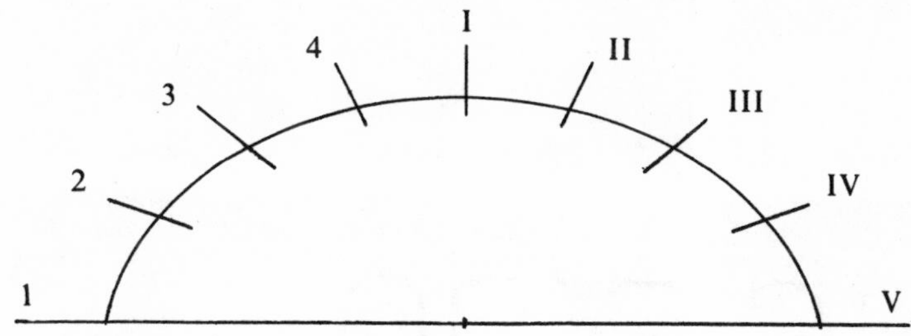

Legend

I: Large upper-case roman / Helmut Faerber
II: Medium upper-case italic / Askar Khaled
III: Small upper-case italic / Manfred Blank
IV: Medium upper-case roman / Georges Goldfayn
V: Small upper-case roman / Michel Delahaye

1: Large lower-case roman / Danièle Huillet
2: Large lower-case italic / Marilù Parolini
3: Small lower-case italic / Andrea Spingler
4: Small lower-case roman / Dominique Villain

Toute révolution
est un coup de dés.
(Jules Michelet)
Every revolution
is a throw of dice.
TO THE DEAD OF THE COMMUNE
21-28 MAY 1871
WILL NOT
A simple
insinuation

WERE IT TO BEGIN AND CEASE
POÈME
UN COUP DE DÉS JAMAIS N'ABOLIRA LE HASARD
par
STÉPHANE MALLARMÉ

1. Every revolution
is a throw of dice.

- -

2. A THROW OF DICE

3. NEVER

- -

4. EVEN WHEN CAST IN ETERNAL
CIRCUMSTANCES

5. FROM THE DEPTH OF A SHIPWRECK

- -

6. BE IT

- -

7. that

8. the Abyss

9. whitened
slack
furious

10. under an inclination
desperately plane

11. of wing

12. its own

13. in advance
fallen back from a trouble
in raising the flight

14. and covering the gushings
cutting at the root the leaps

15. much inside resumes

16. the shadow buried in the depth
by this alternating sail

17. up to adapting
to the spread

18. its gaping depth
inasmuch as the hull

19. of a vessel

20. leaning to one or the other side

- -

21. THE MASTER

- -

22. out of ancient calculations
where the maneouvre
with age forgotten

23. arisen
inferring

24. once he gripped the tiller

25. from this conflagration
at his feet
of the unanimous horizon

26. that there
prepares itself

27. is tossed and mingles
with the fist which would grasp it

28. as one threatens
a destiny and winds

29. the one number which cannot
be another

30. Spirit
to pitch it
into the tempest

31. refold its division
and pass on proudly

32. hesitates

33. corpse by the arm
kept away from the secret it holds

34. rather
than play

35. as a hoary maniac

36. the game
in the name of the billows

37. one
invades the head
flows as a submissive beard

38. direct shipwreck this
of the man

39. without ship
no matter
where vain

40. ancestrally not to open the hand

41. clenched
beyond the useless head

42. legacy on the disappearance

43. to someone
ambiguous

44. the ulterior demon immemorail

45. having
from null countries
induced

46. the old man toward
this supreme conjunction
with probability

47. he
his puerile shadow

48. caressed and polished
and rendered and washed

49. made supple by the wave
and removed

50. from the hard bones
lost between the planks

51. born
of a frolic

52. the sea through the sire trying
or the sire against the sea

53. an idle fortune

54. Betrothal

55. whose

56. gushed out veil of illusion
their obsession

57. like the ghost of a gesture

58. will stagger
sink

59. madness

- -

60. WILL NOT ABOLISH

- -

61. AS IF

- -

62. A simple
insinuation

63. wreathed around silence
with irony

64. or
the mystery

65. hurled
howled

66. into some nearby whirl
of hilarity and horror

67. hovers
around the gulf

68. without strewing it
or fleeing

69. and cradles it virgin sign

- -

70. AS IF

- -

71. solitary feather bewildered

72. save
that a midnight cap
meets or grazes it

73. and immobilizes

74. to the velvet crumpled
by a dark guffaw

75. this rigid whiteness

76. derisive

77. in opposition to the sky

78. too much

79. not to mark

80. exiguously

81. whoever

82. bitter prince of the reef

83. dons it as the heroic

84. irresistible but contained

85. by his small virile reason

86. in thunder

87. worried
expiatory and pubescent

88. dumb laugh

89. that

- -

90. IF

- -

91. The lucid and lordly crest
of vertigo

92. on the invisible brow
sparkles

93. then overshades

94. a tiny gloomy stature
upright

95. in her siren's wrench

96. the time
for slapping

97. by impatient ultimate scales
bifurcated

98. a rock

99. false manor
suddenly
evaporated in mists

100. which imposed
a boundary to the infinite

-   - - - - - - - - - - -

101. IT WAS

- -

102. issued starrily

- -

103. THE NUMBER

- -

104. WERE IT TO EXIST

- -

105. other than as
scattered hallucination of agony

- -

106. WERE IT TO BEGIN AND CEASE

- -

107. emerging but denied and
closed once appeared

108. finally

109. by some profusion shed in rarity

- -

110. WERE IT TO BE CIPHERED

- -

111. evidence of the sum
inasmuch as one

- -

112. WERE IT TO LIGHT UP

- -

113. IT WOULD BE

- -

114. worse

115. no
more nor less
indifferently but as much

- -

116. CHANCE

- -

117. Falls
     the feather

118. rythmic suspense of the baleful

119. to enshroud itself
     in the original foams

120. whence lately its delirium
     sprang up to a summit

121. withered

122. by the identical neutrality
     of the gulf

- -

123. NOTHING

- -

124. of the memorable crisis
     where

125. the event might have been
     accomplished in view of
     every null result

126. human

- -

127. WILL HAVE TAKEN PLACE

- -

128. an ordinary elevation
     pours forth absence

- -

129. BUT THE PLACE

- -

130. lower rippling whatever
as if to disperse the empty act

131. abruptly which else
by its lie

132. might have founded
perdition

133. in these regions
of the vague

134. in which every reality dissolves

- -

135. EXCEPT

- -

136. in the height

- -

137. MAYBE

- -

138. as far as a site
merges with beyond

139. outside the interest
signalled as to it

140. in general

141. according to such an obliquity
by such a declivity

142. of fires

143. toward

144. it must be

145. the Septentrion also North

- -

146. A CONSTELLATION

- -

147. cold from forgetfulness and disuse

148. not so much

149. that it does not enumerate

150. on some vacant and upper surface

151. the successive shock

152. sidereally

153. of a total account in formation

154. watching
doubting
rolling

155. glinting and meditating

156. before stopping
at some last point
which consecrates it

157. Every Thought
emits a Throw of Dice

- -

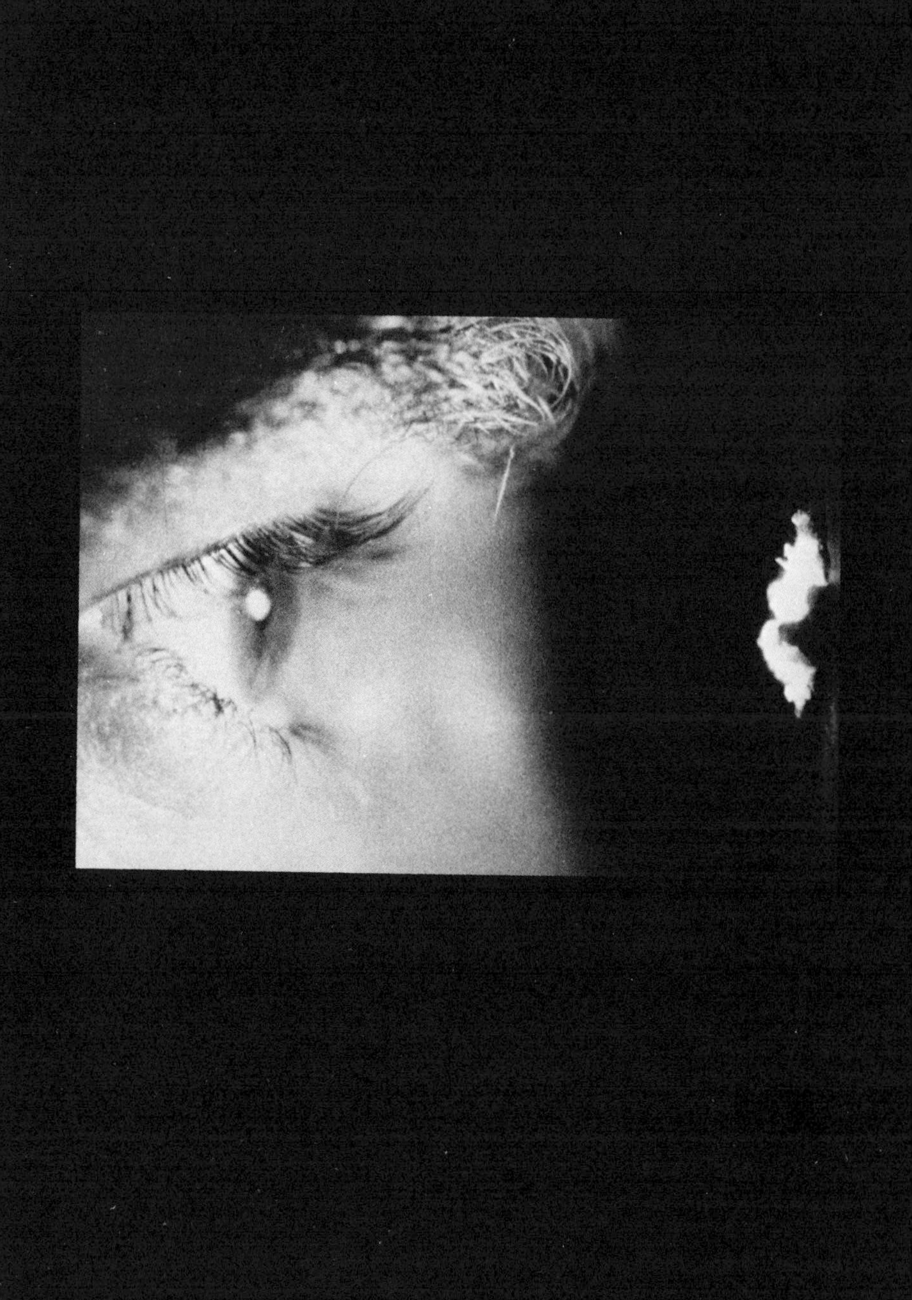

Blinking, Flickering, and Flashing of the Black-and-White Film

Marc Vernet

In her eyes I could see passing sometimes the hope, sometimes the recollection, perhaps the regret of joys I was unacquainted with...and since I could perceive only their gleam in her eyes, I could not see anymore of them than can be seen by the spectator who has not been allowed to enter the theatre auditorium, and who, with his nose pressed against the window-pane of the entrance door, cannot see anything that is happening on the stage.

Marcel Proust

I. *TWISTS*

About the title

"Black-and-white" is hyphenated because it is not so much a question of their opposition as it is of their conjunction, their fusion—one in the other, at the same time.

"Blinking, Flickering, and Flashing," thinking first of Gaston Bachelard, of his work entitled *la Flamme d'une chandelle.* Bachelard saw in this term the sound effect of the blinking of the eye, of the movement of the eyelids, the mimicking of the tenuous, wet sound that punctuates the brief masking of the eye. Thinking also of *Pierrot le Fou,* the scene in which, at the exit of Paris, on the edge of the highway at nightfall, the only thing that can be seen of a parked car is a single blinking light, while the driver and his woman passenger are, we suppose, kissing.

*"Me fascine, la bonne"**

There is a family snapshot in *Roland Barthes* by Roland Barthes[1] whose only caption is the brief phrase, "Fascinating me, the maid." It

*Translator's note: I have left the title of this section in French, partly because it is a slip of the pen—Barthes' actual words are, "Me fascine, au fond, la bonne." The elimination of the phrase "au fond," which positions the object of fascination, is strange, particularly since the whole question of the position of the fetish object is so central to this essay. Richard Howard's translation reads, "What fascinates me here: the maid." Another rendering might be, "Fascinating me, in the background, is the figure of the maid."

is an almost empty photograph, since it does not really represent a figure, as the woman in the foreground is not named or identified, nor does it really represent a scene, if you except the tiny one of the cat escaping from the nonetheless tightly clutched arms. There is nothing here to provoke the imaginary, except in the corner, in the background, the maid pointed out by Barthes.

Now, here is the first enigma—that maid did not fascinate me, nor did she function for me as an eye-catcher. So what was there about her? Let us see.

The solid white mass of the apron against the darkness of the corridor. Between the flatness of the apron and the obscure depths of the corridor, a face is emerging in a few lines, out of the darkness, a face just barely caressed by the light and devoured by shadow, a face that lacks reality, like one in a photograph that is being developed and whose elements are just beginning to emerge in discontinuous masses, in isolated spots.

A silhouette posed in the frame of the doorway, a feminine form, a hollow form filling a hollow form, a phantom figure hovering on a threshold, an awkward figure not daring to show herself but appearing just the same, torn as she is between self-effacement and curiosity. It is a figure which strongly resembles that of Barthes himself, seen in another photograph (p. 37 in the French edition, p. 33 in the English language translation), where, draped in white and petrified with stage fright, he is playing the role of Darios.

The maid—she belongs to the bourgeois environment, but she does not enter its representation—if she appears there, it is on the outskirts.

Watching the scene in which her employers are having their picture taken, she is in a position that is symmetrical with the photographer's. She is taken in, inadvertently, as it were, by his eye, but she in turn is taking him in with hers—she is a containing content, an observed spectator, a watching sight. For me she is the paradigm of the man standing in the doorway in the background of Velasquez's *Las Meninas,* who is turning around to look at the scene he seems to be leaving.[2]

The maid is the inverted double of the photographer, and of the person looking at the photograph. But she is also the inverted double of the grandmother, of whom she is both the repetition and the *negative.* Her negative, because while the grandmother is a massive figure in the foreground, a dark mass with a white head, the maid is a slim figure in the background, a white mass with a dark head. She is a repetition, because on the one hand she is not unlike the figure of the mother (see, for example, the frontispiece photograph in the French edition—p. 11 in the English language translation), and, on the other hand, because she is a figure positioned as a *reclame**, in the technical sense of the term. In music, the *reclame* is that part of the response that is repeated after the versicle. In typography, it is a mark placed in the margin of the text, indicating the point at which the composition or the reading is to be picked up and continued. The figure of the maid is that trace of work in the family photograph, a secondary, unwanted figure, and with which the reading of the picture concludes, but from which that reading bounces back and starts up again for a new ordering. And since my work here will be concerned in part with the difference between the sexes and fetishism in film and cinematic apparatus, I cannot pass up the opportunity to point out this happy coincidence provided by the French language—while *la reclame* is the response in musical terminology and the mark indicating where the reading stops and is begun again in typography, in falconry, *le reclame* is the signal used to call the bird of prey back to the lure.

The maid—a white mass against a black background, framed by the white of the doorway, white in black, black in white—it's a photograph in the photograph.

She is a detail annexed to the "subject" (a grandmotherly figure), a white spot watching me and who draws my eye towards the edge of the photograph and into the depth of the space, to the back of the depth, only to send it immediately back to me like a mirror. Two-dimensionality is turned into three-dimensionality, and the vanishing point of the perspective view leads me back to where I am standing—in front of the photograph and outside of it. The maid here occupies what is called in perspective the "principal point" or "point of view," which is the projection of the eye onto the plane of the picture, and where, in central projection, the parallels converge. It is a point symmetrical with the eye of the spectator, where representation is at the same time founded and annihilated, it is a spot blinking, flickering, flashing in the background of the scene.

The apparatus

At several points in this text the reader will see what my work owes to the research of Raymond Bellour. But it also depends on an examination of the cinematic apparatus as it is proposed by Jean-Louis Baudry and as developed by Christian Metz in *le Signifiant Imaginaire,* with

*Translator's note: It will quickly become clear to the reader of this translation that the French word *reclame* covers a list of several separate and distinct terms in English. But Vernet is playing here upon the fact that this same word, *reclame,* has a multiplicity of distinct meanings in French. Therefore the word has been left untranslated throughout this paragraph. The English equivalent for *reclame* as a musical term is "response" or "responsory." The term in typography is "catchword." I have been unable to find the English equivalent for *reclame* as a term of falconry.

that idea of an unauthorized voyeurism which does not have the counterpart of the exhibitionism of the object observed and in which the voyeur, who is concealed, derives comfort from not being seen.

In Metz's text, as in Baudry's, the parallel with the mirror stage makes it possible to establish an analogy between the undeveloped motivity of the infant and the latent motivity of the film spectator. Now it seems to me that this latent motivity is not so much a matter of lack of coordination or muscular relaxation as it is of paralysis, of that sudden stroke spoken of by Jean-Louis Schefer[3], or of that stiffening mentioned by Freud in connection with the effect produced by the sight of the head of Medusa, which is an erection of the entire body in an effort to deny the castration which the fascinating head represents.

Now, Medusa watches me. In what way would the cinematic apparatus eliminate this gaze, why would it differ profoundly from the pictorial apparatus, about which Foucault, Lacan[4], and Damisch[5] assert that, from the background of the perspective view, from behind the picture, as in Brunelleschi's device, or from behind the foliage of things, as in Tintoretto's *Suzanna and the Elders* in Vienna, "that" looks at me and "that" nails me to the spot.* Furthermore, just as Rosolato does for the fetishist[6], Lacan introduces into the voyeurist apparatus a third eye, the one which takes me by surprise and "pins me down" at the moment when I look through the keyhole.

Thus it seems to me that the famous "law" prohibiting actors from looking directly into the camera is not so imposing as all that, and that it is even quite regularly transgressed, either openly, as in Ozu's films or in musical comedies, or furtively, in the classic film, as Raymond Bellour has demonstrated in his analysis of *Marnie*[7], or indirectly by an anonymous eye which can be attributed neither to an actor nor to a character.

The Problem of the Film Noir

In another study[8] I have attempted to show how the narrative structure of the film noir sets up a circuit in which, after it has been shown, exhibited, something (which may be either the evidence, the solution of the mystery, the hero's strength, or the plot of the story) is made to disappear, to be concealed, hidden for the benefit of its opposite. These two initial movements of the film noir form the basis for a narrative economy operating by means of denial, a denial which will continue to function throughout the whole story until its final resolution.

*Translator's note: The *Ça* ("that") is the term used in French psychoanalytic terminology to designate what in English is called "the Id." Thus, the concluding clause of this sentence contains an obvious allusion to the Lacanian watchword, *"Ça parle."*

But in the very resolution in which the original denial is abolished, a second denial is created, replacing the first one. The film noir would then function partially, on the basis of its narrative organization, according to the mode of fetishism and the threat of castration.

In this essay I wish to make a brief attempt at showing how this fetishism-of-the-spectator, this fetishistic organization (which Barthes has already related to the system of the enigma in *S/Z)* actually shapes many "levels" of the film noir and how a reflection on film sequences[9] leads, through their textual analysis, to a reflection which is no longer only about the film, but also about the genre to which it belongs, about the movements of the cinematic signifier and the apparatus in general. This moreover is the reason why, in its planning stages, this essay bore the title, "The Diegesis of the Apparatus."

The fetish and the object of perspective

In a commentary on Freud's Fetishism,[10] Guy Rosolato develops an analysis from which I would like to summarize a few points here, in order to make my own subject clearer. First of all, Rosolato shows that the fetish represents the maternal penis and *at the same time* its absence, and that it is thus the presentation of an absence, the mark of a lack. Thus the fetish object is paired with a "perspective object" to which it refers us and which refers us back to it, in an endless rebounding, in an unlimited interlocking movement. The fetish is thus situated at a point between its maximum erotic power and its effacement to the bare minimum, in a vanishing point moving back and forth between these two extremes. For Rosolato the characteristic feature of the fetish is its ability to be turned inside out, like the finger of a glove, by an oscillating movement between the container and the contents, between full and empty. If the fetish object is an object which eludes us, it is because it simultaneously bares itself and hides itself, it puts itself forward and conceals itself, it stands out and withdraws into itself.

In addition, one of the attributes of the fetish is its lustre, its shining quality. It may be shiny by nature (a slicker, a polished shoe...), but above all, the fetishist is able, at will, to bestow that shiny lustre upon the fetish object, and to take it away from it, so that objects of the drabbest appearance can receive it and become fetishes. The shiny lustre and its concealment thus contribute to the precarious situation, to the intermittent quality of the fetish.

Another point—the shiny lustre of the fetish is that of the penis in a state of maximum erection, mirroring my own desire and non-castration. But, Rosolato notes, "It is important...for the object finally to lose its power, to vanish in its metonymic dwindling, not only at the end of the scenario, but virtually from its beginning, in a position of permanent 'disavowal'."

Finally, the fetish and its lustre are related in several ways to the eye of the beholder:

—the shiny lustre of the fetish is to be considered in connection with the prevalence of the visual in the pervert, a prevalence which is itself a function of a fear of contact which is a manifestation of the dialectic of the desire to be touched by the mother and the threat of castration that follows from that desire.

—the shiny lustre of the fetish is inscribed in the exchange between mother and child, in which the child watches the mother's eyes for signs of seduction, approval, or condemnation. Rosolato insists in this connection on the extremely unreliable nature of the intention being looked for in the eyes, on the ambiguity and the very tenuous quality of its significance and interpretation.

—the shiny lustre of the fetish remains "simultaneously at the mercy of and the vector of a *possible anonymous eye,* impossible to identify and always implied, and which is that of the phallic father, a consequence of the pleasure obtained and which pursues its removal.

II. *SPOTS*

Diegetic elements of the film noir

Without returning to the subject of the enigma, of the mystery to be solved which will make it possible to tell the good guys from the bad guys, a certain number of elements can be identified in the film noir whose status is homologous with that of the fetish.

Night and Rain on the one hand give the objects represented that "necessary" shiny lustre and that required tenuousness, and on the other hand they set up an image which is marked by sharp contrasts and is at the same time uncertain, difficult to decipher. The luminous spot, very visible, is empty; so is the zone in shadow unless it conceals a presence. In both cases, my eye finds itself drawn behind appearances, beyond what is represented, in order to know and foresee whether or not something is masked there. The image, reduced to black masses and white spots, is a trap for the eye, which is sent endlessly back and forth from black to white, absolute colors which each in their own way can abolish representation in the fade-out in which nothing is any longer discernible. Night and rain make representation unstable, fading—the image may jell, or it may dissolve.

Night (as a diegetic element) and masses of black are to be considered in relation to the fear of contact, for, in the kind of spaces they depict, the sense of touch can precede the sense of sight, expectations can be foiled by a surprise, the hero can be attached before he can see who is attacking him (cf. the murder of Archer at the beginning of *The Maltese Falcon).* The space of night is a space in which the detective, who has everything to gain from seeing without being seen, can be seen without seeing, as the darkness conceals the gleaming surface of an eye or a weapon.

The Character of the Bitch oscillates between the sublime and the vile, she is an attractive murderess who is both revealed and condemned when she pulls out her revolver (see the endings of *The Maltese Falcon* and *The Lady from Shanghai,* of *Double Indemnity,* and the role played in *The Big Sleep* by the younger sister, a perverse adolescent who takes up the initial metaphor of orchids, magnificent flowers which bloom in the midst of filth.).

The Clue is at the same time a tiny detail, a bit of debris (a scrap of torn paper, a cigarette butt, a fingerprint, a furtive gesture...) and a treasure, because it alone can explain everything. The clue, which can only be spotted by the trained eye of the detective (the "private eye"), oscillates between a maximum charge of meaning and a ludicrous opacity. Like the purloined letter, it has the full share of that secret quality stressed by Rosolato and which inscribes it in a vanishing point where, at the very moment it emerges, it can "disconnect" and vanish to the horizon of the story—it never reveals its full meaning on the spot and always leads to a subsequent confirmation which can only lead to the discovery of a new clue which, it too, will lead... *The Big Sleep* provides a concentrated example of this in the scene of Geiger's murder, in the receding movement described by the roll of film Marlowe is looking for. That movement takes the form of an alternating series: the opaque bulb of the flash camera; the black and empty stare of the Chinese sculpture (a mirror image of Miss Sternwood's gaze); the solid wooden head which turns out to be hollow; the camera concealed inside it (a contained object containing a film...which has disappeared—all that remains is a black recess in the depths of which shines the camera lens). The receding movement described by the roll of film (a black and opaque clue which should shed light on the mystery by revealing the scenes photographed with the flash camera) is itself only a repetition of the receding movement of the space of the house which in the preceding moments has been discovered to contain a hidden room. In the unfolding of the diegetic process, that is also the moment in which the hero, taken by surprise, sees his strength and skill reduced to nothing.

The Raincoat (from Bogart to Peter Falk), wrinkled, soiled by the rain, but impenetrable, protecting its wearer from contact and from wounds, a soft but impervious armor, which is both a screen and a container (Rosolato compares it moreover to the mirror penetrated by images but whose surface remains unaltered) and in which the silhouette of the threatened hero is invaginated.

It is in fact the sign of a possible attack; a protection which invokes a threat, a lusterless receptacle for possible blows (from an assailant or from the constant rain). It is the exemplary attribute of that fear of contact characteristic of the pervert. In the film noir this fear designates other scenes, like the fantasy of the "a child is being beaten" type, scenes in which the hero, paralysed, witnesses an act of violence in which one of his friends is the victim—the poisoning of the little informer in the empty offices of *The Big Sleep,* the beating up and murder of the fairgrounds employee in *Ride the Pink Horse,* which the hero watches as he crouches among the horses of the merry-go-round.

The Headlights of Black Cars which conceal, behind their blinding light and within the indecipherable space of the car, the face and eyes of the driver. There again, the spectator's eye is both deficient and displaced, since he is called upon to distinguish the contents of the car at the very moment when he is hypnotized by the glare of the headlights.

Dark glasses, among others, those put on by Mrs. Dietrichson in *Double Indemnity,* when her lover discovers that she is capable of a double murder, and which replace the unreliable expressiveness of the eyes with a fixed and inexorable gaze, removed from exchange, the gaze of a third party which can only deceive my own.

In his analysis of *Psycho* [11] Raymond Bellour very rightly links the dark glasses worn by the motorcycle cop who surprises the "guilty woman" to the sunken eye sockets of the embalmed mother discovered in the cellar. In the same scene Bellour identifies the white light of the light bulb with the material substance of the movie screen, thus bringing to light an apparatus in which the figure of the mother is symmetrical with the spectator in the movie theatre. But while that analysis is as brilliant as it is irrefragable, it also seems to me that the white of the lightbulb, of the screen, counterbalances the mother's sunken eye sockets. It is their counterpart and their denial, an intense white which reverses the beam of the projector to turn it on the spectator in a dead stare, a white and anonymous gaze, that of the father and the Law. The spectator is from that moment indeed the mother's double, not only in that he watches the screen as she does, but also in that *he is watched* by the screen. If the situation is really symmetrical, then the enucleation of the mother corresponds on one hand to the castration of the spectator and on the other to the integrity of the mirror-screen which for a fleeting moment demonstrates that for its part it remains intact.

Here is what emerges for me out of the shifting patterns formed by these recurring diegetic elements of the film noir. Black-and-white is simply the representative, in the diegesis, of the enigma structure, of the fetishist economy, and of the cinematic apparatus. In the form of these elements, what the film noir dramatizes, what it diegetisizes, is none other than cinematic representation itself, none other than the uncertain status of the moving perspective image. In this case it would simply be, as Foucault indicates, the representation of representation. A notch would then be skipped—the screen itself would occupy the position of the fetish and would assume its function, that of the absent-present phallus, riddled with images and serving as a support for the semi-relief of depth, while all the while remaining intact, impervious.

Film image, perspective image

With the film noir we are dealing with an unstable image, one that is always threatened with disappearance, seized in a dizzying space between total darkness and blinding whiteness (a night scene, or amnesia, a gunshot, or the harsh light of a flashlight), in an oscillation that is rigorously fixed and concentrated in the tenuousness of the reflection, of the shining spot, of the sparkling surface. It is an unreliable image, devoured by shadow, reduced to a few spots which "hold" the whole thing together, which I grasp at in order to decipher it, but which at any moment may "run out" on me (in a deceptive fade to black or a brutal surprise flash of white). It is, as Metz puts it, an image which I not only observe but which I also assist, and of which I am not only a witness but also one of the ingredients. There can be no doubt that this movement of the iconographic material must be seen in relation to the suspense effect, in so far as that effect, as I have shown in another study,[12] can only be created through a concealment, through an initial abduction that may always recur at any time; a hovering menace which may at any moment without warning break up my imaginary rapport with the image. This is the image of the film noir (of any film image? of all film images?) which my eye strives to coalesce, to shape, for what it represents as well as the way it is represented, namely, through perspective. Indeed, if I wish to continue to believe in it, and recover in it the desire I am investing in it, I must maintain the illusion of relief, I must maintain the fiction of its three-dimensionality despite the reality of its two-dimensionality, I must maintain belief despite knowledge.

The spot of brilliant light has precisely the function of attracting my eye, beyond the movement of appearances, towards the depths. But in the background of the picture, at the end of the perspective view, there is this eye behind the picture, that fixed stare that dismisses my desire, answering it negatively—the gaze of the father intervening to forbid the appeal to the mother and the dual relationship that is sought. It is a spot of brilliant light in the depths of the image, but it is also a brilliant light that is slightly detached from the objects in the picture and that comes forward, sticking out a bit from the plane of the picture, in a movement like that of a finger of a glove being turned inside out, like a beam of light that is aimed at me and hits me, in my seat, the space of a spectator of moving pictures with no reality. Finally, this bright light, an attribute of the fetish, is also simply a spot of white, an unreadable and unmarked area where representation is abolished to reveal the stubborn nudity of the medium—it is the place of absence, the leftover screen. Behind screen, in front of the screen, on the screen—this flickering spot of light is endlessly oscillating between these three spaces, founding and destabilizing representation in a movement which knows no stop.

Here a whole series of paintings come to mind for me. First of all, Cezanne's still lifes, in particular the late ones, in which, in the midst of acid-toned apples, a white spot persists—beneath the paint, behind it, the unmarked canvas, the painter's apparatus. But in front of the objects, overflowing the table where they are placed, is a tablecloth or a towel. But also, perhaps, floating in their midst, is the evil eye, death, like the lantern in Goya's *The Third of May*. Some of Magritte's paintings too, in particular *The Banquet,* in which the setting sun is *in front of* the trees on the edge of the horizon[13], or the *Empire of Light* series (based on the same principle). Tintoretto's paintings of *Suzanna and the Elders* (in Paris and in Vienna), and, above all, dominating this whole series and connecting it all together, there is *The Jean Arnolfini Wedding Portrait,* by Jan van Eyck, in which a convex mirror, placed between the husband and wife, but on the wall behind them, gives us back the image of the portion of space in front of them and not represented in the scene, a space in which two spectators are standing in a doorway. By means of a paradox that is perfectly logical, since the two spectators are seen in the place and stead of the painter, a Latin inscription above the mirror (and therefore at the back of the room) announces that "Here stood Jan van Eyck." As a spectator I am inscribed in the painting, but the more I enter it, the more I am sent back to my own place, in front of it. I substitute myself for the painter, but I am also substituted for the painting, since at the conclusion of the exchange, it is watching me and it is I who stand out.

It seems to me therefore that a part of the esthetic pleasure experienced in the contemplation of figurative images derives from the subversion, the repeated reversal of the spatial coordinates, in which flatness becomes depth, and the back becomes the front. This spatial movement founds and accompanies a permutation of the positions occupied by the spectator according to a circuit that is endlessly repeated, a circuit in which the observer is by turns the spectator, the picture (in the case of painting), and the painter, the subject of the gaze and its object.

III. *TURNS.*

1. If, therefore, following Raymond Bellour's analyses as well as the preceding passages of this essay, it can be considered that what is set in place and in motion by the diegetic and cinematic apparatus is none other than the desire for the mother and its counterpart, fear of castration, it then appears necessary to stress the following two points.

As a follow-up to the lengthy semiological analysis that has been done of the bases of the impression of reality in cinema, in order to account for its functioning and its strength, it is perhaps now appropriate to turn to a closer study of the "lack of reality" of the motion picture image, inasmuch as its unreliability and its precariousness make this "lack of reality" one of the elements necessary to the diegetic functioning and the involvement of the spectator-participant in what is being shown. By miming its own death through the sporadic appearance of its lack of reality, the force of the impression of reality is strengthened.

If it is true that the film spectacle and the moving perspective picture are to be related to the desire for the mother, and if the pleasure derived from viewing films is linked to the economic structures of the fetish, then that necessarily implies that the Law of the Father must be revealed in that pleasure in the form of the anonymous gaze sent back to the spectator and which both disrupts and reactivates the spectator's dual relationship with the image.

2. Then we need Christian Metz's definition, the concealed voyeur, in Rosolato's sense of the term, that is, a voyeur who is both hidden and revealed, withdrawn and exhibited. The film spectator is part of the show, he is at the same time watching and being watched.

3. If, when it is drawn into the background by the perspective construction (which, according to Panofsky, allows the material surface of the representation to be denied for the benefit of the scene represented), in the end my eye meets this anonymous gaze, in my role of spectator I am barraged, like the screen, by images and light. I am another screen, in the audience, withdrawn, invaded by images but always intact in an inversion of the poles of the apparatus, in which I am no longer anything but the blinded receptacle of the pounding floods of light.

There, no doubt, lies the fascination produced by the *film de scintillement.** I am thinking in particular of the very beautiful conclusion of Werner Nekes's *Makimono* (in my opinion very closely related to the scene on the merry-go-round at the end of Hitchcock's *Strangers on a Train),* in which the alternation of black and white areas on the screen causes the screen to be either entirely eliminated or to overflow its frame entirely. The white light invades the theatre audience completely. The shadows of the spectators are then outlined on the walls, which have turned white; and it is as if they are projected into a two-dimensional space. In this conclusion of *Makimono,* there is a complete subversion of the apparatus—the screen becomes a projector, the theatre becomes the screen, the spectator begins to appear in the space of representation while continuing to be a surface for the reception of light. Here we see, turning back on the spectator, the contact sought and feared through the abolition of the segregation of spaces, but also the threat of castration, a reversal which powerfully reactivates the circuit of permutation of the poles of the structure, just before it is about to be abolished (as in the final test of endurance in fiction films).

This type of ending (of which certain attenuated forms can be found in cinema classics such as Fritz Lang's films, *Ministry of Fear* and *Scarlet Street)* with explosions of light can be contrasted with another possible type of ending—those in which the image seems to "implode" slowly, where the characters go off into the horizon, slowly diminishing until they disappear. In both cases, it is a matter of dispossessing the spectators of their gaze before they leave the theatre.

4. If it is true that through the way it regulates its elements, the *film noir* to a certain degree presents the diegesis of cinematic structure and plays upon it to re-engage, re-involve the affects of the spectators, it could be said that in the *film de scintillement,* the diegesis, or at least what it is partially founded upon, is turned back upon the movements of the apparatus.

The fiction film does not merely tell a story—it tells the story of itself as well. It tells itself, but not so much in the mode of self-reflexiveness (taking itself, within the diegesis, as its object) as is the case in musical comedies, not through the introduction of the means of production into the space represented, but by the regulated movements of the iconographical material itself, through a staging of the apparatus in its spatial, its abstract qualities—a staging in which it stages its own crisis in order to reinforce its hold on the spectator.

Translated by Lee Hildreth

*Translator's note: *film de scintillement* (flicker film) is apparently a term coined by Vernet, in opposition to *film noir.*

NOTES

Three English words have been used to translate the first word of the French title, *Clignotements du Noir-et-Blanc,* because the French word, *clignotement,* covers at least three different words in English—"blinking," "flashing," and "flickering." "Winking" might be added to this list. All of these different senses of *clignotement* are pertinent in this essay.

1. *Roland Barthes,* Roland Barthes, Paris: Seuil, 1975, p. 13; p. 11 in the English translation by Richard Howard, entitled *Barthes on Barthes,* New York, Hill & Wang, 1977.
2. Cf. the analysis Michel Foucault has done of this painting in Chapter 1 of *Les Mots et les choses,* Paris, Gallimard, 1966, p. 19-31.
3. *"L'enfant, l'ange, l'extermination et le crime," Cahiers du cinéma,* no. 302, *juillet-août* 1979.
4. *"Du regard comme objet a." Le Seminaire, livre XI, Le Seuil,* 1973.
5. *"La fissure,"* in press.
6. Cf. infra.
7. *"énoncer"* in *L'analyse du Film,* Editions Albatros, 1980.
8. To be published in *le Cinéma américain, analyses de films,* Flammarion.
9. This lecture was preceded by the showing of an excerpt from Howard Hawks' *The Big Sleep,* the scene of the murder of Geiger in the "Chinese house" at the beginning of the film.
10. *"Le fetichisme dont* se dérobe *l'object,"* in *la Relation d'inconnu,* Gallimard, 1978.
11. "Psychosis, Neurosis, Perversion," op.cit.
12. Op.cit.
13. A study could be done of the pictorial and photographic career of the setting sun and the sun shining through the leaves—the moment when it is at last possible to look at the sun, after it has dominated us, the moment when its maximum of "beauty" corresponds to its imminent extinction in a bit of short-lived suspense.

On February 23, 1912, a young man hiking in the Tyrol discovers a mysterious cave from which emanate beautiful sounds. Fascinated by the music, he enters and follows corridors which lead him to various rooms filled with young people, talking, gambling, smoking, making love. He pursues his exploration until he notices obscene graffiti scribbled on the wall. Intrigued, he enters another room and discovers a group of people lying on the floor wearing strange head bands, grasping frantically at imaginary figures, and in a state of feeling sexually excited. He picks up one of the strange machines...Not too well versed in mechanics, I could not give you any detail about the characteristics of the machine, nor the theoretical data which determined its construction.

The function of this machine was first of all to abstract a portion of space from time and fix it within it at a particular moment and for only a few minutes, because the machine was not very powerful, and secondly, to render visible and tangible for whoever put on the head band the portion of time brought back to life.

Thus, I was able to look, feel, in a word, to do my thing with the body which was at my arm's reach while this body remained totally unaware of my presence, being itself devoid of any reality...The body which I was holding in my arms was so much to my taste that I took advantage of it generously without its suspecting anything. It was a beautiful dark-haired woman, voluptuous, with a white skin filled with so many delicate veins that it appeared to be blue, the same adorable sea blue as the foam in which Aphrodite was condensed. As she seemed to be pushing something away with her two hands at the level of her breasts, I imagined that it was the white and supple body of the Swan who will never sing, and that she was Leda, mother of the Disooures. She soon disappeared when the machine stopped, and I went away slowly, overcome by my good fortune.

Apollinaire "Le Roi Lune" (1902-1908)

The Fiction Film and Its Spectator: A Metapsychological Study

Christian Metz

The dreamer does not know that he is dreaming; the film spectator knows that he is at the movies: this is the first and principal difference between the filmic and oneiric situations. We sometimes speak of the illusion of reality in one or the other, but true illusion belongs to the dream and to it alone. In the case of the cinema it is better to limit oneself, as I have done until now, to remarking the existence of a certain *impression* of reality.

However, the gap between the two states sometimes tends to diminish. At the movies affective participation, depending on the fiction of the film and the spectator's personality, can become very lively, and *perceptual transference* then increases by a degree for brief instants of fleeting intensity. The subject's consciousness of the filmic situation as such starts to become a bit murky and to waver, although this slippage, easily begun, is never carried to its conclusion in ordinary circumstances.

I am not thinking so much of those film shows (some still exist[1]) where one can see the spectators, often young children, sometimes adults, rise from their seats, gesticulate, shout encouragement to the hero of the story, and insult the "bad guy": manifestations, in general, less disorderly than they seem: it is the institution of cinema itself, in certain of its sociological variants (i.e., the audience of children, the rural audience, the audience with little schooling, the community audience where everybody in the theater knows everybody else), that provides for, sanctions, and integrates them. If we want to understand them, we must take account of the conscious game-playing and group demands, the *encouragement given to the spectacle* by the play of motor activity. To this extent, the expenditure of muscular energy (voice and gesture) signifies almost the opposite of what it might first suggest to the observer fresh from the big city and its anonymous and silent movie theaters. It does not necessarily indicate that the audience is a little further down the road of true illusion. Rather, we have here one of those intrinsically ambivalent behaviors in which a single action, with double roots, expresses simultaneously virtually opposite tendencies. The subject actively invading the diegesis[2] through a motor outburst was intitially aroused by a first step, modest as it is—*prescribed* as it is, necessarily, by the indigenous rituals of the film audience—a first step toward confusing film and reality. But the outburst itself, once it has been set in motion (an outburst, moreover, which is most often collective), works to dissipate the budding confusion by returning the subjects to their rightful activity, which is not that of the protagonists as it is evolving on the screen: the latter do not assent to the spectacle. To exaggerate things so as to see them better, we might say that what begins as *acting out* ends as *action*. (We shall thus distinguish two main types of motor outburst, those that escape reality testing and those that remain under its control.) The spectator lets himself be carried away—perhaps deceived, for the space of a second—by the anagogic powers belonging to a diegetic film, and he begins to act; but it is precisely this action that awakens him, pulls him back from his brief lapse into a kind of sleep, where the action had its root, and ends up by restoring the distance between the film and him. It accomplishes this to the extent that is develops into a behavior of approval: approval of the spectacle as such and not necessarily of its quality, still less of all its diegetic features; approval brought from without to an imaginary tale by a person performing real actions to this purpose.

If we consider its possible economic conditions (in the Freudian sense of the term[3]), the attitude of the "good audience," the exuberant audience, or the audience of children, displays, in a milder form, something in common with somnambulism: it can be defined, at least in the first of its two stages, as a particular type of motor conduct characteristically released by sleep or by its fleeting, outlined homologue. This relationship can be enlightening as a contribution to a metapsychology of the filmic state, but it quickly finds its limits, since the enthusiastic audience is awakened by its actions whereas the somnambulist is not (it is therefore in their second stages that the two processes differ). Moreover, it is not certain that the somnambulist is dreaming, whereas in the case of the spectator entering into the action, the lapse into sleep is simultaneously a lapse into dreaming. Now we know that the dream, which escapes reality testing, does not escape consciousness (rather, it constitutes one of the major activities of the conscious person); the dissociation of "motoricity" from consciousness is therefore capable of going further in certain cases of somnambulism than in audience behaviors of the "intervening" type.[4]

Other conditions, less spectacular than those of the shouting audience, are necessary in order for perceptual transference, the dreamlike and sleepy confusion of film and reality, still very far from its total fulfillment, to become any more stable. The adult spectator, who belongs to a social group that watches films seated and silent—he, in short (that other sort of native), who is neither a child nor childlike—finds himself without defenses, if the film touches him profoundly or if he is in a state of fatigue or emotional turmoil, etc., against those brief moments of mental seesawing which each of us has experienced and which bring him a step closer to true illusion. This approach to a strong (or stronger) type of belief in the diegesis is a bit like the brief and quickly passing dizziness that drivers feel toward the end of a long night journey (of which film is one). In the two situations, when the second state, the brief psychical giddiness, ends, the subject not coincidentally has the feeling of "waking up": this is because he has furtively engaged in the state of sleeping and dreaming. The spectator thus will have dreamt a little bit of the film: not because that bit was missing and he imagined it: it actually appeared in the *bande,*[5] and this, not something else, is what the subject saw; but he saw it while dreaming.

The spectator who, as our society prescribes, is immobile and silent does not have the opportunity to "shake off" his budding dream, as one would remove the dust from a garment, through a motor outburst. This is undoubtedly why he pushes perceptual transference a bit further than do audiences who actively invade the diegesis (there is material here for a socioanalytic typology of the different ways of *attending* a film screening). We can therefore suppose that it is the same quantum of energy that serves in one case to nourish action and in the other to hypercathect perception to the point of touching off a *paradoxical hallucination;* a halluncination because of its tendency to confuse distinct levels of reality and because of a slight temporary unsteadiness in the play of reality testing as an ego function,[6] and paradoxical because it lacks the characteristic proper to a true hallucination of wholly endogenous psychical production: the subject, for an instant, has hallucinated what was really there, what at the same moment he in fact perceived: the images and sounds of the film.

In the cases of which we have just spoken, and doubtless in others too, the spectator of a novelistic *[romanesque]* film no longer quite knows that he is at the movies. It also happens, conversely, that the dreamer up to a certain point knows that he is dreaming—for instance, in the intermediary states between sleep and waking, especially at the beginning and end of the night (or when deep sleep steals away, leaving only incomplete, heavy, and fragmentary shreds), and more generally at all those times when thoughts like "I am in the middle of a dream" or "This is only a dream" spring to mind, thoughts which, by a single and double movement, come to be integrated in the dream of which they form a part, and in the process open a gap in the hermetic sealing-off that ordinarily defines dreaming.[7] By virtue of their specific cleavage, *visees*[8] of this kind resemble the special regimens of filmic perception already discussed. It is in their gaps rather than in their more normal functioning that the filmic state and the oneiric state tend to converge (but the gaps themselves suggest a kinship at once less close and more permanent): in the one case, perceptual transference is ruptured and less of a piece than in the rest of the dream; in the other, it sets its limit a bit more insistently than in the rest of the film.

Freud attributed the gaps in the dream to a complex interaction between different metapsychological, and in particular topographical, agencies.[9] In principle, the ego wants to sleep: to sleep and therefore, if necessary, to dream (to dream deeply). In effect, when a wish rises from the unconscious, the dream presents itself as the only means of satisfying the wish without setting in motion the process of waking up. But the unconscious part of the ego, the repressing agency (the "defense"), in accord with the superego which inspires it, constantly stays in a state of semiwakefulness, while the repressed, and the forbidden more generally, against which, indeed, the unconscious part of the ego is commissioned to defend, also remain wakeful and active, or at least capable of activation, even during sleep. The unconscious, in its double aspect of repressed and repressing (i.e., unconscious of the id and unconscious of the ego), never really sleeps, and what we call sleep is an economic modification principally affecting the preconscious and conscious.[10] The wakefulness of one part of the ego, which permits the other part to go on sleeping, usually assumes the form of censorship (itself inseparable from "the dreamwork" and the manifest characteristics of the dream flux); this censorship, as we know, attends even the deepest dreams, those where perceptual transference is total and the impression of dreaming absent, those in short which are entirely compatible with sleep. But it can also happen that this agency of self-observation and self-surveillance[11] may be led to interrupt sleep to various degrees, the two contrary effects proceeding from the same defensive mission carried out in different circumstances.[12] Such a dream creates too much fear; the censorship, in its initial stage, has failed to sweeten the content of the dream sufficiently, so that its second intervention tends to consist in stopping the dream and sleep along with it. Certain nightmares wake one up (more or less), as do certain excessively pleasureable dreams; certain insomnias are the work of the ego, which, frightened by the prospect of its dreams, prefers to renounce sleep.[13] Given a lesser degree of violence in the internal conflict and therefore a lesser degree of wakefulness, this is the same process that is responsible for the various operations of consciousness in which the subject is sufficiently asleep for his dream to continue but sufficiently awake to know that it is only a dream—thus approaching a very common filmic situation—or again when he exercises an intentioned influence over the very unfolding of the dream,[14] for example, substituting for anticipated sequences another, more satisfying or less frightening, version (we have here something like a film with *alternative* versions, and cinema sometimes offers constructions of this kind.).[15]

These different situations have a point in common. They stem from an active intervention of the agency which sleeps only partially, the unconscious ego; it is this that more or less energetically awakens the sleeping agency, the preconscious ego. In other cases, which in a sense end up with the same result, it is the characteristic rhythms of the latter that come directly into play: it is not still entirely asleep, or it has already started to be so no longer, as in the "intermediary states" of evening and morning. As for the function of *consciousness,* let us recall that it sleeps only when sleep is dreamless. Dreams, even when accompanied by deep sleep, wake it up and put it to work, for the final text of its productions is conscious. Truly deep sleep (which does not exist) would be a psychical regimen in which all the agencies slept. We can speak of "deep sleep," in a relative and practical sense, in two circumstances: when the dream is accompanied by no consciousness of being a dream, and *a fortiori* when sleep is dreamless. These two situations taken together cover almost all the cases that ordinary language calls "deep sleep" (or simply "sleep", without qualification). They correspond to the maximal degree of sleep of which the psychical apparatus in its normal functioning is capable.

These metapsychological mechanisms are obviously complex, much more so than this cavalier summary indicates, but I shall retain only their implied common basis: that the *visee* of deep dreaming, the total illusion of reality, supposes deep sleep in the sense just defined. We know how much Freud insisted on this close correlation between dream and sleep (devoting a special study to it in addition to *The Interpretation of Dreams* itself), a correlation going well beyond the simple visible evidence, since it is not only external (i.e., "We dream only while sleeping"), but because the internal process of the dream is predicated in its particulars on the economic conditions of sleep.[16] As a corollary, each slackening in the full exercise of perceptual transference corresponds to a weakening of sleep, to a certain manner or degree of waking. Given our perspective, all this can be summarized as follows: the degree of illusion of reality is inversely proportional to that of *wakefulness.*

This formulation will perhaps be of help in better understanding the filmic state, setting it in relation to the oneiric state as a complex mixture of similarities and differences. In contrast to the ordinary activities of life, the filmic state as induced by traditional fiction films (and in this respect it is true that these films demobilize their spectators) is marked by a general tendency to lower wakefulness, to take a step in the direction of sleep and dreaming. When one has not had enough sleep, dozing off is usually more a danger during the projection of a film than before or even afterwards. The narrative film does not incite one to action, and if it is like a mirror, this is not only, as has been said,[17] by virtue of playing the scenes Italian style or of the vanishing point of monocular perspective, which puts the spectator-subject in a position to admire himself like a god, or because it reactivates in us the conditions belonging to the mirror phase in Lacan's sense (i.e., heightened perception and lowered motoricity)[18]—it is also and more directly, even if the two things are linked, because it encourages narcissistic withdrawal and receptiveness to phantasy which, when pushed further, enter into the definition of dreaming and sleep:[19] withdrawal of the libido into the ego, temporary suspension of concern for the exterior world as well as object cathexes, at least in their real form. In this respect, the novelistic film, a mill of images and sounds overfeeding our zones of shadow and irresponsibility, is a machine for grinding up affectivity and inhibiting action. In the filmic state, this diminution of wakefulness admits (at least) two distinct degrees. The first is constituted in a quite general way and consists in the very fact of the impression of reality, assuredly different from the illusion of reality, but nonetheless its far-off beginning; and all diegetic films, quite apart from their content and their degree of "realism," characteristically play on this impression, draw their specific charm and power from it, and are made for this purpose. One step further in the lowering of wakefulness, and we have the special regimens of filmic perception of which I spoke at the outset. They intervene in a more fleeting, episodic fashion; they move a bit further toward genuine illusion (though without ever reaching it) during the brief instant of a psychical giddiness.

It remains that the spectator almost always knows that he is at the movies, the dreamer almost never that he is dreaming. Beyond the intermediary cases, discreet indicators of a kinship at once more profound and dialectical, the fiction film and the dream remain separated, if we consider each of them in its entirety, by an important and regular difference in the degree of perceptual transference; the impression and illusion remain distinct. The maintenance of this distinction in ordinary operations, as well as its weakening in borderline cases, has one and the same cause, which is sleep or its absence. The filmic and oneiric states tend to converge when the spectator begins to doze off *[s'endormir]* (although ordinary language at this stage does not speak of "sleep" *[sommeil]*), or when the dreamer begins to wake up. But the dominant situation is that in which film and dream are not confounded: this is because the film spectator is a man awake, whereas the dreamer is a man asleep.

II

The second major difference between the filmic and oneiric *visees* derives strictly from the first. Filmic perception *is* a real perception (is really a perception); it is not reducible to an internal psychical process. The spectator receives images and sounds offered as the representation of something other than themselves, of a diegetic universe, but remaining true images and sounds capable of reaching other spectators as well, whereas the oneiric flux can reach the consciousness of no one but the dreamer. The projection of the film cannot begin before the reels arrive: nothing of this sort is required for the dream to be set in motion. The film image belongs to that class of "real images" (tableaux, drawings, engravings, etc.) which psychologists oppose to mental images. The difference between the two is what separates perception from imagination in the terms of a phenomenology of consciousness. The production of the dream consists of a series of operations remaining from start to finish within the psychical apparatus. In a behaviorist system one would say that what characterizes filmic perception is that it requires a stimulus, whereas oneiric "perception" does not.

The *delusion coefficient* is therefore very superior in the dream: doubly superior, because the subject "believes" more deeply, and because what he believes in is less "true." But in another sense (and we shall return to this), the diegetic delusion, less powerful in the absolute, is, when related to its circumstances, more singular, perhaps more formidable, because it is the delusion of a man awake. The oneiric delusion has been partly neutralized, ever since man dreamt, by the bromide that "this was only a dream." This time-honored method of trivialization, despite such equivalents as "it's just a movie," is harder to apply to the filmic delusion, since we are not asleep at the movies, and we know it.

With its authentic images and sounds, the novelistic film helps nourish the subject's phantasy flux and irrigates the figurations of his wish; it is not to be doubted that the classical cinema is among other things a practical means of affective fulfillment. (But we should not forget that it is not alone in playing this very ancient and far from contemptible role: all *fiction*—what Freud calls "fancy"[20]—even in arts commonly thought nobler, serves this same purpose, which an empty moralism, preoccupied with decorum, would like to distinguish from "authentic art.") Inasmuch as it proposes behavioral schemes and libidinal prototypes, corporal postures, types of dress, models of free behavior or seduction, and is the initiating authority for a perpetual adolescence, the classical film has taken, relay fashion, the historical place of the grand-epoch, nineteenth-century novel (itself descended from the ancient epic); it fills the same social function, a function which the twentieth-century novel, less and less diegetic and representational, tends partly to abandon.

We observe, however, that film narratives *[récits]* often thwart the imagination. Given certain combinations of film and spectator, they are liable to induce reactions in which affective irritation or phantasmic allergy appear, and which are nothing other, whatever rationalization the subject gives to them, than frustrations classically resulting in aggressivity against the frustrating agent, here the film itself. The spectator maintains with the film an object relation (good or bad object), and films, as indicated by the current and enigmatic formulas we use after seeing them, are things that we "like" or "don't like." The liveliness of these reactions in certain cases, and the very existence of *filmic unpleasure,* only serve to confirm the kinship of fiction film and phantasy. Common experience shows that film very often divides the opinions of people who otherwise nearly always react in unison (but let me add, and this is an additional confirmation, that these divergences generally manage to even themselves out when phantasy adjustment is at work since birth and is pursued progressively: when two person see the film together, this is to say that each of them is alone without being so).

From the topographical point of view, filmic unpleasure can arise, depending on the circumstances, from two distinct sources, and sometimes from their convergent action. It can arise on the side of the id when the id is insufficiently nourished by the diegesis of the film; instinctual satisfaction is stingily dealt out, and we have then a case of frustration in the proper sense (actual frustration, in Freudian terms): hence films that seem to us "dull" or "boring" or "ordinary," etc. But aggressivity against the film—whose conscious form in both cases consists in declaring that one has not liked it, that is to say, that it has been a bad object—can result equally from an intervention of the superego and the defenses of the ego, which are frightened and counterattack when, on the other hand, the satisfaction of the id has been too lively, as sometimes happens with films "in bad taste" (taste then becomes an excellent alibi), or extremist, or childish, or sentimental, or sado-pornographic films, etc., in a word, films against which we defend ourselves (at least when we have been touched) by smiling or laughing, by an allegation of stupidity, grotesqueness, or "lack of verisimilitude." In short, if a subject is to "like" a film, the detail of the diegesis must sufficiently please his conscious and unconscious phantasies to permit him a certain instinctual satisfaction, and this satisfaction must stay within certain limits, must not pass the point at which anguish and rejection would be mobilized. In other words, the spectator's defenses (or at least the processes of edulcoration and symbolic substitution which are sufficiently efficacious functional equivalents for them) must be integrated with the very content of the film by one of those happy accidents that also preside over the relations between people and the "encounters" of life, in such a way that the subject can avoid activating his own defenses, which would inevitably be translated into antipathy for the film. In short, every time a fiction film has not been liked, it is because it has been liked too much, or not enough, or both.

Whatever the psychical paths that produce it, filmic unpleasure is a thing that exists: certain spectators do not like certain films. The fiction cinema, which in principle caters to the phantasy, can also thwart it: one person might not have imagined heroes of the particular physiognomy or stature that the screen offers to his perception and that he cannot retouch; he is secretly annoyed that the plot does not take the course he hoped for; he "doesn't see things that way." Those spectators whom the intellectual (a native too often ignored) considers naive do not hesitate to say that they dislike a film because it ends badly or because it is too bold, too unfeeling, too sad, etc.; if they were any more ingenuous they would tell us quite clearly that the film is bad "because it's the nice tall blond man who should have survived" or "because the two farmers should have been able to understand each other and be reconciled" (these are only random examples, but many conversations about movies are of this order, even the majority if we consider the population of spectators as a whole). The intellectual protests, this time rightly, that the characters of the film, as long as they are presented thus, are part of its raw content and cannot constitute criteria of evaluation. But he would be doubly naive if he forgot, or if he concealed from himself, that something in him—which is better left hidden but never entirely disappears—responds to films in the same way. These phenomena of *phantasy deception* are particularly apparent when an already known novel is brought to the screen. The reader of the novel, following the characteristic and singular paths of his desire, proceeds to give complete visual clothing to the words he reads, and when he sees the film, he wishes very strongly to recover this (in fact to *see it again,* by virtue of that implacable force of repetition that inhabits desire, driving the child to play unceasingly with the same toy, the adolescent to listen unceasingly to the same record, before abandoning it for the next, which in its turn will fill a portion of his days). But the reader of the novel will not always reencounter his film, since what he has before him in the actual film is now somebody else's phantasy, a thing rarely sympathetic (to the extent that when it becomes so, it inspires love).

Let us add here a second great difference between the filmic state and the oneiric state. As hallucinatory wish-fulfillment, the fiction film is less *certain* than the dream; it fails more often at its ordinary mission. This is because it is not really hallucinatory. It rests on true perceptions which the subject cannot fashion to his liking, on images and sounds imposed on him from without. The dream responds to the wish with more exactitude and regularity: devoid of exterior material, it is assured of never colliding with reality (and reality includes other people's phantasy). It is like a film which has been "shot" from beginning to end by the very subject of the wish, and equally of fear, a singular film by virtue of its censorship and omissions as much as its expressed content, cut to the measure of its unique spectator (this is another sort of *découpage*[21]), a spectator who is also the *auteur* and has every reason to be content with it, since one is never so well served as by oneself.

In Freudian theory, the dream, along with the hallucination strictly defined and the other special regimens of consciousness (Meynert's *amentia*, etc.), belongs to a particular group of economic situations, the "hallucinatory psychoses of desire."[22] Under this heading Freud grouped the diverse and precise conditions in which an absent object can be hallucinated if its presence is desired with enough force. This is to say that it cannot give unpleasure, at least in itself (second reactions to the hallucination can of course be painful). The diegetic film, on the other hand, which in certain respects is still of the order of phantasy, also belongs to the *order of reality*. It exhibits one of reality's major characteristics: in relation to the wish (and to the fear which is the other face of the wish), it can "turn out" more or less well; it is not fundamentally their accomplice; it can become so only after the fact, through an encounter or adjustment whose success is never guaranteed: it can please or displease, like the real, and because it is part of the real. Thus, compared to the dream, which is more strongly bound to the pure pleasure principle, the filmic state rests rather on the reality principle: keeping pleasure for its ultimate goal, it admits sometimes long and arduous tactical detours by way of unpleasure felt as such. This difference in psychical effect derives from an entirely material difference, the presence in the film, without equivalent in the dream, of images and sounds chemically inscribed on an external support, that is to say, the very existence of the film as "recording" and as *bande*.

The physical reality of the film, a simple and important fact, is not without relation to the first problem considered in this study, that of sleep and waking. The hallucinatory process can establish itself, in the normal state, only in the economic conditions of sleep.[23] In the waking situation, and therefore in the cinematographic situation, the most common path of the psychical excitations traces out a one-way line, a directed line which is Freud's "progressive path." The impulses originate in the external world (daily surroundings or filmic *bande*); they reach the psychical apparatus via its perceptual extremity (i.e., the system of perception-consciousness), and finally come to be inscribed in the form of mnemic traces in a less peripheral psychical system, which is sometimes the preconscious ("memories" in the ordinary sense of the word), and sometimes the unconscious, with its own memory, when the case involves impressions of the world that have been repressed after reception. This itinerary goes, then, from the external toward the internal. In sleep and in dreams, the route is the reverse; the "regressive path"[24] has as a point of departure the preconscious and the unconscious, as a point of arrival the illusion of perception. The driving power of the dream is the unconscious wish,[25] linked to repressed childhood memories; it is itself reactivated, through associations of affects and ideas, by more recent, unrepressed, preconscious memories ("the day's residues"); these two incitements, once reunited, constitute the dream's preconscious wish.[26] It is, therefore, a group of memories, preconscious and unconscious, that set off the whole process, and it is these memories, remodeled and transformed by the censorship, the "dreamwork," the imaginary adjunctions, etc., that tend to be deployed in the terminal (manifest) content of the oneiric apprehension. But in order to arrive at this apprehension with its singular power of illusion, the mnemic traces, bearers of the wish, must be hypercathected to the point of hallucination, that is to say, up to the point of vividness where they are confused with perceptions: to the point, in sum, where they activate, if not the sense organs in their ordinary physiological functioning, at least the system of perception insofar as it is a specific psychical agency and *visee de conscience.* Thus the regressive path has perception as its point of arrival, but its particular characteristic is to cathect it from within (this is the very definition of hallucinatory psychosis), whereas usually perception is cathected from without, a feature which establishes it as true perception. Freud recalls that certain activities of waking life, such as visualizing meditation or the voluntary evocation of memories,[27] also rest on the principle of regression, but in these cases regression is arrested before its conclusion, for the memory and the mental image are here clearly recognized by the subject, who does not take them to be perceptions. What is lacking in these *visees* is the last stage of the regressive process, the properly hallucinatory stage, that which continues until it reaches the perceptual function from within on the basis of representations that are purely psychical but highly charged with desire. Complete regression is therefore possible, apart from pathological cases, only in the state of sleep, and this is also why the film spectator, a person who is not asleep, remains incapable of true hallucination even when the fiction is of a kind to stir his desires strongly. In the waking state, the regressive flux, when it appears, runs up against a nearly uninterrupted progressive counter-flux more powerful than it[28] which prevents it from going to its conclusion. Sleep, however, suspends this inverse thrust by stopping the perceptions and thus frees the way for the regressive impressions, which can go to the end of their proper route. In the filmic state, which is one of the variants of the waking state, this classical analysis is fully confirmed and its formulations do not have to be modified but simply made precise: the counter-flux (which is here particularly rich, pressing, continuous) is that of the film itself, of the real images and sounds which cathect perception from without.

But if this is the case, our problem is displaced and our interrogation must take a new tack. What remains to be understood in terms of economy is that the filmic state, despite wakefulness and counter-flux, leaves room for the beginnings of regression, of which I have already spoken, and is marked by more or less consistent psychical thrusts in the direction of perceptual transference and paradoxical hallucination. More fundamentally, it is the impression of reality itself, and therefore the possibility of a certain affective satisfaction by way of the diegesis, that presupposes the beginning of regression, since this impression is nothing other than a general tendency (stillborn or more developed, depending on the case) to perceive as true and external the events and the heroes of the fiction rather than the images and sounds belonging purely to the screening process (which are, nonetheless, the only real impression): a tendency, in short, to perceive as real the represented and not the representer (the technological medium of the representation), to pass over the latter without seeing it for what it is, to press on blindly. If the film shows a galloping horse, we have the impression of seeing a galloping horse and not the moving spots of light which evoke a galloping horse. One touches here on the great and classic difficulty of interpretation that all *representation* poses. In the conditions peculiar to the cinema, it can be stated thus: how does the spectator effect the mental leap which alone can lead him from the perceptual donnee, consisting of moving visual and sonic impressions, to the constitution of a fictional universe, from an objectively real but denied signifier to an imaginary but psychologically real signified? It is true that a regressive outline a bit like this one is also established in other waking states, such as memory evocation, but this still tells us nothing (especially since conditions there are obviously extremely different) about the particular forms that clothe this phenomenon in a case like the filmic state, where it has not been studied from this point of view.

The progressive path defined by Freud also admits of a variation (a bifurcation, rather) which this text has until now left aside.[29] In waking life, action, that is to say, the ego function that consists of modifying the real in the direction of the wish, requires a complete perceptual regulation preceding and permanently accompanying it. In order to grasp an object, it is necessary to have seen, and to be seeing, it. Thus all day long, impressions from without reach the psychical apparatus through the door of perception, and "go out again" (so to speak) in the form of motor activity directed back toward the world. If the dream is predicated on sleep, this then is also because sleep suspends all action and thus results in blocking the motor outlet, an exutory that, by contrast, remains constantly available in the waking state and helps considerably in impeding regression by absorbing through muscular modification all sorts of excitations which, without it, have a greater tendency to flow back toward the perceptual outlet, which is precisely what they do in dreams.

The filmic situation brings with it certain elements of motor inhibition, and it is in this respect a kind of sleep in miniature, a waking sleep. The spectator is relatively immobile; he is plunged into a relative darkness, and, above all, he is not unaware of the spectaclelike nature of the film object and the cinema institution in their historically constituted form: he has decided in advance to conduct himself as a spectator (a function from which he takes his name), a spectator and not an actor (the actors have their assigned place, which is elsewhere: on the other side of the film); for the duration of the projection he puts off any plan of action. (Movie theaters are of course also used for other purposes, but to the extent that they are, their occupants have ceased to be spectators and have voluntarily abandoned the filmic state for a sort of behavior belonging to reality. . . .) In the case of the true spectator, motor manifestations are few:[30] shifting around in the seat, more or less conscious modification of facial expression, occasional comment under the breath, laughing (if the film, intentionally or not, provokes it), pursuing intermittent verbal or gestural relations (in the case of spectators in couples or groups) with the person in the next seat, etc. The institutional situation of the spectacle inherently prevents motor conduct from following its normal course very far, even in cases where the diegesis of the film is in a position to invoke active extensions of it (i.e., erotic sequences, sequences of political mobilization, etc.; this is where these genres contradict themselves in their pseudo-rupture of the fiction and could, in a sense, whether desirable or not, truly begin to exist as *films* only if the *cinema* as a ritual were profoundly changed, in particular with respect to the customary forms of the "screening" [*"seance,"* a word denoting "sitting down"—Tr.] itself; it is also in this regard that so-called specialized screenings or film tracts possess, in default of subtlety or charm, more coherence and honesty). In ordinary screening conditions, as everyone has had the opportunity to observe, the subject who has fallen prey to the filmic state (most of all when the grip of the fiction on his phantasy is sufficiently strong) feels numb, and spectators at the exit, brutally rejected by the black belly of the theater into the glaring and mischievous light of the lobby, sometimes have the bewildered expression (happy and unhappy) of people waking up. To leave the movies is a little like getting up: not always easy (except if the film was really indifferent).

The filmic state thus embodies in a weaker form certain economic conditions of sleep. It remains a variant of the waking situation but less remote from sleep than most of the others. Here at a new turn in the road, with the partial blockage of the motor outlet, we again come across the notion of a lessened wakefulness, initially proposed in reference to the perceptual conditions of the filmic state (the two things go together, sleep inhibitng perception and action simultaneously). The psychical energy which, in other circumstances of waking life, would be dissipated in action is, by contrast, conserved, even if by necessity, in the case of the cinema spectator. It tends to follow other itineraries of discharge, by virtue of the pleasure principle, which always seeks to liquidate stases. It tends to turn back in the direction of the perceptual agency, to appropriate the regressive path, to occupy itself hypercathecting perception from within. And since the film at the same moment characteristically offers rich nourishment to this perception from without, complete regression of the oneiric kind is obstructed to the profit of a sort of semiregression representing another type of economic equilibrium, differing in its dosage but equally marked and characteristic. What defines this equilibrium is a *double reinforcement* of the perceptual function, simultaneously from without and within: apart from the filmic state, there are few situations in which a subject receives particularly dense and organized impressions from without at the same moment that his immobility predisposes him to "hyper-receive" *["sur-recevoir"]* them from within. The classical film plays on this pincer action, the two branches of which it has itself set up. It is the double reinforcement which renders possible the impression of reality; it is thanks to it that the spectator, starting from the material on the screen, the only thing given him at the outset (i.e., the spots of light in movement within a rectangle, the sounds and words coming from nowhere) tends to become capable of a certain degree of *belief* in the reality of an imaginary world whose signs are furnished him, capable of fiction, in sum. For the fictional capacity, as we too often forget, is not exclusively (or primarily) the capacity—unequally shared and for this reason prized by aesthetes—to invent fiction; it is above all the historically constituted and much more widespread existence of a regimen of socially regulated psychical functioning, to which we rightly give the name of fiction. Before being an art, fiction is a fact (a fact of which certain art forms take possession).

The relation between this fictional capacity and the film of narrative representation is close and mutual. The diegetic cinema as an institution could not function—and it would not therefore have begun to exist, whereas in fact it has scarcely begun to disappear and even today accounts for the biggest share of production, good or bad—if the spectator, already "prepared" by the older arts of representation (the novel, representational painting, etc.) and by the Aristotelian tradition of Western art in general, were not capable of adopting in a stable and voluntarily renewed fashion the special regimen of perception that we are trying to analyze here in Freudian terms. But inversely, the existence of a movie industry which produces abundantly and ceaselessly trades on the psychical effect which renders it possible and profitable (possible because profitable), works to stabilize this effect, differentiate it, frame it, enclose it, and keep it alive by offering it a continued possibility of satisfaction; thus the industry ends up by reproducing its own conditions of possibility. Moreover, although the fictional capacity was already at the root of all the mimetic arts (and although the very notion of diegesis, contrary to what certain people believe, goes back to Greek philosophy, to Aristotle and Plato, and not to the semiology of the cinema), it remains true that film, as I have tried to show elsewhere in a more phenomenological vein,[31] produces an impression of reality much more vivid than does the novel or the theater, since the inherent nature of the cinematographic signifier, with its particularly "faithful" *["ressemblantes"]* photographic images, with the real presence of movement and sound, etc., has for a result the inflection of the fiction phenomenon, however ancient, in the direction of historically more recent and socially specific forms.

III

The set of differences between fiction film and dream, and also therefore the set of their partial resemblances, may be organized around three great facts issuing, each in its own way, from the difference between waking and sleep: first, the *unequal knowledge of the subject* with respect to what he is doing; second, the presence or absence of a real perceptual object; and third, an important characteristic of the textual content itself (text of the film or dream), about which we are now going to speak. The diegetic film is in general considerably more "logical" and "constructed" than the dream. Fantastic or marvelous films, the most unrealistic films, are very often only films that obey another logic, a genre logic (like the realistic film itself), a set of ground rules which they have laid down at the outset (genres are institutions) and within which they are perfectly coherent. It rarely happens that we find in a film narrative that impression of *true absurdity* commonly felt before the memory of our own dreams or accounts of dreams, that very specific, very recognizable impression (from which intentionally absurd films, like the "literature of the absurd" of not long ago, remain so remote) wherein at once enter the internal obscurity of the elements and the confusion of their assemblage, the enigmatic brilliance of the zones that the wish dazzles and the dark, swarming shipwreck of the almost forgotten segments, the sensation of tension and relaxation, the suspected outcropping of a buried order and the evidence of an authentic incoherence, an incoherence which, unlike that of films that aspire to delirium, is not a labored addition but the very core of the text.

The psychologist Rene Zazzo,[32] touching on the basis of a repeated remark of Freud's, rightly affirms that the manifest content of a dream, if it were strictly transposed to the screen, would make an unintelligible film. A film, I may add, truly unintelligible (an object in fact very rare), and not one of those avant-garde or experimental films which, as the enlightened audience knows, it is appropriate at once to understand and not to understand (not understanding being the better way to understand and too much effort at understanding being the height of misunderstanding, etc.). These films, whose objective social function is to answer the naively puzzled wish of certain intellectuals for nonnaivete, have integrated within their institutional regimen of intelligibility a certain dose of elegant and coded unintelligibility, in such a way that their very unintelligibility is in return intelligible. What is in question here is again a genre, and one which illustrates the contrary of what it would like to show; it reveals how difficult it is for a film to achieve true absurdity, pure incomprehensibility, that very thing which our most ordinary dreams, at least in certain sequences, achieve directly and effortlessly. It is undoubtedly for the same reason that "dream sequences" in narrative films are nearly always so unbelievable.

We encounter here the problem of the secondary revision.[33] In his various writings, Freud gives somewhat different accounts of the exact moment that the secondary revision intervenes within the complete production process of the dream (i.e., the dreamwork). Sometimes he considers that it comes into play toward the end, [34] following the condensations, displacements, and various "figurations," and that its function is to put a hasty, last-moment logical facade over the illogical productions of the primary process. Sometimes he situates it perceptibly upstream[35] at the level of the dream thoughts themselves or of a choice retroactively made among them. Finally (and this is the most probable hypothesis), he sometimes refuses to assign it a segmental position within a quasi-chronology[36] and considers that the different processes resulting in the manifest dream occur in a tangle, that is to say, in a manner at once alternating, successive, and simultaneous. (There is also the case where a phantasy, therefore a mental object by definition secondary, is integrated as in the manifest dream; we shall come back to this.) But in any case, what remains is that the secondary process is only one of the forces whose combinations and compromises determine the conscious content of the dream and that its entire weight is very often less that that of other concurrent mechanisms (condensations, displacements, figurations), all under the control of the primary process. This is surely why "dream logic" (the logic of the oneiric diegesis) is truly alien, and why one object can instantly transform itself into another without provoking the dreamer's astonishment until he wakes up, why a silhouette can be *clearly* recognized as being (being, not "representing") two persons at once, whom the dreamer, without further confusion, at the same moment considers distinct, etc. Between the logic of the most "absurd" film and that of the dream, there will always remain a difference, because in the latter what is astonishing does not astonish and consequently nothing is absurd: whence, precisely, the astonishment and the impression of the absurd one feels on waking.

The primary process rests on the "pure" pleasure principle, uncorrected by the reality principle, and under this title it aims at the maximal and immediate discharge of psychical excitations (affects, representations, "thoughts," etc.). All the itineraries of energy discharge are therefore good for it, and it is the basis of condensation and displacement, which are non-bound paths; in displacement, for example, the entire psychical charge is transposed from one object to another without being bound by the constraints of reality that make two objects substantially distinct and not susceptible to total equivalence. The secondary process, which on the other hand obeys the reality principle, always consists in fixing certain paths of thought (i.e., bound energy) and preventing the discharge of impressions by other routes; this is the very definition of the various logics of waking, that is, of the various logics (simply) if we take the word in its usual sense. But since the primary process belongs to the unconscious, its characteristic operations are shielded from direct observation, and we can know them, or at least have an idea of them, only thanks to privileged cases such as the symptom, the slip, and acting out *[acting]*, etc., in which the outcomes of these specific routes (but not the routes themselves) become conscious and manifest.

Among these privileged cases, one of the principal ones is the dream. It has a further privilege in that it is the only one that is neither neurotic, like the symptom or acting out, nor excessively minor, like slips and bungled acts. In sum, for the primary "logic" to result in conscious productions of any importance, in a normal situation the conditions of the dream, therefore of sleep, are necessary. It is sleep, more than the dream itself, which suspends the exercise of the reality principle,[37] since the sleeping subject does not have any real task to accomplish. And when he is awake (when he is, for example, watching or making a film), the secondary process succeeds in recovering all its psychical paths, thoughts, feelings, and actions, so that the primary process, which remains its permament basis, ceases to achieve directly observable results, since everything observable, before becoming so, must pass through the secondary logic, which is that of the conscious.

From the point of view of the cinema analyst, everything happens then as if the secondary revision (which in the production-perception of the dream is only one force among others, and not the principal one) became in the production and perception of the film the dominant, omnipresent force, the architect of the *mental milieu* itself, the milieu and the place *[lieu]* where the film is delivered and received. When we trace the obscure kinship relations (interwoven as they are by differences) of the film and the dream, we come upon that unique and methodologically attractive object, that theoretical monster, namely, a dream in which the secondary revision does nearly everything by itself, a dream where the primary process plays only a furtive and intermittent role, a role of gap-maker, a role of *escape:* a dream, in short, like life. That is to say (we always come back to this), the dream of a man awake, a man who knows that he is dreaming and who consequently knows that he is not dreaming, who knows that he is at the movies, *who knows that he is not sleeping:* since if a man who is sleeping is a man who does not know that he is sleeping, a man who knows that he is not sleeping is a man who is not sleeping.

What conditions must be met in order that we may experience this specific impression of true absurdity? They are precise, and Freud often alludes to them.[38] An unconscious production, largely dominated by the primary process, must be directly presented to the conscious aperception; it is this brutal transplantation from one milieu to another, this uprooting, which provokes the conscious feeling of absurdity: as when we evoke, when awake, the memory of our own dreams. In the case of film, these conditions are not met; one of them is (the presentation to the conscious agency), but the other is not, since what is presented is not a direct production of the unconscious, or at least is not any more so than are the ordinary discourses and actions of life. This is why the film, a production of a man awake presented to a man awake, cannot help being "constructed," logical, and felt as such.

However, the filmic flux resembles the oneiric flux more than other productions of waking resemble it. It is received, as we have said, in a state of lessened wakefulness. Its signifier (images accompanied by sound and movement) inherently confers on it a certain affinity with the dream, for it coincides directly with one of the major features of the oneiric signifier, "imaged" expression, the consideration of representability, to use Freud's term. It is true that the image can organize itself—and that it does so most often, in the cinema as elsewhere, when caught up in the constraints of communication and the pressures of culture[39]—in figures as "bound," as secondary as those of language (and which classical semiology, with its linguistic inspiration, is in a good position to grasp). But it is also true, as Jean Francois Lyotard has rightly insisted,[40] that the image resists being swallowed up whole in these logical assemblages and that something within it has the tendency to escape. In every "language," the characteristics inherent in the physical medium of the signifier *[matière du signifiant]*, as I have noted at another level in *Language and Cinema*,[41] have a certain influence on the type of logic tending to inform the texts (this is the problem of "specificities" considered at the plane of formal configurations). The unconscious neither thinks nor discourses; it figures itself forth in images; conversely, every image remains vulnerable to the attraction, varying in strength according to the case, of the primary process and its characteristic modalities of concatenation. Language itself, not to be confused with *langue*, often undergoes this attraction, as we see in poetry, and Freud has shown[42] that dreams or certain symptoms treat representations of words as representations of things. The image, because of its nature, because of its kinship with the unconscious, is a bit more exposed to this attraction. (What is at issue, however, is only a difference of immediacy, and we should be .cautious about reinstating on this basis the psychodramatic antagonism between words and images, a great mythic theme of a certain "audio-visual" ideology that forgets the force of social conditionings exerted in common on the different means of expression.)

When we consider more particularly the narrative fiction cinema, which is only one of the various possible cinemas, this kinship of film and dream—a kinship of the signifier—is doubled by a supplementary affinity involving the signified. For it is also characteristic of the dream (and of the phantasy—a point to which we shall return) that it consists of a *story.* Of course there are stories and there are stories. The film story always unfolds clearly (or the obscurity, at least, is always accidental and secondary); it is a *told* story, a story, in short, that implies an action of narration *[récit].*[43] The dream story is a "pure" story, a story without an act of narration, emerging in turmoil or shadow, a story that no narrative process has *formed* (deformed), a story from nowhere, which nobody tells to nobody. And nevertheless, still a story: in the dream as in the film there are not only images; there is, clearly or confusedly woven by the images themselves, a succession, whether organized or chaotic, of places, actions, moments, characters.

Thus we shall have to consider more closely the exact nature (also, the limits) of the primary operations floating on the surface of the "secondarized" chain of filmic discourse:[44] a formidable job with research requirements that forbid taking it on here, where we would like to be content with marking its place at the heart of a vaster problem, that of the cinematographic fiction in relation to waking and sleep. Nonetheless, we must say straight off that certain of the most specific, and at the same time the most common, figures of cinematographic expression carry within them, starting with their "technical" and literal definition, something not unrelated to condensation and displacement. To take a single example, the very banality of which gives it an importance neither exceptional nor uncharacteristic, the superimposition and the lap-dissolve[45]—though "redeemed" in the punctuation codes, which weaken what is strange and disquieting in them[46]—rest on mental paths where a certain primary-order unboundness *[deliason]* is maintained. The superimposition characteristically effects a sort of equivalence between two distinct objects: a partial equivalence, simply discursive and metaphoric (a "bringing together," which the act of expression *[l'énonciation]* produces) as long as the spectator, in a process smacking of rationalization, secondarizes it at the same moment that he reads it (that he binds it). A more profound equivalence, an authentic equivalence, in a total sense, insofar as the spectator also receives it in a more immediately affective fashion. Between these two contradictory and simultaneous types of reception, whose mode of psychical coexistence I have elsewhere tried to explain,[47] the relation is one of cleaving and denial. Somewhere within him the spectator takes the superimposition seriously; he sees in it something other than a familiar and neutralized artifice of filmic discourse; he *believes* in the real equivalence of the two objects superimposed on the screen (or at least in some magically transitive bond between them). He believes in this more or less: economically, the force belonging to one of the modes of reception is in a variable relation with the force of the other: certain spectators are more censored (or are so more when faced with a given superimposition); certain superimpositions are more convincing, etc. The fact of equivalence remains—equivalence that the film *figures forth* directly, without indicating "like," "such as," or "at the same moment. . .," as language would—equivalence that thus appears a mixture of condensation and displacement. In the case of the lap-dissolve, which is a superimposition drawn further in the direction of consecutive order (in that one image ends up replacing the other), the primary equivalence of the two motifs includes a bit less condensation and a bit more displacement. But the two figures have this in common: that up to a certain point they put into play the transference of a psychical charge from one object to another (contrary to the tendency of all everyday logic), and that in them can be read in outline (or residue) form the propensity characteristic of the primary process to abolish the very duality of objects, that is to say, to establish, outside the divisions imposed by reality, the short and magical circuits that the impatient wish requires. Thus the fiction film consoles us with common impossibilities.

The study of phenomena of this kind, whether in cinematographic language itself or in the formal operations of a given film, leads us back via one of its extremities to the unconscious of the filmmaker (or of the cinema); this is the side of the "sender." But the other extremity (the "receiver," that is to say, the filmic state) is equally interesting to consider. What is remarkable in this regard is that the appearance in the film of these more or less primary figures generally provokes little astonishment and confusion in the spectator. That they may be immediately subsumed in a secondary narrative logic does not explain everything; neither does historical familiarization or acculturation to the cinema. They retain, it would seem, enough of the unfamiliar for us to have anticipated a more immediate, profound, and widespread rejection (for there are traces of it among certain spectators in relation to certain films), a rejection capable of taking diverse forms: explicit protest, laughing as a polyvalent defense and all-purpose protection, aggression perpetrated inwardly against the film (or, on the other hand, among depressives, extreme perplexity), the strong impression of illogicality. None of these reactions is unexampled but no more is any the rule, and even when they are produced, it is most often, as we said earlier, in response to the phantasy content of the film and not to what remains of the primary process in filmic expression as such in certain of its operations capable of conveying more than one content. This is because, to tell the truth, it is characteristic of these operations in the machinery of fiction to be self-effacing, to work for the benefit of the diegesis, to "inflate" belief and activate its hold on the emotions at the cost of their own abasement, in accord with a process of *belief transference* to which I have devoted a separate study.[48] This factor is one of those that permit us to understand why the rejection of primary configurations is not more frequent, why the film object does not surprise the spectator, why it is not an intrinsic scandal.

We now see that the filmic state combines within itself two contrary and yet convergent processes leading by inverse routes to the same result, that absence of astonishment which research should find a little more astonishing. Absence of astonishment because the film is on the whole secondary and the spectator on the whole awake, with the result that they are on an equal footing; but also, insofar as cinematic discourse is perforated by primary emergences, because the spectator is a bit less awake than in other circumstance (the equal footing is maintained then, but on another foot): thus a sort of compromise is created, a middle level of wakefulness, itself institutionalized in the classical cinema, where film and spectator succeed in being regulated one by the other and both by an identical or similar degree of secondarization. The spectator, during the projection, puts himself into a state of lessened alertness (he is at a show; nothing can happen to him); in performing the social act of "going to the movies," he is motivated in advance to lower his ego defenses a notch and not to reject what he would reject elsewhere. He is capable, in a very limited and yet singular measure, of a certain tolerance for the conscious manifestation of the primary process. Undoubtedly, this is not the only case where he is so (there is also alcoholic intoxication, exaltation, etc.). But it is deservedly one of them, with particular conditions not to be found in the others: theatrical situation, presence of a materialized fiction, etc. Among the different regimens of waking, the filmic state is one of those least unlike sleep and dreaming, dreamful sleep.

IV

In trying to specify the relations between the filmic state and the oneiric state, the partial kinships and incomplete differences, we encounter at every step the problem of sleep, its absence, or its intermediate degrees. Thus we are inevitably led to introduce a new term into the analysis, the daydream, which, like the filmic state and unlike the dream, is a waking activity. When in French we wish more clearly to distinguish the dream *[rêve]* and the daydream *[rêverie]*, we call the latter, in a stiff and in fact redundant syntagm, the "waking daydream" *[rêverie eveillée"]*. This is Freud's "Tagtraum," the daytime dream *[rêve de jour]*, in short the *conscious phantasy*. (We know that the phantasy, conscious or unconscious, can also be integrated within a dream whose manifest content it comprises; but in this case, it loses certain characteristics of the phantasy and takes on certain characteristics of the dream; it is therefore the non-oneiric phantasy that is now in question).

The first three parts of this study have already indicated, though in a negative and hollow fashion, some of the features linking the diegetic film to the daydream, for they are often the same ones that separate it from the dream. We shall content ourselves with approaching them from the other direction (necessarily displacing them) and filling them out where necessary.

It is noteworthy, first of all, that the degree and manner of logical coherence of the novelistic film are rather like those of the "petit roman" or "story," which are Freud's terms for the conscious phantasy,[49] that is to say, that the relation of forces between the secondary revision and the various primary operations is perceptibly the same in both cases. A likeness which does not depend, as we might first suppose, on the fact that the film and the daydream are both conscious productions, since the dream is so too and yet is much less logical. It is not, therefore, the specific coefficient of coming-to-consciousness (consciousness in its descriptive, not topographical, sense) which intervenes here; coming-to-consciousness, or its absence, is an exponent affecting the final product of a psychical process, whereas the relative resemblance of the film and the daydream can be understood only at the level of the modes of production. Not that these modes are identical in the two cases. But we shall see that through their very difference they succeed in reconverging, at least with respect to the final degree of secondary coherence.

If film is a logical construction, it is because it is the product of men awake, filmmakers as well as spectators, whose mental operations are those of the conscious and preconscious. These operations therefore constitute the psychical agency which we can consider as directly producing the film. Although the driving force of the psychical processes in general, among them the making and viewing of films, is always of an unconscious order, there still exists an important difference between such cases as the symptom or the dream, where the primary mechanisms work in a relatively open way, and those where they are by contrast more completely hidden. In the second group appear the clearest of the waking activities, provided they are not too neurotic. To define them (and film along with them) as *preconscious productions* has therefore a sense that is not absolute and requires specification: we mean by this that between the unconscious forces where they take root and the manifest process in which they result (discourse, action, etc.), the interposed transformational relay, that is to say, the preconscious and conscious operations, in the end constitutes the agency that does the greatest share of the work and does it in such a way that the visible result is rather different—rather *distanced* (keeping the word's force as passive participle)—from the original source and from the type of logic belonging to it: thus it is in the ordinary processes of life in society and in the greater part of the productions of culture.

The conscious phantasy—or rather, simply the phantasy in its different conscious and unconscious versions, inseparable from each other and grouped in "families"—is rooted in the unconscious in a fashion that is more direct and that follows a shorter circuit. It belongs more to the unconscious system (the unconscious in its topographical sense), even when its manifestations, or certain among them, have access to consciousness, for it is thematically close to the ideational representative of the instinct and energetically close to the instinct's affective representative;[50] whence its disturbing seductive power when aroused by a film or something else. This kinship with the instinctual sources enters into the very definition of the phantasy flux, with the result that we can see there (in the relative sense stated above) a production of the unconscious. It assuredly is that, but is nonetheless distinguished from other productions of the unconscious, the dream, the symptom, etc.—and this is the second element of the definition—by its internal logic, wherein there appears the inherent mark of the preconscious and of the secondary process: the phantasy is directly organized as a relatively coherent story (or scene) whose actions, characters, places, and sometimes moments are connected and do not disclaim the logic of the narrative or representative arts (we know that "logical dreams"[51] are often those whose manifest content, in whole or in part, coincides with a whole phantasy or a whole segment of a phantasy). Thus, although phantasy is always near the unconscious by virtue of its content, and although the conscious phantasy is only a slightly more distant version, a budding prolongation (a "derivative," as we say) of the unconscious phantasy, nonetheless phantasy (even in its submerged parts) always carries the more or less clear imprint of the preconscious in its modes of "composition" and formal layout; this is why Freud saw it as a sort of hybrid.[52] This internal duality characterizes the conscious as well as the unconscious manifestations of one and the same seed of phantasy thrust, but the degree of secondariness obviously tends to grow when one of the germinations crosses the threshold of consciousness and thus becomes accessible to the daydream. When the daydream takes hold of it, we can even establish in certain cases a kind of intentional intervention by the subject, which is like the first stage in drafting a film scenario; the daydream is born of a conscious phantasy, already coherent in its manner but often brief, instantaneous, and fleeting in its recognizable and unwished (recognizable because unwished, because always a bit compulsive) intensity; the act of daydreaming as such often tends to consist in artificially prolonging the emergence of the phantasy for a few additional moments, thanks to a rhetorical and narrative amplification which for its part is fully wished and has already the character of diegetic composition. (We see that the daydream and the conscious phantasy are not entirely confounded; rather, the form is the direct prolongation of the latter.)

The filmic flux is more explicit than that of the daydream, *a fortiori* than that of the conscious phantasy. It cannot be otherwise since film supposes a material fabrication that obliges one to choose each element in all the detail of its perceptible appearance, whereas the daydream, a purely mental fabrication, can tolerate more vague and "blank" spaces. But this is a difference of precision, a difference in the degree of realization, one might say, and not in the degree of secondariness, or in any case much less so than in the difference between the film and the dream. The "little stories" that we tell ourselves somewhat resemble, by virtue of their coherence of the directly diegetic sort, the big stories that story films tell us (whence the enduring success of the latter). It is rare that the narrative line as a whole in a fiction film actually puts one in mind of a dream; it is frequent, even the rule, that it broadly conforms to the *novelistic formula [formule romanesque]* characteristic of the daydream, of the "fancy" in Freud's sense (Freud defined the term precisely by reference to artistic works of representation[53]).

This typological kinship is often doubled by a real filiation of a genetic order, although this more directly causal connection is not indispensable to the resemblance and is less often in evidence. Certain fiction films have more than "the air" of a daydream; they derive directly from the daydreams of their author (here again we meet Freud's "fancy"): films that we call "autobiographical," works of narcissistic filmmakers or young creators particularly full of themselves, show little resistance to the desire to "put everything" into their film;[54] but this is also true in a more distanced and less adolescent form of narrative films whose explicit donnee has nothing autobiographical about it, and, at the limit, of all fiction films, and even others, since no one would produce anything without his phantasies. Nevertheless, when the relation of the work to the phantasy is not established at too manifest a level, it is not any closer or more characteristic than in any other action of life; this is notably the case when the inspiring phantasy is unconscious, so that its mark in the film is considerably transposed (but this can also be the case, by a deliberate step backward, when the phantasy is conscious). We can say therefore that there are indeed films that in this sense do not proceed from their author's phantasies or daydreams.

The degree of secondarization and its essentially diegetic manner are not the only features linking the classical film and the daydream. The filmic state and the conscious phantasy equally suppose a rather similar degree of wakefulness. They are both established at an intermediary point between minimal wakefulness (sleep and dream) and maximal wakefulness, prevailing in the execution of practical tasks actively directed toward a real goal. An intermediary but not median degree, since it is on balance closer to waking, and moreover forms part of it (this is because we conventionally designate as a waking state the whole higher part of the scale of wakefulness together with the totality of its internal degrees). The median degree would be situated lower than that of the daydream or film; it would correspond to certain states which precede or immediately follow sleep in the strict sense of the word.

In the filmic state as in the daydream, perceptual transference stops before its conclusion, true illusion is wanting, the imaginary remains felt as such; just as the spectator knows that he is watching a film, the daydream knows that it is a daydream. Regression is exhausted in both cases before reaching the perceptual agency; the subject does not confuse the representations with perceptions, but clearly maintains their status as representations: mental representations in the daydream,[55] and in the film representation of a fictional world through real perceptions (not to speak of true daydreams, mental images recognized as such, accompanying the viewing of the film and embroidered around it; they are never taken for real; on the other hand, the subject sometimes has trouble distinguishing them from the diegesis, but this is precisely because both belong to a rather closely related mode of the imaginary). In all of this, the filmic state and the conscious phantasy clearly belong to waking.

To waking but not to its most characteristic manifestations. It suffices to compare them to other states of waking and notably to those summarized by the word *activity* in its ordinary sense, with its connotation of doing things and moving about. Film viewing, like daydreaming, is rooted in contemplation and not in action. Both suppose a temporary, largely voluntary, change in economy by which the subject suspends his object cathexes or at least renounces opening a real outlet for them, and withdraws for a time to a more narcissistic base (more introverted, to the extent that the phantasies remain concerned with objects),[56] as sleeping and dreaming cause him to do to a greater degree. Both have a certain power to relax, an attenuated metapsychological equivalent of the refreshing power that belongs to sleep and defines its function. Both are performed in a certain solitude (correlative of the re-narcissification), which circumstances can render delicious or bitter; we know that active participation in a collective task does not encourage daydreaming and that immersion in the filmic fiction (in the "projection," so well named) has the effect, stronger in proportion as the film is pleasing, of separating groups or couples who entered the theater together and sometimes have a certain difficulty reachieving that togetherness when they leave. (People with good personal rapport find it necessary to agree to have a moment of silence here so that the first words they exchange are not jarring: although these words may comment on the film, they mark its end, for they bring with them activity, waking, companionship. This is because in a certain sense one is always alone at the movies, again a little as in sleep.)

Thanks to this relative lowering of wakefulness, the filmic state and the daydream allow the primary process to emerge up to a certain point, which is rather similar in the two cases. We have said earlier what such cinematographic figures owe to a modest step in the direction of regression. The primary power of the superimposition, for example, has something very deadened, very exhausted about it when compared to that of condensation or displacement, its properly oneiric homologues. But if we consider these same operations in the daydream, the degree of belief that they meet with on the subject's part perceptibly diminishes, and thus is brought nearer to that which a film superimposition can arouse. The conscious phantasy superimposes two faces for the fun of it, without believing in their substantial fusion (which is no cause for doubt in the dream), and nevertheless believing in it a little, since the daydream is a step in the direction of dreaming. This divided operation, naive and crafty at the same time, wherein a bit of the wish is reconciled with a bit of reality thanks to a bit of magic, is in the end rather close to that on which the subject's psychical attention is modeled when he is confronted with a cinematographic superimposition like the traditional one of the faces of lover and beloved.

If the film is akin to the daydream with respect to secondarization and wakefulness, it is separated from it by an irreducible third trait, the materialization, lacking in the daydream and in phantasy generally, of the images and sounds. In this respect the daydream, wherein the representation remains mental, is on the same side as the dream, and the two are jointly opposed to the filmic state. This opposition, already noted in connection with the dream, takes on another sense when it is the daydream with which the film is compared.

The dreaming subject believes that he is perceiving. Passing from the dream to the filmic state, he can only be a loser, and even doubly so: the images are not his; they can therefore displease him, and he believes in them less strongly, despite their objective reality, than he believed in those of his dream, since the power of the latter attained the point of actual illusion. In terms of wish fulfillment, the film is twice inferior to the dream: it is alien, it is felt as "less true."

In relation to the daydream, the balance is shifted. There remains the liability of an external imposition (an imposition, in short), and the subject is in general less satisfied with films that he sees than with daydreams he manufactures. (The case of the filmmaker here differs from that of the spectator; or rather, he is the only spectator for whom the film is not another person's phantasy but an externalized prolongation of his own.) On the other hand, we do not give more credence to our phatasies than to the fiction of the film, since true illusion is not be be had in either case; the affective benefit offered by the film is therefore not inferior on this point to that of the daydream. It is a question in both cases of a pseudo-belief, a consented-to simulation. Thus the material existence of the filmic images (along with all that issues from it: stronger impression of reality, superiority of perceptual precision and therefore of the power of *incarnation,* etc.) helps recover some advantages that compensate more or less completely for the images' immediately alien origin: their profound conformity to one's own phantasy is never guaranteed, but when chance permits this to a sufficient degree, the satisfaction—the feeling of a little miracle, as in the state of share amorous passion—results in a sort of *effect,* rare by nature, which can be defined as the temporary rupture of a quite ordinary solitude. This is the specific joy of receiving from the external world images that are usually internal, images that are familiar or not very far from familiar, of seeing them inscribed in a physical location (the screen), of discovering in this way something almost realizable in them, which was not expected, of feeling for a moment that they are perhaps not inseparable from the tonality which oftenest attends them, from that common and accepted yet slightly despairing impression of the impossible.

In the social life of our age, the fiction film enters into functional competion with the daydream, a competition in which it is sometimes victorious by virtue of the trump cards of which we have just spoken. This is one of the sources of "cinephilia" in its ardent forms, the *love of the cinema,* a phenomenon requiring explanation, especially when we recognize the intensity it can attain among certain people. By contrast, the competition between film and dream as techniques of affective satisfaction is less lively, less sharp: it still exists, since both play this role, but they play it at more widely differing moments and according to less similar regimens of illusion: the dream responds more to the pure wish in its original madness; the film is a more reasonable and

measured satisfaction wherein enters a larger share of compromise. Filmic pleasure itself, in order to establish itself as pleasure, requires many prior assumptions: that this is only the cinema, that other people exist, etc. (The dream does not make so many of these.) Thus the neurotic in a crisis often abandons movie theaters when previously he frequented them: what he sees there is already too remote from him, fatiguing, tiresome. (This occasional cinephobia, not to be confused with calm and permanent abstentions, is a degree more neurotic than the badly controlled cinephilia of which it is the reversal; in cinephilia, the incipient hypertrophy of introversion and narcissism would remain hospitable to external contributions, which the crisis renders suddenly unbearable.)

If the film and the daydream are in more direct competition than the film and the dream, if they ceaselessly encroach upon each other, it is because they occur at a point of adaptation to reality—or at a point of regression, to look at it from the other direction—which is nearly the same; it is because they occur at the same *moment* (same moment in ontogeny, same moment in the diurnal cycle): the dream belongs to childhood and the night; the film and the daydream are more adult and belong to the day, but not midday—to the evening, rather.

V

The filmic state which I have tried to describe is not the only possible one; it does not include all of the rather diverse *visees de conscience* that a person can adopt before a film. Thus the proposed analysis would badly suit the frames of mind of a film critic or a semiologist actively researching, in the course of a professional viewing (shot-by-shot study, etc.), certain well specified features of the film, putting himself by this means into a state of maximal wakefulness, a work state; it is clear that perceptual transference, regression, and degree of belief in his case will be much weaker, and that he will perhaps retain something of this mind-set when he goes to the movies for fun. What is in question in this case is no longer the filmic state which cinema as an institution in its ordinary functioning plays upon, anticipates, foresees, and favors. The film analyst by his very activity places himself in this respect outside the institution.

Moreover, the preceding description concerns only certain geographical forms of the institution itself, those that are valid in Western countries. The cinema as a whole, insofar as it is a social fact, and therefore also the psychological state of the ordinary spectator, can take on appearances very different from those to which we are accustomed. We have only attempted *one* ethnography of the filmic state, among others remaining to be done (for which Freudian notions would be perhaps less helpful and certainly less directly useful, since they were established, despite their pretension to universality, in an observational field with cultural limits). There are societies where the cinema scarcely exists, as in certain regions of black Africa outside the cities; there are also civilizations which like ours are great producers and consumers of fiction films (e.g., Egypt, India, Japan, etc.) but where the social context is sufficiently remote from ours to forbid us, in the absence of a specialized study, any extrapolated proposition with respect to the significance that the very act of *going to the movies* can assume there.

A third limitation, often recalled along the way: the only films in question were narrative (or fictional, or diegetic, or novelistic, or representational, or traditional, or classical, etc.—terms which we purposely used as provisional synonyms but which from other points of view must be distinguished). Most films shot today, good or bad, original or not, "commercial" or not, have as a common characteristic that they tell a story; in this measure they all belong to one and the same *genre,* which is, rather, a sort of "super-genre" ["sur-genre"], since certain of its internal divisions (not all: there are narrative but unclassifiable films) themselves constitute genres: the Western, the gangster film, etc. The real meaning of these films, especially the most complex of them, is not reducible to this anecdote, and one of the most interesting modes of assessment is precisely that which, when faced with a story film, bases itself on everything that outruns the story. However, a narrative kernel remains present in nearly all films—in those where it constitutes the main point as in many others where the main point, even if located elsewhere, hinges on it in various fashions: on it, under it, around it, in its gaps, sometimes in opposition to it—and this fact itself must also be understood, this very broad historical and social collusion of cinema and narrative.[57] It serves no purpose constantly to repeat that the "only interesting cinema," the only cinema that one likes, is precisely that which does not tell a story: an attitude common in certain groups and not without its avant-gardist aestheticism, precipitate revolutionism, or desire for originality at any price. Can we imagine a historian with republican sympathies who for this reason would judge the study of absolute monarchy useless?

Here again we encounter the need for a *criticism* of the diegetic cinema. "Criticism" in a sense neither necessarily nor uniformly polemical, since this cinema, like every cultural formation, is composed of important works side by side with mass-produced goods. Critical analysis of the traditional film consists above all in refusing to see it as the natural outcome of some univeral and timeless essence or vocation of the cinema, in making it appear as one cinema among other possible ones, in unmasking the objective conditions of possibility of its functioning, which are masked by its very functioning, *for* its very functioning.

This machinery has economic and financial gears, directly sociological gears, and also psychological gears. At the center of the latter, we always encounter afresh the impression of reality, the classical problem of filmological research. In an article (already cited) which owed its title to this,[58] I attacked the problem, in 1965, with the tools of phenomenology and experimental psychology. This is because the impression of reality results partly from the physical (perceptual) nature of the cinematographic signifier: images obtained by photographic means and therefore particularly "faithful" *["fidèles"]* in their function as effigies, presence of sound and movement that are already a bit more than effigies since their "reproduction" on the screen is as rich in sensory features as their production outside a film, etc. The impression of reality is founded, then, on certain objective resemblances between what is perceived in the film and what is perceived in daily life, resemblances still imperfect but less so than they are in most of the other arts. However, I remarked also that the similarity of the stimuli does not explain everything, since what characterizes, and even defines, the impression of reality is that it works to the benefit of the imaginary and not of the material which represents it (that is, precisely, the stimulus): in theater this material is even more "similar" *["ressemblant"]* than in movies, but this is surely why the theatrical fiction has a lesser psychological power as reality than the film diegesis. Consequently, the impression of reality can be studied not only by comparison with perception but also by relation to the various kinds of fictional perceptions, the chief of which, apart from the representational arts, are the dream and the phantasy. If cinematographic fabulations are endowed with this sort of credibility, which has struck every author and compels observation, this is at once, and contradictorily, because the psychical situation in which they are received involves certain features of reality and certain features of the daydream and the dream, which also belong to the pseudo-real. The theoretical contribution of psychology (study of perception, study of the conscious), with its extensions into classical filmology, ought therefore to be complemented by that of metapsychology, which can play a part, like linguistics (which it does not supplant), in renovating filmology.

To the extent that the impression of reality is linked to the perceptual features of the signifier, it characterizes all films, diegetic or not, but insofar as it participates in the *fiction-effect,* it belongs to narrative films and to them alone. It is before such films that the spectator adopts a very particular *visee de conscience* which is confounded neither with that of the dream, nor with that of the daydream, nor with that of real perception, but which retains a little of all three, and is installed, so to speak, at the center of the traingle that they mark out: a type of looking whose status is at once hybrid and precise and which establishes itself as the strict correlative of a certain kind of looked-at object (the psychoanalytic problem thus hinges on a historical problem). Faced with this cultural object, which is the fiction film, the impression of reality, the impression of the dream, and the impression of the daydream cease to be contradictory and mutually exclusive, as they are ordinarily, in order to enter into new relations wherein their usual distinctness, while not exactly annulled, admits an unprecedented configuration leaving room at once for straddling, alternating balance, partial overlapping, recalibration, and ongoing circulation among the three: authorizing, in sum, a sort of central and moving zone of intersection where all three can "reencounter" each other on a singular territory, a confused territory which is common to them and yet does not abolish their distinctness. A reencounter which is possible only around a pseudo-real (a diegesis): around a *place* consisting of actions, objects, persons, a time and a space (a place similar in this respect to the real), but which presents itself of its own accord as a vast simulation, a nonreal real; a "milieu" with all the structures of the real and lacking (in a permanent, explicit fashion) only the specific exponent of real being. The fiction thus possesses the strange power of momentarily reconciling three very different regimens of consciousness, for the very characteristics that define the fiction have the effect of driving it, hammering it like a wedge into the narrowest and most central of their interstices: the diegesis has something of the real since it imitates it, something of the daydream and the dream since they imitate the real. The *novelistic* as a whole, with its cinematographic extensions, enriched and complicated by auditory and visual perception (absent in the novel), is nothing other than the systematic exploitation of this region of reencounters and manifold passages.

If films which are not *at all* narrative (there are in fact rather few of these) should one day become more numerous and persuasive, the first effect of this evolution would be to dismiss, at a single stroke, the threefold play of reality, dream, and phantasy, and therefore the unique mixture of these three mirrors through which the filmic state is now defined, a state that history will sweep up in its transformations as it does all the formations of culture.

Translated by Alfred Guzzetti

NOTES

1. For example, in the villages or small towns of countries like France or Italy.

2. [Diegesis is Metz's term for the fictional world depicted in a narrative film. It is, as he writes in *Film Language,* tr. Michael Taylor (New York, 1974), p. 98, "the sum of a film's denotation: the narration itself, but also the fictional space and time dimensions implied in and by the narrative, and consequently the characters, the landscape, the events, and other narrative elements, in so far as they are considered in their denoted aspect." Tr.]

3. [Economic conditions are those relating to the quantifiable instinctual energy in the psychical processes. Freud's metapsychology also includes the topographical, consisting either of the conscious and preconscious, or id, ego, and superego; and the dynamic, consisting of conflicts and interactions of forces. For more complete definitions of these and other Freudian terms from a French perspective, see J. Laplanche and J.-B. Pontalis, *The Language of Psychoanalysis,* tr. Donald Nicholson-Smith (New York, 1973). Tr.]

4. Freud, "A Metapsychological Supplement to the Theory of Dreams," *The Standard Edition of the Complete Psychological Works of Sigmund Freud* (London, 1953-73), XIV, 226-27. Hereafter cited as *Standard Ed.*

5. [In Metz's terminology, film is described materially as the combination of a *bande sonore* ("sound track") and *bande-images* ("image track"). Tr.]

6. "Institution of the ego," in Freud's term ("A Metapsychological Supplement to the Theory of Dreams," *Standard Ed.,* XIV, 233-34).

7. Freud, *The Interpretation of Dreams, Standard Ed.,* V, 488-89.

8. [*Visee* or *visee de conscience* (roughly, "orientation of consciousness"), a term borrowed from Sartre, is that which is by definition opposed to the content of consciousness. As Metz explains, "If I see an apple in front of me and if I imagine an apple, the content of consciousness is the same in the two cases, but there are two different *visées:* in the first case, I *'vise'* the apple as present (this is what we call perception), in the second as absent (this is what we call imagination, hope, regret, desire, etc.). I can also *'vise'* it as past (this is memory). The principal *visées* of consciousness (for the same content) are: present-real (to perceive), past-real (to remember), past-unreal (to regret), present-unreal (to imagine), future-real (to decide), future-unreal (to hope), etc." Tr.]

9. Freud, "On Narcissism: An Introduction," *Standard Ed.,* XIV, 95-97; *The Interpretation of Dreams, Standard Ed.,* V, 572.

10. *The Interpretation of Dreams, Standard Ed.,* V, 571-72; "A

Metapsychological Supplement to the Theory of Dreams," *Standard Ed.*, XIV, 224-25.

11. "On Narcissism: An Introduction," *Standard Ed.*, XIV, 95-97.

12. *The Interpretation of Dreams, Standard Ed.*, V, 579-80.

13. Freud, "Mourning and Melancholia," *Standard Ed.*, XIV, 252-53; "A Metapsychological Supplement to the Theory of Dreams," *Standard Ed., XIV, 225.*

14. *The Interpretation of Dreams, Standard Ed.*, V, 572.

15. In *Film Language*, pp. 217-18, I tried to analyze, under the heading "potential sequence," one of these construction, which appears in Jean-Luc Godard's-film, *Pierrot le Fou*. [For a critique of Metz's analysis, see my essay "Christian Metz and the Semiology of the Cinema," *Journal of Modern Literature*, 3 (Apr. 1973), 302ff. Tr.]

16. "A Metapsychological Supplement to the Theory of Dreams" in its entirety and esp. *Standard Ed.*, XIV, 234-35.

17. Jean Louis Baudry, "Ideological Effects of the Basic Cinematographic Apparatus," *Film Quarterly*, 28, No. 2 (Winter 1974-75), 39-47.

18. Jacques Lacan, "Le stade du miroir comme formateur de la fonction du je," *Ecrits (Paris: Seuil, 1966), pp. 93-100, tr. by Jean Roussel as "The Mirror-Phase as Formative of the Function of the 'I,' " New Left Review* 51 (Sept.-Oct. 1968), 71-77. [Lacan's term refers to a developmental phase occurring approximately between the ages of six to eighteen months in which the infant, though still helpless and uncoordinated, anticipates mastery of his body; this imaginative apprehension of bodily unity is indicated by his joy in perceiving his reflection in a mirror. Tr.]

19. "On Narcissism: An Introduction," *Standard Ed.*, XIV, 82-83: "A Metapsychological Supplement to the Theory of Dreams," *Standard Ed.*, XIV, 222-23.

20. Freud, *Introductory Lectures on Psycho-analysis, Standard Ed.*, XVI, 375-77.

21. [*Coup* being the word for a "cut," *découpage*, a word with no English equivalent, refers to the division of the action into shots. Tr.]

22. "A Metapsychological Supplement to the Theory of Dreams," *Standard Ed.*, XIV, 229-30.

23. *The Interpretation of Dreams, Standard Ed.*, V, 543-44.

24. *Ibid*, pp. 533-49; "A Metapsychological Supplement to the Theory of Dreams," *Standard Ed.*, XIV, 226-28.

25. *The Interpretation of Dreams*, esp. *Standard Ed.*, XIV, 226.

26. "A Metapsychological Supplement to the Theory of Dreams," *Standard Ed.*, XIV, 226.

27. *The Interpretation of Dreams, Standard Ed.,* V, 543; "A Metapsychological Supplement to the Theory of Dreams," *Standard Ed.,* XIV, 230-31; "The Ego and the Id," *Standard Ed.,* XIX, 19-20.
28. *The Interpretation of Dreams, Standard Ed.,* V, 543-44.
29. *Ibid.*
30. According to the psychologist Henri Wallon, the sum of a spectator's impressions during the projection of a film is divided into two clearly separated and unequally weighted series, which he calls respectively "visual series" ("diegetic series" would be a better term) and "proprioceptive series" (the sense, persisting in a weakened form, of one's own body and therefore of the real world). Cf. "L'acte perceptif et le cinema," *Revue internationale de Filmogie* (Paris), No. 13 (Apr.-Jun. 1953).
31. ["On the Impression of Reality in the Cinema," *Film Language,* pp. 3-15. Tr.]
32. "Une experience sur la comprehension du film," *Revue internationale de Filmologie,* 2, No. 6, 160.
33. [In Freud the primary process is associated with the unconscious and the pleasure principle, the secondary process with the conscious and preconscious and the reality principle. Secondary revision reorders a dream so as to reduce its appearance of absurdity and disconnectedness and give it a coherence like that of the daydream. Tr.]
34. "A Metapsychological Supplement to the Theory of Dreams, *Standard Ed.,* XIV, 229; *The Interpretation of Dreams, Standard Ed.,* V, 575.
35. *The Interpretation of Dreams, Standard Ed.,* V, 592-95, 489-90.
36. *Ibid.,* pp. 498-99, 575-76.
37. "A Metapsychological Supplement to the Theory of Dreams," *Standard Ed.,* XIV, 233-34.
38. In particular in *The Interpretation of Dreams, Standard Ed.,* V, 431-33, 528-29 (concerning psychotic discourses), 530-31, 595-96 (concerning condensation), etc.
39. On this point see Text 7 ("Au-delà de l'analogue, l'image) of my *Essais sur la signification au cinéma,* Vol. II (Klincksieck, 1973).
40. *Discours, figure* (Klincksieck, 1971).
41. *Language and Cinema,* tr. Donna Jean Umiker-Seboek (The Hague, 1974), pp. 161-83, esp. pp 170-73.
42. Freud, "The Unconscious," *Standard Ed.,* XIV, 197-99; "A Metapsychological Supplement to the Theory of Dreams," *Standard Ed.,* XIV, 229; *The Interpretation of Dreams, Standard Ed.,* IV, 295-304.
43. See *Film Language,* pp. 20-21.
44. Research in this direction has already begun; cf. esp. Thierry

Kuntzel, "Le travail du film," *Communications 19* (Ecole Pratique des Hautes Etudes et Editions du Seuil, 1972), pp. 25-39.

45. [A superimposition looks like a double exposure, although strictly speaking a double exposure is made at the time of shooting and a superimposition at the time of printing. Good examples of superimposition occur toward the end of Pasolini's *Medea.* A lap-dissolve (or simply, a dissolve) consists of the fade-out of one shot superimposed on the fade-in of a new shot. Tr.]

46. I made a modest study of these punctuation codes in an article entitled "Ponctuations et demarcations dans le film de diegese" (rpt. in *Essais sur la signification au cinéma,* II, 111-37).

47. In "Trucage et cinema," *Essais sur la signification au cinéma* II, 173-92.

48. *Ibid.*

49. Freud also employs others: the English word "daydream," "reve" in the French sense of a daytime dream, that is to say, precisely a "reverie" *(The Interpretation of Dreams, Standard Ed.,* V, 491-92 and n. 2 on p. 491). [Freud glosses the German *Tagtraum* with the French "petits romans" and the English "stories." Tr.]

50. ["Ideational representative" and "affective representative" are Freud's terms for the delegates of the instinct in the respective spheres of ideas and affect. Tr.]

51. *The Interpretation of Dreams, Standard Ed.,* V, 490-92.

52. Or "half breed" ("The Unconscious," *Standard Ed.,* XIV, 190-91). In the same passage Freud insists on the fact that the phantasy stock remains always unconscious, even if certain of the formations extending it have access to consciousness. In *The Interpretation of Dreams, Standard Ed.,* V, 491-92, the author stresses that the conscious phantasy and the unconscious phantasy strongly resemble each other in their internal characteristics and structures; their difference is one of content only; the unconscious phantasies are those in which the wish is expressed in a clearer or more urgent fashion and which have undergone repression of this fact.

53. *Introductory Lectures on Psycho-analysis, Standard Ed.,* XVI, 376: the artist draws his inspiration from his "day-dreams"; he understands, too, how to tone them down so that they do not easily betray their origin from proscribed sources. Furthermore, he possesses the mysterious power of *shaping some particular material* until it has become a faithful image of his phantasy..." (my italics).

54. [Possibly an allusion to Godard's article, "One Should Put Everything into a Film," *Godard on Godard,* ed. Jean Narboni and Tom Milne (New York, 1972), pp. 238-39. Tr.]

55. "The Ego and the Id," *Standard Ed.,* XIX, 20; "A Metapsychological Supplement to the Theory of Dreams," *Standard Ed.,*

XIV, 230-31; *The Interpretation of Dreams, Standard Ed.*, V, 542-43.
56. "On Narcissism: An Introduction," *Standard Ed.*, XIV, 74; Freud reproaches Jung for using the notion of introversion in too vague and general a sense; it should be reserved for cases where the libido has abandoned the real object for the phantasy object but has remained directed toward an object [rather than toward the ego]. When the libido flows back from the object into the ego and no longer into the imaginary object, we can speak of (secondary) narcissism. Along the path of disengagement from the object, narcissism represents a step beyond introversion.
57. Cf. *Film Language*, pp. 44-49 and 185-227 ("The Modern Cinema and Narrativity").
58. "On the Impression of Reality in the Cinema," *Film Language*, pp. 3-15.

..They might come in now, the builders, the destroyers—they might come as soon as they would. At the end of two flights he had dropped to another zone, and from the middle of the third, with only one more left, he recognised the influence of the lower windows, of half-drawn blinds, of the occasional gleam of street-lamps, of the glazed spaces of the vestibule. This was the bottom of the sea, which showed an illumination of its own and which he even saw paved—when at a given moment he drew up to sink a long look over the banisters—with the marble squares of his childhood. By that time indubitably he felt, as he might have said in a commoner cause, better; it had allowed him to stop and draw breath, and the ease increased with the sight of the old black-and-white slabs. But what he most felt was that now surely, with the element of impunity pulling him as by hard firm hands, the case was settled for what he might have seen above had he dared that last look. The closed door, blessedly remote now, was still closed—and he had only in short to reach that of the house.

He came down further, he crossed the passage forming the access to the last flight; and if here again he stopped an instant it was almost for the sharpness of the thrill of assured escape, It made him shut his eyes—which opened again to the straight slope of the remainder of the stairs. Here was impunity still, but impunity almost excessive; inasmuch as the side-lights and the high fan-tracery of the entrance were glimmering straight into the hall; an appearance produced, he the next instant saw, by the fact that the vestibule gaped wide, that the hinged halves of the inner door had been thrown far back. Out of that again the question sprang at him, making his eyes, as he felt, half-start from his head, as they had done, at the top of the house, before the sign of the other door. If he had left that one open, hadn't he left this one closed, and wasn't he now in most immed'' iate presence of some inconceivable occult activity? It was as sharp, the question, as a knife in his side, but the answer hung fire still and seemed to lose itself in the vague darkness to which the thin admitted dawn, glimmering archwise over the whole outer door, made a semicircular margin, a cold silvery nimbus that seemed to play a little as he looked—to shift and expand and contract.

It was as if there had been something within it, protected by indistinctness and corresponding in extent with the opaque surface behind, the painted panels of the last barrier to his escape, of which the key was in his pocket. The indistinctness mocked him even while he stared, affected him as somehow shrouding or challenging certitude, so that after faltering an instant on his step he let himself go with the sense that here was at last something to meet, to touch, to take, to know—something all unnatural and dreadful, but to advance upon which was the condition for him either of liberation or o supreme defeat. The penumbra, dense and dark, was the virtual screen of a figure which stood in it as still as some image erect in a niche or as some black-vizored sentinel guarding a treasure. Brydon was to know afterwards, was to recall and make out, the particular thing he had believed during the rest of his descent. He saw, in its great grey glimmering margin, the central vagueness diminish, and he felt it to be taking the very form toward which, for so many days, the passion of his curiosity had yearned. It gloomed, it loomed, it was something, it was somebody, the prodigy of a personal presence.

Rigid and conscious, spectral yet human, a man of his own substance and stature waited there ot measure himself with his power to dismay. This only could it be—this only till he recognised, with his advance, that what made the place dim was the pair of raised hands that covered it and in which, so far from being offered in defiance, it was buried as for dark deprecation. So Brydon, before him, took him in with eve fact of him now, in the higher light, hard and acute—his planted stillness, his vivid truth, his grizzled bent head and white masking hands, his queer actuality of evening-dress, of dangling double eye-glass, of gleaming silk lappet and white linen, of pearl button and gold watch-guard and polished shoe. No portrait by a great modern master could have presented him with more intensity, thrust him out of his frame with more art, as if there had been "treatment," of the consummate sort, in his every shade and salience. The revulsion, for our friend; had become, before he knew it, immense—this drop; in the act of apprehension, to the sense of his adversary's inscrutable manoeuvre. That meaning at least, while he gaped, it offered him; for he could but gape at his other self in this other anguish, gape as a proof that he, standing there for the achieved, the enjoued, the triumphant life, couldn't be faced in his triumph. Wasn't the proof in the splendid covering hands, strong and completely spread?—so spread and so intentional that, in spite of a special verity that surpassed every other, the fact that one of these hands had lost two fingers, which were reduced to stumps, as if accidentally shot away, the face was effectually guarded and saved.

"Saved," though, would it be?—Brydon breathed his wonder till the very impunity of his attitude and the very insistence of his eyes produced, as he felt, a sudden stir which showed the next instant as a deeper portent, while the head raised itself, the betrayal of a braver purpose. The hands, as he looked, began to move; to open, then, as if deciding in a flash, dropped from the face and left it uncovered and presented. Horror, with the sight, had leaped into Brydon!s throat, gasping there in a sound he couldn't utter; for the bared identity was too hideous as his, and his glare was the passion of his protest. The face, that face, Spencer Brydon's?—he searched it still, but looking *away from it in dismay and denial; falling straight from his height of sublimity. It was unknown, inconceivable, awful, disconnected from any possibility—! He had been "sold," he inwardly moaned, stalking such game as this: the presence before him was a presence, the horror within him a horror, but the waste of his nights had been only grotesque and the success of his adventure an irony. Such an identity fitted his at* no *point, made its alternative monstrous. A thousand times yes, as it came upon him nearer now—the face was the face of a stranger. It came upon him nearer now, quite as one of those expanding fantastic images projected by the magic lantern of childhood; for the stranger, whoever he might be, evil, odious, blatant, vulgar, had advanced as for aggression, and he knew himself give ground. Then harder pressed still, sick with the force of his shock, and falling back as under the hot breath and the roused passion of a life larger than his own, a rage of personality before which his own collapsed, he felt the whole vision turn to darkness and his very feet give way. His head went round; he was going; he had gone.*

Henry James

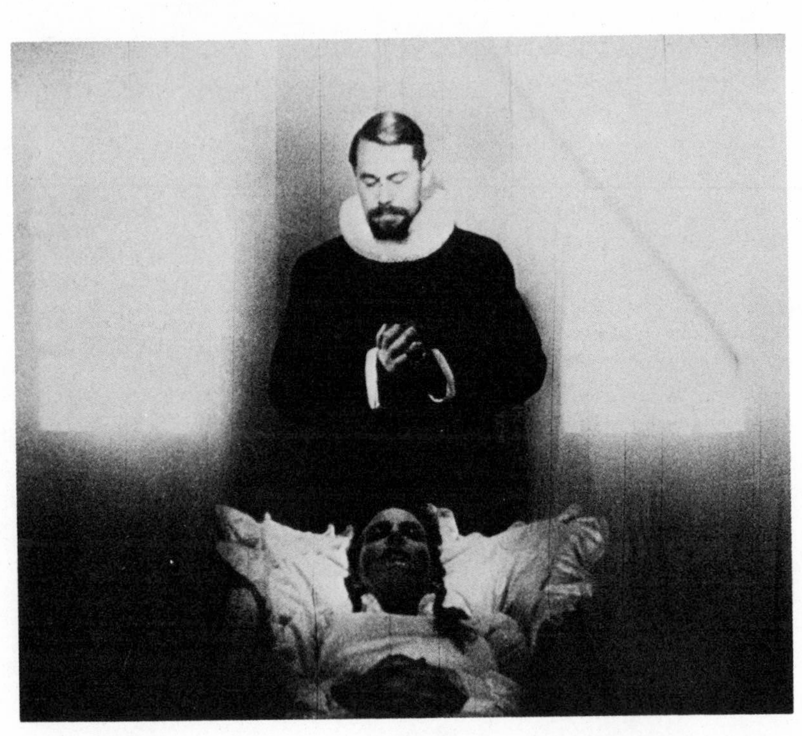

The Lure of Psychoanalysis in Film Theory

Bertrand Augst

One of the most persistent criticism directed at the "old" semiology of cinema, and particularly at the research inspired by Christian Metz's early work, is that its reliance on the social sciences and linguistics represents an unwarranted extrapolation of scientific procedures in a field which has traditionally borrowed methods and critical concepts from philosophy, art and literary criticism. Metz's most recent publication will not reassure his critics. Not only has Metz not renounced his earlier positions, he has radically altered the context of traditional debate in film criticism by integrating psychoanalysis into the "old" semiology. What he now considers the legitimate domain of the semiology of cinema is "the semio-psychoanalysis of cinema."

This development is not without parallel in other disciplines, especially literary studies. However, what is different about the assimilation of psychoanalysis into film theory is that this assimilation has been entirely determined by the internal logic of the field's evolution. According to Metz, classical semiology and psychoanalysis complement one another because both are "sciences of the symbolic and are even, come to think of it, the only two sciences whose immediate and sole object is the fact of signification as such...(Metz, "The Imaginary Signifier"[1]).

No one has claimed, certainly not Metz, that semiology would provide a magic solution to all the unresolved difficulties of film criticism; it has barely begun to delimit its proper space of inquiry. For one thing, it has called attention to the limitations of traditional film criticism and the need to develop a methodology and a theoretical model better suited to the analysis of systems as complex as film. More importantly, however, by providing a methodology which has made possible a finer description of film processes, the semiology of cinema has brought to light heretofore ill-defined characteristics of film discourse that assign to it a privileged place among other cultural objects.

Inexplicably, since the invention of cinema, only the simulation of reality produced by moving images has been the object of critical interest. Critics have almost completely ignored the fact that since the cinematographic apparatus is primarily directed toward the spectator, the simulation effect has more to do with states, or effects on subjects, than with the reproduction of the real. Film theory ought to concern itself with the film itself, the author of the film and the spectator—the "real" subject for whom the film is made. No one will deny that these three elements are interdependent. Together, they constitute a "simulation apparatus" designed to create an impression of reality, but which has the characteristic of being more than a replica of the real.

Obviously, no single element can alone account for the effect of cinema, and to a certain extent, it is not possible to emphasize one element over the others: unlike other forms of expression, the cinematographic apparatus transforms the relationship between its three basic elements in the very instance of its operation. In cinema that other subject of the film, the author, must conceal his presence in the enunciation apparatus in order for the spectator to have the illusion that *he* is the real subject of the film-object which he perceives on the screen. For its part, the film through which this operation is accomplished must become transparent in order to engage the spectator's consciousness.

The Narrative

For the past fifteen years, Christian Metz has been engaged in a systematic analysis of the complex operations of the cinema-machine. Continuing research initially undertaken in the early 50s, Metz soon shifted away from the phenomenological perspectives of his early studies on perceptual psychology, to draw from semiology a more rigorous methodology to delineate with greater precision the specific structuring process of film images. This led him to identify some of the major film codes. Without the spectator however, the film process is not complete; indeed, it cannot exist. Thus the second phase of Metz's work examines film's metapsychological complement, which alone can provide the theoretical framework for studying the psychical situation that characterizes the film state created by narrative cinema.

Metz insists that "The Fiction Film and Its Spectator" is concerned with only one attitude adopted before a film—that of a naive spectator, not an analyst—and that it is valid for only "certain geographical forms of the institution itself," one mostly prevalent in Western countries. In short, he has attempted only "one ethnography of the filmic state among others remaining to be done (for which the Freudian notions would be perhaps less helpful)" ("The Fiction Film and Its Spectator"). Metz's cautious warning against any "extrapolated proposition with respect to the significance of going to the movies can assume" in such countries as Egypt, Japan or India, underlines the existence of narrative cinema as a social fact in Western countries. The merging of cinema and narrativity would have never occurred, except before being an art, "fiction is a fact." The spectator "starting from the material on the screen" tends to believe in the reality of an imaginary because he has already been prepared by older arts of representation. There is a close affinity between the spectator's fictional capacity and the film of narrative representation, and it is only because of this "close and mutual" relation that the diegetic cinema can function as an institution.

The emergence of what was to become the "King's highway of filmic expression," "the feature-length film of novelistic fiction," was a development which had not been foreseen by the pioneers of "cinematographic language." No one imagined that cinema could evolve into a story-telling machine. "The merging of the cinema and narrativity was a great fact, which was by no means predestined—nor was it strictly fortuitous. It was historical and social, a fact of civilization (to use a formula dear to the sociologist Marcel Mauss)" (Metz, *Film Language. A Semiotics of the Cinema*).

This fact is central to the development of contemporary film theory not only because it conditioned the later evolution of the film as "a semiological reality," but also because, in final analysis, it differentiates the semiology of cinema from other film theories. Much of Metz's work has been devoted to narrative cinema because what we have come to experience as cinema results from a precarious balance between carefully regulated effects produced by an intricate apparatus (mechanical, optical, conceptual and psychical) and various regimes of fiction inherited from the nineteenth-century novel. From the merging of cinema and narrativity a new form of film evolved, culminating in the classic Hollywood films of the 30s. One of the essays included in Metz's recent book on film and psychoanalysis is devoted to the aspect of the cinematographic apparatus which endows these "cinematographic fabulations" with a unique credibility. They create a psychical situation in which features of reality, dream and daydream are combined in a pseudo-reality which nevertheless remains apart from each of these three states of consciousness.

The Filmic State

Phenomenology and experimental psychology could adequately describe the impression of reality only as a phenomenon apart from its function in narrative representation. However, to the extent that it is linked "to the perceptual features of the signifier, it characterizes all films, diegetic or not: but, insofar as it participates in the fiction-effect, it belongs to narrative films and to them alone." Metz here is no longer solely concerned with the perceptual phenomenon, but rather with the problem of how the spectator can make the mental leap from the audio-visual perception of moving visual and sonic impressions, "to the constitution of a fictional universe"—how the spectator becomes "capable of a certain degree of belief in the reality of an imaginary world whose signs are furnished, capable of fiction..." ("The Imaginary Signifier").

The answer becomes apparent when the filmic state is compared to dreaming, with which it shares a number of characteristics without nevertheless being equivalent to it. True illusion belongs to dream alone, while the spectator in the filmic state perceives an *impression* of reality. However, "the degree of illusion of reality is inversely proportional to that of wakefulness;" the filmic state, marked by a general lowering of wakefulness, is thus indeed similar to dream and sleeping. It is here that the narrative provides a support indispensible to any filmic state that we have come to associate with cinema. The narrative encourages narcissistic withdrawal and the spectator's receptiveness to phantasy. Pushed a little further, these terms become part of the definition of sleep and dreaming: "withdrawal of the libido into the ego, temporary suspension of concern for the exterior world as well as object cathexes" ("The Imaginary Signifier"). Overstimulating "our zones of shadow and irresponsibility," the narrative film is a machine best suited for "grinding up affectivity and inhibiting action."

To these two factors that contribute to the lowering of wakefulness (the impression of reality, which, although different from true illusion of reality, is nevertheless "its far-off beginning," and fiction, which, among other things, does not incite the spectator to action) one should perhaps also add various forms of hypnosis—from the prehypnoid state described by Barthes, induced by the physical situation of the spectator in the theater, to the complex operations of the fiction taking advantage of the implicit presence of the apparatus as transitional mechanisms to trigger variable degrees of hypnosis. Yet only when the spectator falls asleep do the filmic state and oneiric states converge.

The "delusion coefficient" of mental images is higher than those of film because the subject believes more deeply and because "what he believes in is less true." But, on the other hand, the delusion created by filmic fiction is more "singular and powerful because it is the delusion of a man awake" ("The Imaginary Signifier"). Additionally, unlike dream and the hallucinatory psychoses of desire, film can cause negative reactions in some spectators.

It remains true, nevertheless, that the phantasy deception of dream is greater than that of film because film is not really hallucinatory. It is therefore less likely to succeed in its design than dream. Aside from pathological cases, complete regression is only possible in the states of sleep. Being awake, the spectator remains incapable of true hallucination even when he is deeply affected by the fiction which the film offers to his desire. Yet, one detects the beginning of regression in the filmic state because the spectator tends to perceive as true and external the events and characters of the fiction rather than the images and sounds of the actual projection of the film. The impression of reality is perceived as real, "the represented and not the representer."

Though fundamentally opposed, film and daydream are both halfway between sleep and wakefulness—coming from opposite ends. For both, true illusion never occurs, and the images are always felt as images. There is no confusion between perception and representation. In both instances, the lowering of wakefulness allows, up to a point, the primary process to emerge. Film, however, is more organized and logical than the conscious phantasy. The materialization of its images and sounds compensates for their "alien origin" (alien because they do not emerge from our phantasies). Daydreaming and film both offer a pseudo-belief, a simulation willingly accepted. True illusion is lacking in both cases, but the materialization of the filmic images produces a stronger impression of reality, "a greater perceptual precision and therefore a greater power of *incarnation*" than daydreaming has.

It is therefore not surprising that for Metz, narrative cinema emerges as the dominant mode of cinema, since what we experience as the cinema-effect attains its optimal power of fascination over the spectator when the impression of reality is supported, indeed intensified by the fiction-effect. Narrative cinema is thus capable of creating a particular regime of consciousness which imitates the real, dream and daydreaming without duplicating them. "The fiction thus possesses the strange power of momentarily reconciling three very different regimes of consciousness, for the very characteristics that define fiction have the effect of driving it, hammering it like a wedge into the narrowest and most central of their interstices..." ("The Fiction Film and Its Spectator").

The Enunciation Apparatus

As a cultural object, fiction film occupies a special place among other simulation machines devised by man in the course of the development of Western culture, specifically since the eighteenth century. One may well imagine that someday new forms of fiction film will emerge and displace the current model perfected by the Hollywood machine in the 30s and the 40s. But this cannot take place without major changes in society. It may be argued that, by definition, fiction cannot change significantly because it fulfills a unique function in society. Metz's analysis established beyond any doubt that film theory cannot evolve if it considers the phenomenon of the impression of reality and its effects on the spectator as two separate elements.

It is theoretically possible that other forms of cinema can occupy as prevalent a place in the cinematographic apparatus as narrative film does, but much remains to be done to determine the conditions of existence of such cinematographic forms. Suprisingly, Metz speculates at the end of his essay that history will sweep up the narrative film, since it is a cultural formation, in "its transformation as it does all the formations of culture."

One must succeed in giving to the public the impression that he really sees as though through the key hole of the screen...I am not looking for anything, except life.

Dreyer, Interview (1927)

This assumes that the cinema of representation is like all other cultural formations. But Metz's own work suggests quite the opposite. The combination of the fourfold play of reality, dream, phantasy and fiction constitutes a very particular type of discourse. Specific codes, rules and conventions differentiate this type of discourse from other narrative systems, although it is evident that it allows considerable variations dictated by geographic, social or personal differences.

Among the mechanisms which support the fiction effect of classic narrative films, it is becoming increasingly evident that one mechanism occupies a prominent place in the enunciation apparatus. Raymond Bellour has analyzed one extreme example of this mechanism in Hitchcock's manipulation of the look in *Marnie,* the object of which is to privilege the object of desire 'by exploiting the mechanism of the lure...[whereby cinema] becomes the condition of orgastic pleasure in setting up a mirror construction endlessly refracted, the irreducible gap of the scopic drive. Pleasure is the image that must be assimilated, retrieved, the impossible real, like murder, in which we find the sadistic reversal of pleasure" ("Hitchcock the Enunciator"). Taking another example of the work of enunciation in classical films, again in the "perverse structuration" of one of Hitchcock's darkest films, *Psycho,* Bellour has argued that in the elaboration of the trajectory of fiction, the cinematographic apparatus constitutes itself as "the institution of perversion" par excellence.

This form of the cinema of representation, as found in one of its purest manifestations in Hitchcock's films, raises a larger question with respect to the function of cinema as a cultural object, more precisely as a discourse formation. It is undoubtedly premature to risk an answer to this question, since so little is really known about the specific effects of the cinema of representation. Yet, the dominant position of Hollywood cinema in contemporary culture, and not exclusively American culture, points to the fact that it occupies an important place in the history of the apparatus of sexuality as it developed since the end of the nineteenth century. In its very principle, the cinematographic apparatus mimics the relationship between power and sexuality to the point that it can be taken as the central metaphor of the reversal mechanism whereby power secures its authority. It is only to the extent that it constitutes itself as the discourse of an other that cinema can constitute itself as discourse. The spectator must believe, or feign to believe, that *he is* the subject of the discourse projected on the screen. It is therefore doubtful that narrative cinema can be displaced by other cultural formations in the near future. Coming after a long line of simulation machines, it can only yield to more powerful and intrinsically more perverse apparatuses.

The ending [*of* Rear Window] *is agonizing. American women scream and can't tolerate the anguish of this film. All the spectators scream, and that makes me very happy, it amuses me a lot; even now, that kind of thing is alot of fun for me. On that score, I am not as serious as the public. I must confess that when I hear them scream, I find that comical.*

Hitchcock "Interview with Chabrol and Truffaut"

Historically, economically and ideologically, the predominance of fiction films has long been recognized by traditional criticism. By shifting the emphasis of his analysis to the interaction between the filmic image and the spectator, Metz has shown that other approaches are not only possible but necessary to undertake the description of the cinema-effect. Film theory must therefore include, by definition, a metapsychology of the spectator.

The Impression of Reality

Important as it is, Metz's study of the fiction and its spectator is only a small part of a much larger problem which is at the center of all theoretical reflections on the nature of cinema: the phenomenon of the impression of reality and its intrinsic part in the signifying process of cinema. From a theoretical standpoint, the phenomenological description of this perceptual phenomenon must be related to the semiological description of its effects within the cinematographic apparatus. Metz's original solution is to recognize that the nature of the relationship between the film-text and its spectator is fundamentally different from those established by other forms of expression.

To begin with, unlike other "texts," the film-text is literally, in Bellour's phrase, "unattainable." It cannot be seized, it cannot be cited, in fact, it eludes the spectator's reach in order to constitute itself as text. But more importantly, it must conceal all traces of its operations in order to overcome the spectator's vigilance and to instill a particular state of consciousness in which he will experience a strong impression of reality. It must engage the spectator's *imaginary* as intensely as possible without at the same time preventing him from disengaging himself from the fascination of the image. It must create a precarious balance between two regimes of beliefs.

The impression of reality occupies a central place in the cinema-machine because it is a lure. "I am locked in on the image as though I were caught in the famous dual relationship which established the imaginary. The image is there before me, for my benefit: coalescent (signifier and signified perfectly blended), analogical, global, pregnant: it is a perfect lure. I pounce upon it as an animal snatches up a lifelike rag." (Barthes "Upon Leaving the Movie Theater"). Riveted to the mirror-screen by this impression of reality, the spectator hesitates. He knows that the pseudonaturalness of the scene before his eyes is only an image, yet...in the filmic state, the blurring of the clear distinction between the images perceived, the lure, and the perceiving subject, incorporates the subject into the process of signification. The spectator and its imaginary are thus part of the same signifier, the signifier of cinema.

The psychical apparatus and the basic cinematographic apparatus are thus joined by the impression of reality as the two complementary sides of a mirror through which the impression manifests itself in the production of the filmic text. To the extent that cinema is indeed, in Metz's words, "a technique of the imaginary," film theory must turn to psychoanalysis to describe the operations which pertain to the "imaginary signifier." Far from being a departure from Metz's earlier theoretical orientation strongly influenced by linguistics, the "new" semiology is in fact its necessary complement. Metz's irritation at the suggestion that his reliance on Freudian psychoanalysis constitutes a radical shift in the development of his work is perfectly understandable, because such a conclusion ignores what is perhaps his most important contribution to the field: the description of the mechanisms whereby the imaginary invests the impression of reality in the process of becoming the imaginary signifier.

It is true that, heavily indebted to linguistic methodology, "classical semiology," in its first effort to establish itself as a rigorous field of research, did concern itself almost exclusively with "the immanent analysis of the cinematographic language." The new semiology reintroduces the spectator-subject in the cinematographic process, assigns to him the central place in the apparatus. Undoubtedly, Lacan, Barthes and Kristeva influenced the reorientation of the semiology of cinema, especially with respect to the place of the subject in the mechanism of enunciation.

The old semiology did make a major contribution to film studies. It provided a much needed methodology. It made it possible to debunk what Barthes called many years ago "the ideological fraud," the perpetual confusion of Nature and History that characterizes so much of our perception of contemporary culture, and more profoundly so in cinema. The influence of linguistics was to create "an effect of discourse" by revealing that beyond the distinction between the signified and the signifier, "something else" was linking them in a form of discourse. Extending to filmic images Lacan's comments about the relationship between reading and the text, one could say that the signified is not what we see. What we see is the signifier, "the signified that's the effect of the signifier."

The Film as Discourse

Film is not a language. Having come to terms with this linguistic metaphor that for the last fifty years has been the basis of all major film theories, Metz succeeded in establishing that film is an effect of discourse. Just as the distinction between the acoustic image of a word and its meaning is guaranteed by scientific discourse, so that image and its signifier are distinguished. But beyond that, there is something else, something which could not even be defined without psychoanal ysis. "How does meaning get into the image? Where does it end? And if it ends, what is there *beyond?"* (Barthes' "The Rhetoric of the Image"). These questions are still relevant; some have been partially answered by the "old" semiology. What needed a better answer is the question of how the image engages the spectator's imaginary, or, to put it in Metz's terms, how does the cinema-machine create "a signifier effect?"

The impact of Saussurian and American structural linguistics on the early phase of semiology has been sufficiently commented upon to warrant only being mentioned. There is, however, one aspect of Metz's debt to linguistics which must be stressed not only because it played a major part in the development of his early work, but also because it enabled him to link his analysis of the cinematographic signifier (the identification and the description of the various codes which interact in filmic systems) to the much broader concept of "signifier of cinema," part of which includes the imaginary signifier.

For me, this opposition between characters and objects is absolutely fundamental, it reflects the problems of the ordinary person caught up in extraordinary situations. It is the conflict of all drama. That's why humor is important. Humor is the elimination of dignity, the disappearance of normality, it is what is abnormal. The spectators who go to the movies lead a normal life. They go to see extraordinary things, nightmares. For me, cinema is not a slice of life, it is a slice of cake.

Hitchcock "Interview with Chabrol and Truffaut"

The second half of "The Imaginary Signifier" is devoted to the study of three specific instances in which the signifier pertains to the imaginary. Or rather, Metz approaches the specific characteristic of cinema as an institutionalized signifier from three different perspectives: specular identification, voyeurism and exhibitionism, and fetishism.(9)

Stating that cinema has often been described as "a technique of the imaginary," linked historically to the development of capitalism and to the development of industrial civilization, Metz stresses the double meaning in which the word imaginary must be understood. There is first of all the usual sense because most films are narrative fictions and also because photography and phonography are bases of all films, and therefore by definition imaginary. The second meaning of "imaginary" is to be taken in Lacan's use of the term "in which the imaginary, opposed to the symbolic but constantly imbricated with it, designates the basic lure of the ego, the definitive imprint of a *before* the Oedipus complex (which also continues after it), the durable mark of the mirror which alienates man in his own reflection and makes him the double of his double, the subterranean persistence of the exclusive relation to the mother, desire as a pure effect of lack and endless pursuit, the initial core of the unconscious (primal repression). All this is undoubtedly reactivated by the actions of that *other mirror,* the cinema screen, in this respect a psychical substitute, a prosthesis for our primarily dislocated limbs." (15)

Metz is certainly right in stressing the fact that the main difficulty here is to relate the complex ramifications of the imaginary to the signifier. As in the case of Hjelmsev, Metz draws freely from Lacan's work to fit some key concepts to his theory. *Imaginary* is frequently used in its two meanings simultaneously. We may return to the central part of his analysis by restating the question that he himself frequently asks: "among the pertinent features of the cinematographic signifier, which differentiate cinema from literature, painting etc., what are those which, because of their nature, call most directly on the type of knowledge that psychoanalysis alone can provide?"(46) At the risk of oversimplifying excessively the cautious and meticulous progression of his distinctions, I will attempt to sum up in a somewhat lapidary fashion the main distinguishing features of the *imaginary signifier.* In order to emphasize the specific link between film theory and psychoanalysis.

Each means of expression engages perception to a variable degree of intensity, determined by the number of their sensorial registers and the status of the perceptions transmitted by their signifier. The perception register of literature, for example, is much more limited than that of painting or photography, but the register of both is narrower than those of other art forms which also include auditory perception, time and movement, as in the case of the theater or of the opera. Quantitatively, cinema is "more" perceptual than many forms of expression because it calls upon, "mobilizes" a larger number of axes of perception. It appears to contain the signifiers of the other arts and thus, it has often been argued, especially in the early twenties, that it is in fact a synthesis of the major art forms. However, this perceptual advantage is immediately reversed as soon as its sensorial registers are considered not in terms of number, but from the point of view of status. The perception offered by spectacles like the theater, dance, or the opera, have a distinct advantage over cinema in at least one respect: they are presented in a *real* space while cinema only offers *images*. In this perspective, cinema is the least perceptual among the arts because all the perceptions presented to the eye and to the ear are, in a sense, all false; "rather, the activity of perception in it is real (cinema is not a phantasy), but what is perceived is not really the object, it is its shadow, its phantom, its double, its *replica* in a new kind of mirror."(48) Thus, cinema is profoundly determined by the dual character of its signifier: "an uncommon perceptual intensity, but one stamped to an unusual degree with the unreality in its very principle. In the very moment it engages our perception more intensely than any other means of expression, cinema also pushes us into the imaginary all the more compelling that it is in most instances redoubled by the fiction effect of its content."(48)

As the inventory of the specific conditions required for the "normal" perception of filmic images is refined, and the particular interaction between the various conditions that their perception requires is better understood, the complexity and seemingly unlimited detours of the signifier becomes more readily apparent. The difficulty raised by such a study however arises from the fact that the cinema effect is produced by a large diversity of codes which simultaneously engage the spectator's vigilance in many ways not always isolatable from one another. One often has the impression that the successful functioning of the cinema-machine depends on the interrelationships between these codes and the effects they produce in order to establish a delicate balance between the physical conditions of the screening, the film and its faction, the spectator's physical and psychological aptitude for letting himself be captured by the lure of the imaginary.

If there is an instance where semiology and psychoanalysis become mutually complementary, it is at this point in the description of the signifier of cinema, that extraordinary moment when "false" perception of images really perceived turns into (become) that other imaginary, the glance turned into the evil eye. "It is the signifier itself, and as a whole, that is recorded, that is absence: a little roll of film-strip...which "contains' vast landscapes..." (47) The special condition of perception, real in its very absence, precipitates, so to speak, the return of the imaginary. Unlike the mirror, the screen mirror—a mirror without its silvering— does not reflect the image of the subject. The spectator is no longer a child, and furthermore he has already undergone the experience of the mirror and the recognition of his own body as that of an Other. Unlike the child in front of the mirror, the spectator is absent from the screen, and therefore cannot identify himself to himself as object, but only to objects—which are there eventually by a redoubling effect, he may identify with the characters at the level of the fiction of the film—objects which exist without him. Unlike the child's experience in the mirror, the spectator does not take any part in the perceived, he is *"all perceiving."* He is absent from the screen image, but present in the movie theater, hearing and listening, receiving the film which is being made through him (he is making the film); he is the "constitutive instance...of the cinema signifier." He knows he is watching a film, he has chosen the theater, the time, paid for his seat. He knows that what he sees is imaginary, he knows that he is the one who is seeing the film; "in other words, the spectator *identifies* with himself, with himself as a pure act of perception...as condition of possibility of the perceived hence as a kind of transcendental subject, anterior to any *there is."* (51) He knows that he is not dreaming or hallucinating just as he knows that there is a projector behind his head projecting images against a wall which is not the fourth wall of the theater. He also knows that these images order themselves in his head; he knows that he is the place where this imaginary which is really perceived "accedes to the symbolic" by asserting itself as "the signifier of a certain institutionalized social activity called 'the cinema'." (51)

Metz's reference to the mirror phase and to Lacan's distinction between the imaginary and the Symbolic should not be construed as implying that the imaginary signifier of cinema can in any way be assimilated to the imaginary in psychoanalysis. The comparison between the primary identification of the mirror and the identificatory processes of cinema are very different. To begin with, the spectator must have "known the primordial mirror" because the imaginary of cinema does presuppose the Symbolic since it is itself clearly on the side of the Symbolic. The spectator must perceive the photographed object as absent and its photograph as present, and the "presence of this absence as signifying," in order to understand the film, just in the same way as he must identify with the character and yet know that he is not that character in order to understand the fiction film. It is therefore imperative to differentiate sharply between the primary identification in cinematographic psychoanalysis and in psychoanalysis, since in the second instance the primary identification is really a secondary identification—the screen-mirror is already on the side of the Symbolic. However, in a cinematographic perspective, the distinction between primary and secondary identification must be preserved because, there is also a secondary identification in cinema, especially in fiction films. The primary identification in cinema thus constitutes the permanent (hence primary) identification of the cinema signifier, i.e. the identifcatory process which establishes the signifier itself and with it, the position of the spectator. The spectator "identifies himself to himself" as "pure act of perception," as trancendental subject.

> The "reality mimed by the cinema is thus first of all that of a "self." But, because the reflected image is not that of the body itself but that of a world already given as meaning, one can distinguish two levels of identification...Thus the spectator identifies less with what is represented, the spectacle itself, than with what stages the spectacle, makes it seen, obliging him to see what it sees; this is exactly the function taken over by the camera as a sort of relay. Just as the mirror assembles the fragmented body in a sort of imaginary integration of the self, the transcendental self unites the discontinuous fragments of phenomena, of lived experience, into unifying meaning...the ideological mechanism at work in the cinema seems thus to be concentrated in the relationship between the camera and the subject. The question is whether the former will permit the latter to constitute and seize itself in a particular mode of specular reflection. Ultimately, the forms of narrative adopted, the contents of the image are of little importance, so long as an identification remains possible.

The primary identification of cinema is not limited to the identification of the camera, it extends and supports other types of identifications which are in effect the sub-codes of the primary identification which characterizes the cinematographic effect in its basic principle, i.e. the code. These sub-codes are variants, more specific configurations of the "permanent" more primary identification of cinema.

Some of these sub-codes are relatively well understood because they have long been the subject of study in traditional film theory: subjective images, off-screen space, the mechanism of the look of the characters, the *défilement,* to mention the more obvious operations determined by the basic cinematographic apparatus. One of the main functions of many of these sub-codes is to reinforce, and in some sense stabilize the primary identification of the spectator to the signifier of cinema. The mechanism of the look for example, plays an important role in creating an effect of continuity in fiction films by articulating the looks of the characters in such a way as to give the spectator the impression that the imaginary space of fiction is homogeneous in spite of the constant transformation of the diegetic space in which the characters are situated. Yet, on-screen space can be repeatedly altered by the movements of the characters within the frame, the movements of the camera, or the entrances and exits of the characters in the field of vision of the camera which contribute extensively to the establishment of an off-screen space. Among the well-established conventions of the mechanism of the look of the characters is the one which proscribes the characters from looking directly at the spectator (the camera). Not only does such a look undermine the secondary identification of the spectator with the character by collapsing the possible position of another character off-screen and that of the spectator in the theater, but it does also lessen the primary identification to the extent that it calls excessive attention to the presence of the apparatus as such. Off-screen space which is established by the eyeline of the characters (among many other devices) plays another important function in extending the spectator's identification. He too is absent from the screen, thus, the off-screen character becomes his delegate, a kind of relay between the spectator and the characters which are in the on-screen space.

> What emerges here in filigree is the specific function fulfilled by cinema as support and instrument of ideology. It constitutes the "subject" by the illusory delimitation of a central location —whether this be that of a god or of any substitute. It is an apparatus destined to obtain a precise ideological effect, necessary to the dominant ideology: creating a fantasmatization of the subject, it collaborates with a marked efficacity in the maintenance of idealism. (10)

Having examined some of the specific characteristics of the institutionalized signifier of cinema as constituted by the specular identification, Metz examines this mechanism of identification in a second perspective: voyeurism. For the object to be perceived, there must also be a desire to see: "cinema is only possible through the perceptual passions: the desire to see (scopic drive, scopophilia, voyeurism)." (59) The desire to see and to hear are considered more specifically on the side of the Imaginary because they are more dependent on the lack. Unlike other more "organic needs," sexual drives do not have a very stable relationship with their object. They can therefore be more easily satisfied outside their objects, as in the case of sublimation, for example. However if sexual drives are more accomodating, they also remain more or less unsatisfied even when they reach their object. "Desire is very quickly reborn after the brief vertigo of its apparent extinction, it is largely sustained by desire, it has its own rhythms, often independent of the pleasure obtained..." (60) It pursues an imaginary object through the intermediary of multiple real objects which are all substitute and therefore interchangeable. To the extent that the "perceiving drive" (the desire to see and to hear) "concretely represents the absence of its object in the distance at which it maintains it," they also have a special relationship with the "absence of this object." (60) All these features however are common to all the means of expression based on seeing and hearing. Cinema differs from them in that the mechanism of the lack is intensified by the fact that cinema offers a much more varied spectacle, a much denser object to the perceiving drive. Furthermore, the imaginary signifier of cinema has a greater affinity with the imaginary because, unlike that of the theater, it is also unreal. It will be recalled that the signifier of cinema is in its very constitution simultaneously more and less perceptual than other means of expression, the theater for example. The perceptions it presents are all, in some sense, false. Thus, Metz speaks of "a double withdrawal," of the object of desire because, in cinema, what "remains in the distance is no longer the object itself, it is a delegate he has sent/the spectator/while itself withdrawing." (60) The fundamental difference between the "scopic regime" of cinema and that of the other forms of expression lies in the absence of the object seen. In the theater, as in the case of "domestic voyeurism," and various intermediary types of exhibitionism, the seen is implicitly presumed to be more consenting, more cooperative. The main function of the signifier of cinema is to re-place the absent object with a new representation of the lack, "the physical absence of the object seen." Unlike the voyeurism of the theater, the voyeurism of cinema establishes itself without the consent of the object seen, by definition. The spectator is really alone, or rather alone with other voyeurs in the theater. His voyeurism is of a very different kind because he is looking at something that "lets itself be seen without presenting itself to be seen." (63) This too, is an additional justification for the convention which proscribes the actor (character) from looking at the spectator (camera).

This is why Metz refers to cinematographic voyeurism as *"unauthorized* scopophilia," and argues that it has a direct affinity with the primal scene.

The fact that in cinema the object perceived is real but absent, the fact that the cinema signifier is the least perceptual among the various forms of expression have other implications which are best brought when it is compared to voyeurism in the theater. There is of course the keyhole effect of the screen and the darkness of the room and the quasi-hypnoid effect it has. Their differences however are much more pronounced in three specific ways: their public, their existence as institutions, and their relation to fiction.

The spectator of cinema is more radically alone since the object seen is not present in the theater. Consequently, the audience in a movie theater does not really constitute a collectivity. The space in cinema is also more radically heterogeneous than in the theater where the audience shares the "real" space with the actors. The filmic space on the contrary is totally cut-off from the spectator. Furthermore, because it is really absent, the object seen ignores its spectator more completely. In cinema, the separation between the screen space and the space of the theater is more total than that created by any line of footlights. "For its spectator the film unfolds in that simultaneously quite close and definitely inaccessible 'elsewhere' in which the child *sees* the gambols of the parental couple, who are similarly ignorant of it and leave it alone, a pure onlooker whose participation is inconceivable. In this respect the signifier of cinema is Oedipal in type." (64)

One of the implications of the "unauthorized" aspect of cinematographic voyeurism is that it retains a more "shame-faced" quality that theatrical voyeurism does not have because "it tends towards a reconciled and community-orientated practice of the scopic perversion." (65) Yet, cinema is "authorized" in its institutionalized aspect which, for Metz, associates it with certain other practices which are at the same time legal and clandestine.

Finally, the signifier of cinema lends itself more readily to fiction because it too is absent. While "the dialectical relationship between a real instance and an imaginary instance" is characteristic of all forms of fiction, the *"regime of credence"* adopted by the spectator varies significantly from one fictional technique to another. In cinema, the representation is imaginary while in the theater it is real.

"Thus, theatrical fiction is experienced more...a set of real actions intended to evoke something unreal, whereas cinematic fiction is rather experienced as the quasi-real presence of that unreal itself." (66) Since the signifier is already more on the side of the imaginary, it is more easily absorbed by the diegesis of the film and thus less perceptible as such. In cinema, "the balance is established slightly closer to the represented, slightly further away from the representation." This is also why, the theater of fiction is more dependent on the actor, and cinema more on characters. This difference could be explained by the fact that in the theater the same part may be interpreted by different actors while in cinema it is always performed by the same actor. The reason for this is obvious. In cinema, the representation of the actor, its "reflection, is recorded, fixed forever in the material of the signifier." Once again, the particular nature of the cinema signifier determines the specific effect of its fiction.

The perceptual nature of the signifier of cinema affects the regime of cinematographic voyeurism so as to determine a particular type of *regime of credence* which, in final analysis, constitutes the underlying principle of the cinematographic institution. I shall return to this point to consider the wider implications of this very general principle after discussing Metz's third approach to the specific characteristic of the imaginary signifier: fetishism.

The central argument of this section rests on two aspects of fetishism: "the problems of belief (disavowal) and that of the fetish itself, the latter more immediately linked to direct or sublimated erotogenicity." Drawing more specifically from Freud's essay on "negation," and "fetishism," and from Mannoni's analysis of the mechanism of disavowal and its application to the theater, Metz concludes that fetishism is generally considered as "perversion" *par excellence* because it is often part of other perversions. More importantly, fetishism, like these perversions is "based on...the avoidance of castration," but it is also their model. "To sum up, the fetish signifies the penis as absent, it is its negative signifier; supplementing it, it puts a 'fullness' in place of a lack, but in doing so it also affirms the lack. It resumes within it the structure of disavowal and multiple beliefs." (69)

Undeniably, the problems of belief are at the basis of a cinematographic psychoanalysis. Repeatedly, irrespective of the axes of approach, specular identification or voyeurism, one always returns to the fundamental problem of the *regime of credence*. Obviously, cinema is not the only form of expression where it is called upon to play a decisive role, in modulating the rapports between the spectator (reader) and the object perceived. With cinema, it is more radically implicated by the very nature of the signifier. The spectator is never duped by represented fiction. He knows very well that the fiction on the screen is nothing more than a fiction. However, the combined "work" of codes, effects, and interlocking operations which intervene in the inflections of the signifier regulate the balance between belief and disbelief. Given the expected reward of a forthcoming pleasure, the spectator is willing to play the game and accept the make-believe as what it pretends to be. The spectator of course pretends that he is not deceived. Yet, someone is deceived. Mannoni has shown that that someone is none other than that other part of the spectator's ego. Comparing the varying degree of similarities between the imaginary and conventions in traditional theatrical forms and games, Mannoni points out that "if we are victims of an illusion in the theater or confronted by masks, it appears that we nevertheless need someone who, for our own satisfaction, will be taken by this illusion. It seems that everything is contrived in such a way as to create this illusion, but in someone else, as if we are "in on it" with the actors." It is easy to guess who the "we" really is. "Long ago people believed in masks." Long ago, that is to say, in our childhood, continues Mannoni, suggesting that the "someone" which in us resembles the child that we have been, somehow continues to live in some guise; could not that someone, be that part of ourselves, partially withdrawn, who would be the place of illusion which we do not quite understand?'' That part of ourselves which is taken in by illusion is often literally represented in the theater (and cinema). When the presence of that other part of the credulous spectator is overtly represented, it is no longer necessary to look for him. Hence the presence of those character/spectators in Shakespeare, Corneille, Pirandello. Mannoni thus establishes a three-term situation: the spectator, the character/actor, and the other part of us who *does* believe. It should pointed out that he also hastens to add that the spectator's situation is not unlike that of dreams. Mannoni recalls that Freud did not hesitate to assert that, in dreams in which we are aware that we are dreaming, we always know that we are dreaming ''just as we always know that, when we are asleep, that knowledge is withheld from us.'' In the theater, what is kept away from us, or what we are tempted to attribute to ''someone else,'' is what Freud called ''the agency of dream'' Theatrical illusion cannot be explained away as a problem of belief. ''The expression 'to believe in masks' would be meaningless if it were interpreted as a belief in something real or true.'' If we take masks for real faces, the mask effect disappears entirely. ''The mask does not pass for something other than what it is, but it has the power to evoke images of fantasy''' To believe in masks implies that, long ago, ''at a certain time, (during childhood), the imaginary reigned in a different manner than in adulthood.'' For the adult, the ''mask effects'' and those of the theater are only possible because of the presence of the process of disavowal. In the theater, the illusion must not be true, ''and that we know that it is not true, in order for the images of the unconscious to be really free. It is at this point that the theater rejoins the symbolic role. It would be in its entirety like the form of negation, the symbol of negation whereby the return of the repressed becomes possible in its disavowed form.''

Cinema in its ''unreal'' perceptual form poses a major difficulty. While in the theater the *regime of credence* is almost continuously modulated by the ''real'' nature of the signifier—the presence of the real in the creation of the fiction effect—in cinema the quasi-absence of the signifier undermines the stabilization of the imaginary.

In fiction films especially the fiction presents itself in a particular regime of the signifier which seeks precisely to render its presence invisible, effacing the traces of its own work. The ''affinity'' between fiction and the imaginary signifier in cinema conceals the markers of the fiction effect. The more transparent the work of the signifier is, the more difficult it is for the spectator to ascertain that the object perceived is really fiction, which results very likely in a lowering of the credence regime. This in turn, hampers the free play of the other spectator's imaginary. The apparatus must therefore compensate for the excess of transparency of some of the features of the signifier of cinema in order to maintain the balance necessary for the smooth unfolding of the fiction effect.

From the scratches on the surface of the film-strip going through the projector gate, to the uncomfortable seats of the theater, many elements threaten the balance maintained by the process of disavowal. The cinema-machine, like the spectator, is at once extremely delicate and robust. The apparatus, the film-text, the spectator, all must conspire to produce that expected pleasure given by the "good object." By definition, the spectator of cinema can never escape the magnetic fascination achieved by the imaginary signifier, unless he is able to "take off", in the double sense of the term proposed by Barthes, i.e. in the way his body relates to the block of darkness which surrounds him. The combined effect of the complex machinery of the apparatus, and that includes the spectator's psychic apparatus, is so designed by the institution which it supports to engage the spectator in the lure of its imaginary. One may partially succeed in reducing the attraction of this lure, but never escape it totally. This is why it is so difficult for political films as well as experimental films to escape completely from the effects of dominant cinema.

The second manifestation of fetishism, to return to Metz's final point, the fetish itself, is obviously directly related to the whole apparatus of cinema, the technique of cinema. "Properly speaking, the fetish, like the cinematographic apparatus, is a prop, the prop that disavows a lack and in doing so affirms it without saying so. A prop too, which is, as it were, *deposited* on the body of the object, a prop which is the penis since it negates its absence, and hence a partial object that makes the whole object lovable and desirable." Cinema functions as a fetish in its technical apparatus, in its technical performance, "as a feat." Cinephiles and film connoisseurs are obvious fetishists, but so is the ordinary spectator who lets himself be taken away by the fiction film but also admires it the quality of its technique. For Metz, the fetish is linked to the "good object." The fetish protects it from the threat of the lack and reinstates it. The fetish is the physical side of cinema, and film equipment is by far more complex and more important than in the other art forms: after all, cinema is also an industry." (Malraux)

Metz emphasizes the fact that the fetish plays an important role in cinema. "Because it attempts to disavow the evidence provided by the senses, the fetish is evidence that this evidence has indeed been *recorded* (like a tape in the memory." (73) It has both a disavowal value, and "a knowledge value." Fetishism of technique is particularly developed in the "real connoisseur" of cinema, and that includes the critic and the theoretician, who pursues his interrogation of technique" to symbolize the fetish, hence to maintain it while dissolving it—an interest which motivates his studying it." (73) Metz devotes many pages to the particular desire of the theoretician of cinema, and the necessary relation to it as a "good object" in a rigorous and pointed effort of self-criticism, of his need to know what contribution psychoanalysis can make to the study of the imaginary signifier. But after all, "concern for the signifier in the cinema derives from a form of fetishism which has taken up a position as far as possible on the side of knowledge." (74)

These three approaches to the cinema signifier are far from exhausting the possible contribution of psychoanalysis to cinema. More recent work has been concerned with other forms of perversions for example, or the place of the Oedipus complex in the articulation of the film narrative, as well as other types of analyses which pertain to psychoanalysis, such as hypnosis. Metz's essays do not exhaust the potential developments of the new semiology. He lays out the perimeter of a new film theory, but leaves a large space at the center which can only be filled by extensive textual studies which alone will provide the necessary verification of the complex operation of the signifier of cinema and its broader implications. It should also be kept in mind that the two components of semi-psychoanalysis, linguistics and psychoanalysis, need to be complemented by a third perspective "which is as it were their common and permanent background: the direct studies of societies, historical criticism, the examination of infrastructures." (28) To this, one might also suggest, a fourth perspective; the theory of Symbolism, in the wake of the work of anthropologists like Dan Sperber.

Like Barthes, Metz turned to Hjemslev *(Prolegomena to a Theory of Language)* to develop a model better suited than Saussurian linguistics to describe complex semiotic systems. One of the concepts which came to occupy a central place in the semiology of cinema is the concept of matter of expression derived from Hjemslev's distinction between form/purport and substance. Cinema could then be described as combining five different matters of expression segmented by codes of variable sizes and degrees of specificity, many of which it also shared with other forms of expression.

It is evident, however, that the very existence of the cinematographic signifier presupposes an earlier stage in its constitution as signifier. This stage, which corresponds to a large extent to what Jean-Louis Baudry called the "basic cinematographic apparatus," is more specifically concerned with "the specular space of the movie theater,

Cinema is a remarkable stimulant. It acts directly upon the grey matter of the brain. Once the flavor of a will have been properly blended with the psychic ingredient which it withholds, it will leave the theater far behind...Nothing comes between the work and us. The distinguishing feature of cinema is to be a harmless and direct poison, an injection of morphine. This is why the subject matter of film must not be inferior to the intrinsic power of cinema: it partakes of the marvelous.

Artaud "Reply to an Inquiry" (1929)

the real presence of photography, the real absence of the photographed object, the mechanism of identification and projection, etc. in short, a socio-historical mechanism without which cinema could not even exist and which psychoanalysis seems to me perfectly suited to dismantle. It is the possibility for the code to exist: it does not affect in any way its content." (*Ça/Cinema,* 7/8 "Entretien avec Christian Metz") Thus, Metz's use of psychoanalysis is neither a change nor a reversal of his earlier position, as has been absurdly asserted by his critics, but merely a continuation of his semiological analysis. The film itself is part of the apparatus, and so is the spectator. The one presupposes the other; both relate directly to the same apparatus but in different ways. The imaginary signifier is no less an intrinsic part of the signifier of cinema than any of its other distinctive features, but to the extent that it pertains to the *imaginary,* it falls outside the pertinence of semiological inquiry. Because it introduces a unique characteristic of cinema as a technique of the imaginary, it may be considered the most important feature of the cinema signifier since it affects in a fundamental way the "coefficient of signification" which differentiates it from that produced by any other type of apparatus. In the logic of Metz's system, psychoanalysis and semiology describe complementary aspects of the matter of expression.

Cinema is after all a matter of ideology, and spectators share the ideology of the films offered them. "They fill up the cinemas and so the machine keeps on running." The spectator facilitates the birth of the film, helps it to survive. The film is made to exist in the spectator, to be watched by him in a way that pretends not to be aware that it is being watched. The film *is* and *is not* exhibitionistic. The commerce between the two partners of the perverse couple is unilateral, unlike other forms of voyeurism where it is by definition bilateral. The film offers itself to the gaze of the spectator without returning his gaze, without acknowledging the presence of the voyeur for whom it exhibits itself and without whose gaze it could not exist. It knows that the spectator is there, and that the spectator is there because he knows that the film cannot return his glance. It does not want to know.

"It is this fundamental disavowal which has motivated the development of classic cinema in the direction of 'narration,' which has relentlessly erased the discursive support to turn it into a beautiful object offered without its knowledge to our pleasure (and, literally, against its will), turning it into an object whose seamless periphery cannot be burst open into a inside/outside, a subject capable of saying yes!"

Borrowing a distinction from Benveniste between narration and discourse, Metz argues that the traditional film presents itself as narration, not as discourse. For Benveniste, discourse explicitly includes a subject "I" or a reference to it, while the narrative is characterized by the absence of any reference to a narrator. The former is "subjective," the latter "objective." Considered in this perspective, film can be defined as a form of discourse—because after all someone is the real subject of the film for a public—which erases "all the marks of enunciation, and disguises itself as narration." However, the marks of the subject of enunciation have carefully been removed so that the film can in turn pass itself as the discourse of someone else: the spectator's. The voyeurism of cinema removes the markers of the "real" subject of enunciation in order to make it possible for that other subject to believe that, in the process of giving birth to the film, he is the real subject. Through it, however, the entire cinematographic institution speaks.

The emergence of cinema as a social institution and its stabilization in the classic Hollywood model is not an accident. The Cinema was invented at a crucial point in the development of the systems of representation which since the Renaissance have sought to secure their ascendancy over the "subject's" freedom. Among all the instruments of power, cinema is undoubtedly the most finely tooled for ideology to secure and perpetuate its control.[2]

NOTES

1. The three other articles collected in *Le Signifiant imaginaire* deal with other modalities of the imaginary and other aspects of the signifier from other perspectives. "The Fiction Film and Its Spectator: A Metapsychological Study," examines the affinities between the fiction film and dream: that type of film is a "machine, at once historico-ideological and psychoanalytic...designed to arouse the pleasure of the spectator. It may not always function properly each time it is used (as is the case of other machines), but objectively, it is well suited to stimulate that pleasure by means of economically well-measured similarities and differences with dream or phantasy." "History/Discourse, Note on Two Voyeurisms" explores the relationship

between the spectator and the screen image briefly discussed in "The Imaginary Signifier." Finally, the long essay "Metaphor/Metonymy or the Imaginary Referent," approaches the signifier from the perspective of a relatively narrow aspect of the film-text, or more exactly, one small but absolutely fundamental facet of the film-work. The four essays included in *Le Signifiant imaginaire* will be published in England by Macmillan and in this country by Purdue University Press at the end of 1981.

2. For an interesting discussion of the strategies of power and literature, see Leo Bersani's review of Foucault's *Surveiller et punir: naissance de la prison* and *La Volonte de savoir,* vol. I of *Histoire de la sexualité* (1976), in *Diacritics* (September 1975).

BIBLIOGRAPHY

Film as Art by Rudolf Arnheim, University of California Press, 1966.

L'Effet cinema by Jean-Louis Baudry, Editions Albatros, 1978.

"Hitchcock, the Enunciator" by Raymond Bellour, *Camera Obscura,* no. 2, 1977.

"Neurosis, Psychosis, Perversion" by Raymond Bellour, *Camera Obscura,* no. 3, forthcoming.

Communications, "Psychanalyse et cinema," no. 23, 1975. Edited by C. Metz, R. Bellour and T. Kuntzel.

Film and the Narrative Tradition by John L. Fell, University of Oklahoma Press, 1974.

Film Language: A Semiotics of the Cinema by Christian Metz, Oxford University Press, 1974. Originally published as *Essais sur la signification au cinema,* vol. 1, 1968.

Language and Cinema, by Christian Metz, Mouton, 1974. Originally published as *Language et cinéma,* 1971.

Le Signifiant imaginaire by Christian Metz, Union Generale d'Editions, collection 10/8, no. 1134, 1977.

The Photoplay by Hugo Munsterberg, Appleton and Company, 1916. Reprinted by Arno Press and the New York Times, 1970.

Movie-Made America: A Social History of American Movies by Robert Sklar, Random House, 1975.

Four Fundamental Concepts of Psychoanalysis by Jacques Lacan, Hobart Press, 1977. Originally published as *Les Quatres concepts fondamentaux de le psychanalyse.*

La Volonté de savoir by Michel Foucault; Gallimard, 1976.